# LOVE'S FINAL SUNRISE

CROSSRIVER BOOKS BY
CATHERINE ULRICH BRAKEFIELD

### DESTINY SERIES

*Swept into Destiny*
*Destiny's Whirlwind*
*Destiny of Heart*
*Waltz with Destiny*

### OTHER TITLES

*Love's Final Sunrise*
*Wilted Dandelions*

# LOVE'S FINAL SUNRISE

CATHERINE ULRICH
BRAKEFIELD

ST JOSEPH, MISSOURI USA

LOVE'S FINAL SUNRISE
Copyright © Catherine Ulrich Brakefield

Paperback ISBN: 978-1-936501-69-4

All rights reserved. No part of this publication may be reproduced or transmitted in any form or by any means, electronic, mechanical, photocopying, recording, or otherwise, without written permission of the publisher. Published by CrossRiver Media Group, 4810 Gene Field Rd. #2, St. Joseph, MO 64506. CrossRiverMedia.com

Scripture taken from the New King James Version®. Copyright © 1982 by Thomas Nelson. Used by permission. All rights reserved.

Scriptures marked KJV are taken from the KING JAMES VERSION (KJV): KING JAMES VERSION, public domain.

This book is a work of fiction. Names, places, characters, and incidents are either products of the author's imagination or used fictitiously. Any similarity to actual people, organizations, or events is coincidental.

The opinions expressed in our published works are those of the author(s) and do not reflect the opinions of CrossRiver Media Group or its Editors nor constitute endorsement of said opinions.

For more on Catherine Ulrich Brakefield, visit CatherineUlrichBrakefield.com

Editor: Debra L. Butterfield
Cover Design: Tamara Clymer
Cover Image: ID 184390970 © Leola Durant | Dreamstime.com
Printed in the United States of America

*This book is dedicated to Christ's elect.
May Love's Final Sunrise educate, encourage,
and enrich you to a better understanding of
the love Christ has for His children!*

"[F]alse christs and false prophets will rise
and show great signs and wonders to deceive,
if possible, even the elect." Matthew 24:24

# PREFACE

There are opposing views on whether the rapture will occur pretribulation, midtrib, or posttrib.

According to the pretrib view, Christ will come just before the seven-year tribulation and secretly take the Church, then after the seven years, He will return.

According to the midtrib view, the rapture will take place during the tribulation, but before the three-and-a-half-year reign of the antichrist.

And according to the posttrib view, the rapture will take place at the end of the three-and-a-half-year reign of the antichrist as told in Matthew 24:30, before Armageddon and the seven last plagues.

But no one knows that day or hour when Jesus will return, not even the angels in heaven (see Matthew 24:36). In the Holy Bible, as the prophets foretold the birth of our Savior, Jesus Christ, our Lord God gave His followers a road map in Revelation, Daniel, Ezekiel, Matthew, Luke, 1 & 2 Thessalonians, 2 Peter, and Corinthians of when to expect certain events.

Throughout the Scriptures, God never took His people *out* of calamity but provided ways for them to *endure*. For example: Noah and the flood, Daniel in the lion's den, David fleeing from Saul. There are countless stories throughout history of endurance, such as the Christians suffering persecution during the Dark Ages. The early Christians throughout Rome and the Middle East suffered unto death for their convictions.

Jesus tells us in Matthew 25 regarding the parable of the wise and foolish virgins, preparation cannot be borrowed. You need to ready your heart to be right with God and not be a superficial or foolish disciple. *Love's Final Sunrise* shows Ruth learning new Amish skills, preparing for her role in a new society, reading her Bible daily, as we, too, must learn to do to prepare for our Lord's return.

Your faith will always determine your destination. *Love's Final Sunrise* shows Joshua and Ruth standing up for their Christian beliefs against the unbeliever and dogmatically persevering. God will give us a way when there seems no way to survive.

Jesus tells us to be ready, to watch for His return. Delays test our faith, and monetary pleasures entice us. In the parable of the talents in Matthew 25, Ruth learns to rejoice over what she has and not her need. She faithfully invests her time, talents, and services to those people God places before her willing hands, showing a diligent and fruitful servant.

Current news headlines draw us closer to the end of this age. "Watch therefore, for you know neither the day nor the hour in which the Son of Man is coming" (Matthew 25:12).

# PROLOGUE

Ruth Jessup was fed up with New York City. A reporter for one of the city's most prestigious newspapers, the highlight of her five-year employment was when she wrote the headline, "The United States Negotiates Israel's Shared Peace Agreement." Yes, Israel's prime minister and Pakistan had come together, and the long-prophesied temple was built within that year.

However, her liberal editor-in-chief couldn't dwell on that. After the temple was complete, a whirlwind of crises exploded across the landscape of the world. The next three-and-a-half-years produced more worldwide pandemics. The stock markets plummeted. The grocery store shelves across the country were drastically depleted with shortages of meat, fish, bleach, cleaning supplies, masks, gowns, and toilet paper. Churches couldn't meet. Banks couldn't operate. Retail stores closed.

Her editor demanded she write watered-down versions of the facts. How could she? "The public has eyes." Doctors, nurses, and pharmacists came down with the dreaded plague. Hospitals refused visitors. Patients were denied their loved ones' support. Everything that wasn't mandatory for emergency use was ordered closed. Funeral homes were pushed to their limits. The death toll rose, and there were no places to house the bodies but in closed ice-skating rinks. Retail, barber, beauty, veterinary, and many small-chain grocery stores ceased operations.

People were laid off and wondered if they would have jobs to return to.

Meat processing plants closed because employees came down with the virus. Dairy farmers were forced to dump their milk, with no way to get it to market. Grocery store chains panicked to keep their store shelves stocked.

Just when things were getting better and stores and banks were reopening, an unprecedented cyber-attack added additional fear to Americans. The attack stopped pipelines from distributing their gasoline and brought cars to a standstill, oftentimes in the middle of nowhere. Meatpacking plants were next hit. They couldn't produce their meats—who was doing this?

Ruth came close to losing her life twice, reporting on the riots. Stores were looted, buildings were burned to the ground. Police were spit on, shot at, and precincts were burned and abandoned. Endorsed by her news media, a left-wing dignitary from the European Union arose to power. He enacted a European currency, and nations sighed in relief.

With the Abraham Accord peace agreement enacted with Israel and Pakistan, the Temple Mount seemed always to be in the headlines. The world economy was in an upswing.

However, not to be outdone with what was happening in Europe, which created a massive database on their citizens, the US president decided that in order to protect the public from another pandemic, House Bill H.R. 6666 was voted into law. This would be linked through their cell phones. Everyone was ordered to receive a national ID Number and was placed into a national database. This would help citizens who traveled abroad. However, the government could track where individuals were, and who they had been with. That was enough for Ruth Jessup. She tossed her cell in the garbage. She had had enough of being a New Yorker.

Could her Gran's predictions have come true? Religious freedoms across the globe were threatened. Hangings and beheadings were a common occurrence in Iran and Muslim countries.

Ruth landed a job in Cassell City, Michigan, as editor-in-chief.

# LOVE'S FINAL SUNRISE

And with the latest pandemic under control, the United States and the rest of the world's economy returned to limited normalcy, and people seemed more at ease. Still, pestilences and pandemics lurched upon the timetable of uncertainty with every turn of the calendar month. Two fanatical men in Jerusalem claimed they were causing them!

In the small town of Cassell and with the sudden upswing of a stabilizing economy, businesses reopened, the stock market surged, people were reemployed, and the public was optimistic at what appeared as normalcy, except for the catastrophic swing of climate disasters blamed on global warming.

Ruth sighed with relief as the world economy and the good old USA's stock market surged. Writing about the current events became easier with the recent upswing, and she threw herself into her work.

Thankfully, Gran turned out to be wrong about the antichrist starting a one world order. Ruth had made the right move stepping away from the topsy-turvy streets of New York and into some stability. She planned to begin a new life in Michigan. No more crazy parties, booze binges, and riotous living for her. She settled comfortably into her new seat as editor-in-chief of the *Cassell City Herald* and joined the local hunt club for recreation where she met the handsome lawyer Rex Rollins. The only thing left to complete her happiness was convincing her grandmother to live with her. She prayed Gran could lead her away from her dirty past, guide her to forgiveness, and find the peace she so yearned for. Then the unexplainable happened.

# One

*"But the path of the just is like the shining sun, That shines ever brighter unto the perfect day. The way of the wicked is like darkness; They do not know what makes them stumble." Proverbs 4:18–19 NKJV*

Hoods covered the black-robed men, and a pitch-dark bonnet concealed a woman's face. Fear gripped Ruth Jessup's throat as the wind whipped her hair against her wet cheeks like a whip. Then out of the darkness galloped a milk-white stallion spouting fire from its nostrils…

Ruth bolted from her covers. Perspiration peppered her brow, and the folds of her pj's clung to her like wet laundry. She hoped a change of scenery might end her nightmares. She peeked out her bedroom window to the lawns and stables below. Well, that idea didn't work so well.

The barns and this old Amish farmhouse reminded her of life with Gran. *I can't believe she's dead.*

The trees outside bowed low to the probing of the wind, and the eaves of the old house croaked in reply. *What happened, Gran? They never found the motorist who hit you.*

Ruth and the Marcellus Hunt Club members arrived last evening at the Johansson Bed & Breakfast in Owenson during a downpour that left the Michigan countryside in a blanket of fog. Now that she was up, she might as well get dressed and saddle her mare for the meet.

Her horse, Hosanna, appeared glad to stretch her legs as much as she. They clipped down the drive in a ground-covering trot. Like the mist, the mystery of her grandmother's death swirled around her. "You knew I'd be back. I always come back." In the wee corridors of Ruth's mind, she heard Gran's gentle voice. "Ruth, life never turns out the way you planned. If you don't seek the truth—you'll not find it. Avoid the broad road, follow the narrow. It'll be hard. The little-used always are." Gran had a smile that could light up the darkest night. "Remember, dear one, obey God, follow His commandments, and complete your calling—to the end of your road."

Ruth seesawed her bottom lip with her teeth. "The end of my road." The police said it was an accident. "Was it, Gran?" An anonymous person had written Ruth two days before Gran died. "Your Grossmutter needs you. Stop running—and come home."

A week ago this Sunday since Gran died—she always rose well before sunrise and reveled in the quiet, unhurried life of her Ohio Mennonite neighbors.

Ruth slowed her horse to a walk. "Guess I'm more like my grandmother than I thought." But she desired her own sunrise. Then there was that little—yeah, right, that *little* thing that mushroomed like a helium balloon rises.

She patted her horse's neck. "Maybe we should head back, huh, girl?" As she changed her direction, a sea of fog floated toward her. She shivered. "Well, unless you remember where the Johansson farmhouse is…we're lost, Hosanna."

Like a painter would his canvas, her eyes covered the landscape. Dark and light shadows swept the cultivated fields, which were flat as a pancake. Deep irrigation ditches gaped open on either side of the narrow road like graves awaiting a corpse. She recalled Gran's casket being lowered into the ground. The steel shoes of her horse grated on the gravel like the promises Ruth had made and never kept.

A flash of lightning crossed over her, and an aurora of greens, yellows, and pinks illuminated the sky. Like in the Catskills of New York, they floated there for what seemed a timeless moment.

Spotting an enclosed carriage about a half-mile ahead, she urged her mare into a clipping trot. "He might know where the Johansson farmhouse is."

She fixed her eyes on the black box on wheels with the solitary reflector. The few people she met in Owenson were strange. Even stranger than the Mennonites in Ohio.

She'd learned from Mr. Johansson, the owner of the bed and breakfast house she was staying at, that their Amish Ordnung strictly adhered to the Old Order. Which meant they lived like their ancestors of the 1800s. It was like being in an hourglass frozen in time, with no cars, electricity, or indoor plumbing. Johansson explained, "Our lifestyle keeps us from the temptations and worldly views of the twenty-first century."

Neat trick if it worked.

The swinging yellow beams of two lanterns ahead of her brought her back to the urgency of finding the Johansson farmhouse.

Reaching the enclosed carriage, she leaned forward on her horse. "Hello."

"Whoa," the man said. The large Standardbred horse stomped his foot impatiently.

"Does Michigan usually experience this type of aurora?"

"Is that what that is, an aurora?"

"Yes. I've seen auroras in New York, but never brought on with a bolt of lightning." She rested back in her saddle. "Uh, do you happen to know the fastest way to the Johansson farm?"

"Follow this road until it bends to the left, then turn right on Peak. It will take you there."

Her curiosity got the better of her. "How do your people get the news without a radio or television?"

The man poked his head around the corner of his carriage. His well-tanned face constricted into tiny laugh lines like a cork on a wine bottle. "We rely on you English." His chuckle escaped through the click he bestowed to his horse. "Giddy up." The horse's shod hooves resonated a rhythmic beat, pounding a fast-paced clip as hurried as the man's attitude.

Ruth reined up her horse. Not very sociable. Well, what did I expect, asking for a polite conversation with a guy driving a mirror-image of a century-old hearse? She urged her horse into a canter.

---

Joshua heard the galloping hooves of the horse before he saw the woman's backside leave him in her wake with not a passing glance. She's a good rider, attractive too, though it was hard to see the color of her hair captured by that hairnet. The velvet-black helmet covering her head emphasized her large, expressive eyes. "She has a bite to her, I suspect."

He pulled on his beard thoughtfully. Her turned-up nose gave her just the right amount of sassiness too. It was easy to spot both horse and rider, even in the dark. Her mare's shiny white coat shone like a spotlight for a half-mile in the moon's glow. Her slender silhouette, set off by her snug riding coat, displayed just the right measure of curves. Only, something didn't feel right. What would make a lady like her ride alone before the dawn?

But he shouldn't be pointing fingers. He selected this lonely stretch of road knowing he'd not meet another person. His kerosene lanterns, hung on each side of his black carriage, swung in the rhythm of his Standardbred's clipping gate.

Perhaps she was looking for something—or someone? He could relate to that. Maybe she'd had a falling out with her boyfriend—or possibly a husband? His thoughts submerged into the undertow of the past.

Sometimes he thought he heard her—his beloved Sara. But, no, 'twas only a passing remembrance of her laughter and her soft steps in the small hours of night—his mind playing tricks with his emotions. No, he couldn't do anything about that.

He needed to focus his attention on what he could change—like the crops. Life wasn't getting any easier for an Amish farmer, what with the pestilences, droughts, and that last epidemic that had swept their land. He heard tell the entire world got it. The hospitals had to use schoolrooms void of students. Everyone had been ordered to stay in their homes. Still, the dreaded plague had insinuated its black claws of death into old and young, leaving wives without husbands and children without parents.

Joshua had a distant relative in Nebraska who wrote him and said the pandemic was as bad as the locusts that got in his wheat crop. Still, he counted himself blessed. It was only one crop, and they'd brought the pests under control. Unlike the pandemic.

At least the locusts in Nebraska weren't in the millions, the number that swarmed India and Africa a couple of months before. Alerted by a noise behind him, he jerked from his reverie with a jolt.

The rumbling grew increasingly closer, coming fast—a vehicle. The headlights floated past him and down the road, distorting the image of his horse and buggy. He looked for a place to pull over. His dear friend lost his life a fortnight before to a speeding car that hit him in the backside of his buggy. He and his horse died instantly; his wife was thrown from the buggy and still in the hospital.

The roar grew increasingly louder, he glanced back—a big semi-truck. The headlights lit him up like the fourth of July firecracker he'd once sent off.

The driver wasn't slowing down. He could spook Joshua's horse, especially if the truck was carrying gravel. Rocks sometimes fell off a fast-moving truck without the cover fastened tight. The roar became deafening. Seeing a lane jagging into a narrow road, he pulled into it and kept his horse busy, turning her around in a nearby field, then pulled up the sideroad to wait for his assailant. His Standardbred could see where the noise came from, making her less likely to spook seeing the object in front, instead of to her rear.

Three blasts from the driver's horn affirmed the driver knew of his existence. It seemed to imply, "Get out of my way, or else I'll mow you down."

The lights of the semi cast ghost-like images across the landscape. A deep irrigation ditch only inches away from Joshua's wheel gaped at him. His horse whinnied, prancing in her bindings. He jumped down and took hold of her bridle. "Easy, girl, it'll pass us soon." Running his hand down her neck, he whispered soothingly, "It'll be all right, you'll see."

Stinging gravel peppered him and his horse as the massive semi hauling two gravel trains, the cover of the last partly open, roared by them. In the glow of the truck's headlights, he could see the silhouette of the lady on her horse.

There was no place for her to go. Joshua jumped into the driver's seat and slapped the reins. "Haw!"

The semi-truck headlights landed on the lady's horse. The mare neighed and rose on her front legs, bounced down, and then upwards in a half-rear. Her neigh sliced through the truck's roar and echoed down the road to Joshua as rocks of various sizes slid from the gravel trains, pelting woman and horse as it passed. The animal reared a third time, striking out at her would-be assailant, the truck.

"God, help me!" the lady yelled. The mare struggled to gain a hold in the soft dirt along the irrigation ditch.

Joshua jumped down. A gasp escaped the lady's lips as he swung her down. His horse whinnied. Her horse answered.

The sand along the side of the irrigation ditch shifted. The mare whinnied shrilly. He'd never heard such a cry for help from a horse before. Losing the battle, her legs buckled beneath her.

"Hosanna!" the woman cried.

A whiff of saddle soap and wood smoke whisked past Ruth's nose. Pebbles and debris tumbled down the steep ditch. Caught in a slow, agonizing moment, she watched Hosanna's thousand-pound body fall sideways as the sand and gravel beneath her legs crumbled away.

A lone, frightening whinny echoed in the unbearable silence. Hosanna landed backward, her saddle digging into the mud and water like a rudder on a ship. The Amish man ran down the steep ditch after the horse, jumping over the rocks and mounds of dirt. He reached for Hosanna's reins before she got them tangled in her thrashing hooves.

Coughing spasms rattled Ruth's throat. She was standing on the side of the road and Hosanna's tumble into the ditch dust. She shielded her eyes from the particles and started down.

"Stay there." The man spoke in soothing undertones to her frightened horse. Now lying on her side, her hooves thrashed the bank, her nostrils flared scarlet red.

What if Hosanna broke a leg, maybe severed a tendon? Pathetic sobs pulsated through Ruth's chest. *This is all my fault.*

Her mare rolled over and got to her knees. The man stroked her sweat-drenched neck. He guided Hosanna slowly up the steep sides of the irrigation ditch.

Ruth brushed the mud away from her horse's face as a line of sunlight sent its golden rays across the horizon. She blinked. She'd never seen a sunrise so vivid. The man's silhouette was shrouded in the flaxen color. Everywhere she looked, the eastern sky glowed. The man busied himself with running his solid hands over Hosanna's forelegs.

What must this stranger think of her? "I feel so stupid." Ruth wiped away the dirt as best she could from Hosanna. "I couldn't sleep. So, I saddled my horse and rode out. I…I'm with the hunt."

The stranger didn't answer. Ruth couldn't make out his face. He was a silhouette, a shadow encased with the brilliant aurora of the rising sun. She felt her mare relax beneath her hands. Hosanna nuzzled Ruth's shoulder as if to say, go on, introduce yourself.

"I'm Ruth Jessup." She tilted her head back. *It's him—that man in the hearse.* He was taller than she'd imagined. "Thank you, sir. What would I have done if you—?"

"The same."

"Uh, I suppose." *I can't blame him for thinking the worst of me.* She cleared her throat.

He removed his straw hat. A mass of sun-streaked yellow hair fell across his broad forehead, and the bluest eyes she'd ever seen stared into hers.

"I'm Joshua Stutzman."

"I was warming up my horse for the hunt when I passed you. Then this big semi-truck came out of nowhere and blew his horn—"

"Dumm," the man said. His square jaw relinquished to a large smile.

"Oh, I know, it was a dumb thing for me to do."

"The driver was dumm. Many English drivers know nothing about animals."

"I know. Motorists think horses can't feel the gravel their tires throw. Listen to me; I act like we're from different worlds. English? Say, I always wondered why the Mennonite and Amish call us English. Why not Americans?"

He placed his hat on his head. "Because we are Americans too. So, we call those people outside of our Amish community English. We are different, yet similar."

"You know more about horses than most English riders, me included."

"Danke. You'll be fine?" The soft texture of his voice soothed her like it had her horse.

Me? He's worried about me.

The man pointed to her dirt-caked sleeve and the cut on her face. "Your arm and your face are cut and bleeding." His boots grated the stones as he stepped toward her.

Ruth moved away. Was this an Amish custom, a biblical thing? The Mennonites she'd known were different from him. She touched her hairline, feeling the wet, oozy blood. A Good Samaritan thing Gran talked of in the Bible. No one ever worried about her. Well, Gran did. But that was in another lifetime.

Still, Ruth was done with God. Gran was dead. So was Ruth's real mother and with them everything she ever loved, including Jesus. "I'm fine, thank you."

He captured her thoughts with a knowing glance. "Ja? You sure?"

She didn't answer. She did not need to.

He offered her his handkerchief. She clasped it, stroking her forehead with the cloth. Had God brought this Amish man? Her psychologist father claimed God is non-existent.

Ruth waved her hand in front of her face as if to shoo that thought away. Where was God when my mother died, and when my father married that woman?

Looking puzzled, Joshua said, "Anything you want to talk about?"

She probably sounded like some blubbering schoolgirl. Couldn't blame him. She was acting like one. "Is this the road to the Johanssons'?"

"Ja. But watch for the fork that is less traveled. It will take you to his barns first."

"Are the Johanssons Amish, like you?"

"Ja. But I think they want to be like you English."

"Oh? Is it possible to leave the Amish community? I mean, wouldn't something bad happen to them?"

"I was raised Amish. I left when I turned eighteen."

"So, you like to run away too."

He crossed his arms and studied her. "I didn't run away. I had questions I needed to answer about myself. Besides, I needed to decide if the Amish lifestyle was true to my calling. I returned to help my Mutter when my Dat died. I didn't see the need to leave. I'm thirty-three. You, I figure, must be twenty-five?"

"Uh, twenty-eight, and I'm not sure I understand—your calling? What—"

"You'll find it in here." He tapped his chest, then summed up his assessment of her with six words. "What are you afraid to confront?"

"Me?" She avoided his look. She was fourteen when a hit-and-run driver killed her mother. On her fifteenth birthday, her father remarried a divorced woman with two children—a fourteen-year-old girl and an eleven-year-old boy. So began Ruth's habit of running away when life didn't suit her.

"Could be you're running away...from your calling? You can't hide from Him or His Son. God will keep pricking your conscience until you admit you have a need."

She grabbed her stirrup leather and flung it over her saddle, then pulled up the flap to tighten the saddle's girth. How did he know that? She glanced over her shoulder. His eyes felt as if they bored a hole into the back of her head. She didn't enjoy knowing he saw a road map into her innermost thoughts. A bullfrog croaked not more than two inches from her boots, and she jumped.

"That frog won't bother you. Ja, you know this. So, what has you upset? Me asking about your calling? We all have one. It is our destiny, our reason for being born."

She attempted an amused laugh. It came out a pathetic guffaw. "Calling, yeah, right. My grandmother often said, 'The earth is our battlegrounds; the life hereafter is where our eternal home awaits, and the Holy Bible is our road map to get us there.'" Why did I say that?

"Ja, this is true. Where is your grandmother now?"

"Dead. A hit-and-run motorist rammed her carriage when her buggy supposedly strayed to the center of the road. They think she might have had a heart attack."

She pinched her eyes shut, blocking the picture of Gran's funeral last Sunday and the words she overheard a woman say to another. "Mother Ruth died of a broken heart."

The scene etched her memory like an epic movie with no happy ending in sight. The Mennonite women, dressed in floor-length black dresses, with their black bonnets shadowing their faces, had not noticed Ruth standing there beneath a weeping willow tree. Or if they had, to them, she didn't exist.

Why should she care? So, they blamed her for Gran's death. She blamed herself too. There. She admitted it. Her words came out as raspy as that bullfrog. "I'll head on back to the stable now. Can we keep this incident between the two of us?"

He touched the brim of his hat. "Ja, between us."

# Two

*"Therefore when you see the 'abomination of desolation' spoken of by Daniel the prophet, standing in the holy place...then let those who are in Judea flee to the mountains....And let him who is in the field not go back to get his clothes." Matthew 24:15,16,18 NKJV*

"Mamm, tell the men I'll be in the south field," Joshua said.

His mother, Martha, smiled, glancing down at the boy in her arms. "Did you forget something?"

Joshua took the steps to the front porch two at a time. Sweeping his son up, he planted a kiss on his forehead. Josh Jr. smiled.

Joshua's eyes couldn't get enough of his son. Meeting the English woman made him remember.

He hadn't planned to stay after Dad died. He had returned for the funeral and then stayed to help his mother harvest the crops for the winter months. Then it happened.

He made the blunder of glancing into those deep aqua eyes of Sara Lapp. He knew then. His heart would lead him down a road he thought a dead end.

Martha hugged her ample arms around her middle. "You going to stand there and stare down at your son all morning?"

He understood. Empty arms, a grandmother's lament. He handed his son back to her. "Best be on my way." Jumping down the steps, he sprang onto his wagon seat. His horses walked forward, then trotted down the lane without being prompted. The old springs of the wagon squeaked in protest beneath his weight. The bed of the empty wagon bounced down the rough trail leading to the hayfield. He paid little heed. His thoughts were tumbling back to another time.

It was a day much like this one when he saw Sara galloping across the field, bareback upon her Haflinger stallion, the skirt of her dress flapping in the breezes of her steed's galloping hooves. Sara looked as free as a bird and as headstrong as her pa's old bull.

She had not given him a second glance at church. She ignored him at the frolic's house raising. But as God would have it, Joshua had been the one to save her precious Haflinger when she'd driven him too close to an irrigation ditch that foggy morning.

That incident had rooted his roving feet back in Amish territory for good. He'd found his destiny that moment, but his calling—that was another thing. In the Amish world, he'd done the unspeakable. In the English world, God had forgiven him, and what's more, quickened his heart to understand he might be called again to defend his countrymen. What did it mean that God, in all His omnipotent glory, knew what lay ahead better than he did?

Seeing the tranquil blue of his son's eyes, he knew meeting Sara was no accident, nor was his life here with his people. It was a miracle Joshua managed to be there at all to save Sara and her horse. He felt certain of his future that day. He'd been on that road traveling north, toward town, back to his old job. God had other plans for him.

He rubbed his cheek, imagining the warmth of Sara's lips that early morning some five years previous when God united them in holy matrimony. Sara proved anything but dull. She was like a rosebud before marriage and a full-bloomed flower afterward. His young wife proved full of aromas he never imagined existed. They lived in an atmosphere of quiet tranquility and harmony that living away from the hustle and bustle of the industrial age can bring to a young married couple.

The only thing he missed from leaving the English life were the ice cubes jiggling in his water glass, clinking together as he drank down the cooling lemonade on a hot summer day.

But, if he were honest, he did miss the luxury of keeping his backside warm in the frigid Michigan winters while doing his business. He never dawdled in the outhouse on a brisk winter eve, that was for sure.

"Whoa." He laid down the reins and stared over the field of freshly cut hay, ready to be loaded on the wagons. It proved a challenging year to get up hay, what with all the rain they had had. But it was worth it. This was their second cutting. It looked about as thick as their first.

His five-foot sickle had done a good job. He'd brought his side-rake to windrow the hay. Now it was ready for the hay loader. After jumping down, he hooked up the fork rake he would pull behind the wagon.

The forks and the conveyor would grab up the hay. Spinning from the force of the horses in motion, the forks would then drop the hay onto the wagon. Hmm, I guess that's why we call this contraption a hay loader. However, not all the labor was mechanical.

Haying proved exhausting work performed often during one of the hottest days of the year. But a full barn was better than a cool dip in a sparkling brook. Better than a bank full of money, knowing your animals would have their winter feed.

A sudden reverie came to him. "That was the same spot where I saved my Sara that day. About the same place I saved that English lady." He jumped onto the wagon and clicked to the horses, the forks' noise creating a rhythm to his thoughts. "What do you suppose God is up to, Betsy?" he said to his lead horse.

It was as sure as he was standing on the bed of his wagon, pushing the hay off toward the sides, that the English lady had a powerful lot heaped on her plate. He could tell by the way she acted she didn't know which way to turn. Her words lingered in his mind.

"The way that dirt gave way beneath my horse gets me to thinking what an earthquake must feel like. Why do you think all these hurricanes and pestilences are happening? Some of my friends and people I work with say it could be the sign that the end of the world is coming. My grandmother often talked about this. Now I wish I listened. Will we fall off into an abyss someday?"

"The world won't end. The life we live will change, but the devil, he will get tossed out and thrown into the bottomless pit along with his followers."

She'd rolled back on her heels, her equilibrium askew, dizzy, like someone twirled her around a half-dozen times. He had to reach out and steady her.

"Then you believe in that devil stuff?" Her eyes fastened on his face like a burr to his saddle blanket.

"Because it's true."

She'd jumped into her saddle, angry at what he'd said. "You sound like my grandmother."

*No, Ruth is not angry at me—but at herself.*

She hesitated. "I appreciate your honesty. I'm having trouble keeping a steady toehold on this life. What with my new job, I don't need to hear about an approaching doomsday. I have all I can handle." Then she rode away.

"Whoa." Joshua jumped off the wagon and pitchforked the loose hay that had fallen off the wagon along the sides.

The other men helping with the harvest had started at the Lapp farm but should arrive soon. For now, he needed to fill in the edges of the flatbed wagon to hold the pile of hay dropped by the rake filling the center of the wagon.

Resting, he folded his hand over the stem of his pitchfork and muttered, "Ruth Jessup needs answers I can't give, Lord." He bowed his head and prayed. "Lord Jesus, I don't know much more than I've told ya. Please show her the way back to You, like You did me, Lord. Amen."

※

The countryside stretched before Ruth in a patchwork of golden wheat fields and vibrant green hay that resembled the squares on Gran's quilt. The conversations rose and fell like waves on a choppy sea.

Scarlet and black coats of the Marcellus Hunt Club riders blended with the pageantry of baying hounds and neighing horses. The smells of horseflesh and leather, timothy and clover, intoxicated Ruth's nostrils, transporting her back to the 1800s when fox hunting was an avid sport practiced in Britain and America. Their accommodations added to the Old World allure.

Her bedroom had a little nine-by-ten mirror hanging over a sink basin near a pitcher perched like an owl on an ivory-colored doily. She could have all the cold water she wanted. But hot water was in another room heated by a wood burner.

Her friend Maggie, whose bedroom was next to hers, attacked this new experience of living in a bygone century with eager anticipation. The glow of kerosene lamps perched on walls and resting on side tables added to the allure and romantic suspense that at any moment their handsome hero might appear.

Seeing her friends Maggie and Jane galloping up, she could just imagine what new adventure they had found. "Ruth, have you heard that Judea is under attack?" Jane said, slightly out of breath.

Maggie's nails dug through Ruth's coat. Maggie now had her full attention.

"Right. The Jordan Valley in the West Bank where those Jewish settlements are—"

"Yes!" Petite brunette Maggie liked everyone, and everyone loved her. Come to think of it, for good-humored Maggie to get involved with anything not related to *Vogue* magazine was an accomplishment.

"What about the United Nations' shared agreement that Palestine and Israel signed?" Ruth's heart thumped against her rib cage. "The International Community, including the European Union and the United Nations, agreed on this peace treaty. And what's his name of the European World Community who's heading it all?" Oh, come on now, she'd just written that piece for the *Cassell Herald*. "Well, that European dignitary said there would be no more wars."

"All I know is what my sister called and said, and what I found on my iPhone late last evening before I lost my battery power this morning. The Judeans are running for their lives," Jane said. "Sis says it's all over the television news stations. Gee, what a time to be in the wilderness without any electricity. How do the Johanssons and these Amish survive?"

"I can't believe it. I thought this terrorist thing was over," Ruth said.

Maggie leaned forward. "And you'll never guess where the Jews are fleeing to—"

"The mountains?"

"What? How did you know, Ruth?" Maggie's mouth gaped open.

Jane rode closer. "Some environmentalists say it's the only safe place to be in a nuclear attack."

"I remember my grandmother talking about the 'abomination of desolation' and the Jews fleeing from Judea, and the book of Revelation." Ruth hesitated before saying more. Should she continue? Would they listen?

"A Christian stopped me before I went into Coral Gables last Friday night," Maggie said. "He told me now was the time to get right with God before it was too late. I sort of laughed it off. He told me it was no laughing matter. That all these plagues, earthquakes, locust, and droughts are because of us sexually immoral people who worship our material idols and not the triune God."

"I heard those two men turned the Nile River to blood!" Maggie said. "They testified that Jesus was the Messiah. The Son of God. Some devout Christians praised God and prayed and asked the men to turn the river back to normal—and they did. Oh, and the Christians kept quoting some Bible verse asking Jesus for mercy. The two prophets said that the people must stop their murders, their sorceries, their thefts, and their sexual immorality."

"What do you suppose he meant by that?" Jane said.

"Maybe that God wants more than just our lip service." Ruth avoided their stares. "Anyway, that's what those two men on the Mount of Olives babbled over and over, that everyone needs to repent. But I heard they're gone now."

"And am I glad," Jane said.

"Only, now," Ruth said, "The Bible says the Great—"

"Hello?" Rex, who now galloped up, pointed to something in a distant field.

Two horses hooked up to some sort of hay/rake contraption pulling a wagon came into Ruth's peripheral vision. An Amish man walked alongside the wagon tossing up hay. The horses worked their way down the rows of newly cut hay, their reins dangling on the wagon bed.

"I can't believe what I'm seeing." Rex sneered. "How do you suppose they like it, knowing the rest of us can use modern conveniences? They're stuck in the eighteenth century, using horse-drawn carts to harvest their crops."

"Very well, I should think." Ruth clearly noted the irrigation ditches bordering the fields, marveling that Hosanna had survived with only a few minor cuts on her stomach.

"Say, what's got into you lately?" Rex leaned closer, his eyes staring into her face. "Where did you go early this morning? I don't care for you traipsing across this countryside without me."

"You don't own me, Rex." Ruth scowled.

Jane moved uncomfortably in her saddle. She tapped Ruth on the sleeve of her hunt coat, sending her a beware glance. "Well, we've got to run. Ha, ha, no pun intended."

Maggie glared at Rex. "Look, Ruth, we need to talk." Her deep blues swayed from Rex back to Ruth.

"Wha—" Ruth said.

"Not now." Jane's glance flashed a warning. "After the hunt."

Rex watched Maggie and Jane ride away. "What do you suppose they meant by those remarks?"

What's up with Rex? Why was he being so possessive? Ruth stared out over the field.

The Amish man jumped up on his wagon and pitchforked the loose hay to the sides—tedious work. The day hailed a hot one for September. Ruth could feel the heat rising from the grassy turf.

"Last place you'd find me." Rex grunted. "Working like some hired field hand. Poor suckers, you know they're only educated through the eighth grade."

"There's something natural about drawing from the rich black dirt and eating the fruits of one's labor."

"Dirt…rich? What has come over you, Ruthie?"

"Well, he doesn't have to worry about a boss firing him." She never noticed Rex's possessiveness before, or the way he frowned when someone crossed him. Neither one was flattering. "Think about it, Rex. That Amish farmer doesn't have to pretend to accept or embrace his boss's liberal viewpoints. I wonder what it's like, having beliefs worth believing in and living by them."

"What on earth are you talking about?"

"Evidently, nothing you're interested in understanding."

The early morning dream and the incident on the road troubled her. She told no one about the semi-truck or the Amish man. She couldn't escape the feeling that some divine power had heard her when she cried out for Jesus. Nonsense. God never was there for her before, so why today?

She witnessed to her dad, stepmother, and her two stepsiblings until she wore out her Bible. Her Christian education abruptly ended with Gran. She climbed the steps into a secular college and remembered feeling alone and deserted. *Oh, why God, if you are omniscient, did you allow a hit-and-run driver to kill Gran and my mother?*

"Earth to Ruthie...Just what's got into you today?"

Rex smiled his flirtatious cheeky grin that made women swoon with anticipation. *Does he ever get tired of playing the charming card?* She'd known him for a year. And from what the other hunt members told her, he'd joined the hunt club a short two months before she had. Being serious appeared to bore him.

"We could learn from the Amish, Rex. They take their religious beliefs seriously. Materialism doesn't factor into what's profoundly important to them—like family and God."

"Learn what?" he said. "How to make a fire with two sticks or how to muck out a cattle barn? Get real. These Amish are backward. What's so bad about the way we live?"

"Maybe if I had my mother longer, I'd feel differently. Humph! Stepmom is inflexible, like a frozen pond in February. She refers to my dad by his surname. Jessup! What wife does that sort of thing? I still miss Mother—she was caring and loving. The total opposite of Stepmother."

Rex shrugged. "You can't possibly hold the idea this Amish world is a better alternative to ours."

"I'm sometimes overwhelmed by all of this—worldliness. And they are not backward, far from it. I know that for a fact, you see—"

"Yes, you already told me about your grandmother who lived near the Mennonites and followed their lifestyle."

"If you ever bothered to pick up a Bible, you'd see that what was written over two thousand years ago is happening now."

"Garbage. All of this is a coincidence. That's all. And, of course, global warming has a lot to do with it."

"Right, global warming, how could I have forgotten the answer to all our weather problems. And the answer to all our woes." Ruth leaned forward. "But know this, in the last days perilous times will come. For men will be lovers of themselves, lovers of money, boasters, proud, blasphemers, disobedient to parents—"

"Ruthie, quit that."

"They aren't my words, but the Bible's." She tilted her head questioningly and smiled. "You have to admit, doesn't that sound like our generation?"

Rex shrugged. "I can't believe you're caught up in this Christian thing again. Your grandmother turned her back on you. Get over her death and move on with your life."

She didn't realize how much she remembered from her earlier biblical training until this morning. A window of her past had reopened that she hesitated to shut.

After this morning's event, she saw herself and Rex in a different light. Where would she be now if she'd listened to God's wisdom? "Don't get me wrong. I'm the chief of sinners."

Rex shifted in his saddle and looked around, evidently bored silly with her ramblings. "I think—" The huntsman's horn echoed through the countryside. "Come on, the hunt is starting."

Rex galloped after the huntsman and hounds. Ruth took one last look at the Amish man. Suddenly one horse fell to its knees. She reined up her mare.

Rex must have glanced back. Small wonder he even cared. He galloped back to her side and yelled, "What's wrong now?" His face contorted like a bulldog ready to bite. She felt tempted to yell back, but instead, smiled sweetly.

"I can't figure you out. Do you want to hunt or watch some stupid Amish guy pitchforking an entire field?"

She related to Rex's feelings more than hers. She couldn't explain it. Maybe when that Amish guy pulled her to safety, he shook some sense into her. "I think that man's in trouble. You go on. I'll catch up."

She ignored his swear words. His cussing never bothered her before. She remembered the feeling of being alone—and in need. She urged Hosanna to jump a narrow ditch and soon stood alongside the Amish farmer.

The man, bent over his horse, hadn't noticed her approach. "Sir, can I be of assistance?" No answer. "Sir?" His 1800s-style denim pants had large blue buttons on the yoke. He wore no belt. His suspenders ran up the front and along the back of his bright-blue cotton shirt. She could just make out his hair beneath his straw hat—the color of wheat before harvest—and a trim beard ran along the bridge of his chin.

The man rose. "Come on, Betsy." The mare obediently took a step. Then running his hand down her foreleg and up again to her shoulder, he patted her neck and whispered something in German.

Maybe she should leave. After all, what could she do? She saw the hunting party enter a wooded field. If she didn't leave now, she wouldn't find them.

The Amish man brushed the dirt off his knees and squinted at her through the bright rays of the sun perched just over her shoulder. He removed his straw hat. Ruth gasped.

"It's you." She snapped her fingers. "Ah, don't tell me. Yes, Joshua Stutzman. Is your horse all right?"

"Ja. But Betsy won't be able to work today." He patted his mare's neck affectionately. "Her heart's willing enough, but she needs to rest."

His voice had a melody of its own, kind of soft, foreign. Maybe because they speak Pennsylvania Dutch? No wonder he managed to coax her horse and his Betsy into doing his wishes.

"Can I help?" After all, she could hardly abandon him.

"You can save me a trip." He lifted his arm and pointed down the dirt road. "Could you ride to the white farmhouse with the picket fence out front? It is down away. Ask for Mr. Lapp. Tell him to bring his spare horse. I will wait here. Got nothin' better to do. Oh, and keep this between the two of us?"

His eyes sparkled back into hers, and she laughed. "Guess I did sound a little foolish." She felt her cheeks burning. "This looks like a back-breaking job that would take days to finish in this heat."

"I'll have it up today." He unbuckled the leather straps, unhooking Betsy. The horse limped off to graze to her heart's content on the grass. "The men will be here shortly. We work the fields together. Many harvesters make the work go faster, and we will have a good gathering after, but it won't be as big as our frolics."

She had no idea what a gathering or a frolic was, but evidently this Amish man was looking forward to it, so it must be like some party. "I guess you must take this delay in stride, right? No use worrying about it."

"I don't think there is."

"Can I bring you something, water, perhaps?"

"I have my lunch."

Wow. She'd almost forgotten. She couldn't leave without telling him first—or did he know? "You don't have television or cell phones, but one of you must have a battery-operated radio, right?"

"Nee."

"Then you don't know. Judea in Israel is under attack; the residents are fleeing to the mountains," Ruth said. Bits about what she learned earlier in the Bible about what Jesus prophesied popped up irregularly. "What do you think will happen next?"

Joshua rested back on the lip of the wagon and pushed his straw hat from his forehead, looking out over the landscape. "If the Jews are fleeing into the mountains, then we are into Matthew 24 'Therefore when you see the *abomination of desolation* spoken of by Daniel the prophet, standing in the holy place…then let those who are in Judea flee into the mountains—'"

"What exactly is the abomination of desolation?"

"They are pagan sacrifices."

"I remember reading something about that European Union organizer stopping the sacrifices."

"The Bible prophesied that in the book of Daniel, 'he shall bring an end to sacrifice and offering.'"

"That European man of the United Nations was to assure the peace agreement between Israel and Pakistan—"

"We will know for certain it is the antichrist if he sets himself in the temple and says he is the true god. As prophesied, 'he will sit as God in the temple, saying that he is God.'"

"Wow. You know your Scripture verses." She clicked her fingers together. "I know the news was saying something about how great he'd be as a world leader. But I thought it was all some crazy joke."

"It's not."

She felt as if someone had hit her in the gut. The cry of the hunt horn broke her thoughts. Riders and hounds reappeared to the north, jumping over an irrigation ditch.

"Gran spoke about an antichrist that would take over the world. No one could buy or sell without a kind of tattoo." She snapped her fingers as she thought. "It signifies a name. No. It was a number."

"Six six six, and everyone must take that number either on their forehead or hand, and no one can buy or sell without it." He took a step closer, his eyes solemn. "If you take that mark, you will not be admitted into God's kingdom. You will have chosen allegiance to Satan and not the triune God."

"No one in my world is going to believe that will happen. Not in a million trillion years."

He stroked her horse's neck gently. "Do you believe in God and His only begotten Son, Christ Jesus?"

"Yes. I, I loved listening to Bible stories as a child. Then I grew up."

"Your faith will determine your destination."

"This sounds like a science-fiction flick." She chewed on her lower lip. "I can't believe this is really happening in the twenty-first century."

"God is in control. And you worrying over this is interest paid on trouble that often never happens the way you think."

"Really?"

"Worry shows weak faith."

She shrugged. What does an Amish farmer know? "Well, after all, people thought Hitler was the antichrist—"

"Ja, and Jesus tells us to watch and be diligent, delays will come."

She sat back in her saddle. There was something familiar about what he said. Had she lost sight of God because of her impatience? "About those delays—"

"They test our faith. We must rejoice over what we have—not what we want. Because faith without works is worthless. God's two prophets warned us to repent and accept Jesus as our Savior. Now it is that dragon, Satan's turn. He knows his time is short. He will try to crush the Christians, God's elect, making war against those who keep the commandments of God and have the testimony of Jesus."

"Really?"

"Read it for yourself, it's found in Revelation 12:17."

Truth was often a bitter pill for Ruth to swallow. "If what you say is true, then it's all about sheep and goats—what do you think my classification is?"

He rubbed his chin with his thumb. "I wish you hadn't asked me that."

"Thanks a bunch! Well, I better get going to the Lapps and get you help." Then she mumbled to herself, "Wish someone could help *me*."

# Three

*"Who then is a faithful and wise servant, whom his master made ruler over his household, to give them food in due season? Blessed is that servant whom his master, when he comes, will find so doing." Matthew 24:45–46*

Had Joshua's words frightened Ruth, or was it the scowling man she introduced to him as Rex Rollins?
Before Ruth's mare took three steps, Rex Rollins had ridden up, yelling her name. Her face resembled the doe Joshua had come across in a bear trap once.

"Hey, Joshua," Lapp said, watching the hunt gallop away to the notes of the huntsman's horn. "It's *gut* to see you've kept yourself busy." He glanced at the half-full wagon.

Joshua laughed. "Ja, I had to, what with you lollygaggers sleeping till high noon."

"Well, Coz, looks like you weren't lonely. Lapp said an English gal came to his place pleading you needed help bad. Was she pretty?" His cousin Benny Stutzman liked to know the news before it got out of a person's mouth. Joshua planned to keep Ruth to himself for as long as possible.

"Johansson has got himself a nice little business with those English. Maybe Joshua plans to do the same, Benny," Lapp said.

Eying Joshua, Benny swooped up a blade of timothy from the ground and placed it in his mouth, chewing slowly. "I got me a feeling that English woman could be trouble for you, Coz. I could tell how the English man galloped down the road looking for her that he didn't like it much, her spending time with you. Do you think they could be married or maybe engaged?"

Engaged? That thought hadn't occurred to Joshua. He bent over, raking the hay into rows. It was none of his concern one way or the other. Still, the thought of Ruth being any closer than a friend to this Rex guy unnerved him.

Benny pulled his rig beside Joshua's. Joshua set his expression blank before his cousin's alert eyes.

"Ja." Benny rubbed his chin, his brows puckering as though pulled together by a string.

Was his cousin worried he'd get wedded to the wrong woman, an English one to boot, and leave the Ordnung? Joshua worked his way down the rows of hay. Once the hay was on the wagons, the men would drive the horses to the barn. Using a gasoline-powered bailer, the men would bail up the hay. Then send it up on the conveyor into the barn, where the stackers would stack it.

"Say, you give any thought yet to who you want to court?" Benny asked.

Joshua grunted. "You tend to your courting, Benny, and I'll tend to mine. Besides, it's hard to think anyone could fill my wife's shoes."

"Sara was special, for certain." Benny continued to chew on a blade of timothy. "But the way I see it, your son needs a Mutter. You need to be thinking of someone. Not that Martha isn't doing a fine job, but it's—"

"You haven't been married once, and you want me to marry again?" He knew his cousin meant good from the things he said. But he knew what it was like to see the best part of Sara's goodness in his son.

Meeting Ruth reminded him of his former life. Was he doing the right thing for his son? Raising him in the English world would give little Josh more choices. There was little chance of him learning a trade here, other than that of a farmer, carpenter, storekeeper, or blacksmith.

Those first few years living in the English world had their periods of difficulty. He learned new skills and ways of making a living and along the way, discovered a good bunch about himself. He learned he couldn't work his way to heaven. After living with the English for ten years, he witnessed the worst—and the best about mankind.

Amish and English, the two lifestyles were in constant battle with each other now that his Sara had left for her ever-after home. He had his doubts if he belonged with these gentle people. He couldn't call himself one of them in that regard. Ruth's face popped up unexpectedly. She was powerfully troubled over something—or someone. He understood and had a feeling it was that man Rex Rollins.

---

Ruth led her mare toward the waiting box stall. She checked to make sure Hosanna had plenty of hay and water, all the while pondering Joshua's words.

The Son of God will return to Earth to set up His kingdom after the Antichrist's reign. She remembered hearing that in Bible class. It didn't sound so scary then. But the way Joshua told it, times would get worse before Jesus' return. She picked up her grooming tools and started brushing her horse.

Her grandfather had told her about Hitler and what he did to the Jews in Europe. Would it be that way during the Antichrist's three-and-a-half years? She shuddered to think of that happening to her. After all, God loved everyone. Only—the Jews did suffer for their faith.

"I know God exists. I'm not like Rex," she whispered to Hosanna. "And when I come back to the fold, God will let me in." She shrugged. Could be before she snatched her last breath. *God loves me, and He'll understand.* After all, she didn't kill anyone or do mean things like Hitler and Stalin. She was having too much fun with her friends to change right now.

"I saw what a Christian's life was like through my hard-working mother and Gran." She had to admit, Dad was a better person as a Christian living among his Mennonite neighbors.

She was her father's daughter because she liked the party life too. "Hosanna, today we reciprocated the good deed Joshua did for us earlier. Surely that gives me points in God's book."

She'd met enough fanatical Christians in her lifetime to recognize Joshua as one. That whole end-of-the-age thing was too strange to be real. How was a person supposed to live? If she didn't receive the 666 mark, she wouldn't be able to work. She continued to groom Hosanna in big sweeping strokes of her brush. Metal shoes hitting cement click-clocked down the aisle. Rex waved to her, taking his horse to the end of the stable where his horse's box stall was.

She waved back absentmindedly, her thoughts on her earlier conversation with Joshua. "If I can't work, how am I going to pay my mortgage, pay your board bill, Hosanna—or eat? God wouldn't send me to hell because I didn't want us to starve."

Gran taught her she needed to accept Jesus and be born again into God's kingdom.

She rubbed her fingers along the coarse bristles of the grooming brush. Making a commitment like that was a big step. She'd be giving up her wild drinking parties. For years, she witnessed to Stepmother and her step-siblings and got nowhere. "I proved a lousy Christian; however, I excel as a party girl."

"Finished." She put away her grooming tools, hugged Hosanna, then whispered, "Thanks for listening, girl." She opened the stall door and gazed out at the milling crowd of happy-go-lucky riders. God would understand. He knew her best of all. He made her what she was—a happy, fun-loving gal who loved her booze.

Ruth joined a group of riders walking toward the farmhouse. Rex lounged a few feet away, smoking a cigarette. She linked arms with him and smiled coquettishly. "Hi there, good-looking."

His wavy black hair and flirty dimples were the most admirable features of his handsome face. His well-built physique fit his hunt coat like a glove, accenting his broad shoulders and chiseled waistline. The hours he spent at the gym were as evident as the confidence in his gleaming eyes.

"You look proud of yourself. Was that your good deed for the year?"

Ruth squeezed his arm. "I thought I'd apply this morning's good deed to the previous year, seeing how I haven't done anything like that for some time."

"Rex." Maggie stepped forward. She clutched Ruth's free arm. "If you would excuse us, I want to show Ruth this beautiful parlor done up in eighteenth-century heirlooms."

His eyes traveled up Maggie's form. "That doesn't interest me in the least." He tilted his chin and sent a spiral of smoke above their heads.

Guiding Ruth into the parlor of the antique farmhouse, Maggie frowned. "What are you talking to him for?" She glanced over her shoulder, making sure Rex hadn't followed them.

"Why not?" Ruth couldn't understand Maggie's disapproval. Her easy-going nature always boosted every party.

Maggie glanced over her shoulder again. Her mouth puckered into unaccustomed lines about her full lips as she spoke in hushed tones. "Talk to Jane." She looked around the crowded group of riders thumping their riding boots against the farmhouse's hardwood floor.

Maggie didn't need to worry about anyone overhearing them. Ruth could hardly hear her. The riders' laughter, tinkling of wine glasses, and loud voices spilled through the doorways of the other rooms.

Fidgeting with her stock tie, Maggie glanced around. Both spotted Jane, deep in conversation with Rex.

"I can't believe they made up." Maggie rolled her eyes toward the ceiling. "You should have seen that black eye, Rex—"

"Jane, quit with the teasing looks." Rex's words were loud enough to hear clear across the room.

Women endlessly buzzed like bees around him. Today was no exception. Rex was in his element, captivating the attention of two riders, Jane and Ellen Marie, whose beautiful hazel eyes were always mascara tipped, even after the hunt's rigorous cross-country rides. Ellen Marie's sassy lips gleamed in rose hues, wet and luscious, up at Rex.

He placed a finger on his tight collar and stock tie sporting the fourteen-karat gold pin.

"Ellen Marie makes every unsuspecting male go weak at the knees," Ruth whispered, bending closer to Maggie. "Whatever had bothered Jane before, seems forgotten. Check out the exchange of glances between them now."

"I can't believe this." Maggie tipped her glass to her pink lips. "No one here knows much about Rex Rollins. I've checked with the other guys. 'He hasn't been part of our hunt long enough,' that's what Jim said."

Could Maggie simply be jealous that Rex hadn't noticed her today? After all, Rex first dated Maggie, until Ruth came into the picture. She sent her friend an apologetic smile. "Rex is my private tour guide. He's shown me the sights since I came from New York to Cassell City. Nothing serious."

Rex met Maggie's gaze. She held hold of Ruth's arm and spun away. "Follow me."

Maggie led her to a secluded dark corner of the sizable oval-shaped room. "I dated Rex about a month ago and enjoyed two weeks of utter terror until he decided to leech himself onto you." Maggie's eyes glistened with something resembling fear. That can't be. Ruth turned away.

Maggie shook her. "Listen. I know what I'm talking about. He came here from California. Beneath that handsome demeanor of his, he's got a fiery temper that would give the devil competition. When he doesn't get his way—"

"For real?" Ruth felt speechless. Rex was the one who had befriended her, helping her to find a horse, making her feel welcomed in a new state.

"And when he starts drinking—watch out. He's downright vicious." Maggie hugged her arms and stroked them as if she was comforting herself that now she was safe, all the while staring into Ruth's face. "I can see my words are falling on deaf ears. Don't say I didn't warn you." She plucked an hors d'oeuvre off a server's tray and swallowed it down. "Some women can't see past a man's good looks and suave personality, or is it his pocketbook?"

"Oh, no, it's not that." Ruth sighed. There were a few instances where she'd noticed a hint of a temper. Maggie must be worried; she never drank or ate like that unless she was. "I'll be careful. I promise."

Rex made his way toward them. Maggie hurried away. His hot breath sent chills down Ruth's neck. "What did she say about me?"

Ruth glanced at Maggie trying to blend into the crowd and at Rex's scowling face. "Why do you think we were talking about you?" She emptied her glass. She didn't plan to lose Maggie's friendship, and Rex looked like he was ready to spit nails. Ruth smiled pleasantly. "Just that you're one great lawyer, which I said I knew because you told me so. I trust you. Haven't I proved that to you already?"

"Yeah, that's right," Rex replied, but he kept his cool eyes on Maggie's back. "No one better lock horns with me. I never lose. If something should go wrong, you better believe I'll find a way of getting even."

"I'm starving, Rex. How about you?" Ruth said.

He flashed her a quick smile. "Shall we stroll toward the dining room?" He offered her his arm. "I see your glass is empty; you want another drink?"

# Four

*"Enter by the narrow gate; for wide is the gate and broad is the way that leads to destruction, and there are many who go in by it. Because narrow is the gate and difficult is the way which leads to life, and there are few who find it." Matthew 7:13–14*

Through brunch and dinner, Ruth's stomach felt tied in knots. Rex hadn't left Ruth's side. What Maggie had told her put out her antennas. Why had she allowed Rex to talk her into naming him as her beneficiary of her new house should something happen to her? But what other option did she have she? She wasn't going to leave her holdings to her dad. He had disowned her, and Gran was dead. There was no one left.

She burped. Rex kept her wine glass filled, and she'd drank too much. She had hoped that a stroll around the grounds might help her clear her head. Taking deep breaths, she gazed out over the countryside of fields and barns. She'd forgotten how she enjoyed smelling clover and snapdragons all mingled together in a delightful bouquet.

"Are you as bored as I am?" Rex pivoted her closer. His long strides were intimidating her shorter ones. She staggered from side to side, pushing into him. "I think my next article will be about the Amish lifestyle."

"Are you insane?"

Leaving the west lanes where the tractors drove to the fields, the barn and the house loomed toward them. She swayed off the gravel path, and he grabbed her arm.

"You okay?" Rex's soothing tones told her someone was within hearing distance. She glanced up at their host. Mr. Johansson strolled a short three feet ahead of them.

Johansson spent the afternoon welcoming the Marcellus Hunt Club onto his fifty-acre estate. He showed the hunt members his many outbuildings and expansive ten-room mansion complete with swimming pool and tennis court. He had purchased the farm in an estate auction.

She blinked, focusing her foggy gaze. "Mr. Johansson?"

He turned.

"Are you tired of being Amish? I mean, it's a whole lot of dos and don'ts and what for, right? Why live in the dark ages when you can live like us?"

He fingered his beard. "Ever since I bought this place, the devil plagues me with that question. He gave me an earful about not changing this place. Still, I didn't feel right not to make the changes the Ordnung demanded."

He grinned at her. "Some Amish feel I'm an English want-a-be, especially now since I married an English woman. Yet, I feel it." Slapping his chest. "God is still with me and my business. I've taken out the plumbing, disconnected the electricity, and filtered that swimming pool over there with solar and my gasoline generator. I'm following God's will by opening the main house as a bed and breakfast.

"My wife and I took the *dawdi haus;* that's what we call the grandparents' house, and you Englishers call the guest house. I don't like seeing the alcohol guzzling, but my wife is right. It's not our duty to judge another person. God does that. Hopefully, by our example, you Englishers will see another life. A better way to live."

Ruth smiled, swaying slightly. "Why, yes I certainly do."

"I go to church, read my Bible, and follow God's Ten Commandments," Johansson said. "Englishers have told me they understand about the plain life, staying here and why too much worldliness and not enough of Jesus is not good." He searched her face as if he needed her to understand his meaning. "God has a plan for me, and I'm willing to wait and see what that is."

"I've been thinking that life is not made better for abandoning our relationship with God." Ruth bit down on her bottom lip, recalling her encounter with Joshua. "But you don't act like them."

"How would you know how the Amish act?" Rex interjected. "Oh, you mean that tall, well-built guy pitchforking hay? You better keep—"

"What are you upset about?" Mr. Johansson glanced curiously at Rex.

Like a chameleon changes colors, Rex reversed his stance. His good-humored disposition emerged. "Ruthie's thinking about writing a piece on you Amish. Do you mind if Ruthie and I take a stroll around your grounds?"

"I thought that's what you *were* doing."

Rex wasn't fooling Mr. Johansson.

Ruth inhaled deeply, enjoying the smells and sights of the vast acres of harvested golden wheat and emerald alfalfa fields. Walking alongside Rex, she pretended she hadn't noticed the jealousy Rex displayed over Joshua. So, I'd better keep my eyes from wandering—from his arrogant self? Maggie is right. Rex's temperaments changed as quickly as a woman changes her shoes to match her dress. She hugged her hunt coat closer. The temperature had dipped drastically—as had her opinion of Rex.

"You can't find this afternoon anything but boring," Rex whispered, eyeing the large burly physique of their host now a few yards away.

"I'm enjoying learning about the Amish community."

"What's so interesting about a bunch of people who live in the past?"

Ruth kept her voice low so Mr. Johansson couldn't hear their conversation. "Haven't you listened to our host? He could leave but has respect for Amish values. I see another side to our materialistic society. That Amish man I helped today enjoyed his work and spoke of neighbors helping one another with their crops. Couldn't we learn to help one another without asking for pay? Just be a true neighbor and not seek recompense?"

Suddenly the grass mingled with the sky—Ruth shook her head, steadying her steps. "I think I'll write an article about the work and religious ethics of the Amish community."

"I don't want my girl doing a piece on some silly religious cult." Rex turned her roughly.

Her head spun like a kid's toy top. "I'm not—"

"You are—" his face came within an inch of hers, "mine. And you'll do what I tell you to do." His breath reeked with liquor.

"I'm not." She struggled to free her arm from his vice-like grip. "I do what I want and go where I like."

"Face it. You're a coward." Rex spat in her ear. "You run from relationships when people get too real."

She struggled beneath his iron grip.

"Everything all right, Ruth?" Phillip and Johansson, on their way toward the barn, were not more than three feet away.

"Fine." She thrust her arms from Rex's reach and smiled back. As they strolled away, she whispered, "In the morning, I'll probably see a bruise there from your fingers, Rex."

Rex pinched his nose. "What did you do? Swallow a case of wine during brunch and dinner?"

"You should talk." But Rex was right. Who was she to be prudish? She'd consumed as much as he had. And could he be right? Was she a coward? Is that the reason she ran? Afraid to face the truth about herself?

"Sorry about how I acted. What do you say I make it up to you? I'll drive you around, and we can see more of the sights before it gets dark?" Rex said.

"What about our horses? Don't we need to start back to Cassell City? Most of the hunt members have left."

"I've arranged it with Mr. Johansson to keep our horses here overnight. We'll get a room in town." Rex caressed her hair.

Ruth did a sidestep. "What's wrong with staying here—in our separate rooms? I'm sure Mr. Johansson will be happy to put us up for another night. Besides, you know how I feel about sex before marriage."

He smirked, a look that displayed his disbelief. "When did you grow so high and mighty? You said you didn't believe in all that God stuff."

"I'm not, I mean, I don't. I was brought up that way by my mother and my grandmother. They were biblical." She paused. The memories of her rape by a so-called religious boy flashed through her mind.

"Anyways, my grandmother warned me not to let go of my virginity until I marry. And—"

"Wait." Rex reached for her. "You're through with God."

"I am." Ruth struggled to release her arm from Rex's grip. "Quit, you're bruising my arm."

"You're wearing your hunt jacket."

"I can feel your anger in your grip! You want me to prove it? I'll take off my jacket and show you."

Rex's fingers dug deeper.

"Let go of my arm."

He winched down on her arm more. She brought her other hand up and pushed against his chest.

"What's gotten into you?" he snapped.

"Reality." Ruth stepped back. "I want to end our relationship, Rex."

Mr. Johansson and the huntsman, Phillip, had gone to the barn after the hounds. Well, she didn't need them or anyone.

She took off at a staggering jog toward the porch. Rex overtook her and forcibly turned her. His face was an ugly dark red. His voice whispered venom in her ear. "I give the orders. Remember that." Suddenly, his focus reverted to someone behind her. His facial features changed back into his charming self. "Ruthie dear, you sure you want to leave on our sightseeing cruise, now? If so, I'll run and get my keys and a jacket for you. It's getting too cold for you to be wearing that thin hunt coat."

Ruth hugged her arms to her chest. What's got into to Rex? Maybe what Maggie said upset him. A couple of yards away, Mr. Johansson and Phillip strolled toward them.

Rex smiled at Mr. Johansson. "Ruthie loves this place. We might get a room in town tonight—or I might. Ruthie thinks she wants to stay here. What's the best road to take to see this quaint community?"

It must be the alcohol. She lifted the palm of her hand to her mouth and breathed. Wow, I need some black coffee. Ouch. She rubbed her arm where Rex had manhandled her. *I hope Rex chooses a deserted road, or we both might be spending the night in some drainage ditch.*

※

The harvesting done, Joshua carried his son in the crook of his arm with their plates balanced in his other hand as he followed his mother to their seats. When did dishes loaded with chicken, potatoes, fresh vegetables, and cornbread weigh so much? His arms ached from the nine or so hours of raking, stacking, and lifting. The weight of Josh Jr., just past his first birthday, felt good.

"Martha, I was wondering if you need me to help you with your canning?"

Beth directed her words to Martha, but her sparkling smile addressed him. He nodded. "*Gut* to see you, Beth."

She nodded shyly.

"I feel you should know. I'm still in mourning for my Sara—"

"Ja, Beth knows this." Martha stepped between them. "As the Good Book says, 'Then shall the virgin rejoice in the dance…For I will turn their mourning to joy—'"

"I think Jeremiah had a different purpose in writing that," Joshua said.

Martha's mouth puckered into a knowing smirk. "It's all gut. Here, Joshua, I'll take those plates. Why don't you go and help Beth get her food? We can sit and enjoy a gut meal together, ja?"

Beth giggled. Her little kapp hat framed her oval face like a portrait. Her deep-blue dress matched the color of her round eyes. She had stepped into grade school when he was leaving school. Then her family moved to the next district. He remembered Beth was small then, and she barely came to his chest now.

Of all the eligible men, why him? She couldn't be over twenty if she were a day. "Did Benny send you over here?"

Beth glanced at Martha as if trying to discern how to answer.

# LOVE'S FINAL SUNRISE

"Joshua." Martha's eyes narrowed.

He felt ten years old again. He knew a setup when he saw one.

"Go help her. I'll save you both a seat next to me. Beth's family came over from the next county to help harvest our crop. You can introduce her to the other neighbors here." Turning to Beth, Martha said, "Are your parents still thinking about moving here?"

"Ja." She glanced up at him shyly.

"Son." Martha nodded toward the food line.

"*Danke*, Joshua, but don't let your food grow cold; I can fetch a plate myself."

"No problem." His stomach growled, and he hoped no one else heard. He glanced at his vittles longingly. He couldn't make out the plate for all the food piled on it.

With one last lingering look, he led Beth toward the lengthening food line. He'd been so busy doing his fields and the neighbors' that he hadn't bothered to stop when Benny introduced the Stoltzfus family to the others.

"Say, what happened? Did you jump in the creek with your shirt on?" Benny slapped him on the back, slightly winded from jogging up to him.

"Feels that way. I doubt I smell the better for being washed in—"

"Gut, I see you met Beth." Joshua's cousin tallied up Beth with one sweep of his sharp brown eyes. "How did you like babysitting Josh Jr. while Martha and the other women did the cooking for this gathering?"

"He's a fine little one, sure enough. Gut as gold and hardly needed tending. I was able to help peel the potatoes and prepare the meal."

The two of them struck up a companionable conversation immediately. Joshua didn't need to fill in the gaps with his idle chatter. Besides, their banter gave him a chance to overlook the sea of helpers who had come out to do the grueling work of haying for his and the adjoining fields. Now that their families had arrived, the meal turned out to be more of a frolic than he would have thought.

The time Joshua spent with the English was a stark contrast. He made his wages by building houses while going to school. Frequently, constructing a building would take months.

When an Amish neighbor needed a house or barn built, the neighbors would get it done in a day or two—the basement already dug and cement blocked. Time was precious, so the men worked hard nailing up the frame and roof, and often, they completed the entire construction in a day. Then a frolic would happen afterward, a lot like this one.

Frolics were much like English parties. Only, with the English, their parties and get-togethers were planned, sometimes months in advance. The intent baffled him. Who cared which house or party was the best?

Beth's musical laughter broke into his thoughts. Josh Jr. would like a mother as pretty as her. Her eyes were twirling a dance step all their own. Whatever Benny said about him hit her funny bone.

"I was telling Beth that the Mactonishes didn't come out to help, and I feel bad for them. They didn't come to the last two house or barn raisings either. Nor did they come to the harvesting, after we did theirs a week before. So, I wonder how long it will take before they learn the lesson of gratitude and giving."

"It's the Golden Rule," Beth said. "Only in reverse."

"When you were working in the English world, didn't one English man tell you their Golden Rule was, 'Do unto others before they can do unto you'?" Benny said.

Joshua nodded. "More than one told me that." He looked down at his dusty shoes, his conscience pricking him. He reached for their plates. "I must admit that the Christian English were doing unto others without a plan of reaping any pleasures from their toil—only the heavenly kind. Giving their time and money to a person in need. Be it here in the States or elsewhere."

"Ja?" Beth said.

Somewhat taken back by her willingness to know his experiences, he continued. "With television, internet, and cell phones, it's easy to see the happenings anywhere you care to see." Three men, one older than the other two, made their way toward him.

"The introductions of Beth's *Vater* and *Bruders* are about to begin."

# LOVE'S FINAL SUNRISE

Benny slapped Joshua on the shoulder and snickered.

# Five

*"Beware of false prophets, who come to you in sheep's clothing, but inwardly they are ravenous wolves. You will know them by their fruits." Mathew 7:15-16*

The steaming coffee warmed Ruth's hands. She sipped it and marveled at the stars shining clear and bright overhead. "Don't you love it here, Rex? It's so beautifully natural, and there's a peace I've never felt before."

Rex's Jeep hit a bump in the road. Good thing she thought to take her Thermos, or she'd be wearing her coffee right about now. He swigged another drink from his bottle. Slowing down, he turned into what looked like a field.

"You promised me you'd stay on the dirt roads."

"Relax, Ruthie. The way you're acting I'd think you didn't trust me."

She seesawed her bottom lip with her teeth. He hasn't stopped drinking since we got in the car. That was over twenty minutes ago. "Rex, it's getting late, and you wanted to get a room for the night in town."

"What are you worried about? Relax."

"I'm worried about what Johansson will think, me coming in after midnight."

"Exactly what I want him to think." Rex lifted the bottle to his lips. He shook it. "Empty." He rolled down his window and tossed it out.

"Don't do that. A horse could step on it and—"

"Then they get cut up, so what?" He reached beneath his seat. "Why worry over some stupid farmers and their dumb horses?"

The crackle of paper ended with Rex pulling out another bottle. Then he threw the bag out the window. Grass scraped the bottom of his Jeep. The headlights cast irregular beams across the hayfield. His tire hit a rut, and her head bumped the top of the roof. He swore, driving wildly, like a half-crazed teen out for a death ride.

For the third time in her life, she didn't feel in control. The first time was when her mother died. The second, when she learned she was pregnant and her grandmother—What was it she always said? That's right, "Cry out to Jesus, Ruth, when you get in trouble. Remember, He died for you. He loves you enough to bleed for—"

*Me.* Ruth closed her eyes. Right, love everyone. Only, the world doesn't reward a Goody-Two-Shoes. She'd never forget when she mimicked her half-sister and half-brother's example and hugged her new mother. Right then, she learned the truth.

Her stepmother pulled away. "Look, I'm not *your* mother. You can call me Harriet, understand?"

Harriet could turn her affections on and off like a water faucet. When Ruth's dad was around, she was all huggy and kissy with Ruth, but when her dad wasn't around, Harriet was a cold block of ice.

She gave Ruth her first sip of vodka. "Fifteen's not too soon to taste the finer things of life," she told Ruth.

Dad never thought about her mother anymore after he married Harriet. The gulping sounds of Rex blurred with the shuddering noise of the Jeep slowing. Memories, oh, why couldn't she forget?

Life wasn't fair. She tried to be a good stepdaughter and help her stepmother in washing clothes and not arguing when it came her time to do the dishes, hoping Dad would notice.

She needed a hug. But, no, no hug. Harriet, who lay around and drank all day, got the hugs and kisses. Because Ruth knew God, her stepmother figured she could do anything to Ruth she liked. Forgiveness is the basis of a Christian's creed, right? Ruth folded her hands in her lap, she didn't think having that abortion would affect her so hard.

Afterward, there was no one she could turn to—not even Gran. Through tears, Gran called Ruth a murderer. Her pride prohibited her from telling Gran that her stepmother drove her—Harriet made all the arrangements and assured her there was no other alternative. Her dad would never forgive her. Stepmother promised never to tell her daddy that she had gotten *that way*.

Little had Ruth realized that secret would be her stepmother's tool against her. Christian love, right, Stepmother laughed at her, told her that all she had to do was keep reading her Bible and all the bad memories would go poof and be gone.

"I was too late to tell Gran I was sorry, too late to say I'd made a mistake. Did I tell you that I wanted to go back home, to take care of my grandmother? She was getting up in age and needed me."

"Yeah, you still sniveling over that?" Rex turned. "Your grandmother didn't love you. All that mumbo jumbo thou-shalt-not rubbish is for suckers."

"I guess you're right," Ruth said with a sigh. "I'm not a Christian any longer, and this job has worked out nicely for me too."

The Jeep rolled to a stop. Rex turned the key off. No light but the stars, not a noise but their breathing. "Hey, quit hogging the bottle. Give me some."

He handed it to her. "That's my girl."

Ruth tilted her head back and let the liquid run down her throat, noting with satisfaction that she managed to drink about a quarter of the bottle. She burped. "Didn't I tell you not to call me your girl? I'm my own person. Remember that." Ruth felt the heat of the liquor. She coughed, wiping her eyes. "Why'd you stop the car?"

"We can drink and count the stars." Rex slid closer, taking the bottle from her. "Now, you know what happens when you get too much alcohol."

Ruth burped again. "What? I get tipsy?"

"Remember what happened after my boss's party last week?" Rex's arm went around her.

Ruth smiled, burped, and lifted a forefinger. "Oh, I remember now,

I puked, right out your car window, right?"

Rex's face bent forward. His wet lips moistened her forehead, then her nose, then her cheek.

Ruth laid her head back, feeling Rex kiss her mouth. Rex's hot fingers flipped the buttons on her hunt jacket, then traveled to her throat and unfastened her hunt collar, working down to the buttons of her shirt.

"Now, I told you—"

"And I told you, I've had enough of your puritanical ways. I've waited longer than usual, Ruthie, and it's time to pay up."

"Pay up?" Ruth lifted her head. Rex's eyes shone in the night like two glistening coals, his mouth an ugly scowl. "Don't mess with me. It will be better for you to…relinquish. That way, you won't get hurt."

"What? What are you implying?" She shoved him away.

"You think you're so smart. Just because you've made editor-in-chief of that little *Cassell Herald* doesn't give you a reason to boss people around. Your high-and-mighty ways don't cut it." His fingers gripped her belt.

"Leave that alone."

He slapped her hard across the mouth.

Ruth gasped and shook her head, feeling the blood caused by Rex's ring, oozing from the corner of her lips. "You can't treat me like this. You'll see. I have the power of the pen on my side."

"Hah. It'll be my word against yours."

Her belt unfastened, he ripped open her clasp and started to work on her zipper.

"No, you don't." She hit him in the face. He punched her back in the gut.

"Aw…" She doubled over in pain.

He lifted her chin. Staring into her face. "Ruthie, I don't want to hurt you."

"Really? You could have fooled me."

"It doesn't have to be like this." He bent forward.

She grasped the door handle. With one thrust, she tumbled out onto the grass with Rex on top of her. They rolled around on the dewy field until Rex sneered wickedly. "My little pussy cat has turned into quite a hell-cat." Dirt and debris filled her nostrils. Rex grabbed her face and slapped it like a punching ball.

She screamed. "Jesus, help me!" With her last ounce of strength, she brought up her arm and sent her fist smack into his perfect mouth, and just as quickly, she thrust her knee against his groin. While he reeled in pain, she used the heel of her riding boot to push him onto his back.

Then she kicked him hard again.

He lay there, stunned.

She jumped up and ran toward the woods, sliding on the dew-covered grass. Riding boots made great weapons, but they made terrible running shoes.

Breathing deeply, trying to still her labored breathes, she hid behind a massive oak and waited.

"I think you broke my tooth. When I find you, you're going to wish you'd never been born. I'll have you begging for mercy. You wait and see, Ruthie, my girl!"

Ruth held her breath. He was so close she could touch him—but that was the last thing she'd do. Why hadn't she thought to pick up a rock or stick to use as a weapon?

"You'll learn what it means to rile me. What does the Bible say? Yeah, 'a tooth for a tooth.' I'm going to break every tooth in your mouth." His sinister laugh echoed through the woods. "One guess who that hit and run driver was that killed your grandmother—yours truly!"

Ruth covered her mouth before her cry erupted.

"Hmm, I ran over your grandmother and made it look like an accident. Yeah, maybe I should kill Ruthie here and blame her death on a wild animal—no, what about that Amish man?" Rex muttered a drunken conversation with himself. "I'll have to figure out the details later."

As he walked past her, she bit down on her fist. She felt her wet tears streaming down her cheeks, splattering the leaves. He's gone. She crumbled into the decayed and moldy leaves, the foulness inflaming her nostrils. God, if You're real, help me. I can't see him, but he'll be back. This is Your last chance, Jesus, or else I'm a dead person heading straight for the fires of hell.

Shaking and on all fours like a beaten and wounded animal, she fumbled in the leaves for a branch, something, anything to defend herself.

She heard a sound and huddled down near the gnarled root of a massive tree and held her breath. Nothing. Then she heard him, cursing her name.

Her heart pulsed in her ears, and she feared that somehow Rex would hear it. His heavy steps came closer. Flattening her body against the tree, she closed her eyes and waited. A noise to the right of her. A deer? It bolted into the woods. Rex's lumbering steps followed it.

She ran out from behind the tree, running deeper into the darkness and the sheltering cloak of woods in the opposite direction from Rex. Gasping, she ran down a bank to a babbling brook. Wading in, she headed eastward. Her mouth dry, she cupped water into her hands and sipped, panting. She strained to hear him. Is that a car? Is he trying to drive his Jeep through the woods?

Something moved above her in the leaves. She climbed up the opposite bank, her hands clawing at the soft earth, her feet frantically scraping a toe hold in the bank, without success. She was trapped, trapped like a rabbit in a snare.

She glanced downstream. The only noise was the babbling water washing over the rocks. An owl hooted. What did that mean? Ruth thought back to what Dad told her when they'd gone hunting together. She listened. Nothing. She went east, hoping to find a place to cross the stream.

A deer jumped before her. More afraid of the wild thing barging in on them than the lone human that could reach out and touch her—Rex's Jeep rammed through the underbrush like a bulldozer, destroying everything in its wake. "Wow, I'm a dead person."

Running downstream, she attacked the bank again, clawing and kicking her way up. A field stretched out beneath the star-drenched sky

## LOVE'S FINAL SUNRISE

above her—and woods. Yes, she could see the tops of the trees swaying in the night. "I'll have to run across the field and to the other side before Rex gets here." She ran as hard as she could, her heart pounding faster than her feet. She gasped for air. Her lungs ached, and her tired legs wanted to fold. Her riding boots were so heavy. She couldn't run anymore—but she had to. With her last ounce of strength and running on pure adrenalin, she sprinted on.

She had fifty yards left to go. Setting her eyes on her intended goal, yes, she could do this, just a little further. "Ah!" She'd stumbled into an irrigation ditch and landed hard at the bottom with a thud, hitting her head on a rock. Bright lights flashed before her eyes, then—darkness.

# Six

*"Let no one deceive you by any means; for that Day will not come unless the falling away comes first, and the man of sin is revealed, the son of perdition, who opposes and exalts himself over all that is called God or that is worshiped, so that he sits as God in the temple of God, showing himself that he is God."* 2 Thessalonians 2:3–4

The sky, as clear as a mountain brook, stretched out before Joshua's eyes and met the golden furrows of his harvested wheat fields that glistened in the early morning dew. "It's like a handshake from the Almighty seeing earth and sky meet, my fields plentiful with the fruit of my labors," he muttered to himself.

The grating of rubber wheels on gravel muffled the noise of his rooster cuckooing. In his peripheral vision, he saw the 1980ish police vehicle roll to a stop nearby. Why did they drive that antique and not one of their newer models?

Joshua watched as Mr. Johansson and Sheriff Baker exited the vehicle. Mr. Johansson's sprawling six-foot build and 200-pound body cast a large shadow across the ground. Sheriff Baker trailed him, his legs working double-time to keep up with Johansson. Baker's belt bulged with his guns and a set of handcuffs. His two-way radio fastened on his shoulder, squawked loudly.

"We're looking for a woman, Joshua, an English girl, named Ruth Jessup. She's about five foot six and probably about 120 or so pounds. She was part of that Marcell Hunt Club that went through here Saturday," said Sheriff Baker. His booming voice sent Joshua's head swirling. Ruth, wasn't that the name of the lady he rescued the day before?

"Ja, Ruth mentioned to me that she met an Amish man, was that you?" Johansson asked.

Joshua's heart pounded in his ears as if the burly Amish farmer of Swedish and German immigrants had hit him over the head with his fist.

"I did help a rider Saturday morning. When she left, she was fine, so, what happened to her?"

Johansson shrugged. "I don't know. She returned from the hunt and left in a car with another hunt member. She told me she would be back that evening and said she'd like to stay the night in her same room. But she didn't come back. Now here it is Monday and no trace of her. Her horse is still in my barn."

Sheriff Baker took out his notepad, glanced down, then looked up at him. "Rex Rollins says you might know her whereabouts."

"I tell you, Sheriff, it's Rex who did something to Ruth. They went out on a drive, and he returned, but she didn't. He gave me a no-account reason—just handed me some bills to keep her horse at my place for another day. Said that knowing Ruth, she'd show up sooner, if not later. Rex said she would have one terrible hangover from last night's binge. That she loves to hit the bottle."

"She does?" Joshua said.

Johansson removed his hat and rubbed his neck. "This is all so strange. She didn't come across like that to me. The last thing she asked for was a thermos of hot coffee."

"What did that Rex gent say to that?" Joshua said.

"That I don't know her like he does." Johansson turned to Sheriff Baker. "I tell you; we are on a wild goose chase here. That Rex guy is hiding something. I don't care if he is a lawyer. They can murder like the next person, only easier."

"I gotta follow all the leads." Sheriff Baker walked closer to Joshua, then narrowed his eyes. "When was the last time you saw Ruth Jessup?"

"I was getting ready to harvest my crop. I had some trouble with my lead horse. She rode to the next-door neighbors and got help. After that, she rode away with Rex Rollins, and I swear, that's the last I saw her."

"Ja, I know a lady when I see one," Johansson said. "I also can recognize a polecat when I meet one, and that is—"

"Stop!" Sheriff Baker sounded like a traffic cop. Even looked like one, especially when he threw up his hand as if it held a stop sign. Joshua chuckled despite his concern for Ruth. Sheriff Baker couldn't compete with Johansson's volley of words.

"I'm conducting this search. I only allowed you to ride along 'cause you reported Ruth missing and knew where this Amish man was that Rollins mentioned in his statement."

"See here, you wouldn't have a missing person report filed if it wasn't for me."

"She isn't missing until twenty-four hours. I'm doing you a favor."

"What? Don't you count Sundays? Some favor," grumbled Johansson. "After all, it was Rex like some snake wound around her arm, feeding her booze, and it was his face that looked like it seen some nails."

"Nails?" Baker asked.

"Fingernails, Sheriff."

Sheriff Baker flipped through the pages of his notebook. "Rex said he got those scratches from a thorn bush while on the hunt that morning. His horse knocked out his tooth." The Sheriff turned. "Do you remember any scratches when he got back from the hunt?"

"Nope."

Sheriff Baker's startled look conveyed his surprise.

"I can feel it. Ruth's either badly hurt or—dead." Johansson shook his head. "This is unlike her not to return. If for any other reason, for her horse."

"She's mighty protective over her mare." Joshua hunched his shoulders, recalling Ruth's tears streaming down her cheeks for fear she'd hurt her Arabian.

The sheriff muttered into his outdated walkie-talkie. "Check around town and see if there is anyone dressed in tan hunt pants and a black blazer resembling the girl in the missing person's report." The sheriff signed off. "Maybe someone has seen her wandering around."

"You know what I wish?" Johansson bent down and picked out a pebble from the drive, tossing the stone around in his fingers.

"What?"

"You'd kept Rex here for more questioning and not let him go back to Cassell City so quick. Did he mention her next of kin?"

"Uh…" Baker shrugged. "Only himself. I'm to contact him when we find her."

"What?" Mr. Johansson blurted.

"Look, I can't hold someone on speculation. I know where to contact him if I need to. He says the girl is prone to running away, that he'd only known her for a couple of months."

Johansson locked his arms across his robust chest. "So, how could Rex's horse hurt his mouth when he wasn't riding him that evening? His mouth was fine at the brunch."

"What was wrong with his mouth? Oh, yeah, right. A missing tooth." Baker fumbled through his notes, his fingers shaky. "Look, we're getting off on a tangent here. I came to interview Joshua, not rehash what I interviewed Rollins on."

"I've got a funny feeling about all this," Joshua said. "I don't think Johansson is far-fetched on his accusations." Ruth seemed worried about Rex suddenly galloping up Saturday during the hunt. "I noticed Mr. Rollins being a little gruff in his conversations with Ruth Jessup."

Mr. Johansson's brows peaked like snowdrifts in January. "Ja! What did I tell you?"

"I asked Rollins about his missing tooth…and the scratches on his face and neck." The sheriff glanced down at his notebook. "He got the scratches from a bramble bush, and his horse hit him in the head, the reason for the lost tooth."

"A lie. It's all a lie." Mr. Johansson flung his hand in the air. "I smell a rat. A big six-foot rat of a lawyer who thinks he can sweet-talk his way out of anything. There's more to that little gal not being here than he's saying, Sheriff."

"Now, you just wait! Or—"

"Or what? We've got a name for men like Rollins."

"Mr. Johansson, we need to work together and find out everything we can as to what happened to Miss Jessup. She might have gone into town."

The shrill noise of sirens blasted down the road and turned into Joshua's driveway. "Look a here. I guess we won't need to worry anymore," Sheriff Baker said.

Officer Smith's door flew open, and he jumped out of his outdated squad car, resting his right hand on his firearm. "The world has gone mad, rip-roaring mad."

"Uh, good morning to you too, Smith." Baker said. "So, you found Miss Jessup? Asleep in some field no doubt? Is that the reason you laid on the siren?"

"Who's Jessup?"

"The woman I sent the message about an hour ago, you know." Sheriff Baker tapped his phone.

"I didn't get anything but static. Our electricity is still out, and the generator quit working about an hour ago."

"So, what's with the sirens?" Johansson squinted, then turned to the sheriff, lowering his voice to a whisper. "Did he get into the juice? It's kind of early for that, don't you think?"

Baker leaned over to take a whiff of Smith's breath.

Officer Smith paused. "I'm fine. That's as far as I can go right now with being fine when I found out we're not the only ones without electricity."

"What are you talking about?" Sheriff Baker said.

"I'll tell ya, that blaze of light we saw illuminate the sky we thought was lightning Saturday morning wasn't lightning." Officer Smith eyed Joshua and Johansson.

"Go ahead. They have a right to know, too. What was it?"

"The rumor going around is it was an electromagnetic pulse attack that knocked us off the grid. No power, no electricity anywhere, and the talk is it's going on throughout the country—maybe even the world."

Johansson rocked back on his heels. "I'll be hogtied and horse-whipped. And you're tellin' me the whole of the USA has lost their electricity?"

"It's kind of hard to say," Officer Smith said.

Baker rubbed his chin. "With no televisions or radios, I don't know how we'll get any news."

"You know what this means, that NASA guy my wife was telling me about," Johansson said, "you know the one spouting out about that electromagnetic pulse device thing and that he could stop all forms of electricity—was telling the truth."

Sheriff Baker pushed him aside. "Get real. You don't know that for certain."

"What my wife said is true. The country will have to live like us Amish or perish. With no electricity and gas to run your cars, what else can you do? It's a page out of Revelation, I tell ya!"

Sheriff Baker shrugged. "It won't last long; they'll get our electricity up and running."

"You'd better hope they do, or else you'll be getting your mail by pony express."

"Come on, Smith, let's go into town and see if we can find Miss Jessup. Most likely, she's at some restaurant, eating breakfast."

Joshua and Johansson watched them leave.

"Ruth is not in town; she's out there someplace." Johansson waved his arm across the fields. "I feel it in my bones."

Joshua nodded. Ruth's face flashed before his mind's eye. He knew what he needed to do. He placed a comforting hand on his friend's shoulder. "I believe we need to pray that our good Lord keeps her safe until I can find her."

☀

"Oh, my head." Ruth blinked into the bright sunlight warming her face after the frigid night she had endured. How long had she lain here? "Why am I in a drainage ditch?" Sliding forward, she wrenched. A pain traveled from shoulder to thigh. "Ouch!"

A noise as loud as a flock of geese flying north captured her attention. Six large birds circled overhead. Are they? No, they couldn't be—vultures? What could they be after?

"Me!" She clawed the loose dirt, frantically struggling to her feet. "Ouch!" Plopping back down into her prison of dirt and roots, she held her throbbing ankle. Hard to do with her stiff boot wrapping it like a corset from below the knee to her foot. "Oh, it hurts." She rocked back and forth; her ankle pulsed against the ridged restrictions. "If I take my hunt boot off, I'll never get it back on." No chance of that. She needed a boot jack to pull it off. "I have to get out of this ditch first."

She inched herself out of the deep irrigation ditch with her good leg. "Made it." Exhausted, she lay on her belly and slithered along the ground. The clammy cold dampness of dirt and leaves scraped her chest. Why is my blouse open? Quickly she buttoned it with the few buttons that remained. What happened to me? Where am I?

What's wrong with me? Why can't I remember? The vultures swooped lower. "I'm not dead, you ugly things—at least not yet." She waved her arms. "Get your breakfast elsewhere!" Her yell came out more like a croak. She'd better save what little voice she had left to hail a car. Endless farm acres met her gaze. No cars, no houses, nothingness.

To the left of her stretched miles of field. To the right, a forest. No help there—only more hungry animals looking to her to supply them breakfast.

Half crawling and half sliding, grabbing a handful of dirt and grass to pull herself along, she inched her way into the plowed field. A stick would be handy. She could probably manage to stand and—She glanced at the forest and shuddered, hearing the vultures overhead.

Hours dropped away, leaving her weak as a newborn colt. Her mouth felt as dry as the Sahara Desert. She couldn't remember when she'd eaten last. Maybe she should look for a road? But something kept telling her to hide. Why? What happened to me? The landscape started to spin. She buried her head on the dirty sleeve of her blouse. I'll lie here for a minute. The sun felt so warm, so comforting. Closing her eyes…

The ground beneath her rumbled. She heard the clang of iron meeting steel and rocks, rolling closer. The odor of leather and manure penetrated her nostrils. A wagon pulled by four big sandy-colored horses moved forward. An enormous man stood up on the bed of the wagon and peered down at her. Beggars can't be choosy.

"Please, can you help me?" Her voice sounded alien to her, barely above a whisper. "I'm thirsty. Do you have any water?"

The man reached for a glass jar. He jumped down from his wagon in one fluid motion. The tepid water trickled down her cracked lips, sending instant stabs of pain. She opened her mouth wider, swallowed, and gulped down the delicious liquid that spilled over the corners of her lips and dripped down her jaw to her neck. The man bent closer. "What happened to you?" he said, his voice full of worry.

"I don't know—I can't remember." Her thoughts did not cooperate with her will. Like she was still sleeping, blank, unrecognizable thoughts alien to her. She looked down at her hands, dirt beneath well-manicured, pink-tipped nails. A lady's hands. Her white button-down blouse missed buttons, riding boots—*do I have a horse? Then where is it?*

Nothing made any sense. She scrubbed her hands on her dirty breeches. "Why did I wake up in a drainage ditch? Why am I here in this field?"

The horses stamped impatiently, jiggling their harness. The man stared back at her. Panic wrenched her heart. *What kind of clothes is he wearing? He looks like something from a different world.* Trees, grass, a man with a beard, and a dirty palm stretched out toward her troubled gaze. "Let me help you into my wagon, ja?"

She hesitated. "What year is this? I can't remember anything—do you know who I am?"

# Seven

*"Therefore let us not sleep, as others do, but let us watch and be sober. For those who sleep, sleep at night, and those who get drunk are drunk at night. But let us who are of the day be sober, putting on the breastplate of faith and love, and as a helmet the hope of salvation." 1 Thessalonians 5:8*

Joshua said a quick prayer. Jesus, give me wisdom. Could Johansson's feelings about Rex Rollins be correct? After all, who else could have done this? "Here, let me help you."

Ruth's black eye marred her beautiful face. Her lip was swollen and cut, her cheeks scratched and bleeding. Her hair, hidden beneath her hunt helmet the day before, was free to bounce about her slender shoulders. Thick dark masses of hair matted with dried leaves and twigs shined a blue-black color in the early sunlight. It reminded him of a crow's wing.

"What's wrong with me? Why can't I remember anything?" Her eyes implored his. "I, I, feel woozy. I think I might—"

"No." Too late. He reached for her just as her head dipped. She didn't need to tumble back down in that ditch a second time.

Gathering Ruth into his arms, he muttered, "Poor thing. She fainted." Her limp form was unresponsive to his words. She didn't weigh more than a sack of feed corn. His boots sank into the soft earth of the field as he carried her to his wagon.

He gently laid her on the remnants of the freshly cut hay he'd harvested two days before. That day seemed an eternity ago. What had she done to deserve a beating? The English, he always suspected, could be mean to the opposite sex.

Should he tell Sheriff Baker he found Ruth Jessup? The sheriff would contact Mr. Rollins. And by the looks of her face—Mr. Johansson's concerns were closer to the truth than Rollins' statement.

Should I take her to the nearest hospital? But if the hospital had no electricity, she might be better at his house where his mother could tend to her wounds. And the remnants of the last plague still echoed in the corridors of most hospitals.

He'd met enough English to know they had uncontrollable urges for gambling, liquor, and carousing. A temper was one of the byproducts of their society. His driver was never satisfied with the speed limit or the traffic lights.

Joshua knew of an Amish man whose temper and hard handedness to his wife and daughter made it imperative they call in the bishop. With the English, they called the police. Being a cop in Detroit for a few years, he'd seen it all. Still, he never got used to seeing a woman beaten.

Ruth groaned, then fell back into a restless sleep. He studied her high brow, long lashes, and solid chin that jutted out with the least provocation, which all pointed to an uncompromising face.

He climbed into his wagon, and taking up his smooth leather reins, said to his team of horses, "Let's go home." He did what he told himself he wouldn't do. He looked back.

The dark-haired girl dressed in a snow-white blouse with a scarf tied around her neck like a bandage had been the first hunt rider he'd met. He'd heard from his neighbors that the English were riding up here, but he'd never met one until Saturday.

He'd muttered a quick prayer. "Keep her safe, Lord. She's young and impetuous." He clucked to get his Percherons into a trot. "Ja, reckless, that too. Lord, she's one of Yours, though she may not know it. She needs guidance and Your protection."

His wife had needed help, but the Lord chose not to hear his prayer

# LOVE'S FINAL SUNRISE

for her. Why God?

Joshua closed his eyes. The last picture he had of his beloved Sara alive had been her gasping from pain as she strained to deliver their only child. The doctors at the big hospital had done their best. They kept his premature baby for three weeks until he gained enough weight and could breathe independently. That had been a little over twelve months ago. His little boy was the size of his eight-month-old cousin.

His family wanted him to remarry. Said he must give his baby a *mamm*, and he needed a wife to heal his wounded heart. However, the truth was obvious. They were afraid he'd leave and go back to the English world with Josh Jr.

The bishop suggested he court the Widow Smoker. She needed a husband for her two children. He couldn't. His heart felt raw, a gaping wound that bled for his Sara every time he looked at his son.

"Ruth Jessup, you remind me of my Sara. An English girl reminding me of my little Amish wife." He laughed heartily. The first laugh he'd indulged himself in since his wife's death. He grew quiet, remembering. A tear found its way down his hardened cheeks.

Sara had loved riding bareback in the pre-dawn hours to watch the sunrise crest over their fields. He'd waken, feel the bed still warm from her body, and hurry out the door to see her etched in sun, washing its rays around her slender body. Sara was impetuous and a little reckless too.

The wagon had lulled Ruth into a deeper slumber and him into half-forgotten reveries. What had happened that fateful morning changed his life forever.

Sara had ridden out on the mare she raised from a foal for one last time until after the birth. The midwife had warned her she was nearing her last trimester weeks, and it was time to become a proper mother-to-be. Sara pleaded for one more ride to say goodbye to her *Mädel* ways. The accident had happened at that very spot in the bend of the road where Ruth had her mishap.

A snake had slithered out of the ditch. Sara's mare reared, and she fell off.

Yesterday morning, Joshua rode out in his buggy to ask God *why* yet again. When the semi roared past him, he urged his horse to go faster, fearing the worst. Why God? Why hadn't I been there for my lovely Sara? His bottom lip trembled, and he felt the ever-widening stream of salty tears wetting his cheeks. "It's just like God to explain this to me by me being there to help someone else. Ruth Jessup, you don't know it, but for some reason, God has used your accident to help me forgive myself."

# Eight

*"Set me as a seal upon your heart, As a seal upon your arm; For love is as strong as death, Jealousy as cruel as the grave, Its flames are flames of fire, A most vehement flame."* Song of Solomon 8:6

"Will Betsy be able to plow come spring?" Martha asked her Joshua.

"Nay," he replied. "But she'll make you a good buggy horse."

"A Percheron as a buggy horse?" Martha giggled. The glider rocker made a whooshing noise in rhythm to his mother's sing-song words. His son cradled like a baby in her arms. "Your *Dati* is funny, Josh Jr. But if it is all Betsy can do, it's okay for me and my *boppli*."

"Danke, Mamm. Betsy needs to be of use." Joshua placed another log in the belly of the stove. "That should be gut." He looked down approvingly. Good for heating the rooms, for cooking, and hot water for his coffee tomorrow morning. He stretched and placed a hand to the small of his back. "I'm about ready for my bed. How's my son doing?"

Martha stroked his cheek with the back of one work-worn index finger. "He needs a Mutter's love."

"Then why did God take his Mutter?" Joshua scowled.

"Your attitude won't help, son. Prayers will. And ask God to find Josh Jr. a good mamm."

He knelt by the rocker and kissed his son wrapped in blankets from head to toe.

"Josh is small for his age, but this boppli showed courage, fighting to live. He has his Mutter's determination." Saddened, Martha continued. "He will never know his beautiful Mutter."

"He will, through the stories we will tell him." Joshua swallowed past the lump in his throat. "Sara had a song in her heart, bursting forth like a spring after a hard winter." He rose and walked toward the window over the sink. It was hard each morning to face a new day without Sara. Especially with his son reminding him of his loss.

"God has His reasons, son."

Joshua turned. Martha's tears brimmed over her eyes. His mother's tender heart was like a weathervane. "You always know what I'm thinkin', don't you, Mutter?"

"It's easy to know." Martha wiped at her face with the back of her hand. "Is the woman in our back bedroom the same that rode to the neighbors to fetch another pulling horse?"

"I am sure. She is also the same lady I helped out of the irrigation ditch—where Sara fell."

"Really?" Her head bobbed up. "How did it happen, and why have you not mentioned this until now?"

"A semi-truck came speeding down the road, loaded to the top with gravel. I saw the lady's horse spook and got there quick. Before her horse could topple over on her."

"Is she from around these parts?"

"No, she came with that hunt club that rides here occasionally. Don't know why they find such sport in running a fox to ground."

"Ach, that's what they do."

Joshua nodded. "They had over fifty hounds looking for that fox, and I doubt they caught him. You should see their clothes. Fancy's the word. The men wear red coats, bright as a robin's breast, and shiny black boots with brown tops that haven't seen a field's dirt. The ladies, they wear black coats and black hats, pretty to watch."

"Ja, you met this Mädel again?"

"I saw her with the hunt group that she rode off with. She came back when she saw I was in trouble."

"She's got a good heart, then." Martha looked down at her grandson. "Appears as if God wanted the two of you to meet."

"Don't go looking for signs when they aren't any but a Samaritan doing her duties."

"That being the same place Sara had her mishap and all, it appears to me our Lord is looking out for you. Sara may have left this earth earlier than we expected, but she left you a namesake to remember her by."

Joshua turned toward the window and clung to the bone china sink until his knuckles grew white. "Sara would make sure she did."

"Ja, it is good." Martha glanced toward Josh. "He's doing gut on the goat milk. See, that is God's doin'." She nodded to her son and smiled hopefully. "You want to hold him?"

Joshua glanced back. He saw his mother where his wife should be. That made it harder for him. His heart ached for Sara, especially at night, not feeling her sleeping next to him. An agonizing experience at times, knowing Sara was gone because of his son. She left them behind to make do the best they could.

"You can't hold Sara's death against your boppli. Here, come rock him."

He looked away. Whenever he rocked his son, memories haunted his thoughts with what-ifs. If he'd returned to the English lifestyle, he'd not be feeling this emptiness. Sometimes the selfish side of him wanted to be free of responsibilities, free of the agony of broken dreams.

That day long ago when Joshua shook his dad's hand before leaving the Ordnung, his dad muttered he had a selfish heart. Did he? Was that the reason he shielded his feelings, not wanting to become too attached to his son—or anyone else?

"Got to tend to the livestock." He snatched his hat and bolted out the door to the safe harbor of his stable.

※

What's that noise? With effort, Ruth opened her eyes and focused. An older woman carrying a child stood near a window, a foot from her bed. The woman hummed a tune Ruth had never heard before, rocking a baby. The woman's dark dress came to her ankles. She peered into the child's face, and said, "If only we could be as happy as you."

Glancing out of the window, the woman sighed. "Your Dati is hunching his shoulders against that north wind. Only it's not the north wind he's fighting—he's fighting his feelings. His heart needs time to heal, little boppli."

She clicked her tongue. The noise resembled that of a cackling hen. "Ach, Almighty God, there's suffering goin' on in this haus. A Mutter can do only so much. There is a whole lot that only You can heal with Your grace and love. Ja, 'love is as strong as death; jealously as cruel as the grave.'"

Into what world had Ruth awakened? She needed to get out of here and go home, wherever that was. Swinging her legs over the side of the bed, she attempted to rise. "Oh my." The room swirled like a merry-go-round. She moaned, leaning forward, cradling her head. "Where am I?"

"Willkum."

She glanced up.

Placing the baby on her hip, the woman dipped a cloth into a basin of water. Gently she stroked Ruth's hairline with the washcloth. "You are still bleeding—a little."

"Thank you. Ouch, oh my, I'm sorry," Ruth said, touching the cut on her forehead.

"My name is Martha. Can you remember anything?"

"No." Ruth paused. "I'm sorry for all this trouble. How long have I slept?"

"You've been asleep for nearly a day."

"Ah, that long?" Ruth lowered her head into the palms of her hands. "No wonder I have a headache." She looked up and smiled at the woebegone expression Martha graced her with. "I apologize for being such a child about this. But my face hurts, like it's—bruised. Is it as black and blue as it feels?"

"Ja, and still bleeding in spots." Martha bit her lip. "You need nourishment, some broth?"

"I am hungry." A stab of pain pierced her side, and dizziness overcame her to the point she felt she'd puke. Hugging her arm around the pain gave her a little comfort. "What happened to me? All I can remember is depriving some vultures of their breakfast."

"Ja?" Martha said. "Let me put Josh Jr. down, and I will help you up."

Martha disappeared into another room but came back quickly. "I did manage to get some broth inside of you before you fell asleep earlier." Carefully she helped Ruth up. "Here, lean on me and not on your bad ankle. You must learn to hop on your good leg until your ankle is healed."

Once outside the room, Ruth focused on the iron stove that stood about three feet away from the wall. Across from her was a sink with a window framed with curtains. There was a large kitchen table with numerous chairs and to the table's left was a cluster of chairs. A door gaped open in one corner of the room and revealed a bed, a dresser, and a basin.

Another sink with a small mirror above it was in a small room next to her room. Martha looked to be in her late sixties, wearing a white hat-like thing with strings running down the sides. That looked familiar. She recalled someone wearing one.

She looked for—where's the television, the computer, even a radio? Maybe she was still dreaming. Had she somehow awakened in the eighteenth century?

"Sit here, in the rocker. This should be comfortable for you."

The child cried, and Martha rushed to swoop up the infant, hushing the child in a language unknown to Ruth.

Ruth eased herself against the rocker's spindled back. "This is comfortable." A stab of pain shot through Ruth's leg. "Ouch."

"Be careful, do not hurt your ankle."

"Oh, it doesn't hurt unless I try to use it. Definitely no rocking for a while." Her bound foot and ankle were twice the size of her other one. "I was wearing riding boots. How did you manage to get them off?"

"Joshua removed them," Martha said. "The one was cutting off the circulation to your sprained ankle. He had to cut it off. I'll bring you some broth as soon as I feed Josh Jr."

The front door opened and sent in a burst of cool air. A few parched leaves escaped from the crisp wind outside and blew into the cozy room. Is this tall man with blond hair and blue eyes Joshua? The man carried a whittled-down stick with the crook wrapped in cloth. He walked toward her. "Gut to see you are awake."

"Son, the broth on the stove is for her."

His eyes, void of emotion, looked her over. Hmm, this must be Joshua. Doesn't appear too friendly. The once soft cushioned rocker became too ridged. She moved uncomfortably.

Propping the stick against the table, he walked toward the cupboard, and, removing a bowl, scooped out a generous helping of the broth, setting it down on the table. He picked up the stick and walked over to her. "You want to try the cane? It will help you walk until your ankle heals."

"Will it make me more independent?" That comment brought a smile to his lips. So, he's probably afraid I'll be too much of a burden. Well, not for long, strange man and woman. Ruth took hold. Joshua waited. She hesitated. How hard could this be? Martha, with the child named after his father, joined the man. So, Martha is this man's mother. Where is his wife? Ruth shrugged. No use shoving her nose into something that wasn't any of her business. Using her good leg, she heaved herself up, grabbing onto the walking stick.

"Try it this way." Joshua quickly came alongside to give assistance.

Ruth felt Joshua's hand steady her, careful not to push her off balance, gently tilting her to lean onto the cane. Her arms shook. It was harder than she thought. She snatched a shallow breath and exhaled taking her first step.

Sweat peppered her forehead. Wow, it was more complicated than she thought to hop on one leg and balance her weight on the walking stick.

"Ja, you are doin' gut," Martha encouraged.

Good to have your own personal cheerleader. Ruth grunted, swinging her hip in step with the crutch. "I wish I could remember. Did I know you before my accident?"

"You met my son when your horse shied."

"I did?" Ruth glanced up. Joshua nodded.

"It's good to know I have a horse. Am I a good rider?"

Joshua's eyes shined back into hers humorously. "Ja, you and your horse jumped a drainage ditch and galloped off to help me with my Betsy."

Ruth stopped to rest. Mentally counting the steps to the table. The short four feet seemed to her mind like a mile. Her ankle throbbed. Her armpit hurt, not to mention her ribs. She set her chin. She could do this. She had to do this. Joshua was worried she'd be a burden. Well, she couldn't remember—but felt certain she was more of the independent type.

I gotta be agreeable. Her only hope to know her past was Joshua. "I don't remember my name, not even how I hurt myself. I mean if we met beforehand, did I mention my name?"

He paused, his face a mask. "Nee. I do know your first name, Ruth."

"Well, that's better than nothing." She took another step forward. "Any clue to what happened to me?"

"Clue?" Joshua met her eyes, then glanced at his mother. "Nee."

Hmm, she got the feeling he knew more. "Well, today doesn't seem to be my day." She'd reached the table edge. "We made it—and the soup is still steaming." She laughed. Joshua and Martha joined her.

Joshua helped her into a chair and sat across from her.

Ruth took a hesitant taste. "Thank you for your kindness and, Martha, you're a wonderful cook. I'm much better off here than being dinner to that flock of vultures I met yesterday morning."

"Gut, then we pray a prayer of thanksgiving." Martha grinned at her son and then Ruth. "Ja, son, see how God provides for us." Her smile suddenly turned upside down, staring into Ruth's now startled eyes. "Are you a Mädel or a Frau that found ill favor with her man?"

Ruth looked at Joshua helplessly. "Pardon?"

A deep flush worked its way to Joshua's cheeks. "My mother wants to know if you are single or married. And if you are married, what did you do to make your man beat you so harshly?"

# Nine

*"Though I speak with the tongues of men and of angels, but have not love, I have become sounding brass or a clanging cymbal.... And though I bestow all my goods to feed the poor, and though I give my body to be burned, but have not love, it profits me nothing." 1 Corinthians 13:1, 3*

"What was Mutter thinking?" Joshua muttered as he finished unhooking his team. Much had changed in his life since Ruth came to live with them nearly four weeks ago. He couldn't ignore the feelings growing first like a seed and now a budding plant from the earth of his hurting heart. Ruth was the opposite of Sara, yet similar in spirit. His son had attached himself to her immediately.

Like a turtle, Joshua withdrew into his inner shell for fear his heart would bruise worse from the impact of her leaving them.

Too much lay hidden within Ruth's darkened memory. The brief conversations he'd had with her before her accident heightened his concerns. She spoke about running away. What had she meant by that? Why would she willfully go with a man like Rollins if she did not trust him from the start? She was confusing, and he had his own problems to battle.

His mother felt God had brought her to them. There were instances when Ruth and his son lay asleep that he wanted to tell Mother his conflicting emotions. Something always stopped him. Why?

Was he, too, hoping God sent this stranger into their house to ease his aching heart?

※

"Martha, I've got the better part of the chores." Ruth beamed down at the sleeping child nestled in her arms. Her health had improved day by day. More importantly, she felt needed. Martha gave her the chore of tending to Josh Jr. At first, she worried Josh wouldn't agree to the arrangement. No worries in that department now. Josh's acceptance was the best solace of all.

"Ja, I am glad you enjoy your job." Martha dropped a log into the wood-burning stove and, walking to the cupboard, got out her big cast-iron skillet. "I'm thankful I have an extra pair of hands with the boppli. He misses his Mutter. A child knows." Her kindly eyes swept Ruth's face. "You remind me of her."

"I do? Maybe I knew her. What did she look like?"

"She had bright yellow hair the color of springtime daisies and big blue eyes that could give the sky competition. I miss her cheerfulness and humorous outlook at life's problems most. That's where the similarity is." She hurried to the pantry and drew out two large jars from the curtained room. "I'll have to hurry if I plan on supper being ready before Joshua returns."

Ruth's hand went to her dark hair. Martha had done it up this morning in tight braids and had given her a black kapp that told everyone of her single state. It fit snug on her head and hid most of her hair. Martha explained she had to wear it every day.

Her blouse and breeches were replaced with a dress that resembled Martha's dark blue one. Only hers was a light blue, almost aqua. The dress didn't have buttons but safety pins closing the yoke.

Ruth scratched her forehead. "Ouch." She rested Josh Jr. in the crevice of her arm and walked to the small mirror that hung over the sink they used for washing their hands and face. The mirror afforded a face shot, nothing more. Her reflection showed a bluish knot big as a walnut below her hairline. *Will my bruises ever heal?* The child peeked up at her.

"Yes, I'm still holding you, Josh Jr." A grin creased his little lips as his eyes blinked their way closed again. "He sleeps a lot, doesn't he?"

Martha shuffled toward her and, lifting the blanket she used to wrap him in, smiled down at the fat little pink cheeks of her grandson. "Not for a preemie. Sleep helps him grow."

Martha spent the morning explaining about their Ordnung and the Owenson Amish rules. There was much Ruth didn't know, and questions as to her origin plagued her. "If I was Amish, why was I dressed in those other clothes?" Ruth said while laying Josh Jr. down in his day bed set up in the kitchen, close to the warm stove.

Martha shrugged. "Could be you were from a different Ordnung, one that is more liberal than ours. It could mean you are still young enough to try the English ways before you choose to be Amish as Joshua did." Martha walked away from her boiling pots and to her rocker. "Or it could be you are English. Has anything come back to you yet?"

"No, but I don't feel English. I feel Amish." Desire 99 percent the cause. Seeing Josh Jr. stir, she gently rocked his crib. "I feel secure here." She whispered, "I like being Amish, because I know I am safe here."

The shuffling of boots outside the door alerted the women Joshua had arrived.

"Oh, dear, supper is not ready."

"Can I do anything to help?"

"If Josh Jr. is asleep, can you set the table?"

Taking a last look at the sleeping child nestled like a baby bird in its nest, Ruth hurried to the cupboard.

The door creaked open, letting in a strong breeze that set the checkered tablecloth slapping against the table legs and Ruth's skirt to fluttering. Her heart thumped out of control as the smells of horses, fields, and wheat whispered through the kitchen. The smells of Joshua. His frame shadowed the open doorway, and she looked up, right into his frowning face.

"You—changed." Joshua's deep baritone filled the vacant silence.

"Uh—yes, I did." Would Joshua approve of her attempt to embrace his world? Ruth fumbled with the sash of her apron. The dress had been a little large in areas. She'd done the best she could with gathering it around her waist and bodice. The skirt was too short. Her ankles and feet exposed the dark stockings Martha gave her to wear beneath her dress.

Her voice hummed with the stuttering words of her self-consciousness, cringing beneath Joshua's piercing glance. "Your mother kindly lent me some clean clothes to wear."

"Ja, it is the good neighbor thing to do, son," Martha said, then turned and devoted her full attention to stirring the stew.

Little Josh stirred. "Maybe I should take him to his bed. He might sleep better there." Before she could, Joshua picked up his son.

Martha evidently had not asked permission before giving Ruth Sara's clothes to wear. Joshua rocked his son in his arms and avoided looking at her. "I could change back into my clothes." The tension in the room was as thick as last night's cooked cabbage. She hurried and gathered her clothes from the drying rack.

Martha held up her arm. "Nee, Ruth." Martha's pleasing round body swayed to the rhythm of her stirring. "Those clothes of Sara's were gathering dust in the closet, Joshua."

Mother and son switched to Schwabisch, the language of their Southern German ancestors. Martha had explained to Ruth earlier that it was the language that some English called an old-fashioned interpretation of Pennsylvania Dutch, but that their Ordnung called Old-World German. Martha explained Swabian is how the English say it.

*English or Amish? I must choose what I am.* Still, the last thing she needed to do was upset those living in this tiny household. She needed to stay here until she knew where she belonged. The thought she could be running from someone haunted her dreams last night. Who? She frowned. Now she sounded like the old hoot owl that perched itself outside her window last night.

Joshua carried his son into the bedroom, bent down, and kissed him. Ruth looked away. She hadn't meant to spy on them. She busied herself at the cupboard, selected cups from the lower shelf. Joshua, now at the kitchen sink, rubbed the bar of soap that smelled of roses and lye and scrubbed his hands and arms clear up to his elbows.

This silence between them had to go. "Joshua, your mother explained this morning that the first Mennonite and Amish orders came to America in the 1700s." She set down the cups and saucers. "So, your Ordnung came up with the name English for, how do you put it, outsiders?"

"Ja. This Michigan order was established in 1988. Now we have four church districts with close to a hundred people."

Going back to the cupboard and reaching the highest shelf, she counted out the plates and bowls. She hadn't noticed how high the shelf was. Standing on tiptoes, she carefully took each plate down one at a time; she didn't want to risk a chance of breaking any.

"I can help. Usually, Mutter gives me the chore of getting these plates down." Joshua walked up behind her. She could feel him hesitate. His shadow covered her as he reached above her outstretched arm and selected the remaining china.

"Thank you." Their eyes locked. Joshua hesitated. Slowly, he took her plate, placed it with his, cleared his throat, and walked toward the table.

But not too quickly for her to see his face had turned a deep crimson. *I'm sure it matches my own.* She followed with the silverware.

"Where are the napkins?" Martha said.

Ruth confusingly looked around. "Right, uh, where are they?" *What had come over her? Her mind had turned to mush.*

Martha pointed to the cupboard drawer.

"Oh, right." The sounds of her stocking feet padded across the wood floor. *Sara's shoes had been too small to fit her large feet.*

Joshua sat at his place, the head of the table.

Grabbing *Plain Interests,* he pored over this month's edition. Ruth took a glance at it. "Oh, I can read that." Her curiosity getting the better of her, setting down the cloth napkins, she leaned closer.

"This is written in the English." Reaching over, he picked up his Bible and held it open to her. "Can you read this?"

"Uh...no can't make out one letter from the other. But something feels familiar. I can't place why those letters would."

"This is German, the language of the Mennonites and Amish. For generations, we have passed this down, from father to son. In our household, we only speak Schwabisch. That way, the children learn the language from their youth."

"Thank you for speaking English for me." Humbled, she said, "It must be wonderful to feel so deeply about one's roots."

"Ja, we try to keep the traditions alive the way our Grossvater and Grossmutter taught us to do," Martha said.

Ruth's words tumbled out impulsively. "Could you teach me how to read your Bible?"

Joshua nodded his head slowly, his words but a whisper. "Ja, if you like. I could teach you."

She rose from her bowed position and backed away. Joshua thinks she could be here for some time. Time enough to learn a new language.

"Yes, that, that would be wonderful." But she had a life. Somewhere. "I wonder if anyone misses me? I don't believe I have a child—or a husband." She fumbled with the dangling strings of her cap. "I never thought losing one's memory could be so confusing."

☼

Joshua leaned back on his solid chair. "Ja, you have your own life, and when you remember, you will want to return to that life." It was good to remember that Ruth did not belong here. This truth saddened him.

Ruth helped his mother spoon the steaming stew into bowls. Fresh bread made that morning, string beans, and corn were set on the table along with the stew. "We eat now. Son, say the prayer of thanksgiving."

Thanksgiving? The word got caught in his throat. Was it the food—or Ruth he was thanking God for? A small part of him wished Ruth would not too quickly regain her memory.

Their dog barked, a sudden rap on the door followed. Joshua rose slowly. "Johansson, come on in and have some dinner."

"I've eaten but don't mind sitting down with you for a cup of coffee." His eyes landed on Ruth as quickly as a fly on a horse.

Joshua bit down on his bottom lip. He knew this time would come eventually. Silly of him not to prepare something to say for the occasion. Neighbors dropped by. That's what neighbors do. It might as well be Johansson as anyone else.

"Meet Ruth, Sara's cousin, come over for a visit. She came to help Mamm with the boppli."

"Ja, for sure and certain Martha can use another pair of hands tending to Josh Jr." Johansson sipped his coffee thoughtfully. He accepted a piece of Martha's fresh bread and homemade jam. "Danke." Then kept to his thoughtful self, hardly making a ripple amidst the clanging of spoons and forks amidst the conversation around the supper table.

Joshua heaved a sigh of relief. He wasn't sure Mother would go along with his lie. But it was that or release Ruth to the sheriff and have Rex Rollins get ahold of her. Good that Mother agreed with him.

God, please forgive me for breaking Your ninth commandment.

Mother agreed on the day Joshua brought Ruth home that she'd not contradict her son. But she would confess her sin of lying before the congregation at the proper time. "When I feel sure Ruth is in no danger of being harmed," Mutter had said.

Ruth unknowingly played her role. Dutifully quiet, she kept her eyes focused on her plate. All was fine until Josh Jr. decided to awaken. With the first peal of a scream, Ruth hurried forward as quickly as her mending leg allowed.

The lantern shone clearly on her face when she picked Josh up, the purple imprint of the black eye, the dark bruises that marred her shallow white face, not to mention her limp—and Johansson's sudden gasp and demanding stare spoke more than words. Their charade had come to a climactic conclusion.

"That is gut bread and jam, Martha," Johansson said.

"We have pie for dessert, so don't run off."

"Nee, I'd best be getting on back. I've got to tend to my horses. That lawyer, Mr. Rollins, went and picked up that mare I told you about. I think her name is called Hosanna—"

Ruth gasped. Something like fear gripped her. She clutched Josh close to her chest before sitting down in the rocker with the bottle she had prepared.

"Hosanna." Ruth rolled the name around on her tongue. "That name sounds familiar." Her glance met Johansson's and then dropped to Josh Jr. sitting in her lap.

"Well, I'd best get home." Johansson picked up his hat and shuffled toward the door. "Joshua, can I speak with you privately?"

# Ten

*"Most assuredly, I say to you, unless one is born again, he cannot see the kingdom of God.... That which is born of flesh is flesh, and that which is born of the Spirit is spirit. Do not marvel that I said to you, 'You must be born again.' The wind blows where it wishes, and you hear the sound of it, but cannot tell where it comes from and where it goes. So is everyone who is born of the Spirit." John 3:3,6–8*

The horses' neighs mingled with the scrunching of tires as an old beat-up Ford pulled into Joshua's drive. He didn't bother to look up. He finished fastening the team into their harnesses, ready for a day's work. He heard the passenger door open.

"I hope you didn't have anything you needed to get done today." Johansson stepped closer.

Joshua crossed his arms. He decided he wouldn't allow Johansson or anyone else to take Ruth away until he knew her whole story, or at least until she said she wanted to leave.

The driver got out, an Englisher he'd never met before. A lean man stepped forward. His felt-looking cowboy hat appeared more prominent than his head. He didn't seem to be in a hurry. Hmm, that's strange. Most English were in a mighty hurry to get nowhere.

The Englisher's large hat rested on a full head of hair, and his clean-shaven face broke into a companionable grin. "Hi there. Allow me to introduce myself. I'm Private Investigator Bill Ricker. I've been hired to find Ruth Jessup."

Joshua gritted his teeth. What was Johansson up to? He told him his feelings last Saturday when he'd come at the dinner hour. Right now, Joshua needed to finish his chores. It was already mid-October; shorter days and winter would be upon them soon enough.

They shook hands, and Joshua recalled seeing a boxing match some five years before. They shook hands, too, just before they clobbered each other.

"I could use your help," Ricker said. "I need to find out where Ruth Jessup is. She has a history of running away. At least I hope that's what happened. It's possible some varmint sent her into hiding. If so, I need to find him."

"The detective was hired by Ruth's parents," Johansson explained. "He wants you to go with him to question Mr. Rollins, Joshua. Will you? He asked me to come with him, but I can't. Rollins knows how I feel about him."

"I don't see the need," Joshua said.

Private Investigator Ricker dug a rock up with the toe of his boot. "I understand you lived in my neck of the woods for a spell, so you know the court system and the way we do business in the modern world better than an Amish man like Johansson would."

Ricker crossed his arms and leveled his eyes. "You see, it's like this. I want justice." The private investigator paused, his eyes trailing Joshua's build. "I bet you still have the clothes you came home with, or else I might have some duds that would fit you."

I should have known better than to confide in Johansson about my past English life. "I have a full schedule today."

"Don't need to be now. You name the day, and I'll comply. That is, if I can find the gasoline and this ancient Ford can make the trip."

☀

Joshua tugged at his button-up shirt as Ricker headed to Rex Rollins' office. He'd forgotten how uncomfortable city clothes were. The latest coronavirus scare and the coronal mass ejections caused by that solar storm left the streets about empty of cars. If it was a solar storm that left the electronic devices as useless as a kid's toy, when would the electricity return, and would it stay? Who would have imagined that beautiful aurora everyone saw over a month ago was a CME?

Or was Ricker, right? Was this an electromagnetic pulse (EMP) attack on the nation's electric grid?

Joshua could care less. Electricity wasn't a concern in the Amish world. But what if this was an enemy attack? What would come next? His family and loved ones' welfare were a different matter. He fastened his suit coat and smoothed down his hair to fit neatly in one of Ricker's hats. Squaring his shoulders, he walked up the four flights of stairs with Ricker and toward the offices of Smith & Associates, wondering if he looked the part, or would Rollins recognize him as that dumb Amish farmer?

He wouldn't be the center of attention anyways. He glanced at Ricker. Dressed in his cowboy boots and ornate shirt, Ricker looked more out of place for a classy city like Cassell. Where does he think he is, some farm in Texas?

Ricker strolled into the waiting room as if he was part owner of the business. His booming voice sent everyone within hearing distance staring at him in alarm.

Removing his Stetson, Ricker glanced down at the name displayed on the receptionist's desk. "I would have called, Ms. Cassings, but seeing how your telephone lines are down, can you fit me into Mr. Rollins' schedule?" Ricker leaned over the receptionist's desk and muttered something about Ruth Jessup, then raising his voice added with alarming bluntness, "Little lady, it's simply a matter of life or death."

The pretty young receptionist jumped up, rushed out of her little cubical, knocked on the lawyer's door, and to the reply of the gruff voice on the opposite side, opened it.

Ricker sent Joshua a confident wink, replacing his hat on his head. Joshua frowned back as he listened to the ongoing conversation inside Rollins' office.

"Sir, there is a Private Detective Ricker and his associate here to see you."

"For what case?"

"He's here about your girlfriend, sir, Miss Jessup?"

"First of all, Miss Cassings, Miss Jessup was not my girlfriend. She was a friend I dated briefly."

"Yes, sir." Miss Cassings rested her hand on the doorknob and glanced over her shoulder. Her shoulder-length blonde hair splashed about her cheeks as her head turned from them to her boss.

Rex slammed his palm on the desk, rose, and walked toward her. The detective stepped forward. Rex Rollins changed his aggravated features into one of deference. "That will be all, Miss Cassings."

Rollins extended his arm and smiled, drawing them into his room. "Detective Ricker, what brings you to my office?"

"May I introduce my associate, Mr. Jones. I apologize for our short notice; however, our visit is important."

"Have a seat."

Rex Rollins walked to his desk, waited for them to be seated, and then plopped down in his swivel chair. He leaned his dark head back on his leather chair and swiveled around to view the skyscraper office building across the street.

"Mr. Johansson sent you to me, right?"

"Yes sir," Ricker said.

"A man of his word."

"Mr. Johansson contacted the sheriff's department in Cassell," Ricker said, reading from his notes. "Evidently, the sheriff's department heard from Ruth's closest kin; her father contacted me."

"Ruthie didn't associate with her biological family."

"I understand her father remarried after her mother died from a hit and run driver."

"True, and incredibly sad. But Ruthie is a big girl now. She can take care of herself." Rollins rested back in his chair.

"According to the police report, you were the last person to see Ruth before her disappearance."

"So?" Rollins asserted.

Ricker sent Joshua a sideways glance.

"I understand Ruth Jessup is a client of yours," Ricker said. "She came from New York, purchased a house. Didn't she have mortgage papers drawn up by you?"

"I have many clients, but, yes, I remember Ruth recently had me draw up a deed for a house."

Rollins planted a congenial smirk on his clean-shaven face as he handed over her file.

Detective Ricker pulled out his glasses from his chest pocket, pushed them up the bridge of his nose, and began reading the document. Removing the glasses, he looked at Rollins. His eyes didn't waver. "Looks like you were more than friends. She put your name down here as a beneficiary."

Rollins flashed him a disarming grin.

"How did you get your front tooth knocked out?" Ricker asked.

"My dentist is out of town, and I'm particular about who works on my mouth." He made a beeline toward the built-in bar located at the back of the office and opened the small refrigerator door. A whiff of stale food met Joshua's nose.

"Forgot. Our generator is on the blink along with our electricity." He chose a couple of bottled waters and held them up. "You want a glass of water? Sorry, no ice."

"No thanks," Joshua said. The plastic containers probably carried remnants of the stale odors erupting from the fridge.

"Nothing for me." The detective rested back on his chair, surveying Rollins beneath the brim of his Stetson.

Rollins slammed the door shut. "Something more substantial?" He nodded his head toward bottles of hard liquor sitting on the shelf.

"No, we're fine," Detective Ricker said.

"Well, I could use something right about now." He poured himself whisky and took a sip. "You know, I hate it when someone can see my eyes and I can't see his."

Nice stalling trick. "You haven't answered the detective's question. What happened?" Joshua said. "Your face looks like someone didn't approve of your looks."

"Oh, you mean this?" He pointed to his missing tooth. "I—fell."

"Where?"

"On the sidewalk, I think. It happened a while back," Rollins said, strolling toward his desk.

The private investigator wrote something down in his black book. "You should get that fixed."

"My dentist was vacationing in the Smoky Mountains at the time everyone lost their electricity. He's trying to get back to the city. Not an easy task with half the gas stations out of business. The city's running on generators. Every dentist office has been closed here since the grid went down." Rex plopped down in his oversized swivel chair.

Ricker flipped through his notepad like a sheriff would his colt .44, loading the chambers. "According to Mr. Johansson, and I quote, 'I noticed Mr. Rollins' tooth missing Sunday morning.' He also noticed, and I quote again, 'A whole lot of scratch marks on your cheeks and eyes.' Funny, I didn't notice any sidewalks at Mr. Johansson's."

"You got me, Mr. Detective, dead to rights. I didn't want it to get around the hunt." Rex winked. "You see, it's embarrassing. Been riding before I could walk, and, you see, my—hot-headed mare walloped me in the head. I wished I'd kept my mouth shut. Know what I mean?"

"How about those scratches?"

"Got them running through the underbrush."

Joshua's job on the police force had taught him a thing or two. Rollins was a lawyer from one of the most prestigious firms in the county. Why the amateurish angle? Unless he felt secure over his prestigious position and couldn't believe anyone would consider him a murderer. So, why worry about an iron-clad alibi?

Rex swirled the liquor in his glass methodically. "Mind if I ask you a few questions?"

"Not at all," Ricker said.

"Have you checked out the Amish country? I think that Amish guy nabbed Ruthie. Probably put her in his commune. Everyone knows you can't trust those religious freaks."

Joshua clenched his fists. He was half-right. He did have Ruth. A commune? Is that what this lowlife thinks about people who like to bring up a family instilled with Christian values?

Ricker tipped his Stetson over his forehead and leaned back in his chair. "Rollins, you interest me. One minute Ruth Jessup is an acquaintance, then the next instant I find out that you are a beneficiary for her real estate." As quick as a cat he crouched over Rollins's desk and slapped the papers down in front of his face. "What happened that night?"

"Are you accusing me of foul play?" Rollins said.

"Shouldn't be a problem for you if I am. You don't have anything to hide—"

"No! I don't." Rollins jumped up from his seat like it burned his backside and leaned over his desk. "I have nothing to hide because I didn't harm Ruthie." His lips contorted into a snarl, giving him the appearance of a mad dog.

"So, when you went for your sightseeing drive with Miss Jessup, where did you go?" Ricker persisted.

"I, look, I'll admit Miss Jessup and I were pretty intoxicated. You can ask anyone about that. Snookered. And besides, I brought along a couple more bottles, just in case we got dry." Rex shrugged and held his hands out in a pleading gesture. "Come on. You're a man. Ruthie's one gorgeous trick. Beautiful dark hair and a body that could make a dead man rise from his grave."

Joshua clasped the sides of his armchair. Cool it. A picture of Ruth's bruised face, her pleading eyes, the gentle way she took care of his son appeared before his mind's eye. No man had the right to talk about a woman like that. He bit down on his bottom lip, halting his retort.

"Ruthie's a cute little trick and has a way of flirting that takes the breath out of a man's lungs with a sweep of her dimpled smile." Rollins leaned forward. "Give a guy a break."

"You didn't have a lover's spat?" the detective coaxed. "Maybe a few slaps to cause her to want to walk home?"

"Of course not. Any man with one ounce of red blood left in his blue veins couldn't hurt a sweet little number like Ruthie." Rex sat down, leaning back on his chair, and rocked ever so gently. "You're clueless. You haven't located her or anyone who's seen her. And Mr. and Mrs. Jessup have finally decided to do right by their daughter." He stood, walked around his desk, and rested his bulk on its glassy finish. "That is interesting, seeing how Ruthie had no use for her father—nor especially her stepmother."

The calm, calculating eyes took their time. No evidence pointed any wrong doings to Rex.

The time Joshua spent helping undercover detectives, the mug shots, the morgues, all of it swept over him. He felt sick to his stomach. Too often, the predator got off free.

"Ruthie had a reputation of being on the wild side. She ran away from her parents' home repeatedly during her adolescent years. The gal has a record that runs up and down the charts like a thermometer." Rollins snickered deep in his throat.

Joshua forced himself to listen. What did he really know about the woman who lived in his house and mothered his son?

"Here's more data on the sweet little innocent Ruthie Jessup." Rex Rollins pulled out another file. This one bulging from its manila borders. "Did Mr. and Mrs. Jessup happen to say how many times their daughter ran away? How they often found her visiting the cold cells of police departments on more occasions than not?"

Ricker glanced down to his pad, then up again. "They mentioned it."

"Because of her wild friends, she got herself fired in New York and landed a job in Cassell. The editor at the *New York Times* was so glad to get rid of her that he gave her a five-star review that landed her a job as editor-in-chief at the *Cassell Herald*. Did you check with them?"

"My next stop."

Rex's jaw lowered, his hands poised like a cat ready to pounce on an unsuspecting mouse. "Listen, I'll level with you. Ruth's been around the block more than once.

"I'm not saying she's not a capable journalist. The *Herald* will attest to her reliability and her talent. But a girl with Ruthie's background could change at a moment's notice." Rex snapped his fingers in front of the detective. "Men, drugs, you name it, just like that." He smiled back into Detective Ricker's face.

Rex Rollins pushed his chair closer, the steel bearings on the rollers sounding louder against the plastic mat in the quietness of the room. He grinned. "I would say that should about finish our discussion, gentlemen."

Joshua ached to give this sorry woman-beater a shiner to match the one he gave Ruth.

Joshua recalled the man who had looked down at Joshua from the lofty pinnacle of his horse. The guy oozed conceit and confidence. The problem was the file Ricker was thumbing through. Could Ruth be a chameleon herself? Was the information in there legit?

"Some of these items the Jessups are familiar with: the drugs, running away, the drunk driving. Still, I'd like to know your sources?"

"I am a respected lawyer with an impeccable record. I didn't accumulate these records to hold against Ruthie but to help her. You see, I want Ruthie to find herself a comfortable living here." He turned, rose, and strolled to his big twenty fifth-floor window. "I hoped she would find a love that could change her from a frightened runaway to a fulfilled woman. I was willing to give her that."

Joshua couldn't deny the facts. Ruth trusted Rollins enough to make him a beneficiary. Could it be a lover's spat? Rollins hit her and Ruth ran away. She could have gotten most of those scratches from running through the woods. Rollins was mad and drunk enough to drive away, thinking she'd get a ride from someone.

Rollins glanced down at the pedestrians below. He didn't bother to turn but kept talking with his back to them as if they mattered less than the little people below his window.

"Take my advice, Detective Ricker; check out that Amish community. Ruth spent Saturday afternoon telling me how our society could learn some things from the Amish. Deep down, she's an idealist. Hope for the helpless and all that. Her good intentions were often for misplaced reasons. She could be hiding out with this stranger. You never know about Ruthie. She told me she spent a year in New York as an undercover reporter."

"Well, you've got my attention. So, what did the man look like?" Ricker asked.

Rex looked over his shoulder and grinned at Joshua.

He returned Rollins' stare for stare, not batting an eyelash.

Ricker's pen poised over his notepad. His glasses shone in the sunlight coming from the window.

Rollins smirked. "Tall, well built, dressed in denim, suspenders, a blue shirt, and a straw hat. I couldn't see much of his face for the hat."

"That describes every Amish man in the county. Don't you have anything more you can give us?"

"That explains why you're hounding me. I'm convenient and accessible." Rollins sat down, rubbing his lips with his forefinger. "I don't have her. Mr. Johansson might know more than he's saying."

Joshua had a bad feeling about this. Johansson never held his tongue or temper in check. He'd blurt out Ruth's whereabouts.

Detective Ricker ran his eyes over Rex Rollins like a poker player. "Can you give us a description of the terrain that night? Any fields, streams?"

Rex's face turned red as the apple on his desk. "Some farmer's lane. It was dark. How do you expect me to remember when I was drunk enough to land my car in a ditch—but didn't." He paused, rubbing his temples. "We finished off the bottle of vodka together, then had a little lovemaking, and—brought her to Johansson's place. It's all a bit hazy."

"Her bed wasn't slept in."

"I didn't tuck her in," Rollins said. "How should I know what she did after I dropped her off? She was bent on seeing more of the countryside. Maybe she went for a walk and got lost. Ruthie's innocent in ways I don't like to say, always willing to accept a man at face value. Yet, she had a way of making a man's blood boil in a split second."

Rex walked over and stood facing Joshua, then bent forward and whispered. "I've got to tell you; these Amish men aren't ready for our

Ruthie." He winked. "If you know what I mean."

Joshua balled his fingers into a fist. It would feel so good to knock out another tooth right about now. "Being born a male isn't our choice—being a man, is." He narrowed his eyes. "Not a male pervert, you understand, but a man who controls his feelings."

"Ah." Rex took a step backwards as if he'd had the wind knocked out of his lungs.

Ricker removed his glasses, looking long and fast at Rex, like Ricker was a complacent cowboy ready to rope an ornery steer. "Amish are known for their quiet ways and staunch religious background. You're not suggesting they're holding Ruth against her wishes."

Rex raised his arms. "Ruthie. She likes it rough."

"You've known a few of those naughty girls like Ruth." The Detective rose, taking some papers out of his jacket pocket. "Some have filed complaints against you."

Rex walked away and sat back down in his chair. "Nothing that stuck. Look, I'll come out with you a week from today. That is if I can find the gasoline. I found me enough gasoline to get to Detroit and back—"

"Detroit?" It clicked like a gun in Joshua's head. "To that satanist temple?" The years reversed like a speeding car. He was a cop again investigating a murder scene of four students killed by a fellow classmate. A fifteen-year-old kid who'd entered the house of satanists. The maimed birds he left in the boy's john. The kid knew something evil now filled his soul. He wrote on one class paper, "Help, I can't stop the voices in my head."

Josh looked down at his hands, feeling the helplessness again wash over him. No one understood. Like no one understood the evilness of what was to come.

"Yeah." Rex puffed out his chest. "Detroit's got the largest satanist temple in the whole of the grand old USA! They'll know what's going on in the rest of the world." Rex was on his feet again like something was festering in his head. He paced the room and then stopped before the detective. "Ruthie wanted to stay out all night. I told her I was tired and thought we should get some rooms in town, separate rooms, mind you."

"You are quite the gentlemen," Joshua muttered. And you're like your god, a good deceiver.

"I don't take advantage of a woman when she's been drinking." Rex read the doubt on their faces. "Look, I have a list of clients, judges, even the opposing prosecutors who will vouch for my character. My sin is—I like to help women. There are men out there who will take advantage of a good-looking and innocent girl without conscience. That's not me. No sir. The trouble is, some ladies with questionable morals will take advantage of good-looking men, if you know what I mean. Makeup tales to give them bad reputations."

"Thank you for your time." Ricker stood, pointed to the folders, and said, "May I take these? I can return them to you in a week if that's satisfactory?"

"Keep them. We should have our power back soon; everything in the folder is on my computer. I could hire some bloodhounds to find Ruthie's body." He rubbed his eyes. "I hate to think that my lovely Ruthie could be lying dead in that dirty creek. Heaven forbid."

Rollins patted Private Detective Ricker on his shoulder as he and Joshua left the office, closing the door behind them.

"And I bet he knows just what dirty creek to take those bloodhounds to," Ricker murmured to Joshua as they passed the receptionist.

# Eleven

*"And there shall be a time of trouble, Such as never was since there was a nation, Even to that time. And at that time your people shall be delivered, Every one who is found written in the book. And many of those who sleep in the dust of the earth shall awake, Some to everlasting life, Some to shame and everlasting contempt." Daniel 12:1-2*

Ruth ran nervous fingers down the apron of her dress. Since Joshua left with that detective to Cassell last Thursday, he acted differently toward her.

"Ruth, make sure you bring the ears of late corn you picked to the canning today," Martha said. "I hope it won't taste too tough, it being so late in the season."

"Yes, I have that by the door, ready to be packed in the wagon," Ruth said, then sat across from Joshua and sipped her coffee.

"You probably should have kept it on the stalk and let it mature, so I could feed it to our horses." Joshua's glance darted from her to his mother.

"It's good eating corn, son, and the warmer weather helped mature it."

Ruth grimaced. He avoided saying anything to her, the one who harvested it.

Shoving down his eggs, then sipping the cup dry of his coffee, he rose, stomping toward the door. "Martha, maybe Ruth should stay here with Josh Jr. Might be a virus running around at the canning bee."

"Son, we missed the quilting bee last month because of your concerns. I think it's time for Ruth and Josh Jr. to get out in the sunshine and meet some of the ladies."

"If your mind is made up, I'll get the horse harnessed." Without another word, he left.

Well good riddance to him. No way could she be one of these gentle people. That man could heat her temper to the boiling point without a word being said.

The abrasive noise of steel wheels grinding the stony driveway aggravated her agitated temper further. If she wasn't an Amish woman, then where did she belong? She couldn't adjust to having her hair braided tightly. But—she liked it here, liked the security. Was it the security she liked, or the tall, good-looking daddy of Josh Jr. who acted mad at her for what she had no clue?

Joshua loaded the sweet corn, canning supplies, and baskets of beans, tomatoes, and blackberries in the wagon's bed. He offered Ruth his hand. She hesitated. Callused, stained fingers, an honest man's hand. After the way he ignored her at breakfast this morning, she wanted to slap it away. His mouth did that twisty thing that told her he was laughing at her. She avoided looking at him and took his hand. Using her good leg, she stepped up into the wagon, allowing her just-mended ankle to trail behind.

Joshua's eyes danced their way into hers as he handed his son to her, and she looked away. He directed his comment to Martha. "You have yourself a good Ladies Day now."

"Land sakes," Martha said, "I feel I'm driving a plow with that big old rump staring me in the face."

Joshua and Ruth joined in the laughter. The sound of it sang through the early morning mist around them.

"Giddy up, Betsy." Martha slapped the reins. As the horse clipped down the winding driveway, Ruth's kapp ties flapped against her cheeks like strings on a kite. "You have a pleasant way about you, dear, and a laugh that invites company."

Did Joshua think her laugh pleasant? She peeked over her shoulder. Joshua, his arms crossed against his square chest, smiled back. The warmth from his look flooded her face. Her gaze fell to her lap, into Josh Jr.'s little face.

Martha tittered. "I think my son and Josh Jr. have a lot to do with your happy heart."

Ruth could not deny that, only she'd be happier if she knew what ailed Joshua. She kissed Josh Jr.'s forehead.

His bright blue eyes were wide and alert. "Ach, he's a beautiful child. I couldn't be happier if he were my own. You darling thing. And to think your poor mother will never know."

Martha patted her arm. "There, there, his Mutter knows. The good Lord sets our feet down on the right pathway if we listen to His voice and obey His words. Never doubt His will, dear."

"Yes, I'm beginning to understand that." There wouldn't be a better time than now to ask. "Martha, do you know what I've done to get your son distraught with me?"

She patted her arm. "Not you, his heart. He's afraid to go a step farther, for fear you will remember your past and leave us."

"Oh."

"We'll be at the canning soon. We've done most of it earlier. Just a few straggling vegetables and fruits left to do."

Ruth glanced back at the collection of baskets. The glass jars clicked a resounding tune in their boxes when Martha hit a bump in the road. "Why did Joshua say to enjoy our Ladies Day? I would think canning wouldn't be all that fun?"

"Ha, ha, the menfolk think when we ladies have a get-together and have our coffee and cake and conversation that it is more fun than work. It is true. Many hands make the chores pleasant." Martha glanced toward her. Her sharp eyes never missed anything. Could she see Ruth's nervousness? If someone should ask her name or what she was doing there, what should she say?

"Remember, try not to say much, let me do the talkin'," Martha said.

Ruth had no doubt now. Martha was capable of reading minds.

"I doubt we'll have need of sayin' anything, what with the way news travels here."

Ruth looked at her confused. "How does it travel?"

"You'll see for yourself. Johansson is the best source to spread any around. He's the Paul Revere of our community."

Ruth had reveled in the hospitality of the Stutzmans' for a little over six weeks now. Their entertainment consisted of listening to Bible readings and telling stories. She loved hearing about Jesus, the Man who could walk on water and heal the sick and could foretell the future. She was small work. Jesus could heal her if He hadn't started already.

Ruth's heart felt it would bust with gratefulness. Only a benevolent God could have taken her from a muddy hole and placed her into this loving home.

She bowed her head in silent prayer. "Martha, what if I wasn't a good person? What if God is trying to protect me from myself? Maybe He's pointing me in the right direction and doesn't want me to remember my bad life? Do you think He could be?"

Martha bit her bottom lip. "Ja, could be. Only, I wouldn't worry. This is not your trouble or mine. God tells us in His Good Book that the day's troubles are sufficient, and we are not to worry about the tomorrows."

Pulling up the driveway, she reined the horse to a stop. She climbed down and tied Betsy to the hitching pole alongside five Standardbred horses.

Martha glanced at the large Percheron that, compared to the harness horses, looked gigantic. Reaching for her boxes of jars, she glanced back. "We don't need to worry about our Betsy defending herself."

Ruth laughed, lifted a box, rested it on her hip, placed Josh Jr. on her other hip, and followed Martha through the threshold.

---

John and Ellen Walsh's sprawling porch wrapped around the first floor. The second story had a balcony that overlooked the expansive front yard. Two large rooms met Ruth's eyes. One had a stove and a long table where the women gathered. The large table was laden with clear jars and various pots. Baskets sat on the floor, brimming over with the produce of this year's garden.

"Excuse me, everyone. Please meet Sara's cousin from Ohio, come to visit us, and help tend to the boppli," Ellen said.

Martha knowingly elbowed Ruth. She marveled at how the Amish knew about the goings and comings of everyone without the need of the mail service or modern aids.

"Ellen, how did the quilting go?" Martha asked.

"Gut, but we missed you last month."

"Ja, and I missed not being there."

One of the girls held out a quilt. Ruth marveled at the bright colors and hues. "What is this pattern called?"

"Sunshine and shadows," Martha said.

"My, Josh Jr. is the spitting image of his Dati," Ellen said and held out her hands.

Ruth clutched the child to her as if he were her security blanket and looked imploringly at Martha.

She took the boppli out of her arms and handed Josh Jr. to Ellen.

Josh Jr. opened his eyes. "What beautiful blue eyes, Martha." That was all Ellen could say because Josh Jr. let out a howl of protest to this new face poking into his world. "Oh, my, what a set of lungs that boppli has!"

Ruth held her arms out and soon had Josh Jr. smiling again.

"You are good with the bopplis and kinder." Ellen turned to Martha. "We could use someone with a gift like Ruth's at the gatherings."

A dog barked outside, and the chickens scurried for shelter, warning them a stranger was coming. The sound of rubber tires crunching against the gravel outside confirmed it. The ladies hurried toward the front windows.

"Ach, a police car. What do you think they want?"

Ruth looked out. Flashbacks of a black car sent lightning bolts shaving the dark interiors of her mind. She clutched Josh Jr. closer. Two heavy-set policemen walked toward the house.

Ellen opened the door. She smiled back into their solemn faces. "Willkum."

"Thank you, ma'am." The two policemen, one shorter than the other, walked in. "I'm Sheriff Baker, and this is Officer Roy Smith."

The shorter one, Sheriff Baker, had a wiry mustache that poked out from his cheeks like a bramble on a fence. Removing his hat, he displayed the same thick stringy hair on his head.

Officer Smith was a head taller and much younger than the sheriff. Sheriff Baker elbowed Officer Smith to remove his hat. As the sheriff drew out his pad of paper, his thick leather jacket creaked with every movement of his large arms. Clearing his throat, he unfolded an 8 x 10 sheet and held it up to them. "Have any of you ladies seen this woman?"

"She's in her late twenties. She worked in Cassell for the newspaper as editor-in-chief. She came with the hunt club about six weeks ago. No one has seen her since." Sheriff Baker walked around the room with the photo.

Ruth slipped behind the crowd. She couldn't pinpoint why, but she didn't want these officers to spot her.

Martha stepped forward, took the picture, and studied it. "Ja, she is pretty. What do you think might have happened to her?"

Officer Smith shrugged. "We don't know. Please keep an eye out for her." The policeman took the picture from Martha and shuffled through the crowd, asking every woman, "Have you seen her?"

Ellen took the offered paper. "Not too many English women come around these parts. Have you checked the Community Hospital?" She handed it back to Sheriff Baker.

"Yes, we have. She was last seen here. So, I've got orders to check the Amish community. Anyone remember seeing a stranger?"

"Ja, you." Ellen smiled.

Ada and the ladies chortled. Ellen threw out her arms like she was feeding her chickens. "You're welcome to look around. We have nothin' to hide."

"Much obliged." Sheriff Baker's thick leather boots thumped his way through the rooms.

Martha quietly moved next to her hostess and whispered. "Why did you tell them that? They need a search warrant to investigate your house."

"I'm not hidin' anything. Why should I care?"

Misgivings filtered across Ruth's thoughts; a chill crept up her spine. She's a stranger, and it had been about that time when Joshua found her. When Martha joined her, she whispered, "Could I be the person they're looking for?"

"Nee. It is not you." Martha patted Ruth's hand consolingly. "Stay here. I'll talk to the nice policemen."

"I don't want to leave your side." Ruth held onto Martha's arm like a timid child.

"You'll be fine."

"Please don't leave me."

"Why, *Kind*," Martha said, "You're shaking from head to foot."

"And I can't stop shaking." Ruth snatched a deep breath. "Maybe I should peek at the snapshot? I could see if this English girl looked familiar to me."

Martha put a hand around Ruth's waist. "Not to worry. If this English lady wants to be found, they will find her. Everything will be gut."

The two policemen's boots echoed through the rooms. When they returned, they stopped in front of Martha and Ruth.

"What a cute child," Officer Smith said.

"Ja, this is Josh Jr." Martha cuddled the child. "He's a wonderful gut boy."

"Will you look at those chubby cheeks, Smith?" Baker said. "See how rosy they are. He has good color."

Officer Smith peered down at the sleeping child. "So?"

"That means he's healthy. You'll understand it more once you're married and have a kid of your own."

Smith's large form shadowed Ruth's face. "How old is your boy?"

"He's a year old," Ruth said.

Sheriff Baker frowned. "He's little for his age."

"He came early. He'll catch up with his cousins soon," Martha said.

"Ja." Ruth glanced down at the wooden flooring.

"Keep an eye out for that gal. There might be a reward for her whereabouts," Sheriff Baker said.

"Gut. From her husband?"

Sheriff Baker, who'd started toward the door, stopped, his hand on the door handle. He looked down at his paper. "No, says here she's twenty-eight years old and single. Her parents are offering the reward."

Martha smiled and handed Josh Jr. back to Ruth. The policemen left, and the noise of tires crunching the gravel drifted through the open window. "Why do you think they came here?"

"Probably because they saw all the buggies," Ellen said. "We haven't heard the last from them, I'm thinking. What you suppose has gotten over that English girl, not telling her Mutter where she is? Not good. That English girl should have thought about her poor Mutter."

Ruth clutched Josh Jr. to her chest. Her breath came in gasps. "Maybe the poor girl is hurt. Maybe she can't tell her Mutter. Maybe she has amnesia..." *Why did I say that?*

Five pairs of eyes stared at her. She hunched her shoulders and slinked behind Martha. *Would these policemen handcuff her if she should be this English girl? What had she done?*

"Go about your canning, ladies. My cousin had an experience like that once. You see, one of her young cousins had amnesia, and they searched and searched for her," Martha said.

"Was she a mädel?"

"A Frau and a Mutter. Her husband was worried sick for her. We must get to our canning."

The wood stove sat idle while the portable kerosene stove burned brightly, giving little steam and heat to the cozy room. The aroma of the sliced tomatoes and simmering blackberries blended companionably.

Ruth snipped the ends of the string beans, then cut them into smaller pieces and handed her bowl to Naomi.

Naomi smiled. Seven months pregnant with her seventh child, her eyes sparkled, and her fair complexion seemed aglow with an inner light. She poured water into the bowl, strained the beans, and with a small funnel inserted in the top of the jars, she poured them into pint- and quart-size containers. Her two-year-old's little hands were eager to play with the shiny utensils that had his mother's attention. A mop of blond hair fell helter-skelter into his large blue eyes.

Ruth smiled back at Naomi's five-year-old girl sweeping the floor. She was a lovely more petite version of her mother. The little girl eagerly turned her small hand to handling the too-large-broom in sweeping up the bean fragments cluttering the shiny wooden floor, smiling as she performed her duties.

The beans now in jars, Ella added Himalayan salt and filled the jars three-quarters full of water.

"Martha, set the pressure cooker for ten pounds and the timer to fifteen minutes," Ella said. "After they come out, we'll have to leave them here until they are perfectly cooled. That will set the seals on the jars."

Ruth looked up from washing the dishes and nodded.

Anna peeled the tomatoes and showed Ruth how to dig out the seeds for next year's planting. Then Anna mashed the tomatoes lightly, placed them in a pot, and let them boil.

Ella laid the grinder over the pot, which had seen much use, ground them until they were more liquid, then added salt and pepper to the tomatoes. "This will be the consistency of tomato juice when complete. Good for soups and such. If you wanted tomato sauce, you would have to let it boil longer to thicken it."

The boiling jars hummed a lively tune in the pressure cooker, their rattling melody adding a backdrop to the ladies' conversations.

The tomato aroma mingled with the fruity smells of blackberries bubbling on the stove, and when the berries were removed, Ella added lemon juice, Perma-Flo, and sugar.

"Now we'll do the sweet corn, and afterward we'll have our dinner," Anna said.

The aroma wafting past Ruth's nose smelled heavenly.

She worked up quite an appetite, shucking and cleaning off the cobs. Her troubling thoughts floated away with the aromas. She stopped for a moment to observe the children. The older children took care of their younger siblings, obeying their parents without argument.

Why allow outside concerns to worry her? God can heal all wounds. Could she learn to feed her faith and starve her fears with meaningful work?

After shucking, she tackled the juicy sweet corn with relish, slicing it neatly off the cob. She poured it into pint containers. Ella added the Himalayan salt and water and set the jars into the pressure cooker.

The sliced chicken canned last year was placed in a skillet, fried in flour, and was soon ready for the table. Martha said they canned the tough birds, usually those who were old and past their laying years. "I wonder how it will taste."

Naomi's husband, Norman, came for supper and sat down at the head of the table.

Sweet corn, potato casserole, homemade bread, and sliced tomatoes followed. The curtains on the window fluttered in the autumn breezes as the wives, children, and young single women sat down to eat the bounty of their labors.

Everyone bowed their heads in prayer.

As the food was passed, so did the mouthwatering aromas. Ruth couldn't believe how delicious it was. Even the tough old bird was flavorful and tender. The only cloud hovering around the table was her recurring memory of that dark car.

Like a shadow hounding her heels, thoughts of uniformed men wrapped Ruth's shoulders like a dreary wet shroud and sent shivers traipsing down her spine. She yearned to embrace this peace—but her unknown past bound her in her own locked room.

Norman returned to his work as soon as he finished eating.

As the door shut, Josh Jr. yawned and stretched from the sofa a few feet away. Ruth got up and covered him with the small hand-sewn quilt that had fallen to the floor. He settled beneath its warmth.

Millie walked over and smiled. "Ruth is a distant cousin, on Sara's side? Ja, that's gut, real gut."

"Gut for boppli, too." Martha looked back at Millie.

"And gut for his Dati."

Ruth squirmed beneath their glances. "It is warm in here, I think."

"Ja, but not enough to entice that bloom in your cheeks." Anna and the women giggled.

Martha swerved the conversation to pressing matters. "Officer Smith looks young. Especially to be a policeman. Did he look familiar?"

"Can't say for certain," Anna said. "His first name is Roy. That doesn't say anything to my memory either."

Officer Roy Smith's face popped uninvited into Ruth's thoughts. Her mind swam around looking for a connection. Roy? Where had she heard that name? Pictures flashed through her mind like bolts of lightning.

A tall dark-haired man, his handsome face smiled confidently at her from atop a chestnut gelding. His laughter rang through an early morning mist.

"This corn is gut," Ella said.

"Ja, delicious." Martha fingered the black tablecloth. "You think this would go good with the harvest *rumspringa*?"

Ruth looked. To her, it resembled the evening skies and the stars—it happened at night, and a man had grabbed her harshly, he slapped her across the face. Roy? Not Roy...*Rex!*

She gasped and turned away from the table. The window with the fluttering curtains drew her like a moth to a flame. Yes, yes, she remembered. She ran into the darkness to hide.

"What's the matter, Ruth?" Martha said.

A spasm of shivers crept from her toes to her throbbing forehead.

"You've got yourself a chill." Martha walked her to the table and sat her down. "Ja, what you need is a good cup of herbal tea."

Another bout of shudders traveled through her body.

Josh Jr. was done with sleeping and screamed his disfavor. Ruth rushed toward him, picked the child up, and clutched him to her bosom. Who is Rex? Could she be that missing girl in the picture? Oh, why hadn't she been brave enough to look? Was she a coward? She recalled someone had once called her that.

Ruth glanced down at Josh Jr. who had a set of lungs that could bring the cows home. He smiled up at her, his eyelids drooping.

"Why, the Kind's swimming in his fairyland of boppli dreams," Ada whispered.

Ruth's bottom lip trembled. A tear trickled its way down her cheek. No, I'll not let that bad man get you or me, Josh Jr.

She glanced into Martha's concerned eyes and grinned, handing her Josh Jr. "I'll be all right." She sipped her tea, feeling its healing warmth wash through her body like Jesus' words had to the Samaritan woman at the well. Living water. Yes, that's right! Jesus will protect me through His word. Ruth held up her cup. "This is what I needed."

Ella pushed her speckles up the bridge of her nose. "My *schwester* was like you. Uniformed men made her fearful."

Anna nodded. "She feared any stranger. You know, did I tell you, she got shoved off the road back in '66 by an Englisher driving a bright red pickup?"

"Anna, you should not tell Ruth about that. It is not gut." Ada frowned.

"Why not? It's true," Anna said. "Our Almighty gives us a forewarning, a sort of sixth sense about these things we need to stay clear of. Right to this day, my schwester wishes she'd listened to that dream the Lord gave her the night before and not gotten in her buggy."

Ruth squeezed her eyes shut. Another picture popped before her eyes, not a red truck, but a Jeep Cherokee. Yes, the dark-haired man named Rex hammered his fist in her face while she sat in his car.

☼

Hearing the roar of an engine, Joshua looked up.

"Now, what do you suppose they want?" said Johansson.

They left their pile of wood splitting and met Sheriff Baker and Officer Smith halfway. Sheriff Baker was a friend they could count on. He helped them out when motorists didn't adhere to the speed limits. The

Amish knew they could trust the sheriff. However, Officer Smith was new to the community.

Clearing his throat, Sheriff Baker was the first to speak. "We saw the buggies out front of John and Ellen Walsh's. Officer Smith thought we should drop in and see if any of your ladyfolk had seen this gal in the photo. Hope you don't mind none." The sheriff extended his arm. "Here's one for you, too."

Joshua noticed the sheriff's nervousness. That wasn't like Baker at all. He had spent many an hour in their homes enjoying meals. Even hired some of them for carpentry work. "Something more on your mind?"

Sheriff Baker didn't need a second invite. "Smith and I've been arguing, and seeing you both here when we had an hour to kill, it made sense to me to stop." He crossed his arms. "I'm not sure you people know, but there's a European UN leader in office now, and his place of residence is smack dab on Mount Moriah. In the middle of Israel's holy center."

"You mean the temple mount?" Johansson looked up, startled. "What happened to the peace agreement?

"Ingenious move, this sharing arrangement with the Israelites and the Palestinians, it brought peace to the land for three and a half years!" Sheriff Baker waved his arms. "Then out of the blue, Iran, with help from Russia and China, bombed the West Bank and Judea but not without a fight from our own United States."

"Is that what happened?" Joshua said.

"How much do you know about the economic condition of our country and the world?"

"Not much, Sheriff. We like to keep to ourselves," Joshua said. "We have our share to do taking care of our families."

"I don't blame you one bit." Baker shifted from one foot to the other. "I know some children who grow up without a daddy, sometimes without a mother, raised by their grandparents."

"Ja, it's gut to have strong community support. Our ancestors understood this, so we keep the tradition alive, living as the Good Book intended."

"I'll give you the slam-bang version of the happenings outside your tranquil world. You know about the coronavirus and all those geophysical occurrences of earthquakes, fires, typhoons, tornadoes, locusts, and other pestilences. Then, as if that wasn't enough, the liberals in Washington decided to spend more money that we didn't have, and the grand old USA is, like most nations, flat broke—"

"And now the greatest man that ever lived," Officer Smith interrupted, "is in Europe, and the whole world has an economic plan that everyone embraced, and he—"

"The European Union has." Sheriff Baker corrected.

"You mean the new and affluent Roman Empire, don't you?" Officer Smith's face had turned fire-red. "This empire is a good thing. He's given world peace to us and is feeding the hungry. This UN guy has established order amidst—"

"Don't be so sure about that, Officer Smith. I got a feeling he's up to no good." Sheriff Baker perched his arms on his belt.

Joshua felt the tension escalate between Sheriff Baker and Officer Smith. Neither willing to compromise their beliefs.

"I've been raised in this religion my whole life." Smith rushed on. "The pope is unifying the world, declaring a tolerance of all faiths, pluralism of religion that is acceptable to God. He's met with the Muslim leader and signed a document for world peace. A world religion is better than having these petty religious movements." He raised his arms in exasperation. "Can't you see the good this is going to bring? It's all written down in the Catholic Missal."

"I feel like the good pope is being used by these Muslims. I tell ya, this new UN leader has got his own agenda and speaks out of both sides of his mouth. He changes his words to fit the occasion. He's up to no good," Sheriff Baker declared. "Mark my words, he'll make everyone conform to his ideologies."

"What you're saying makes sense, Sheriff," Johansson said. "Jesus stated in the Bible that He is the way, the truth, and the life. 'No one comes to the Father except through Me.'"

"Ja," Joshua said. "The Bible says, I think it's in Ephesians, there is one Lord, one faith, one baptism and only one God and Father of us all, who is above all, and through all, and in all."

"So, how can the pope say that Muslims are brothers and be of our faith?" Sheriff Baker asked.

"I don't know," Joshua said. "These are fearful times. Christians must know what they believe and why. Be aware. Because if we, or an angel, preach any other gospel…let him be accursed. I know that's in Ephesians someplace too."

"And that's not the half of it. This UN guy who is head of the World Organization wants all nations to register their names, addresses, children, religious affiliation, bank accounts, and vaccinations. Then the authorities will put this into a microchip and insert it into your hand—"

"I heard about that. Don't the Swedes already do that?" Johansson asked.

"Yeah, only now it's on a much larger scale and for a different reason. Riots have sprung out across the country, and we're under martial law. I expect soldiers to arrive any day now, and they could very well be these super soldiers that are part man and part machine. Machine humans with super-vision and internet-brains." The sheriff's walkie-talkie started squawking, and he and Officer Smith hurried away.

Johansson stroked his beard. "What do you make of this, Joshua?"

# Twelve

*"And four great beasts came up from the sea, each different from the other. The first was like a lion, and had eagle's wings. I watched till its wings were plucked off; and it was lifted up from the earth and made to stand on two feet like a man."* Daniel 7:3

"Danke." Joshua took the steaming cup of coffee from Martha. It had begun. The Antichrist and this new world government hadn't wasted any time. Joshua hardly recognized his peaceful community. Two UN soldiers rode bikes up and down Main Street in their little town that consisted of a feed and grocery store, a funeral parlor, and a hardware store. No arrests so far. "I've got to go to a meeting tonight. I'll be at the Johansson house."

Martha's troubled gaze fell on her son, her eyes questioning.

He looked away. How could he deceive his mother?

"Why are you going there, son?"

Joshua rested his hand on her shoulder and felt a shudder travel through her body. "We are in the final stretch now. Daniel tells us when the abomination of desolation is set up there will be one thousand two hundred and ninety days—"

"Until Jesus returns?"

"Ja. Only in Daniel 12:12 God tells him, 'Blessed *is* he who waits, and comes to the one thousand three hundred and thirty-five days.'"

"So, the gut Lord gave Himself some leeway. My, that could be over a month of more waiting. No wonder no one knows the day or the hour, not even the angels, but Almighty God himself."

"Ja, and we've used up sixty-four of those days."

"So why Johansson's? Thought he chose the English over his kind."

"Or is he doing the Lord's bidding? Is that why I left the Ordnung, only to return? Johansson knows the gut side about the outside world, the goings-on better than our people do. He got this meeting together because some of the English are asking for our help. I think *Vater* would agree we need to help. We have stored up gut for these final three and a half years." Joshua continued.

"These English are not asking for our food. They ask for our knowledge, how to live in a world without their modern conveniences, a world that regressed into the 1800s. No one knows the day, nor hour when our Lord returns, but we must not grow impatient watching in anticipation. Nor be like those foolish virgins who were not prepared for their bridegroom's arrival and sadly heard, 'I do not know you.'"

Martha hugged her son close. "Ja, preparation for God's kingdom cannot be borrowed. Not even your own children raised in a godly home can inherit salvation—they must ask for it and accept it on their own. What is going to happen next?"

"We must be the light God has called us to be."

"The Good Book warns us to beware of false prophets," Martha said. "Many will betray one another, and lawlessness will abound, it says so in—"

"How will I know which Englisher I can trust and which I cannot?" Joshua shrugged. "I do not, but God does. He will show me. Meanwhile, we must make provisions to go the distance and be like the five wise virgins in case the bridegroom delays—Jesus is worth the wait."

He picked up his coat. "I feel my calling is to help God's elect not to be deceived in these latter days. Ja, God is planning to shorten the days for His elect during these tryin' times. Some English don't know what the inside of the Bible looks like."

"That is sad, son."

"Ja, our Lord cares about His flock." He shrugged on his coat and hat. Only God knew what he was up against. With his hand on the door handle, he said, "I must do what I can to help them not lose heart and not take the mark of this antichrist."

"Can I come, please?" Ruth said.

He stopped. "Not a gut place for a mädel. I go by myself." He paused, looking around. "I need my Bible."

Ruth hurried into his bedroom and got his Bible. She held it out to him, her eyes gazing questioningly into his. "I might be of use to you. I'm ready to leave."

He hesitated, feeling the cool metal doorknob beneath his fingertips. Was it wrong of him not to want to protect her from the world she ran from? "Ruth, we could be entering the devil's playground tonight. So, beware."

---

Ruth looked around the dimly lit room. She counted forty English men and not nearly as many women. Not having their cell phones, televisions, radios, refrigerators, bathrooms, running water, or electric lights must be hard. A lady told her that most English families showered every day.

The past months had taken their toll on everyone. The odor of sweat and unwashed bodies mingled with the smell of kerosene lamps and wood smoke that hung in the air.

Mr. Johansson, seeing her in the crowd, approached her. "Komme, we need to find some seats." He led her to the front of the room. Joshua found two more chairs.

Johansson pointed to a man who raised his arm the moment Joshua stepped to the front of the large room.

The man, dressed in jeans and a polo shirt, stood. "What I want to know is how do you Amish get your water for cooking and cleaning and take a bath?"

"I can say from being in your world for many years and living in mine now that often it was pure luxury for the Amish farmer to be as clean as the English with their electricity, indoor plumbing, and showers. The English often liked to scratch their funny bone by poking fun at the way we dressed, worked, and played. Look at this new experience as if you are camping out. Only inside your own homes," Joshua said.

Some faces looked frightened. Ruth understood. So did Joshua.

"Some of your faces resemble what a deer looks like when caught grazing in my pasture during deer hunting season."

That got a chuckle from the group.

"You others resemble a coyote, poised, ready to run or, if it must be, fight."

That got a mumble from the crowd. "The rest of you are just plain antsy. You're squirming like you were sitting on an ant bed."

People laughed and patted each other on the back. A little humor never hurt. Joshua looked at Ruth and grinned.

She returned the favor, figuring she was the coyote. Whatever had caused Joshua to doubt her earlier, had dissipated with this new adversity.

"How do you bathe?" one woman yelled out.

"Depends on how you want your bath. If you want a hot one, we have in the back of our wood-burning stove, a metal box attached where we pour water, and this heats up nicely. We use it for washing dishes and such things like bathing. Most of you probably don't have a wood-burning stove. So, you can heat water on your Coleman stove. Some of you probably have this around from when you camp out. Also, any fireplace with a hearth, you can put a pan down and heat water. Don't forget about the sunlight. It can heat water.

Mumblings followed.

"Or else, you could bathe in the closest creek or river."

More mumblings.

"Most of you have wells, right? Good. We can show you how you can hook up your well to a gasoline-driven motor."

"Just how much gasoline are you talking? It's being rationed as we speak."

"I use about a gallon every two months for my needs," Joshua said. "What we do is we start our well, fill up our holding tank and then shut it off. We use the water in our holding tanks for the day."

A man in the back raised his hand.

Joshua nodded for him to speak.

He stood. "I have a portable water filter if anyone needs to borrow it. Also, I have a solar generator kit I'll let you borrow." The man sat back down.

"How do you wash your clothes?" someone said.

"Wash day is something I know little of. I know my Mutter uses a ringer washer and hangs her clothes outside to dry. That makes my clothes in summer smelling nice, like sunshine and fresh air all rolled together."

"What does your mother do during the winter months?"

"She hangs some near the stove and the rest outside. It takes a while to dry outside." Joshua grinned. "Sometimes I have to bang my pants on the doorpost just to get the ice off before bringing it inside to finish drying."

Some of the English laughed.

"After my clothes have been outside and once I thaw and warm them up inside, they're nice and soft. You'll see."

"No, I don't see." Mr. Brinkman, the lumber and storekeeper stood and said, "I don't see why I came to this here meeting. Soon we'll have our electricity up and running, including our televisions, computers, and cell phones. In a couple more weeks, we'll not remember any of this, and know—"

"Know?" Sheriff Baker slammed the door behind him. "You can know this, Brinkman, our life as we knew it is over."

Sheriff Baker walked toward him and handed Joshua a brown wrapped parcel. "Okay, we've got a lot to cover, so let's begin." Sheriff Baker reached into his briefcase, drew out a folder and plopped it down on the table. "We won't be able to buy or sell if we don't take the allegiance."

Mumbles from the over-packed room arose. Sheriff Baker slammed his fist down on the Johanssons' table to silence the room.

"Allegiance to what?" A fiftyish man with a head full of hair and a beard to match yelled out. "From that sorry dictator who perched himself like a god in Israel's temple?"

"What is this guy, some kind of nut?" someone yelled from the back of the room.

"What do you mean allegiance?" another man yelled out. "We're Americans and live in the home of the brave and the land of the free. I don't remember electing him!"

Sheriff Baker banged his fist down on the table again. "Not anymore. There aren't any elections to worry over. We've lost our freedoms with that financial crash that wiped out our savings and that solar storm that no one can explain. The big shots call that storm a coronal mass ejection."

"This is all a bunch of hogwash," someone yelled out. "You got it all wrong. You got this confused with that coronavirus plague that keeps mutating into another worse plague."

"You can call it what you want. It still means no electrical power for any of us." The sheriff glanced over his paperwork. "Looks like I covered the most important facts."

"Thought this was a HEMP attack?" someone else yelled out. What's HEMP?"

"It's a large-scale electromagnetic pulse, which can be produced at high-altitude. High-altitude electromagnetic pulse, HEMP. It's a weapon for cyber warfare or cyber terrorism to disrupt communications," Sheriff Baker said.

"Was that what stopped the Colonial Pipeline and giant meat packing plant back in June of 2021?" the same man asked.

The sheriff shrugged. "Those were just cyber-attacks."

"*Just?* I was in Tennessee when my car ran out of gas, and there were *no* gas stations that had any gasoline left!" the man yelled back.

"Sort of like now?" the sheriff said. "No one is fessing up to this latest attack. Back in 2020, our president tried to explain to the White House the potential threat of an EMP attack on our nation's electric grid. The Pentagon knew about Russia and China but didn't know about North Korea's and Iran's power until they attacked Judea and the

West Bank over a month ago."

"So? That's in Israel. They didn't conquer us," someone yelled.

"No, they didn't, but the president tried to keep the United Nations' stuffed shirts from grabbing more power in the United States. You got to remember, we're no longer a world power. The European Union holds all the cards now."

More mumblings followed. "So, what is this European UN guy asking for?" someone asked.

Joshua and the sheriff sat down heavily on the kitchen chairs Johansson offered them. "I'll say this as politely as I can. You understand that Christians worldwide have had to make sacrifices for what they believe; some have faced prison and death by beheading and hangings. What we say here should not go past these walls, do you understand?"

"Yeah, out with it, Sheriff; you've talked enough to fill a hot-air balloon."

Someone laughed.

"Who said that?" the sheriff demanded, bolting out of his chair.

"Come on, Sheriff Baker," Johansson said. "We can stand hearing the truth for a change."

"It's this big kahuna—you know that UN guy who prefers same-sex unions and wants to punish the Christians who gave him a hard time." Sheriff Baker took a long breath. He lowered his head and rubbed his forehead before he looked up and continued. "I've been ordered to collect your Bibles and religious books and burn them."

"I'd like to see you try!" someone hollered.

"Exactly," Sheriff Baker said. "And if I don't do as they tell me—then my head will be on the chomping block. Washington DC is in chaos. Generators run everything. There's no extra power for the surveillance cameras, and people are burning buildings, looting, and stealing whatever they can get their hands on. Extremists and anarchists blame the Christians and Jews for all these social and geophysical problems.

"I'm telling you to hide. Hide your Bibles and Christian books. Preferably, dig a hole in the yard for them. Having them in your possession could send you to prison." He pointed to a woman a few chairs away from Ruth. "And get rid of those crosses you have dangling around your necks too. That's become a hanging offense. The orders that were passed down to us by some liberals is they plan to search your houses, confiscate your guns—"

"No way! That's an infringement on my rights as a citizen." The crowd grew increasingly hostile.

"Look. I don't like it any more than you do. And remember, tell no one, not even Officer Smith, that I told you. You got that? I think they'll be coming for us soon."

Angry grumblings followed.

"These liberals and followers of this anarchist are gaining by numbers. This European UN dictator is busy killing Christians in Europe who won't take his mark. Our police force is stretched like a rubber band. We can't protect every building, every person. There's going to be more buildings burned, more muggings, more street gangs, and more killings."

"Go on, Sheriff," a man said. "What else have you got?"

Sheriff Baker fumbled through his briefcase. His hands shook so hard he had trouble finding what he sought. "I'll pass this around; read it and pass it back to me."

"Why don't you read it to us and save us some time?"

Sheriff Baker fell back in his chair and dropped his arms to his sides. "Our country is divided. Half for this New World Order guy, and half for the America of old, upholding their Christian heritage."

---

Joshua glanced down at the bold print of the sheriff's notice.

"Can you read it?" the sheriff said to Joshua. "My throat feels as dry as that road out there."

Joshua reached for the paper and stood. He cleared his throat and began. "Before I read this, I'd like to say something."

"Go ahead, Joshua," Johansson encouraged him.

"You came to this meeting tonight because you're Christians seeking survival skills. Some may not know the Bible the way you should. I'd like to read something written over two thousand years ago that speaks about our trouble today." He picked up his Bible and turned to Revelation 12. "'Now when the dragon saw that he had been cast to the earth, he persecuted the woman who gave birth to the male *Child*. But the woman was given two wings of a great eagle, that she might fly into the wilderness to her place, where she is nourished for a time and times and half a time, from the presence of the serpent…he went to make war with the rest of her offspring, who keep the commandments of God and have testimony of Jesus Christ.'

"That's three and a half years. Now this European leader isn't claiming to be Christ—but all signs point to him declaring this soon."

"Do you think that somehow the United States will fight this Antichrist to the bitter end? That would be wonderful gut!" Heydenreich said.

"I can't be sure. But here is where I think we are at in this world saga. Second Thessalonians says something about the coming of the lawless one is according to the working of Satan, and he is a liar and full of deceit and deception."

"But," a woman rose to her feet, "what about the trumpet and the rapture of the church spoken about in Corinthians?"

"You mean the last trumpet?" Joshua clarified.

"Yes!"

"You're referring to 1 Corinthians 15:51 and 52. 'At the last trumpet…the dead will be raised incorruptible, and we shall be changed.' That means, being the last trumpet, this will happen lastly. That's when Jesus returns. You can see this in Revelations 14 and Matthew 24:29 and 31. 'Immediately after the tribulations of those days…And He will gather together His elect from the four winds.'" Joshua paused, but the room remained silent. He turned his attention to the sheriff's paper. "Sheriff Baker's paper is from the UN. Everyone over the age of eight must pledge allegiance to the European Union leader. The oath of allegiance consists of:

"Denouncing your religion, be it Jew, Christ-follower of any denomination. Then they must attend desensitizing classes and learn about the one true god. The new world government will not tolerate religious extremists, and those people hereby are classified as a domestic terrorist.

"As domestic terrorists, they will not have the privilege of a trial. The people's government will confiscate their property and will take their children to a reeducation camp. The worst offenders will face death by beheading."

Someone from the back spoke up. "Sounds like this dictator is trying to frighten us to giving into him without a fight. Like Europe did."

Sheriff Baker raised his arm. "This is serious stuff. This guy means business."

Joshua continued reading. "At such time that you accept this New World Order, you will receive the mark of his name, the number being 666, imbedded either on your forehead or right hand. With this mark, you will continue to perform life's functions, jobs, and purchasing ability without interference.

"Anyone not willing to take the mark cannot buy or sell. They will be removed from their job, their bank accounts and homes confiscated. Further disobedience will make it mandatory for this New World Order to terminate their lives."

Silence engulfed the room. Joshua laid the paper on the desk and sat down. "There's no doubt this European Union leader is the Antichrist. Christians are warned in Revelations 14 not to take the mark because that means he or she has accepted the Antichrist as their god."

A woman stood; the room quieted. "How're we going to live if we can't buy food?"

Words of assent echoed around the room.

Joshua seized his Bible and raised his hand to quiet the room.

"Joshua?" Sheriff Baker said.

"According to Matthew 24, we are now in the tribulation time. Jesus spoke of the abomination of desolation found in the book of Daniel, and it said there would be 1290 days, maybe a little more, before we are caught up with Jesus in the air. Incidentally, that 1290 days is the time and times and half-time I mentioned earlier, which equals three and a half years."

"So, you're saying we have three-and-a-half years to get through, and then this nightmare will be over?" a woman asked.

"Ja, before Jesus comes down to rescue us. Not that He hasn't already, by wiping our sins away when we ask His forgiveness. It'll be the ending to the prayer He told us to pray in the Our Father. 'Thy kingdom come. Thy will be done.' He's goin' to go to war with that Antichrist and his followers, and we'll be in his army! He's going to kick out Satan, and we'll see it happen!"

"Amen!" a man hollered out.

"We've got to hang on for three-and-a-half-years," another man said.

"Right, how are we going to do that?" a woman asked. "I can't draw water without my generator, and last time I was in town, the Shell station said they were nearly empty of gasoline and kerosene, and no trucks had come."

Joshua puckered his lips. "We'd have to think of a sharing plan. That could work."

"What are we going to do with no refrigeration?" someone else interjected.

"We'll do what the Amish do." Sheriff Baker slapped Joshua on his shoulder. "They've lived all their lives without electricity or any modern conveniences. We can do this for three-and-one-half years, right, Joshua?"

Joshua nodded. Were they all staunch Christians? Or would some of them fall, maybe turn in their neighbors and family members?

Was he certain this was his calling? To encourage the elect not to be waylaid by the Antichrist and his deceptiveness? He stood, raising his hands to silence the current of murmurs.

"Go ahead, Joshua, we're listening."

His heart felt like it was in his throat. "We are getting the cart before the horse. We need to decide here and now, are we going to pledge our loyalty to the one true Christ or to the Antichrist? If anyone else thought to bring along their Bible, they are welcome to read along with me. Revelation 14:9: 'If anyone worships the beast and his image, and receives *his* mark on his forehead or on his hand, he himself shall also drink of the wine of the wrath of God, which is poured out full strength into the cup of His indignation.'"

"No way," a woman protested. "This can't be true. God is a God of love; He wouldn't do this to us. And besides, where's the rapture? Christians were supposed to be taken up before all this antichrist stuff happened."

"Could it be that this UN man is the Christ?" a man said.

Mr. Johansson slowly rose from his chair. "Who said that?"

"Me." Mr. Brinkman, the owner of the general store and lumber company walked toward the front. Not more than five foot five, his receding hairline and large paunch were his distinguishing characteristics.

Brinkman's fat fingers fumbled with the brim of his hat as he stood at the front of the room. "Maybe we should sit quiet for a spell. After all, this European UN guy might be an okay fella. Give him a chance. All he desires is peace and harmony. Could be he'll figure out a way of getting our electrical grid working. I need electricity for my store and lumber mill." He shrugged. "After all, that's more of the Christian thing to do than becoming a rebel. Jesus said to turn the other cheek, remember?"

"Jesus warned us not to be deceived," Johansson said. "Right now, this UN man is sitting at the Temple Mount claiming he's God. Can he forgive your sins? Will he sacrifice his life to save yours? That's what the true Christ, the anointed one, does. He gives you His Holy Bible to read and then his Holy Spirit to guide you. And he doesn't make you wear his mark—because he wants you to decide for yourself, whether to believe in Him—or to follow this here Antichrist! Yes, it's your choice where you will spend eternity."

The crowd muttered.

Mr. Brinkman shook his head. "Now, Johansson, you don't know for certain that man has claimed to be God. Hitler thought he was

God. So what? This UN man wants everyone to live in harmony."

"It was him and his allies that sent everyone in the Gaza strip fleeing for their lives! How can you be so deceived?" someone yelled from the back.

"Ja," Johansson stood up. "Guess you didn't read the part Joshua hoped wouldn't apply to anyone here. You must accept Jesus as your Lord or Savior, or else God will allow you to believe this lie because—"

"I guess you think those Jews killing innocent animals and burning them in that temple as a sacrifice is the right thing to do. Huh?" Brinkman took a threatening step forward.

Joshua jumped to his feet, holding high his Bible. "Jesus said not to take this mark. Look, I've sat beside enough death beds to say no one here will escape the jaws of death. And only you decide where your future will be in eternity—heaven or hell."

"Humpf! If you believe *that* stuff," Brinkman said.

Joshua looked at the crowd, but it was Ruth's sweet face he could not pull his eyes away from. "It is not God's will for any to perish."

"Ha!" Mr. Brinkman yelled. "Don't you Christians teach about Jesus being all love and forgiveness?" Brinkman turned to face the crowd in the room and raised his hands. "Look, that holy man, what's his name, says this European guy is *the* one. To believe in him."

"He's got to be the one," a woman said. "I went to church so I wouldn't have to go through the tribulation, so I'd be taken up in the pre-trib rapture, and now that that's passed, I'll be taking the mid-trib rapture—when do you think it will happen? My pastor said the pre-trib rapture would come when Israel built again and began their sacrifices on the Temple Mount. That time has gone. But no rapture."

"You got that right," grumbled another woman dressed in a mini dress. "I had to endure all those plagues and hurricanes. I lost my last house in a flood."

"Right," the first woman said, "so here I am with no electricity and another pandemic hanging over my head."

Joshua was on his feet again, yelling over the murmurs of the crowd. "Revelation 2:17 says, 'To him who overcomes I will give some of the hidden manna to eat.' If there were a pre-tribulation, we would have nothing to overcome? I am certain God will take care of His people through the tribulation period."

"Are you going to believe this guy?" Brinkman said. "Knowledgeable preachers say this UN guy, who is head of the European Union, is the real deal."

Joshua prayed for Jesus to open their eyes to the truth.

"It's a smart move to have those Bibles burned after all." Disgust painted Brinkman's scowling face. "That Book is too full of contradictions to suit me."

A woman stood. "My preacher always spoke of God's love and believing in an earthly life full of good outcomes. I don't see that in what Joshua is quoting. Do you have a different Bible from ours?"

"No ma'am, if you open yours to those Bible passages, you'll see the truth of His Word."

The woman plopped down on her seat. "I don't understand. If those verses were so important to the end times, why didn't my pastor say so?"

The lady in the mini dress stood. "And besides, I've worked all my life for my house and property. I've got me a nice little nest egg, too; I wouldn't want to lose it. Did you happen to get the last issue of *Vogue* magazine? Wow, that latest picture of him was great—he's so handsome. He's supposed to be a descendant of some king way back when." She puckered her lips. "No one that good-looking is a demon. This European UN guy is handsome enough to be a god."

Brinkman snickered. He slithered toward her. "Look, you can come with me and receive your mark, and you'll not have to worry about having your children go hungry or losing everything you worked for."

She drew back. "Oh, but will this mark hurt? I don't like needles."

"Rest assured. I will make certain you receive the super-gentle treatment."

Joshua's arms fell to his side. Ruth squeezed his hand .

"Please don't be discouraged," Joshua yelled out.

He noticed a beam of hope emanating in Ruth's eyes. "Then we know this much about you, Ruth, you are one of God's elect. Now all we have to do is wait." What would be the Antichrist's next move?

# Thirteen

*"O son of man, say to the children of your people: 'The righteousness of the righteous man shall not deliver him in the day of his transgression; as for the wickedness of the wicked, he shall not fall because of it in the day that he turns from his wickedness; nor shall the righteous be able to live because of his righteousness in the day that he sins.'"* Ezekiel 33:12

Golden hues of orange and yellow swept the horizon as the sun slowly appeared over the hills. "What a gut day to glorify the Lord," Ruth said, awed by the sight. The mid-November Sunday admirably displayed the glorious strokes of God's handiwork. Still, something felt amiss in her soul. An emptiness she yearned to fill. Was it her lost past or something else?

Hearing a sound from the bedroom, she hurried to get Josh Jr.'s clothes together to take the trip to the Lapps' farm where the church service would be held.

After last night's meeting, she was confident of one thing. No fence-sitting. Either you were a Christian ready to stand for Jesus, or else you were a follower of that handsome Antichrist. "Hurry, Josh Jr., and get dressed, my ears itch to learn more about Jesus in the Bible this morning."

A knowing smile spread across Martha's wise face. "I see Joshua's meeting went gut for you."

"Is there anything you don't know?" That question burned in Ruth's heart for months now.

"Not me, but the gut Lord knows all." Martha appeared to contemplate her words. "I don't know half of what I wish I knew. We shall soon tread uncharted paths." She fidgeted with the collar of her dress for several seconds. "Each their own, mind you. Each has their weaknesses to contend with."

"Sounds scary." Ruth placed her package beside the door and hurried to gather the basket of fresh bread, cheese, and peanut butter ready to be packed along with the rest of their things. "I wish I could get my hands on an English Bible so I could read the Scriptures along with you in the evenings. That might help me with my walk with the gut Lord."

"Did someone wish for a Bible?" Joshua came down from upstairs, hugging a bundle wrapped in brown paper. He stretched his arm forward, placing the bundle in her hand.

"For me?" Words at this moment felt inadequate. "But—I have nothing for you."

"It is a present, and I want nothing in return but for you to enjoy it, with my gratitude for caring for my son. It was fortunate for me the sheriff found the package at the post office."

"Open it," Martha said. "I grow impatient when I don't know everything."

Ruth hid the package behind her back in glee. "It is gut to know that mamm's have faults, too."

Curiosity got the best of her, however. Ruth tore at the brown paper and string, much like their four-month-old kitten did with their *Plain Truth* newspaper. "It is more than I'd hoped for." She ran her hand over the rich brown leather with the embossed gold letters, Holy Bible. Quickly she opened it. "English! I can read this."

"It's the New King James Version. It has much the same wording as our German Bible."

"Joshua, if you stuck out your chest any further, you'd bust your suspenders."

He laughed. "Mutter, I have plenty of room, see?" He snapped the suspenders with glee.

They made their way to the buggy and were soon on their way. Their Standardbred's clipping gait made a nice backdrop to Ruth's thoughts. Whatever her past, it could not compare to the present. In this bleak time of the Antichrist, she found happiness. Her heart sang for sheer joy as she hugged Josh Jr. closer.

As they rounded the bend to the Lapps' farm, dried stacks of Indian corn near the mailbox greeted them, and colorful mums braved the chilly weather. Emerald grass amidst the bright red and orange leaves of the maple trees decorated the landscape.

A van drew up close behind them, then parked. Unusual. Cars and vans were a rarity with the present gas and electrical shortage.

"Strange they would come here on a Sunday when our shops are closed," Martha said.

"They've been following us." Joshua jumped down in front of the hitching post and turned to help his mother. Ruth handed him Josh Jr. and climbed down. Three men and two women approached Joshua.

"You guys consider yourselves Christians? If so, we got questions needing answers."

"Ja," Joshua said.

"That's a yes? Well, we want to join your church group this morning." The man sported various tattoos and shaved hair along the sides of his head. Another man hung onto his arm. "Yeah. Where do you want us to sit?"

"It is spoken in German. You will not understand anything." Joshua turned to Ruth and his mother. "Go inside the house and get the bishop, please.

"You are willkom to wait," Joshua told the newcomers.

"Sure, we'll wait," the man with the tattoos said.

"Hey." A woman obstructed Ruth from going farther. "Is that what I think it is? A Bible? Don't you know they're outlawed in Europe and soon to be in America?"

Ruth pushed her way past the woman. Another girl, sporting a low-cut dress and dangling bracelets, looped her arm around the woman.

"Say, don't I know you?" the first woman said. Her voice, or was it those eyes, that knowing smirk? Still, Ruth could not recall knowing her, but the woman said otherwise.

"Ruth Jessup, you couldn't forget me." She stepped uncomfortably close.

Ruth hugged Josh Jr. closer. "Nee, I don't know you." The woman repulsed her. Lord, what have I done, where have I been? Is this the reason my mind refuses to recall my past?

Quick as a cat, Joshua moved to her side. "Anything wrong?"

"Joshua, may I go into the house with the other ladies?"

"You? A lady?" The woman laughed, a fiendish sound.

The tattooed man's voice rose an octave louder. "You have to let us attend, according to the Equality Act. Sexual orientation and gender identity is not immoral; hypocrites cannot discriminate against us because of our sexual preference. What do you think about that?"

"I think we will know soon." Joshua grinned. Seeing his bishop approach, he stood aside.

The bishop smiled at the English. He clutched his Bible like a shield in the crook of his arm. "The service is about to begin. It is always said in Schwabisch, a form of German, and we read out of our German Bibles."

"You're doing this because you don't want us to participate! I'll see this establishment—" looking around, he was suddenly speechless. "Where's your church?"

"We do not have a building for our church, we meet at each other's homes every other week for our service."

"So? The government can keep you from meeting if you don't allow us to participate."

The bishop shrugged. "Our children have not been taught the English language yet. Not until they enter school. All they know is Schwabisch. They are taught English and then German in the third grade."

One woman smirked. "We came all this way for what?"

The bishop stepped back, bowed his head, opened his Bible, and thoughtfully walked forward. "We will move in more chairs for you and have an interpreter speak in the English language so you will not be left out of the sermon. My Lord has directed me to talk about an especially joyful topic."

People hurried to their seats. The bishop's eyes were as sharp as an eagle's, and that was nothing compared to his tongue. Ruth did not envy the newcomers sitting to the left side in the front.

"Do you think God cares what you think?" The bishop looked at the Englishers. The interpreter repeated the words.

"How should I know?" the tattooed man replied. "And why should I care?"

"Do you think God cares what I think? Anyone have an answer?" The interpreter repeated the words in English. *Of course not.* Ruth realized she had assumed God would go along with her life choices.

"Nee. God does not care what I think or what society thinks is sin." He looked at the Englishers. "Yet, He loved you enough to send His only Son to rescue you and me from hell—which God created for the devil and his demons.

"God's Son, Christ Jesus, was nailed to the cross for my sins, your sins, and all the people who ever sinned. But the thing is, people don't know they're sinning until they read this Bible. And ignorance is no excuse. If you don't read this, how will you know about the gut blessings that are yours for the asking? First John 3:22 tells us 'whatever we ask we receive from Him, because we keep His commandments and do those things that are pleasing in His sight.' You have a choice where you want to spend eternity—live with God or live with the devil."

"Aw, the devil isn't so bad," the tattooed man said.

"Don't believe that lie, son. Satan deceives. He doesn't dress himself in horns and tail. He disguises himself as pleasing to the eyes, a wonderfully gut peaceful man—his pitchfork is disguised by his lying tongue." The bishop pointed his finger at his congregation. "The devil hates you! Because you were made in God's image. And Satan's vengeful—he wants you to burn in hell with him."

He mopped his brow with his handkerchief and continued. "Jesus, at Gethsemane, saw that cross, felt the nails hammering through his flesh—knowing the pain, humiliation, and agony. Do you know what Jesus thought?"

"I haven't clue," the tattooed man replied sarcastically.

The bishop stepped closer and stared down at the man. "He thought, yes, you're worth it! And a thousand others like you are worth it, because of His great love for you—and for me."

"That's an earful." The man grinned. "And you Christians think we're in the last three-and-a-half years—"

"Those who have been born again into God's kingdom will not receive the mark of the beast. At the end of the tribulation, they will be caught up with Him in the clouds. But those who choose to take the mark of the beast will face Armageddon and the seven last plagues until the wrath of God is complete. Then, sadly, they will follow Satan and his minions into utter darkness and into the lake that burns with fire and brimstone. Trust me, it is a real place, and *you* make that choice. Ahh, but he who overcomes shall inherit all things!"

"Come on, let's get out of here." The tattooed man stood. "You'll be sorry. Wait till you see the trouble we bring you."

"You knew this was a church service, and I'm not through. Sit and listen," the bishop said.

"We are all sinners," the woman said. "You as much as me! So, don't do that holier-than-thou-stuff on us. We believe Jesus is the Son of God, so there."

"You know of Jesus. So do the demons," the bishop replied. "Scripture shows that Jesus cast the unclean spirits out of a man. The demons asked Jesus not to send them to hell. Think of that—they would rather be in a swine's body than in hell. Jesus cast them into some swine, and the swine went mad and ran over a cliff."

"Who's going to cast the demons out of you, bishop man?" the tattooed man yelled. "We are all sinners, and Christians are always ready to point out same-sex sin of the Old Testament, but never their own sins! Why don't you preach on that?"

The bishop nodded. "Gut idea. Congregation, turn to Romans 1:22 and follow along.

"Professing to be wise, they became fools, and changed the glory of the incorruptible God into an image made like corruptible man—and birds and four-footed animals and creeping things. Therefore, God also gave them up to uncleanness, in the lusts of their hearts, to dishonor their bodies among themselves, who exchanged the truth of God for the lie, and worshiped and served the creature rather than the Creator, who is blessed forever."

"So what's your point, Bishop?"

"My point is love begins with loving God with your whole heart. Loving God in that way, you come to understand and learn the true meaning of His words. I feel God inspired Paul to write this for our day."

The grinding wheels of a police car interrupted the bishop. The Englishers saw it, too, through the large picture window. Had they planned this?

Ruth sighed with relief. Praise Jesus, it was Sheriff Baker and not Officer Smith.

The bishop waited for Sheriff Baker to have a seat before preaching again. Ruth marveled at the interpreter, how he managed to keep up with the bishop. Of course, he'd had practice because of her.

"God doesn't spare any words in telling us what He expects of us. He will not tolerate unrighteousness, which incidentally includes liars, sexual immorality, wickedness, covetousness, maliciousness, murder, and strife. No wonder Jesus told his disciples that God will forgive the sinner seventy times seven—if he earnestly asks God for forgiveness. Think of that!"

"Our sins don't look all so bad, now do they preacher?" He kissed his companion on his cheek. "We can have our orgies and drinking and drug binges. And not even I can sin that much." Tattoo man chuckled, looking around. "We can sin, and Jesus has to forgive us."

The bishop sighed. "God doesn't expect us to wallow like a pig in slime repeating our sins over and over, demanding God to forgive them."

"Yeah, I've read that Bible," the woman said. "And I remember it says, by grace alone are you saved."

"Ja, that is in Ephesians 2:8. The Bible also says, 'For we are His workmanship, created in Christ Jesus for good works, which God prepared beforehand that we should walk in them.'"

"Ahh, see, I was right," the woman replied with an arrogant nod to her colleagues.

The bishop smiled. "You know just enough of the Bible to get inoculated, but not enough to get saved. James 4:17, warns us, 'Therefore, to him who knows to do good and does not do *it*, to him it is sin.'"

The woman gasped.

"Do you understand now why God's Son, Jesus Christ, came from heaven to Earth and became the sacrificial lamb for us?"

"Sort of," the companion of the woman said. "I'm saved, well, at least I was, I think."

The companion was seeking the truth. The bishop's kind eyes met hers, his voice understanding. "The best part about God's plan for us and all humanity is knowing He is offering a way to paradise. A place where there is no pain, suffering, humiliation, disease, or death. Forever! Your plan and my plan of redemption.

"All you must do is repent and be born anew. Repent means to make a 180-degree turn from whatever sin has hold of your coattails and accept His plan of salvation for us. Accept it by faith, believing. In John 3:3 and 6 Jesus says, 'Most assuredly, I say to you unless one is born again, he cannot see the kingdom of God.... That which is born of the flesh is flesh, and that which is born of the Spirit is spirit.'"

The bishop looked out at his congregation. "Paul warns us in Romans 1:32: 'knowing the righteous judgment of God, that those who practice such things are deserving of death.' This is your decision to make today. Do you want to share a spot in the lake of fire with Satan—or share eternal life with God and His Son, Jesus Christ?

"Come now, don't wait." He held out his hand, his eyes piercing the each one. The companion stood. The woman attempted to pull her back. "Do you know what you're doing? We can no longer be married."

The companion shook her hand off. "I know." She walked to the front.

The bishop turned to the companion and spoke; the interpreter translated. "Now, repeat after me, 'Lord, I'm a sinner. I ask you to forgive me of my sins. I'll make that 180-degree turn in the opposite direction, and I ask by faith believing that you will walk every step of the way with me, and that Your Holy Spirit will guide me, so I might obtain eternal life and be with You in heaven forever. Amen.'" The companion repeated it right along with the interpreter.

The companion laughed. "I never felt so clean. So—free. Hallelujah!" She looked over at her friend.

She, looking doubtful, said, "Are you certain this is for real?"

"Satan deceived us into believing a lie—now's our chance to flee from lust and the sins of our past lives—and live, really live—for Jesus. I don't want to return to my former life. Jesus will help me. Can't you hear Him calling you?" She held her hand over her heart. "I feel His presence. His loving presence! Oh, how I wish you could come to know such love and peace."

"That's all I need to hear." Ruth was on her feet. "I know what I want." She ran toward the front. She didn't know why or how she knew what she knew. But all she wanted was to rid herself of the muck and stench of the pig pen. Forever.

She stood alongside the tattooed man and woman with the crew cut and dangling bracelets. They smiled, locking arms, the woman's bracelets adding to the chirping of the birds outside the open window. It wasn't long before the other woman joined them and Sheriff Baker.

Ruth felt that peace wash through her body. She wasn't alone anymore. She had the Holy Spirit renewing her spirit and giving her a newfound love for her Creator. She couldn't wait to share her new experience with the man who had brought her to this point in her life, reborn, and living for Jesus Christ.

Joshua stood off in the distance, his face immobile, watching her. His arms wrapped tightly around his son.

# Fourteen

*"But I say unto you that for every idle word men may speak, they will give account of it in the day of judgment. For by your words you will be justified, and by your words you will be condemned." Matthew 12:36–37*

"Johansson, hold her still," Joshua commanded. He had the front of the horse, Johansson the hindquarters. Joshua settled the yearling's head against his shoulder and got the tub of ivermectin ready. He ignored his innermost feelings over a previous conversation pertaining to the woman who said she and Ruth spent many a lonely weekend in bars and such together.

"I think it's more than this horse that's got your dander," Johansson said. "Ja, more like that event last Sunday when that woman said she knew Ruth. I think most will forget it before our next Sunday worshiping. A gut thing we worship every other Sunday. Gives people a longer time to forget."

Not much hope in that if you keep talking it to death. Joshua pushed down on the syringe, squirting the mixture down the yearling's throat. "Gut, I got it in her without her spitting it back out. Glad that worming is done." He led the chestnut into the corral with the other horses. She let out a shrill whinny.

"She's going to be a beaut when she's full-grown," Johansson said.

Joshua stroked her coat. It was growing thicker, like mink it was, with the approaching colder weather. "God takes care of His creatures." Thoughtfully, he released her. She did a half buck and ran to join the herd.

He knew how to make his animals happy. He also knew what his animals needed to stay healthy. Often, like that filly, they fought him, not wanting their medicine. However, without it, they could get terrible worms that could eventually kill them. "Our God is a gut God who knows what we need to be happy and prosperous."

"That must be why God gave us the Ten Commandments and the Bible to follow, a Divine Manual to ensure His creation made in His image would be blessed." Johansson's eyes filled with concern as he looked at Joshua.

"You think it will help Ruth when she recalls her past to know that she's part of God's family now?"

Joshua had seen the way Ruth looked at that woman dressed in man's clothes. Is Ruth's amnesia gone and she's pretending, not wanting to face her past? That idea plagued his thoughts and expanded like Mutter's rising bread.

"Don't hurt to let go now and then to someone over troubling thoughts."

"Words can't make this right." Like porcupine needles, Joshua's conscience pricked him. What about himself? "I think that about covers everyone. I should be gut until spring." He hoped his friend got the hint. He didn't want to talk about Ruth. He didn't want to analyze the people who stormed their church service. Not that he wasn't happy that many came forward and accepted Jesus as their personal Savior that day.

"Sometimes it is easier to forgive oneself a sin than another person, especially if you should, by chance, harbor certain feelings."

Joshua reached for his coat and shoved his arms into the sleeves with deep thrusts. Can't Johansson take a hint? He placed his hat on his head and, with a backward shrug, said, "What do I care what Ruth did before she came here?"

"I think it is because Josh Jr. has grown so fond of her that you're worried. She not knowing her past, a man can't help wondering what else she's done."

Joshua's hands formed fists at his sides. He debated whether to tell Johansson everything about his own tainted past. Oh, the things he'd asked the Almighty to forgive him for. The years he'd spent in the English world, and the sins he'd committed were nearly as many as the stars dimpling a clear midnight sky in July. But he didn't want to remember them. Those things were done in another life, another time.

"Might as well talk to the wind." Johansson shoved his big hands deep into his trouser pants and walked off without saying another word. Lifting himself up, he sat down heavily on the wagon seat and took up the reins.

"Hold up there!" Trotting forward, Joshua thrust out his arm. Feeling the hardened hand much like his own, returning his farewell.

"Ja, I let you think a little more on it and pray you come up with an answer you can live with, Joshua."

He heard the iron shoes of Johansson's horse clicking down the drive, patterning Joshua's beating heart.

Memories flooded his thoughts. If it hadn't been for that church he'd stumbled into one Sunday, he might not have returned. He might not have met his Sara and had Josh Jr. Strange how God works.

That preacher had given a powerful sermon that day. All about the power of the Holy Spirit. Christ had done the work; He'd given him absolute forgiveness and the ability to fight against his personal devil. Yes, Joshua didn't have to work his way to heaven because Christ had. He had accepted God's grace and by faith believed he was saved, not by anything he could do. The apostle Paul said not to set aside the grace of God; for if righteousness *comes* through the law, then Christ died in vain.

So, Joshua had forgiven his dad that day and returned home when he'd received his mother's letter saying Dad had died. Mother and Sara had forgiven him without hesitation for leaving home and not rushing to his dad's bedside when he became ill.

Joshua hadn't told the bishop everything, hadn't admitted he'd gone to Afghanistan, killed men, and then become a policeman and killed again. His mother knew, but he never told Sara. Johansson knew only a little part of his English life. He'd asked God's forgiveness and received it that day, kneeling in that English church.

He punched the wall of the barn. Still, it wasn't the same. He'd heard his son call Ruth his mother. She corrected him, but a heart-wrenching scene followed, seeing his son's face squinch up, his little hands reach for her.

If she *had* regained her memory, what might she be hiding from them?

Then again, if she did have amnesia, what had she done that she might not want to admit, not even to herself? She and he were more alike than he thought.

# Fifteen

> "[A]nd causes the earth and those who dwell in it to worship the first beast, whose deadly wound was healed. He performs great signs, so that he even makes fire come down from heaven on the earth in the sight of men....He was granted power to give breath to the image of the beast, that the image of the beast should both speak and cause as many as would not worship the image of the beast to be killed." Revelation 13:12–15

Ruth scooped up a pair of Joshua's work pants and held them to her. "What's wrong, Joshua? What is it you want to ask me—or won't tell me?"

The sunlight played peek-a-boo, cresting the treetops. Monday's wash would take longer to dry in the cold of the late November weather. Where had the year gone? Josh Jr. had his second birthday. Joshua didn't invite anyone but the immediate family to celebrate.

These were miraculous times. Only Jesus's love could turn the plans of the Antichrist around and help Christians not to succumb to his demands. Churches helped their congregations with food supplies. People were bartering and willingly giving what they had to their neighbors. Sewing circles, canning bees, wood cutting, and whatever it took to help their fellow man get through these three-and-a-half years. Praying, believing, and showing through their Christian deeds that they hadn't lost faith. Yes, people were inspiring each other. And with all the work, the days and months fairly few by. Or was it the Lord's doing? He did promise to shorten the days for the elect's sake. Well, He certainly was a God of His word. She and Joshua barely got a moment to themselves. Joshua helped the English with their planting and reaping, and Ruth helped his mother by going to the English homes to help them with their needle work and teach them how to cook on an open fire.

Joshua's New Zealand White rabbits were more popular. His buck and does kept busy making kits for the English. This way, they could have a supply of fresh meat available to them in their suburban homes. Who would have thought when Joshua sold his rabbits at Easter they would become staples for hungry households. She prayed daily for Christ's miraculous hand to work His will for all concerned.

She pinned the pants to the clothesline, knowing Joshua believed she'd been born again. She never wanted to go back to her old way of life, whatever that was. Dear Lord, what did I leave behind that I don't want to remember? That was the problem—Joshua wanted her to remember her past life, and try as she must, she could not.

The Border collie, Brutus, barked. Josh Jr. awoke. "Oh, did that bad Brutus wake up my little boy?" She hugged him close, dancing with the child to keep him from crying. The clip-clip of a horse as it trotted up the driveway caught her attention.

It was Mr. Heydenreich. His passenger, dressed in a suit, looked out of place. A large cowboy hat adorned his head.

"Ruth, this is Private Investigator Ricker to see Joshua."

"He's not here. No one is home." Ruth squealed out the last words. What was she going to do? The last thing she wanted was to entertain a perfect stranger alone. "Mr. Heydenreich, I'm not certain when Joshua or Martha will return. They went to visit Martha's *schwester*."

"Schwester you say? Who's that?" Ricker said, looking at Ruth closely.

"Schwester is the Amish word for sister," Mr. Heydenreich replied.

"Oh, right. Of course. You'll have to be patient with me," Ricker said with a chuckle in his voice. "It might take me a while to grow accustomed to your language and, um, transportation." The springs of the seat screeched their complaint.

"Have you traveled far?" she asked.

"Oh, about twenty miles," Mr. Heydenreich said.

"Oh, my. If you are not used to a buckboard seat, a two-hour trip can be painful. You are willkum to stay awhile."

"I have customers waiting for me." Mr. Heydenreich eyed his passenger. It was evident to Ruth that Mr. Heydenreich was eager to get back to town and dispose of Mr. Ricker at wherever he was lodging.

"I've paid you enough for four hours of your service," grumbled Mr. Ricker. "I want to wait here and see if Joshua might not be clipping up the driveway soon." He removed his hat and wiped his forehead with his bandana. "I'll pay you well for the additional hours."

"I guess we can rest for a while," Mr. Heydenreich said.

Ruth nodded. "You want to come into the house?"

Mr. Heydenreich grinned. "Before this power failure, we Amish were always hiring the English to drive us around. Now it's the English hiring the Amish to take them places."

"Humpf. Hardly a laughing issue." Ricker's face askew, he climbed out of the carriage, rubbing his backside. "I prefer riding a horse to sitting on a wooden seat for hours. But I couldn't find a horse for rent." He approached Ruth, his eyes sweeping her form. "You've lived here long?"

"Oh, Ruth is kin to Sara, Joshua's deceased wife. Ruth tends to Josh Jr." Heydenreich stroked his beard. "Been here, oh, I'd say little over a year now. That so, Ruth?"

She nodded.

"That so. Well, I'm looking for a woman that's your height, about your age, that went missing a little over a year ago." He held up a poster of a woman with long dark hair and eyes strangely the same color as her own.

The woman's mascaraed eyes stared back at her. She did not appear happy. A half-smile etched the woman's lips, sort of like an afterthought. "It's as if she is afraid to smile openly, worried what someone might think—"

*Insecurity* painted the woman's face. Ruth, clutching Josh Jr., hurried up the stairs to the large white farmhouse without a backward glance.

The resounding heavy boots of Mr. Heydenreich and the sharp cowboy boots of Mr. Ricker followed on her heels. "Please have a seat at the kitchen table."

The wood inside the stove glowed red. Good, still live embers. She put a pot of water on. "What would you prefer, coffee or tea?"

"Coffee is fine for me," Mr. Ricker said.

"Me, too," Mr. Heydenreich replied.

Hearing a noise outside, she hurried to the window. Joshua's horse and carriage trotted up the drive pretty as you please. She sighed with relief.

The large Standardbred clipped up the gravel drive in high fashion and neighed to Heydenreich's mare. Perched in the driver's seat was Joshua. Martha sat next to him.

Ruth strained to hear the argument going on at the table while she watched Joshua help Martha down from the carriage. They would both be in soon.

The kettle on the stove whistled, adding to the general befuddlement of the situation between Mr. Heydenreich and Private Investigator Ricker.

Josh Jr. had fallen asleep in her arms. Ruth hurried to the child's bedroom and placed him gently onto his bed. His golden curls surrounded his angelic face in poetic verse. "You remind me of the cherubims Joshua reads of."

In a flurry, the door flew open, and Martha strutted in, all hustle and bustle, rolling up her sleeves in preparation of showing off her hostess's ability in style. Joshua was right behind her. He stopped and looked at Ruth. "Everything gut?"

Ruth nodded. "Now that I have my boppli down for his nap, I'll come help your Mutter serve the men."

"Ja." Joshua hurried toward the kitchen table.

She heard Joshua open the stove's heavy door and throw in another log.

## LOVE'S FINAL SUNRISE

"Mr. Heydenreich, you going to try and go back into town today?" Joshua said.

"Ja."

"You are welcome to stay overnight," Martha's said, her voice clear as a bell.

Ruth, hesitant to join the strangers, tarried a while longer and covered Josh Jr. with another quilt. Her hands shook. She hoped she didn't look as nervous as she felt. She stroked her hands down either side of her hair and turned toward the doorway. What was she afraid of? Why did she feel her heart race whenever she saw an English stranger? She couldn't hide forever. Josh Jr's door creaked shut behind her.

Joshua glanced at Ruth, then walked toward the big kitchen table, the focal point in the L-shaped kitchen and sitting room. "Mr. Ricker, gut to see you again. Did you acquire any more news since last we met?"

Ruth took their fancy cups down from the top shelf over the stove. "You like milk with your coffee, or do you prefer it black?"

"Black is fine." Ricker withdrew two manila folders from his briefcase. Scanning the labels, he chose the second. "Nothing that gives me a strong clue, Joshua. Here are some more photographs I have of the missing woman. Seems all I've learned is that you were the only one who got a good look at her. I understand she helped you with your lame horse or something to that regard back in September during the fox hunt hosted by Mr. Johansson."

"It's been over a year, but yes, a lady helped me with my horse. But I didn't get a good look at her face. She wore a helmet, and her hair was in a net of sorts."

Martha squeezed Ruth's arm before slicing into an apple pie. Ruth gathered plates and silverware.

Joshua squirmed uneasily in his chair whenever Mr. Riker's gaze fell on her. That was troubling in itself.

"Ruth, they might like some fresh bread too," Martha said. "Could you fetch us some more jam? There's a fresh jar in the basement."

"Wait. I wanted to—"

"She'll be back, Mr. Ricker." Joshua's voice sounded strangely deeper than normal.

Ruth hurried down the stairs, feeling the chilliness of the concrete walls cooling her cheeks. She didn't know if she was this woman who was missing or not. What she did know is that she liked it here and saw no reason to leave. Besides, Josh Jr. needed her and she needed him.

She took as long as she could to select the flavor of jam. Too bad she couldn't stay here until Mr. Ricker left. She walked back up the stairs and into the kitchen.

"Thank you." Martha smiled.

"Who's this?" Mr. Heydenreich said.

Ricker turned his head sideways so he could see the picture. "Oh, that's Mr. Rollins."

Mr. Heydenreich took it between his thumb and forefinger, looking at it more closely. "What does he do for a living?"

"He's a lawyer. As far as we know, he was the last person to see Miss Jessup before she disappeared," Ricker said.

"That's all you have?" Joshua asked.

"I have Mr. Johansson's testimony. Said Rollins was feeding booze to Miss Jessup with no letup. Her father is worried about her. But I haven't been able to find a single clue as to what might have happened to her. No trace of any foul play." Ricker paused, sipping his coffee. "With this European UN guy establishing a New World Order, I'm beginning to wonder if I'll even have a profession left."

"New World Order, is that what they're calling this—" Joshua stopped himself just in time. Did that mean Ricker had received the mark of the Antichrist? "Ah, what is this UN man planning on doing once he's a world power?"

"What do you think?"

Joshua tapped the table with the photo of Rollins. "Did Mr. Rollins, did he send you here?"

"Yes and no. Mr. and Mrs. Jessup want answers. Not even the bloodhounds could find a body, which means Ruth is alive. Remember, Rollins thought some Amish guy kidnapped her."

Mr. Heydenreich guffawed. "We got enough of our own to tend, let alone taking in another. You English are enough to babysit."

Mr. Ricker sent him a sideways frown. "Have you seen something that could shine some light on my investigation on Ruth Jessup?"

Ruth dropped the plate she was carrying to the table.

"Sure. News is learned fast here." Heydenreich rested his arms on the table.

"Her boyfriend, Rex Rollins, had a tooth missing the next morning after Ruth's disappearance and claims his horse did it." He looked up at Ruth, then down at the picture and held up Ruth's picture. "You wouldn't think a little lady like her could have knocked out someone's tooth, now, would you? But Mr. Johannsson swears Rollins had no tooth missing after the hunt that morning. Said it had to have been knocked or kicked out by Ruth—and Rollins swears it was his horse that did it. Anyways, I was getting tired of seeing Rollins looking like a prizefighter and told him to get it taken care of."

"What? The horse?" Heydenreich said.

Was Heydenreich attempting to provoke Ricker into leaving or just being his cantankerous self?

"No, Rollins' missing tooth." Ricker frowned. "Guess with this electrical malfunction, Rollins' dentist can't fix it. But that won't be an excuse soon. The electrical power grid is working in Europe now and most parts of the world. Parts of the United States are having trouble with their power grids and electrical circuits, but they should be up soon."

"Ja, something we know little of," Heydenreich said. "And don't have much use for anyways."

"Good thing for you. I doubt we'll get things back to normal until next year sometime." Ricker took a bite of his apple pie. "Hmm, this is good." He rolled it around in his mouth as if savoring the flavor for as long as he could. "Rollins was supposed to come out here again with me."

He shrugged. "I spent half the morning getting to his office only to find out that he's gone and joined this Antichrist New World Order movement.

Joshua and Heydenreich looked knowingly at each other.

Mr. Ricker's loud slurping filled the silence. He watched them over the rim of his cup. "Good coffee and pie. Is that bread homemade, too?"

"Baked early this morning," Martha said.

He took a piece of bread, spread jam on it, and plopped it in his mouth. "Mmm. And the only suspect we have to Miss Jessup's disappearance might be an Amish man and that's coming from Mr. Rollins." Quizzically, he glanced up at Ruth and then Joshua. "Did you want to see some pictures of the hunt group?" He reached into his briefcase.

Ruth peeked at the photo over Joshua's shoulder. Dark-haired, a confident smile, and the cocky tilt of his head said it all. He was handsome and a charmer, and he knew it. But his eyes, the window into his heart, his eyes were as black as his—soul. "Ahh…" she backed away from the table. Something in Ruth's memory bank jarred open a crack. She'd prefer to keep that door closed.

Ricker's easy-going façade and friendly nature froze cold as an icicle in the middle of January. He leaned back on the wooden chair and crossed his arms.

This couldn't be good. Ruth felt the urge to run. Where?

"How did a nice Amish woman like you meet a man like Rex Rollins?"

"I…don't know. Honestly, it's a feeling." She glanced down at the photo again. "What will happen to him if you don't find this woman?"

"Nothing. No evidence, no conviction. If I get lucky, he'll go to prison for an exceptionally long time." Ricker leaned forward. "Glad to know you're safe—Ruth."

Ricker rubbed his hands together. "Now I'm in the mood for some more pie." He took a big bite and swallowed. "But I doubt this Antichrist will care. He's too busy making images of himself speak. I even heard he makes fire come down from heaven—"

"What?" Joshua said.

Ricker looked around. "I take it you haven't heard?"

"Heard what?" Joshua said.

"About the Antichrist being severely wounded. Everyone thought him dead, and then this religious guy healed him and brought him back to life. People in Europe are following him around like he was the Pied Piper. He's claiming to be God. Most likely, the rest of the world believes he is God. I read that he told the people to make an image of himself; they did. This Antichrist breathed into the statue and brought it to life. The statue even spoke." Ricker shook his head.

"Really?" Joshua said. "That's right out of Revelation 13."

Ricker nodded. "What do you think about this Antichrist and his New World Order?"

"I think we have less than three-and-a-half years before Jesus sends him into the bottomless pit for good."

"You've studied your Bible. You can't be too careful these days. The Antichrist is ordering everyone to receive his 666 mark on their right hand or their forehead. You can't buy or sell without one." He munched on his bread. "He's got a reason for everything. Said that way no one needs to carry cash and credit cards anymore. No way am I buying what he's selling. I wish I could say the same about some of my acquaintances."

Ricker's eyes sparked daggers. He continued. "This Antichrist won't care about bringing to justice Miss Jessup's attacker. They're too busy rounding up good Christian people whose only crime is their love for Jesus. You want to know what I heard in a news brief over the hand radio device at the police station in Cassell this morning?"

A hush filled the room.

"A doctor tried to have this Christian woman abort her baby on some made-up medical condition. Christians and Jews alike are afraid to leave their houses for fear of getting arrested on some trumped-up charge."

"Like what?" Ruth had to know.

"Could be a parking ticket, an expired vaccination…Anyone can come up and say they heard you speak some hate speech or another." Ricker took a sip of his coffee. "Oftentimes, these left-wing liberals are waiting for parishioners outside the church doors. They interrogate them and haul them off to reeducation camps. If they refuse to accept this Antichrist and take his mark, they're beheaded."

"I can't believe this, not in America." Ruth bit down on her bottom lip. She hadn't meant to speak her thoughts.

"Yeah. It's sad to see the individual that complies. He accepts the mark and comes out of one of those reeducation camps drugged. With computer chips in their head that makes them into half man, half machine, a sort of human robot."

"And all these Antichrist endorsers do is wait for an excuse to arrest someone?" Joshua said.

"Right. Mind you, some people in the cities are newcomers out of Europe. They're the instigators that get Americans to receive the mark. They attempt to convince the people that this Antichrist is the god Christians and Jews have been waiting for. That this king of kings wants everyone to come to him and experience true freedom. They don't want the people to know the truth that this Antichrist is a dictator, worse than Hitler and Stalin ever were. This Antichrist is working wonders; he's performing miracles like Jesus did when He was on the earth."

Mr. Heydenreich slowly lowered his coffee cup. "I heard about those beheadings happening in Muslim countries, but I figured that it could never happen here."

"Well, we best take off, Heydenreich. Don't want you to lose any revenue on account of me." Ricker stood, his folder and hat in hand.

"I'll walk you out." Joshua needed to tidy up the issue of Ruth Jessup. Walking toward the buckboard, he stopped Ricker before he mounted the wagon. "Say, Heydenreich, wait here. I want to show Ricker something before he leaves." Inside the barn, they faced each other. "So, what are your plans? You going to tell Ruth's parents? That could put her life in jeopardy."

"I know. She's got amnesia?"

"Yeah."

"Well, seeing how Ruth can't remember who she is—why should I change something the Good Lord seems not want known just yet. She makes a good Amish lady, and these times are trying enough. I don't want Jesus upset by anything I've done in the line or out of the line of my calling."

Josh bowed his head. "Ja, you've shown me God knows best why He kept Ruth from knowing her past. I've been righteously blind, not owning up to my shortcomings and ignoring God's divine knowledge."

"Part of the reason I don't want to tell Ruth's family where she is, is because of her stepmother." Ricker shoved his hands into his trouser pockets. "She has little self-control. She means well but can't seem to keep her thoughts from escaping through the hole in her head."

"A dangerous sin in these times." Joshua watched as Ricker made his way to the wagon and climbed on. Heydenreich slapped the reins, and he and Ricker progressed down the winding driveway.

"A dangerous habit in these times," Joshua muttered to himself.

# Sixteen

*"The coming of the lawless one is according to the working of Satan, with all power, signs, and lying wonders, and with all unrighteous deception among those who perish, because they did not receive the love of the truth, that they might be saved. And for this reason God will send them strong delusion, that they should believe the lie, that they all may be condemned who did not believe the truth but had pleasure in unrighteousness." 2 Thessalonians 2:9-12*

Ruth pounded the mound of dough. A cloud of flour floated into the air. She coughed into her arm and kneaded the mass again. She'd made enough for two loaves. She tore the mound in half and kneaded it again, then rolled it, forming the loaves neatly into the loaf pans she'd readied, all the while thinking over the past year's events. November 30, my, another year has flown by!

Josh had taught the English how to cut ice from the ponds, and how to butcher beef and pigs. Martha had taught many of the English how to plant and can. Some of the English, like Sheriff Baker, traded with them for their eggs, bread, and staples. Josh's Alpine goat business was doing well; the kids were bartered for before they were a day old. Goat milk and cheese commodities in high demand. Their country life provided a hedge around them that the English in the cities didn't have. However, his goats were helping those in the suburbs survive. The two soldiers that had been posted to their town a year before had vanished. No one knew where they went—but no soldiers replaced them.

Unlike last year, Joshua invited all their kin to Josh Jr.'s third birthday. He had to plan it six months in advance because of the mail being so slow. None of the out-of-towners managed to make it, due to the gasoline shortages and the paperwork required get through all the police stops. But everyone who could come had a good time. Considering the upheaval of the Antichrist, it was hard to believe life continued. Still, no strangers came down their roads. Her world was calm and pleasant. Talk was the World Order policemen were having a tough enough time in American cities to worry about the countryside.

She suspected Joshua was keeping much of the bad news out of the house. He spent one afternoon a week at Johansson's farm and didn't share too many conversations.

Now that Josh Jr. was older, Joshua took his son on trips with him to the fields and frequently to the granary, which operated by waterpower as it had for over a hundred years.

Ruth's heart jumped like a jackrabbit in her bosom. She missed his little hand in hers, his sweet head caressing her neck. But it was good that his dad took him places, and she shouldn't be selfish wanting Josh Jr. to remain little so she could have the pleasure of his company.

A scraping noise and a horse's clopping hooves alerted her someone was arriving. Grabbing a towel, she walked to the window. It was Ellen Walsh, come for a visit.

She placed the bread near the warm oven to rise one more time before baking them in the woodstove. A knock on the door said she was right on time to meet their neighbor.

"Willkum." Ruth stepped away from the doorway so Ellen could enter. "Martha isn't back yet from tending to the chickens." Ruth smiled warmly. "Would you like a cup of tea?"

"Ja, that would be gut."

Setting a kettle of water on the stove, Ruth hurried to set the table. Ellen eased herself down on one of the cushioned spindled chairs. "You can feel the chill of winter in the air."

"Ja, we had a frost this morning. Gut thing I brought in the potted plants." The teapot gave off a whistle. Ruth rushed forward, pouring the boiling water into the cups."

"Danke, this will help take the chill out of my bones."

Ruth turned from the pie she was slicing into three pieces and smiled. "I thought this cherry pie might go gut with your tea, but would you prefer a sandwich?"

Ellen nodded. "Ja, my appetite grows larger when it grows colder." She looked around, her eyes sparkling mischievously. "Now that we're alone, I'd like to ask about you and Joshua. You two are getting to be gut friends, ja?"

The silverware Ruth had fell to the floor. "Oh, my. I'm clumsy." Picking them up, she placed them into the sink and opened the drawer to get more.

It seemed everyone's conversation lately revolved around the subject of her and Joshua.

"It is not gut for man to be alone. That's what our Good Book says. Josh Jr. needs a little sister or brother, don't you agree?"

Ruth dashed to the table with silverware and pie. The only way to halt the inevitable list of questions about the goings-on in the Stutzman household was to get Ellen's thoughts elsewhere, away from sharpening her matchmaker skills.

"Besides learning a little more than I have a right to know, I came here for the pieces of cloth Martha said she made for our quilting bee next week." She tilted her head like that old hoot owl outside of Ruth's window. A dimpled smile and a knowing look crept across Ellen's face like dawn across the hillside. "My, your face is very becoming with that shade of red coloring your cheeks. So, answer me this one question. Do you find Joshua attractive?" She sipped her tea. Her eyes sparkled like twin stars leftover from last night's clear skies.

Ruth turned, looking around the kitchen for something to fill her hands. If she stood too close to Ellen Walsh, she would see the truth written on her face. Joshua and Josh Jr. were all she lived for.

The door banged open, and Joshua's decisive steps and the small quicker, lighter steps of Josh Jr. pounded against the oak flooring.

"Mamm!" Josh fairly few into her arms and gave her a big wet kiss on her cheek.

She hugged the child close, breathing in his sunshine curls and earthy clothes. "Ja, did you have a gut time with Dat?"

"We at sheep pens."

"Ja," Joshua said. "The lambs are big now and ready to go to market." Josh started pulling on his dad's trouser leg, his eyes pleading.

"Even the one you and Josh took a shine to?"

He picked up his son and tossed him into the air. "I promised Josh we would keep her if you like and use her for breeding in the spring."

He let Josh down and he ran to Ruth.

She hugged him close. In the warmth of their kitchen, she and Josh had nursed the little lamb that came too early that spring. They had their doubts it would live, so she and Josh prayed over it, then spoon-fed it until it could nurse again.

"Can we? Say yes!" Josh pleaded.

The door banged open for a third time. Martha's face, red with excitement, looked from Ellen then to Joshua.

Ellen spoke first. "I came for the squares of cloth you prepared for our quilting bee next week. I could get them if you tell me where they are and be on my way."

"Sure, Ellen, this way." Martha pulled her along into the sitting room with the big picture window that offered a view of Martha's flower beds.

Joshua bent down and ruffled his son's hair. He frowned into Ruth's startled eyes, but spoke to Josh. "Remember, son, Ruth is not your mamm."

"Oh, I forgot."

"That's all right with me." Ruth hugged him back.

Joshua's eyes turned as hard as granite. "Ja, but not always all right when neighbors come calling. They like to spread the news. Not always gut for us."

Joshua climbed the steps toward the bedrooms. Too bad she couldn't crawl into that lower cupboard she left ajar. He must not feel the way she did about him. If he did, he couldn't look at her that way.

She prayed to the Lord for discernment on what to do. If she could make a little money, she could buy herself a horse and buggy and go to Cassell in search of her parents. Joshua would never accept her until she knew all her past.

"Ellen, wait, I need to tell my son something." Martha left Ellen's side.

"I'll go load these into my wagon," Ellen said. "It's sometimes hard to find enough cloth to use for our quilting bee. Times are hard. I'll come back for the others. I'll be a moment longer and then be on my way."

"Ruth, where's Joshua?" Martha wrung her hands absentmindedly.

Something was wrong, and Josh Jr. felt it too. He clutched the end of Ruth's flour-covered apron and wouldn't let go.

The rapid descent of boots on the stairs told Ruth he had returned. "I'm here. What's wrong?" He clutched his rifle in his hands.

"Joshua, when I was in the chicken coop, I heard the unmistakable noise of gunshots coming from the next farm. Or it could be from a gully over yonder, past our fields? It was hard to tell, the way sounds carry in the country. It wasn't normal. I never heard the like of it. It sounded—like an army. Could it be some of the English practicing their shooting out here? What would they be doing over here at this time of day?"

He turned toward the door, not meeting their looks.

Ruth exchanged glances with Martha; both knew that attitude. It became increasingly familiar with Joshua whenever something he wished not to explain happened in their community.

Martha gave her son's arm a shake. "You don't need to protect us; we can handle the truth. Ellen told me Ella's husband was taken away last night. She thought it was because of a parking ticket he hadn't paid in town. Can you imagine that? Now you can't park your horse and buggy without paying a fee."

A knock. Ellen didn't wait for someone to open the door. "You've got to see this."

They hurried out the door to see ten or twelve Englishers marching two by two down their dirt road, with a rifle wedged against their shoulders. The man in the lead was saying in a loud, boisterous voice, "One, two, three, four, you're in the army now."

"Can't we tell them this is private property?" Martha said.

Joshua crossed his arms. "The road isn't private. Anyone can use it."

"They must have been who I heard," Martha said. "It appears they plan to use our land for their target practice, and we haven't got a whole lot to say about it."

Ruth watched Joshua's eyes grow cold. His jaw locked down like a steel trap around its quarry. "We got rights."

She shuddered. Did the Amish know what they were up against with the English? Ruth had observed enough to know men with tempers and guns could be ruthless.

One of the men marching down the road had curly hair, greying at the temples. His bushy eyebrows and mustache reminded her of someone. His head turned; a large grin swept his face.

"Ruthie! Is that you?"

# Seventeen

*"Then they will deliver you up to tribulation and kill you, and you will be hated by all nations for My name's sake. And then many will be offended, will betray one another, and will hate one another." Matthew 24:9–10*

Joshua plopped down on a kitchen chair, placed his coffee on the table, and waited. He'd allow Riker to do the talking and learn by listening. That group of men marching down their road the other day had everyone in his household in a mild thunderstorm. Was that man Ruth's dad?

Private Investigator Ricker stared blankly out the window. "You Amish have it good here. Keep to yourselves and stay in the country." He shifted his gaze to his coffee cup. "Seeing people herded into vans, taken to reeducation sites gets to me. Best not to mention your faith or that you are a Christian. Nowadays, that's a bad word."

"I could never denounce my faith or my God." Joshua waited. Would Ricker affirm the same belief?

"I know that." Ricker gulped down his coffee. "This change in our culture that any type of blasphemy and sin is good is hard for me to stomach. Right is wrong, and wrong is right, you know what I mean? Has anyone asked you to take the new pledge yet? Humpf! Just another way for people to be drawn into taking that 666 mark."

"No, what about yourself?" Joshua swished his coffee around and stared into it as if reading the swirls. He hesitated to tell Ricker what he knew. After all, it could be a ploy to get him to talk.

"I've managed to be out of the city when they gather up the church people leaving Sunday services. Priests and pastors must send in their written sermons to their townships before stepping up to the pulpit. If there is hate speech of any kind in there, then that pastor or priest is hauled off to jail."

Detective Ricker leaned forward in his chair. "I'm a Christian. Not thou-shalt-not type like you, but I'll be hogtied if I'll give my allegiance to some dude in Europe, and that's what this thing is all about. Those patriots are—"

"Wait." Joshua turned. The noise came from the back of the house. Ruth was returning from the chicken coop, her apron and basket brimming with eggs. Her startled look told them she hadn't known that Private Investigator Ricker had driven up. She quickly turned away, but not before the men noticed the becoming blush on her high cheekbones.

Everyone had turned a year older. Ruth had blossomed in her work in the fields during harvest and spring planting. She relished the work and put herself into every task with wholehearted exuberance.

His son adored her and never failed to go running into her arms with the slightest provocation. The emotions were heartfelt between Josh Jr. and Ruth. More than once, he heard his son call her mamm. He stopped correcting him because of the beautiful smile that filled Ruth's face. That is, only if a neighbor wasn't within listening distance.

Ruth put the eggs in the compartment lined with blocks of ice cut from the lake last winter, then hurried into the kitchen. "Would you like some more coffee? Perhaps a cookie?"

"I never turn down delicious Amish cooking." Ricker grinned back at her like that hyena Joshua once saw at the Detroit Zoo.

Ruth checked the kerosene stove and seeing it lit, turned up the heat and reached for a cup off the pantry shelf.

"Say, Ruth, remember that man who shouted out to you while marching with his volunteer unit?" Ricker said.

"Ja." She turned to face Ricker. Joshua thought her cheeks a little too rosy. Perhaps it was from the heat of the stove.

She brought them a plate of cookies. "I thought you might like these snickerdoodles I baked this morning." She smiled.

Joshua's heart did a somersault. *She's beautiful when she smiles like that.*

"Why don't you sit a spell with us." Ricker grinned warmly up at her.

Joshua felt jealousy jab his chest.

"Ja. I can do that. Most of my chores are finished, and Josh Jr. is down for his nap." She walked to the wood-burning stove and poured herself a cup of tea.

"Now that there are more cars on the road, do you remember driving in traffic?" the detective said. "Maybe red, yellow, and green lights hanging in the middle of the roads like the one in Owenson? How about noises? Like cars and buses and their screeching brakes—"

"Why?" She paused, setting down her cup, and walked over to gaze out the window. "Sounds very noisy compared to our life here."

"How about a computer printing out pages like Martha flips pancakes?"

"Why would I need a computer or a printing machine?" She walked back to the table and sat down across from the detective. Her face became a mask of confusion.

"Because Ruth Jessup worked in an office. You were the editor-in-chief at the Cassell City *Herald* newspaper before your accident."

Her hands shook as she lifted her cup of tea to her mouth. "Me? I am Amish. This lifestyle is all I know."

"Yes, you."

Joshua looked from Ricker to Ruth. *Was he doing her an injustice, not allowing her to return to her way of life?* Here all she did was mundane housework, cooking, canning, planting the garden, weeding, hoeing, picking, washing clothes, and cleaning over and over again.

He folded his hands and studied his broken and chipped nails. *What had he done?* Glancing over, he noticed Ruth's hands, red and chapped by the wash water and cold air. *He needed to keep her safe, and here it was safe.* The thought comforted him, but facts spoke louder than words. He had benefited by having Ruth a part of his family. She was a good worker.

Brutus barked.

"Ach, he could wake up Josh Jr." Ruth ran toward the front door and opened it a crack. "Hush, Brutus."

The clear sounds of a horse and buggy coming up the drive alerted the household of visitors. Johansson sprang from his seat. "Ruth, please, tie my horse. Is Joshua in the house?"

"Ja. With Mr. Ricker."

Joshua never remembered seeing Johansson so frazzled.

"I tell you it's right from Revelation 13, Joshua. People didn't think it could happen, either." Johansson wiped his forehead with his bandana. "I had to go into town for some planting tools, and what do you think I overheard?"

Ricker leaned back in his chair, slapping his hat partway across his forehead. "Bet I can tell you what you heard."

Just then, Ruth and Martha walked through the front door. Ricker turned. Taking his hat off his head, he did a large sweep. The hat could easily be used as a fan or a swatter to swipe at horse flies. "Come on in, ladies. This concerns you."

"I'll be hornswoggled if I take this guy's mark." Johansson slapped the table with his hand. "We've got to do something, Joshua. I got my Frau, sons, and mädels to think about."

"Hold up there," Joshua said. "Start from the beginning."

"They threatened me, Joshua, that if I didn't take that European's mark, and bow down to that Antichrist, I wouldn't be able to buy anything in their store anymore." He leaned closer and whispered. "Then a bunch of these Englishers I've never seen in our town before tried to grab me."

Ricker slurped his coffee and cookie. "So, here's my news. There's a bunch of patriots that have their headquarters up in the hills. They refuse to take the mark. I've managed to avoid the left-wing mob or the World Order Police, the WOP as the Patriots and I call them." Ricker rose.

## LOVE'S FINAL SUNRISE

Joshua followed and walked Ricker toward the door.

Ricker stopped at the door and turned to face Joshua. "Be careful. You don't know who you can trust. I understand the WOP and their spies are everywhere. The worst thing is that the WOP sometimes come in the middle of the night, take the husband or maybe the wife, and leave the rest of the family to wonder what happened to their loved one. That's how they work—with fear. You need to provide a place where your family can hide and stay safe if that should happen here. Start having your neighbors post watchmen. Have them use a lantern if they see anything abnormal and warn their community."

"It sounds to me that you think we're at war," Johansson said.

Ricker nodded. "We are. We are fighting for Jesus Christ against the Antichrist and his thugs." He strolled toward Ruth, his look understanding. "I think it's time I tell your mother not to worry about her stepdaughter. The poor woman has enough to worry about, what with her husband abducted by the WOP last night."

"What?" Ruth stammered out her questions. "I mean, I don't understand."

Ricker searched her face.

"Uh...I don't know if what you say is true—honestly, but if he is my dat, what can we do to help him?" Her eyes implored his. Joshua stepped in front of her, ready to be a human shield against this onslaught of questions.

Ricker chuckled. "I'm not as blind as you think. I'm happy to see Ruth in your safe and protective hands, Joshua. As I told you before, I'll not reveal Ruth's cover." He sighed. "Mr. Jessup is not so lucky. He's in a rehabilitation camp."

"Ja? Where?" Ruth said.

"Pigeon Falls. It's not too far from here, is it, Joshua?"

# Eighteen

*"For then there will be great tribulation, such as has not been since the beginning of the world until this time, no, nor ever shall be. And unless those days were shortened, no flesh would be saved; but for the elect's sake those days will be shortened." Matthew 24:21–22*

Joshua was running late for their meeting. When he spotted Sheriff Baker entering the back door ahead of him, he sighed with relief, threw a blanket over his sweating Standardbred, and hurried in after him.

Sheriff Baker picked a seat next to Johansson's fireplace, rubbing his hands together. "Brrr, it's getting cold."

"Heard we'll have a break in the weather come Thursday," Johansson said. "I called this meeting together today because Joshua asked me to and because we need a plan of action. My wife got a letter smuggled to her about these UN biological super-soldiers who have super-strength and no conscience. They are killing machines and planted in American cities to weed out the Jews and Christians. It's only a matter of time—"

"I heard from my radio source this morning. That's why I was late," Baker said. "Some Americans have formed their own vigilante groups. The UN's going to have their hands full in Detroit, Ann Arbor, and elsewhere, as well as the suburbs. Yep, they've got quite a network going. Even managed to locate those re-education camps. Anyways, I promised my wife I'd ask Joshua's help on a personal matter first before we launch full scale into politics."

"All right, go ahead," Johansson said.

"I need to purchase one of those stoves that cooks, heats, and boils water all with wood. My fireplace can't keep the house heated, and I've run out of gasoline and kerosene. My wind turbines don't run without wind; I've used up the battery. And my solar pack doesn't charge without sunlight. We haven't seen the sun for two weeks. Been one snow squall after another." Sheriff Baker leaned forward as if the fire could give him solace. "Who do I get in touch with?"

"Isn't your electricity back?" Joshua said.

"Can't get it without the mark and anyways, I heard the price quadrupled. Besides, we're at the tail end of the electrical crew's to-do list. Most of the big cities are fixed, but not the small country towns. Meanwhile, I'm freezing in our big house. My wife and I eat, sleep, and read by the glow of our fireplace during these winter months. Boy, do I wish I'd thought to build my house with an open design so that the heat can reach all areas."

"I'll send Heydenreich over. He's got the biggest wagon and the strongest team of drafts." Joshua said. "I'll make sure he brings over the stove, and the men needed to install it. We can't afford to waste time."

He paused, his conscience pricking him. Maybe if he'd told the truth he could have prevented Ruth's dad from getting abducted. "I need to confess that our Ruth is Ruth Jessup, the woman you've been looking for."

"I sort of suspected that all along," Baker said. "I figured she's better off with you than with that lawyer, Rex Rollins."

"Danke. So, what about Mr. Jessup? Did you locate him?"

Baker frowned. "Isn't going to be easy, but if we're going to stage a breakout, plan to break everyone out. What do you say?"

"I'm in," Joshua said. "What do you need?"

"Some dynamite, guns, and men. Who have you got?" Baker turned to Johansson.

"I was afraid you'd ask that," Johansson said. "People are getting skittish; you know what I mean? Sort of afraid of their own shadow. They don't want to get involved. I think they're hoping to try and get along with the World Order Police."

"Divide and conquer, it works every time like it did during those riots we had several years ago that kept popping up in the cities across the country. This civil unrest we're smack dab in isn't helping the situation." Sheriff Baker rested back in his chair, sticking his socked feet out toward the stove.

"Back to basics, I say, or at least until Jesus takes us up," Johansson smirked.

"We need to do what our forefathers did in the Revolutionary War against Britain," Baker said. "Fight the WOP from the hills and swamps, and I've got a hunch there's a group like that."

"This is gut news," Johansson said. "Private Investigator Ricker mentioned one, but how do you get ahold of them when you need to?"

"Good question." Baker took the offered coffee from Johansson's wife. "Thank you, ma'am."

"God has a plan." Joshua sipped his coffee. "Hasn't He already shortened the days?"

"Sure enough," Johansson said. "You can't dawdle getting your chores done. My Frau and I read the Bible by candlelight like we used to read the newspaper—"

"I remember reading my smartphone for all the updates of the news," Baker said. "But I can't have the authorities tracking my whereabouts after HB 6666 passed in our second pandemic. I had to throw my smartphone away. It's the hardest thing I've ever done. I depended on that thing for a conventional telephone, messaging, a camera, weather, and current news updates."

"Check your Bible regularly," Joshua said. "You can about pinpoint the next thing to happen reading it. Like the news, there are a lot of sad things happening. However, the ending is glorious."

"Speaking of which," Baker said, "my radio friend said he witnessed the Patriots in action. Ordinary people doing extraordinary accomplishments, like during the Revolutionary War. Back then, they were called minutemen because people would go about their jobs until someone sounded the bell, or whatever they used, to call everyone together. They sprang into action to rescue families and fight off the British and Indians."

Joshua nodded. "Trouble is, there were Tories, British sympathizers, even back then, and you couldn't trust your neighbor."

"So, you think that's why no one's talking?" Johansson said.

"Could be." Baker stared into the fire. "It's a sad day when we can't trust our neighbors or our coworkers."

"You thinkin' about Officer Smith?" Joshua said.

"Yeah," Baker replied. "I wish I didn't feel so uneasy about him. We could use his help. Well, we have the Patriots, and they operate much like our Revolutionary War ancestors, not revealing their identity and striking when called upon, then escaping through the night, and the next day performing their day jobs. I remember a show called *The Swamp Fox* I watched as a child. It's something like that now."

Joshua stroked his beard. "I like that name, the Patriots. We're patriotic toward our Lord Jesus and Americans."

Baker slapped his hand on his breeches. "I know two men who'll buy into that. They said they'd help any way they could. They'll bring their guns."

"What about that private investigator, Ricker?" Johansson said. "He told us he knows a group who calls themselves the Patriots, let's join them." He leaned back in his big chair. "You going to ask Officer Smith in. After all, he could be an okay gent?"

"I—don't think that's a good idea." Baker squirmed in his chair. "I don't like the way he upholds this New World Order guy. If you say okay, I'll try him out this one time."

"We could use Smith's help." Johansson said, "What about giving him a chance this time and see?"

Baker nodded. "I've been up in Pigeon Falls and mapped the place out. I saw three guards protecting about thirty prisoners. The prisoners looked malnourished and beat up. My computerized squad cars still don't work. Besides, they can tell the WOP where we've been. Anyways, the cars and vans won't have enough room for everyone." Baker stood. "We might need one of your wagons or two to haul them out of there. I doubt they will be able to walk too far on their own."

"We'll use the dirt roads and farm trails to get them home," Joshua said.

"This sounds powerfully complicated," Johansson said. "We'll need someplace to hide them for a spell."

"Got that handled. I know of some cabins up in the forests," Baker said. "We have enough miles of wilderness here to keep them hidden for at least a month. With supplies, they'll do better than at that rehabilitation camp."

"We'd best do it before the snow piles up. I wish we had more people," Johansson said.

"We got to hold on for a couple more years. Hopefully, others will join us," Baker said. "If people lose hope, I'm afraid they'll take the easy way out and accept the mark—especially if the WOP take their loved ones as ransom."

Joshua stirred uncomfortably. "God has His rules, too."

"I know. They can't take the Antichrist's mark. God made that clear. So, we can't stand by and allow Satan to kill us without a fight." Baker punched his fist into his open palm. "It's been born into me living in these United States. If our forefathers could go against a mighty country like Great Britain, we can dodge the chopping block of this Antichrist. We can hide in the forests and defend ourselves the way our ancestors did."

"Count me in. That makes it three." Johansson guffawed. "Besides, I like the odds. We're in the Lord's army."

"And me, that'll even up the score," Joshua said.

"You two are Amish. It's against your religion to fight," Baker said. "I figured I'd use you to haul away the prisoners."

Joshua looked down at his hands, folding and refolding them in fixed concentration. *Lord, should I tell them?* "The way I see it, I don't plan on killing, and I can help. You're willing to get my, I mean Ruth's father, out of that rehabilitation camp. I can't stand by and do nothing."

"What will your Amish people say—you don't know, you might have to kill someone?"

Joshua grinned. "Nothin', because they're not going to know."

"It might work, Joshua," Baker said. "You got any kin in Pigeon Falls? If we can find another man that will help us, you and he could hide me and Smith in the back of your wagon. You can drop us off at the outskirts of the complex. We could run around the back of the building, cut the wire, and get the prisoners out. Maybe we won't have to fire a shot."

"What night you are planning?" Joshua said.

Baker looked from Joshua to Johansson. "I was figuring on Saturday evening. Smith told me the other day that two of the guards like to whoop it up on Saturday evenings in the local bar down in town. That leaves one left to deal with."

"Sounds like a plan," Joshua said. "Snow should be gone and that means no fresh wagon tracks. Let's plan this Saturday. That will give us four days to get our equipment together."

※

The light of the full moon peeked through the small window of Joshua's bedroom and gave enough light for him to grab his boots and coat and tiptoe out of the house. He'd prayed and fasted all day and had Martha do the same. Though he'd not told her of his plans, he knew she suspected something. The only problem, he hadn't found anyone else to help them.

Johansson would drive one wagon. That would mean one of the wagons would have to wait in the woods near the road until they returned. Too many wagons in a sleepy town like Pigeon would alert the World Order police. It was risky, leaving a couple of horses by themselves in the woods. Horses were more valuable than a car now.

"Joshua, I want to help. May I?" Ruth stepped out from beneath the shadow of a rafter.

She was dressed in her kapp, wool shawl, and hard-soled shoes. Joshua had to blink twice to make sure it wasn't his Sara. "Go back into the house."

# LOVE'S FINAL SUNRISE

"No."

"Ach!" This was not his Sara. Joshua grimaced. English women. Just like it for God to give him an English woman with a stubborn nature to boot. "This is no place for a girl to be."

Ruth stepped closer, her soft voice and shallow whisper a direct contrast to his gruff one. "I think we both know I am no girl—but a woman full grown."

Joshua stepped from beneath the shadows of the barn beams. Grabbing her on either side of her arms, he intended to shake some sense into her. Instead, he felt his arms draw her close. Her sweet head fell without misgivings onto his chest. It was then he heard it—her quiet sobs.

"I am a *Dummkopf*—you are ailing?"

"Yes, for my dad." She looked up at him, her eyes moist with unshed tears. "Please let me come. I won't be any trouble, Joshua, please."

Her womanliness and her sweet breath intoxicated the air he breathed. It felt good to hold a woman in his arms again. Only Ruth wasn't just any woman. She was the one who could reel him in like a fish on a hook with a smile—or a tear. "Ach," he whispered in her ear, "I fear for you, my—son has grown fond of you." Her arms caressed his shoulders; she searched his face. "And what about yourself?"

"Ja—me too, very much." He bent closer, her eyes closed, her lips expecting. The moment he had waited so long for had come.

"Whoa," someone said.

It was Johansson and Baker. "Stay here," he whispered to Ruth, pushing her toward the shadows. He stepped forward and lifted his lantern high.

"You got the team hooked up?" Johansson said.

"Ja, one. Where's Smith?"

"Said he'd meet us up there," Baker said, getting off his horse.

Joshua returned to get Betsy. He thought it strange for Smith to go up alone when he could have ridden with them. Still, sometimes what the English did didn't make any sense to him.

"Did you have any luck finding someone to drive the other team?"

Baker said.

"Yes. Me." Ruth stepped out from beneath the shadows.

# Nineteen

*"But as for me, I trust in You, O Lord; I say, "You are my God." My times are in Your hand; Deliver me from the hand of my enemies, and from those who persecute me. Save me for Your mercies' sake." Psalm 31:14–16*

Displeasure etched jagged creases across Joshua's face, like a road map with no end in sight. Ruth smirked. She had learned Joshua's facial features well these past years.

Whenever displeased, as now, his full lips would crinkle at the corners, and his eyes wouldn't meet hers. She'd have to bear the brunt of his anger for a while.

If what Detective Ricker said about her dad was true, she would not be able to live with herself if she didn't help. Her dad. The Lord had answered her prayers. Soon she and Joshua would learn of the blank pages of her past.

She watched Joshua hook up Betsy. Before Baker could unsaddle his horse, Joshua said, "Might be a good idea to bring the horse along, you never know, we might need him."

She sat next to Joshua on the wagon seat like they were husband and wife. That would have pleased her if not for his stony countenance.

He sat ramrod, his profile in the moonlight like carved stone. Only a brief interlude ago he wooed her with his words of endearment. Maybe not so apparent to him, but to her, they were. Did she imagine it? His strong arms warm, inviting, his voice whispering in her ear, his lips so close to hers—she could still feel the effects of their closeness. No, she hadn't imagined it, and she refused to feel intimated by Joshua's behavior.

Ruth rubbed the back of her neck. It had now been over an hour traveling the pitted back roads. It would have been faster if they could have used the paved roads. But Joshua didn't want any passing horse or motorist to spot them. The wagons drew to a halt past the crook in the path.

Ruth made out a tall three-story brick house with blue spruces that loomed around the building like silent sentinels. Stark-looking maples stripped of their autumn foliage etched skeleton-looking shapes before the light of the full moon. A fence ran in front and behind the house and barn.

"This is where we separate company." Baker and Johansson jumped down. Joshua handed her the reins. "Stay here. If anyone should ride by, pretend you're asleep."

"Ja." She had found out a simple yes seemed to please the Amish men most. A grin bent the corners of Joshua's lips. His concerned eyes met hers. "Hmm, ja, my little mädel, stay safe." He took her hand into his and squeezed it. She felt the heat of his burning through her mitten. Then he was gone into the night.

☼

Sheriff Baker shoved a .22 into Joshua's hand. "Take it."

Joshua pocketed it in his coat and followed.

A man moved out from beneath the shadows of the massive gothic architecture of the house. "About time." Smith nodded his head toward the side entrance. "This way. We've got to move fast. The only way to escape is up a ladder through a fire escape." He opened the door then quietly crossed the storage room to another door. "Heard them say they have more people than they can handle here. They're planning on setting up another place in Detroit." He motioned for them to follow him.

Joshua crept down the steep, narrow stone steps. The sounds of children whimpering and women sobbing met his ears before he reached the bottom. His stomach lurched; he'd thought he'd seen just about everything—but this human suffering made him shiver in his boots. As he took his last step, he stepped into something soft and oozy. Was it excrement from the prisioners, water oozing from the cracks in the cement blocks—or blood.

Smith turned on his flashlight, scanning the room. Joshua glanced down curiously. Pools of red spotted the dirt floor. Glancing over at the wrist and ankle chains attached to two poles, his thoughts went a little woozy. What was wrong with him? He was used to gutting a deer, heifer, and hog for his meat and hanging them to dry. But this was *human* blood. He spotted a half-sawed log about eight feet long with a saw lying on top. Dried blood layered its serrated edges. What kind of person could inflict such a barbaric ritual on another human? He didn't need any more explanations as to the intent of these antichrist terrorists. It was written in blood—hate for his Savior, Christ Jesus. Hate for all His beloved children. Christ's elect must endure the Antichrist's vengeance—but not for long.

The beam from Smith's flashlight glistened on chain-link fences. Joshua saw at least twelve ten-by-ten cages made to house dogs and other pets but which now housed women, children, and men who were barefooted and half-clothed. They barely had room to turn and little space to stand, let alone lie down. Half-fearful, half-hoping eyes followed him.

A block of wood stood in the far corner with a large old-fashioned hatchet leaning against it. Reddish stains layered the iron blade as it did the wood that measured twelve by twelve. The hairs on the back of Joshua's neck pricked. "We're here to get you out!"

"Thank you, Jesus!" someone said, and the cheers of the captives followed.

"Come on, let's move. Where are the keys?"

Smith shone his light on Joshua and Baker, then reached into his pocket and pulled out the keys. Joshua and Baker exchanged glances.

Were they walking into a trap? Still, why hadn't the captives yelled out to free them? Something felt amiss—but what? *Lord, send forth your legions to save us.*

"Give me some of those keys," Baker demanded. "What cages do these fit."

"The far end," Smith said. "We got to hurry before the next shift gets here." Walking to the closest row of cages, Smith opened one at a time.

"Okay, no more yelling, group up everyone." Joshua felt suddenly in control. "You there, help this kid up the stairs. Anyone here named Jessup?"

"Yeah, that's me."

"Your daughter is waiting for you in the wagon down the road."

Smith turned. "Get out of here quick. The WOP is coming back to finish—the reeducation process."

A noise from upstairs alerted Joshua that the WOP men had finished their liquid dinner at the bar and returned.

"Skedaddle. Go through the fire escape. I'll finish letting everyone out," Smith said.

"I'm staying to make sure everyone gets out." Joshua couldn't chance anyone left behind in this hellhole. He turned, taking off his coat and wrapping it around a woman who was dressed only in her bra and skirt. "Jessup, help this lady up the steps; she might need to be carried. Here, this child, too."

"Where are the wagons?" Jessup asked.

Joshua gave instructions, and Jessup, carrying the child, made a beeline for the narrow exit and climbed the ladder that surfaced to the top of what used to be a tornado shelter years before. Jessup and his group bent low to the ground as they ran across the courtyard and headed toward the road.

---

Ruth counted twenty bearded mean-looking men, five women, and four children, mostly all barefoot, making their way toward her. Then men wore nothing but a tee-shirt and jeans, the women and children ragged clothes. Johansson was huffing and puffing, all of them resembling prison escapees of the worst caliber.

"Ruthie?" Jessup reached the wagon first.

"Dad?" Was he her dad? They were in each other arms before she could blink.

"Come on, Ruthie. We got to get out of here before those WOP men show up. They'll shoot and ask questions later." He motioned for the men to jump into the wagon bed and help the women and children up.

Looking over her shoulder, she realized the wagon she drove wasn't full. "Wait." She reined up her horse. "We can take more people. Johansson, where's Joshua and Baker?"

"We had to get out because some of the WOP men returned sooner than expected," Jessup said.

Joshua's in there. She felt the breath leave her lungs. And Jessup left him? "You're my dad? Where's your sense of duty? I'm going back to help them." Ruth turned to climb out of the wagon.

"No!" Jessup said.

"I can't leave Joshua."

Johansson, still winded and visibly shaken, moved forward. "We got to go, Ruth. We got to get out of here. Or…we could be captured. It's more horrible than you can imagine in there."

The women and children started crying. Huddling together in their rags, they wrapped the blankets Joshua had brought around their thin shoulders.

"Come on," Jessup hissed.

"But are there other women and children?"

"They're coming." Jessup's hand took the reins from her. Then he whipped Betsy into motion. Soon they were galloping through the small trail.

Ruth held onto the sides of the wagon. This man couldn't be her dad. Then a flashback of Dad denouncing the authority of God caused her to cringe. "How can you turn your back on people who risked their lives for you?"

Jessup's face was frozen in horror, his eyes wide and wild with fright. "You didn't go through what we did. Those WOP men aren't human. I tell you, they're demonic. I watched them saw a man in two! They get immense pleasure torturing us into submitting to their ideology."

Jessup stopped where Johansson said to. Johansson jumped down and walked to Joshua's wagon. "Climb down and split up," Johansson told the ten-odd men in the wagon. "Find someplace in those woods over there to hide until we return with the others."

One man stepped forward. "Can you use my help to drive one of the wagons?"

Jessup jumped down. "It's your funeral. Remember what to look for before trusting someone."

"What to look for? What do you mean?" Ruth asked.

"Those WOP men have 666 tattoos either on their forehead or hand. Often, they cover it up to fool you. But they can't cover it up under an iridescent light. You can see that hedonistic mark as plain as day then."

Ruth jumped down from the wagon, motioning the man to take her place, and walked toward the horse tied up behind her wagon. "I'm going to go back to get us more help. I saw a bar in town. You bring the wagons."

"Get back here!" Jessup said. "I saw the mark on one of them. It's too dangerous. Get back here."

"What?" Johansson said.

Jessup lunged toward her. She backed away from her dad. "What did you see? I mean, can you describe him to me?"

"Yeah," one guy said, jumping down from the wagon. "He was tall, young, and sort of the uppity type. He acts like he's our friend, there to help us escape. Only don't trust him. He's trying to get information. You know, good cop thing. I think he could be a policeman, even has the crew cut of one."

"Officer Smith," Johansson said. "Baker was right!"

Her dad grabbed her. He flung her none too gently back toward the now empty wagon. "I can't allow you to go back and get killed. Your mother would never forgive me."

She pounded him in the head with her fist. That released his grip. "I'm through running away. And I'm through with you. Get back with God, or get out of my life." She jumped onto the horse and galloped back toward town and the old mansion.

---

The WOP guard's fist seemed to come toward Joshua's face in slow motion. He braced for it. Thump! Before he could react, someone kicked him in the groan, and he doubled over with pain. Slammed in the head by something, he landed on his back.

"Tell me who planned this little breakout. Why are you trying to protect them? They left you here to die. Doesn't that mean anything?"

Joshua licked at the warm blood oozing down his chin. He looked over at Baker. He had a cut dangerously close to his eye and a bloody cheek. His nose looked broken. How long had it been? A half-hour, an hour? He looked around at the cages of men, women, and children who still needed rescuing.

"Answer me!"

He was whacked on the head again. Then he blacked out.

---

Joshua woke up to find himself in a small cell. Someone was wiping the blood off his head and what dripped into his eyes. "Baker?"

As his eyes focused, he saw a woman who was wiping away the blood. She backed away and cringed in the corner, staring with frightened eyes at Smith. Joshua coaxed her. "Come on."

From outside the cell, Officer Smith's face, grinning, stared into his. "Come on. I'm going to get you out of here." The lock clicked; the door flew open, banging against the bars of the cage.

"I'll wait here," she said. "Don't trust him and watch your back."

Joshua's mind felt like mush. Something didn't figure. What happened to Baker? Why was this woman acting so strange? All he remembered was he and Baker had been busy opening the far row of cages. And Smith had the keys in his pocket—say, why wasn't Smith banged up like him? Baker had worked at the opposite end of the room. Suddenly the WOP swarmed on all of them like hornets, flooding the stairway. But where had Smith been all through the interrogations? Now, for some reason, Joshua and Baker were separated.

Smith pulled Joshua to his feet. They walked toward the ladder that led to the yard. "Okay, now one step at a time." A distant roll of thunder rumbled across the stark blackness of night. Joshua made it to the top. He reached over to give Smith a hand up. A lightning bolt lit the sky like day—the mark of 666 shone across Smith's hand.

Smith growled low. His hand, like a vice, wrapped Joshua's as he attempted to pull Joshua down. Joshua struggled, but gravity and his 180 pounds worked against him. His body went air-born, thumping down the ten-foot drop into a heap of pain. "Ah!"

He drew several deep breaths and mustered all his strength. He climbed back up the metal ladder, grabbed Smith, and threw him to the ground, pouncing on him. Grabbing Smith's knife from his belt, he rested it at Smith's Adam's apple. "Okay, now I'm going to ask the questions."

"Guess again, Amish." A dozen WOP men surrounded him. They pulled him toward the prison-like dungeon foul with the smell of blood, feces, and vomit. He was strapped into a chair, his head bound to a high-top strap with a metal hat-type apparatus.

---

Tying the horse some ten feet away from the old mansion, Ruth crept toward the light shining out from the cellar door and listened.

"Why, Smith? You had everything going for you, a good pension, people respected you. Why join the WOP?" Joshua said. "And you probably went to church. Right? Why this Antichrist?"

"I got tired of Baker bossing me." His laughter bordered on the hysterical. "And this guy is the real deal! Not that weakling Jesus who wants you to love your enemies. My savior is god, the real deal." Smith doubled his fist and shook it at Joshua. "Our god is powerful, and we will reign with him forever and ever!"

The stench of rotten flesh and human waste swept up toward Ruth. She held her hand to her mouth, leaned forward, and covered her nose. The smell was enough to gag her and cause her to vomit.

She lay flat on her stomach, her eyes following the sound of voices. The lights inside offered her a partial view of Officer Smith as he leaned over Joshua. All she could see was Joshua's arm strapped to something metal.

"Now you'll take orders from me. A few electric shocks will make you see the light," Smith said. "I'll have you begging to take the mark!"

Her heart leapt in her chest in heart-wrenching agony. God help me. She had to find help—before it was too late. She ran to her horse, dug her foot into the stirrup, sprung up, and galloped down the side of the road. *The bar.* It was the only place with lights and with the men she needed.

She flung open the door, huffing, and out of breath. The dim lights made it hard to see—how many men were here?

The men sitting at the bar and side tables turned and looked at her, then resumed their drinking. She stumbled toward them. "I could use your help. The WOP have captured my friends."

Two guys laughed. Their shoulders heaved and rolled like a ship bobbing across a wind-tossed lake. What was wrong with them? Had they lost their feelings of humanity? All she saw was a sea of bearded men heehawing their dirty gritty grins at her.

"I think she might have drunk more than we did. Look, girlie, just what the blue blazes is the WOP?"

☀

"Don't you know you're licked?" Smith hissed. "Now I'll ask you nice like—where does Johansson plan to go with those prisoners? You better do what I ask, or you'll never see your mother or little boy again."

Joshua pushed against the straps. He scowled back at his captor. "I can't believe you would turn on your chief as you have."

"Baker's a fool! Pledging his loyalty to that freak who died on a cross some two thousand years ago."

"Christ Jesus is alive, and you'll get to see Him in the flesh soon enough."

"I serve a greater god. He's the true god! There is no other god but my mine."

---

"You got to believe me," Ruth said. "These are the men from the New World Order. They're grabbing everyone who won't swear allegiance to the Antichrist and receive his mark. Right now, they have innocent Americans in that old mansion up the hill. They'll be starved and tortured, and if they refuse the mark—their heads are chopped off. My friends and I have managed to get a wagonful to safety, but there are more people needing help."

"Look, girlie, they're political offenders of the worst type and mentally unstable." The bartender didn't glance up but continued to wipe the top of his handcrafted wooden bar.

Ruth stared at the bartender's bent head. "So, it's okay that Christians are unlawfully held behind bars without bail, without a trial?" She pounded her fist down on his highly polished bar. "How can you stand there and let this atrocity happen? We are all Americans, one nation under God, remember? If we don't fight for Truth, then all that is left is this hell on Earth."

"The only hell we have here is you Bible-thumping fanatical Christians who can't change with the times." The bartender slapped his wet dishrag into the air, making a snapping noise with the cloth. "Your type of religion doesn't exist anymore, and you better get used to that."

Ruth felt ill-equipped. The Truth was too hard to uphold. Then something Joshua had taught her and read popped up in her thoughts.

"Spiritual amnesia, that's what you have," Ruth yelled. She raised her hand and encompassed the roomful of men. "You've forgotten what our Almighty God has done for us. You've become complacent in your sins, your idolatry, worshipping money and material things over God; you live as you please and if your lady friend gets pregnant, just have that baby aborted—can't you see that you're murdering a baby—an innocent life?

"And you say same-sex relationships are fine. 'Men burning in lust for one another, men with men, women with women, committing what is shameful, going against nature.'

"Then you put Christians in jail so you don't have to hear the truth. Do you call that freedom of religion? Hardly. You think God will forgive everything because you want it that way?" Her eyes swept the room. "You really think God will change His moral compass? To be whatever a slothful and sinful society deems right?"

"Why don't you get out of here before we have you arrested and put in that reeducation place along with those other fanatics?" One man in the corner of the room dressed all in black stood up.

His hands locked into fists; he took a step toward her. She didn't care, her words flooded her mouth before she could stop. "Don't you see this is what Jesus talked about in Matthew 24, we are the last generation? The final curtain is about to draw closed, and you're sitting here getting drunk."

"That's it." The man dressed in black said and started toward her.

Five or six men who had sat quietly talking got up and walked to the back of the room, forced the man to his feet, and then carried him out the back door.

One man sitting by the ornate cherry-wood bar said, "I recall what my granddaddy said about Hitler's concentration camps, hellish places. The German people were much to blame, allowing that to happen in their cities and not doing anything about it."

He slapped the man next to him on the back and jumped to his feet. "Little lady, you make powerful sense. I never did think it was right to throw out what I was taught growing up. I guess I figured I could coast along for a spell. Living was easier if I didn't have to follow all those thou-shalt-nots of the Ten Commandments. I enjoyed listening to preachers who said I could keep on sinning, 'cause God loved me." He chuckled. "I heard one preacher say, God loves us sinners—"

"He does! He cared enough about sinners to put His only Son on the cross for your sins," she pointed to the man at the back of the room, "and your sins." She turned to the bartender. "And your sins!" Winded, as if she'd run a marathon, she paused. The men and woman stared back at her.

"But you have to do your part—you have to repent. That means to turn away from your old life, your old sinful nature, and accept by faith His forgiveness in true repentance. This only comes with the Holy Spirit who convicts and draws you to God—and helps you not to sin again!"

Ruth shook like a leaf on a tree in a windstorm. "God warns us. He says, He who hardens his heart will suddenly be destroyed and without remedy."

She could have heard a pin drop. "He also says there is great rejoicing over one sinner who repents."

"I, for one, am not going to let this happen." One man in a checkered flannel shirt slapped his hand down on the table. "I haven't taken the mark, nor am I about to. I might not be the good Christian I should be, but I am repenting of my past life here and now."

"Sam, you know I got baptized right in that lake over there and asked Jesus into my heart," said the man sitting next to him.

"That's right," Sam said.

"I've backslidden, but I'm not going to let someone dictate to me that I can't believe in Jesus," said Sam's friend.

Sam turned to stare at her. "You think this is true? One guy who was here earlier bragged about his tattoo. Said he can buy and sell all he wants with that tattoo. Is he part of this New World Order?"

The woman who sat at the next table stood and looked at Ruth, then answered for her. "Yeah, looks like that's the way the wind is blowing."

"They'll not send me to no reeducation place, at least not without a fight. I'm still a God-fearing American, and I don't care for some gent with a new idea about religion from some New World Order coming in here and telling me what I can say and believe."

The woman wrapped her heavy wool sweater around her middle. "Say, what you said about God's forgiveness—does it work? Can you feel different, I mean, like you had—"

"A rebirth?" Ruth nodded. "Yes. Have faith in Christ Jesus and believe in that new life—and stay far away from your old life. 'For God did not send His Son into the world to condemn the world, but that the world through Him might be saved.'"

"Okay, little lady, lead the way," Sam said.

"Wait just a minute, Sam. You're going to get this town in a heap of trouble," the bartender said. "They haven't bothered me. Let's not get them riled up. They pay their bills. What am I supposed to live on if I don't comply with their demands? Air?"

Sam slammed his fist on the bar's gleaming surface. "Our time is coming. Those WOP guys confided in me that a group of super-soldiers would soon be here—to educate us. I may not go to church every Sunday like I should and frequent the bars too much. But I always ask God to forgive me and His Son not to give up on me. I'll not let my Savior nor my country down when they need me the most."

"Do you think this New World Order will give up because we want it to?" the bartender said, his color rising in tune to the tremor in his voice.

"Nope. I do not. No sirree." Sam rubbed his stubbled chin. "I recall now what the Bible says about these times. That God's place is with His creation. It might just be that the ending to the Lord's prayer, the Our Father, has come to pass after all. You know it, remember?" He gave his friend a poke with his elbow."

"You mean, 'thy kingdom come. Thy will be done.' That one?"

"That's the one." Sam nodded.

Ruth smiled at the unbelieving bartender. "Jesus is coming, and it's soon. He'll be riding back on a milk-white stallion."

"You're all a bunch of nuts!" The bartender slapped down his towel.

The door banged a resounding solidarity note to the bartender's last retort as they left.

Beneath the shadowed trees, the five men who left earlier appeared. The four men and one woman who followed her out looked at her questioningly.

She needed every able-bodied man she could find. She squared off, lifting her head. "Have you men come to join our fight against these bullies that would wage war on innocent women and children?"

The tallest of the men stepped forward. My, he had to be seven feet tall. She snatched a deep breath.

"Yes, ma'am, we have. We call ourselves the Patriots, and we're a group of volunteers linked with the underground. Ma'am, could you lead the way?"

Nine men and Ruth, her horse in hand, covered the distance to the mansion slinking behind trees and blending into the shadows. She didn't know what to expect, but she couldn't stop now. Then she saw him, her father, leading a band of men. They joined on the house lawn and slinked along to the back of the building.

The tall man, evidently the leader, touched her arm. "Why don't you and your horse stand beneath that tree and stay in the shadows until we take care of matters down below? Here, take this. Only shoot if you're threatened."

☼

Joshua struggled against the straps that bound his arms. The electric shocks had amazingly grown weaker, the generator losing power and eventually dying.

"You need a little more persuasion," Smith said.

A WOP man heated a poker in the flames of the fire he built. He waited until it sizzled and carried it red-hot toward Joshua.

Smith placed a hand on the guard's arm. "Wait. I have a better plan."

He dragged out a mother and child huddled in the corner of a filthy cage.

Joshua was aghast.

# LOVE'S FINAL SUNRISE

"This little girl's name is Nancy."

Her little face was bruised and her clothes were ragged and torn. The half-starved girl looked from Smith to him.

"Say hello," Smith prompted her.

She clung to her mother and opened her mouth. Nothing.

"Oh, I forgot, you can't speak." Smith laughed. "Remember, I'm your friend. Do as I say, and I won't let those bad people hurt you."

Joshua fought against his bindings. "You are wicked through and through, just like the god you serve!"

Smith's face distorted into fiendish lines. "Give me the poker. Mom, your time's up. Pay homage to the one true god, and I'll brand 666 on your forehead. Or face the chopping block."

She stood a little straighter in her soiled clothing. "I belong to Christ Jesus. Him alone do I serve. 'For who can separate us from the love of Christ? Shall tribulation, or distress, or persecution, or famine, or nakedness. Yet in all these things we are more than conquerors through Him who loved us.'"

Smith's maniacal laugh echoed in the damp quarters. He swirled the poker toward the little girl.

She wrote a big J in the air with her finger, then pointed to her heart.

"Little fool." Smith cursed her, then turned to face Joshua. "What will it be? Her, or are you going to tell me where you took my prisoners?"

Time. Joshua needed time. "Untie me. I need to show you. There are no road signs where they went."

Smith motioned to the guard to free Joshua. "Quick, you fool! We're wasting valuable time."

Untied, Joshua flexed his muscles.

"Wait, I want to finish off Baker before we leave." Smith hurried toward an alcove.

Baker, his eyes swollen and bruised, his arm cut and bleeding, was hauled out of a dark pit in the far corner of the room. "Who gets the privilege?" Smith said.

"Me!" A brawny man with arms as round as a fully matured maple tree stepped forward.

Two men stood on either side of Joshua. "Say WOP, should we bind his arms again?"

Smith jeered. "Amish can't fight. It's against their religion."

"Really? This Amish guy belted me in the face not too long ago."

A sudden commotion outside diverted their attention. "What's that?"

Joshua walloped the man on his right, then punched the one on his left, and rushed the WOP ax man like a mad bull and toppled him to the ground. The ax went flying onto the dirt.

Smith reached for the red-hot poker. Joshua managed to grab it first.

Baker's hands were tied, but he managed to kick one WOP man in the groin.

The poker came dangerously close to Joshua's face as he and Smith rolled round and round in the dirt. He felt the hot embers of the fire on his back. He threw his legs up and shoved Smith off of him. The poker lay in the fire, its sizzling heat sending spirals of smoke into the air like a tornado.

Smith got to his feet first, pulled the little girl to him, using her as a human shield, and dragged her toward the burning fire.

The girl's eyes went wide with fright, her bare feet dangerously close to the burning wood. Joshua went red with rage. "Why you filthy, lying—" Joshua leaped through the fire. He seized the girl then tossed her toward her mother, his clothes now aflame. Smith thrust the poker toward Joshua's burning shirt. A large man with glowing yellow hair jumped in front of Joshua, taking the blow meant for him, and sent a powerful punch to Smith's head.

The large man slapped at the flames engulfing Joshua and his clothes. Smoke billowed around him. He coughed, his eyes watering from the fumes and heat. The vapors cleared. He glanced at his arms and chest. Not a single burn anywhere.

A blast of light lit the dark corners of the underground room. The noise of boots on steps filled the room as Jessup and ten other men scrambled down. He didn't know who all these men were, but he was grateful they were here. The group soon had the WOP gagged and locked in the cages.

"Ruth! What are you doing here?" Joshua's pulse quickened. He wrapped her into his arms, shielding her from the bloody scene. Joshua looked at Jessup, and then at the ten men who joined in the fight, and then to Ruth. "Let me guess. It's because of her that you're here."

"You learn fast." Jessup mock punched his jaw. "She's got a powerful wallop when she wants to let go."

"Joshua, I was afraid they'd kill you." Her eyes, pools of emotion, shone into his. If she only knew, she could melt his heart away with one glance.

"Na. I'm too mean." I need to get her and the other women out of here. "Say, where are the wagons?"

"Mine is a quarter mile up the street," Jessup said. "Hidden in a grove."

"Okay, let's get everyone out of those cages." Joshua picked up Nancy, cradling her in his arms. "You want to help me?"

The girl nodded, hugging him. "Thank you, Jesus," she whispered.

"Do you know of anyone else needing freeing?" Joshua asked, Nancy's mother. She showed them where three more children, two teenage boys, a teenage girl, and two women were in another room hidden in the alcove.

"We need to get everyone out," the leader of the men directed the WOP.

"Where do you keep the WOP you capture?" Sheriff Baker asked the leader.

"That's confidential information."

"Okay, I'll accept that. But tell me this, are you one of the bands of Patriots?" Joshua said.

"Yes, sir, we are."

"Where do you come from?" It was Ruth's turn now.

"From round about. We rescue Christians and Jews while waiting for our Lord and Savior to arrive and relieve us of that duty, ma'am."

"Us too." Baker thumped his chest. "We're with you, Patriots."

Joshua glanced out of the pit of the filthy dungeon to the starlit sky above. "And like you, we look forward to being relieved of this duty."

Coming topside, Baker nodded toward the forest. "Johansson is here with the other wagon. Here's hoping we don't get caught. We can take those who live in Owenson with us."

"We'll see what we can do to get the rest who live elsewhere back to their families."

Joshua helped Ruth into the wagon.

With a decisive nod, the seven-foot man with the flaming yellow hair said, "Wish you could learn to obey orders, ma'am. I've got to say, the Holy Spirit was speaking through you tonight."

"Danke." The soft tremor of her voice spoke more than words of her humility. "My name is Ruth. What's yours?"

Joshua recognized the unmistakable gleam erupting in the man's twinkling clear eyes. He felt a stab of jealousy prick his heart. You could almost see right through—

"Call me Gabriel."

"Gabriel, you mean like the angel?" Ruth said.

He tipped his hat to her and disappeared into the shadow of the trees.

"That guy disappeared mighty quick, don't you think?" Sheriff Baker said.

Another of the Patriots and Jessup walked forward.

"Sheriff Baker, do you need me to take the women and children to Owenson?" Jessup said.

"Anyone who wants to help is welcome. We'll need to travel through town."

"Let's get the women and children in the wagon," Joshua directed. "Ruth, I want you to stay with them and keep them quiet. Jessup, can help you drive? I'll take the horse. Wait for me before entering town. Can you do that, I mean wait for me?"

"Ja, but Joshua—" Ruth protested.

He held up his finger. "No buts. I'll explain it later. What I need from you right now is to obey, like a gut Amish—" His thoughts weren't forming like they should with those luminous eyes staring at him. "Frau."

"Wife?"

How had he managed to allow that to escape? "Nee, I don't mean that you are—"

"Ja?"

His blood pumped like fire through his veins. Uppermost in his thoughts were his near miss with death, and she, a pink-cheeked, sweet little Paul Revere, saving him. "I mean, you must not forget you are a mädel?"

"Ja, Joshua. I get it."

"No, you don't," he whispered, sadly watching her drive away.

# Twenty

*"For if you forgive men their trespasses, your heavenly Father will also forgive you. But if you do not forgive men their trespasses, neither will your Father forgive your trespasses." Matthew 6:14–15*

The aromas of turkey, cinnamon, and ginger tickled Ruth's nostrils. Ruth basted the Christmas turkey, closed the oven door, and hurried toward the large picture window. A blanket of newly fallen snow lay like a white down comforter on the grass and lanes. Joshua, what could be keeping you?

A buggy turned into the drive. "They're here." Joshua had gone to fetch her dad and his wife, Harriet, to enjoy Christmas dinner with them.

An ominous dread swirled within her, making her stomach feel queasy. Why? This should be a happy occasion, this reunion with her stepmother. She tried hard to remember. Nothing but a dark hole. Why did her mind refuse to allow her access into the recesses of her past?

The buggy did not disclose its occupants until they disembarked. Her dad, his wife, and two others descended. Who could they be?

"Ruthie! I can't believe it." A slender woman with short blonde hair and a tanned complexion drew Ruth into her arms. "We've found you and are together on this Holy Day. I have been praying for you. So have your sister and brother. Honey, I am so sorry about the way I treated you before. Can you ever, ever forgive me?"

"Certainly." Ruth smiled. Her nerves tickled her backbone. *But for what?*

Harriet's arms clutched Ruth in another embrace that left her gasping for air. For some unknown reason, she wanted to draw away.

Her stepmother, holding her at arm's length, stared into her eyes searchingly. "I've accepted Jesus as my Savior. Finally, I know. You tried so hard to make me see the truth. Come to think of it, it's been a little over four years since I accepted Jesus as my Savior. And now here we are, all together for Christmas dinner. And I brought you presents. Years' worth of presents left beneath the Christmas trees in hopes you'd return home."

"Danke," Ruth said, accepting the brightly wrapped presents.

Another woman stepped forward. "I'm your stepsister, Jane. Do you remember me?"

Ruth shook her head. "Willkum. Danke for the presents."

A man stepped forward. "I'm Paul, your stepbrother." He was a head taller than Ruth. He smiled broadly. "Look at you, all dressed up in Amish clothes and still looking like you could snag a guy without any trouble, just with those gorgeous eyes of yours!"

"Danke." Ruth shifted from one foot to the other. No memories of either Jane or Paul came to her mind. Perhaps it was a good thing.

"Ach, we do not have any presents for you," Ruth said.

Joshua came to her aid. "Amish do not celebrate Christmas like the English."

"Not commercialized like ours, right. I remember," her dad said.

"I have you to thank for rescuing my husband—your father, Ruthie." Tears brimmed Harriet's eyes.

Ruth searched her memory for a piece of the puzzle to insert into the odd-shaped design that this beautiful woman should fit. Jane was close to Ruth's age. Surely, they enjoyed growing up together. Her dad had told her about many things from her past. Much made no sense. Why then did she run away from her dad's home to live with her grandmother? "I, I'm sorry, I had an accident and—"

"My Ruthie." Harriet stepped forward, clutching her heart.

Her stepmother could fit the role of a damsel in distress admirably.

Something clicked. That dramatized charade was familiar.

"I hired Mr. Ricker to find you," Harriet said "He never told me about your amnesia. However, I think I am getting the picture as to why. Often, I do present the wrong image. You see—"

"Oh, Harriet." Dad stepped before her. "Mr. Ricker didn't know. None of us knew. I found Ruthie myself when I was walking down that road with my militia group. At least I thought it was her. Ruthie didn't know me. She came with Josh as part of the rescue group who—"

"Josh is part of the Patriot group? But I thought the Amish were forbidden to fight?" Harriet said.

"No. I mean, he wasn't in the beginning. You see, dear, the Patriots are comprised of people just like you and me who are tired of these New World Order terrorists working for the Antichrist. Like Hitler's army, they wage war on women, children, and whomever they choose, torturing and beheading those who refuse to denounce Jesus and accept the mark. The Patriots have formed their own group. Thank God that Ruth took the initiative to get help, or we might not be here today, celebrating."

Harriet looked at her closely. "Can you remember anything? Your childhood, friends?"

"I am having a hard time remembering our relationship. I'm sorry. Please forgive me, Mother," Ruth said.

"Of course, darling. I understand."

"I must tend to the turkey and dressing. Please sit down and visit with Joshua."

The snow began in earnest. Joshua glanced outside toward his Standardbred, her coat wet and steamy. "Ja, here are a few *Plain Interests*. Now I must unhitch my horse, rub her down, and feed the livestock. I will be back in soon. You might enjoy thumbing through our news."

Ruth took this time to check on her bubbling pots, then checked on the oven. Yes, it burned brightly. Her dressing was near completion, as was the turkey. Martha should be here soon with her sister, and then they would eat.

A noise drifted in from the bedroom. Ruth peeked in at Josh Jr., wishing for just a few more minutes before the child arose. Good, he was still fast asleep. His golden hair gleamed in the half-light shining through the windowpane. Closing his door, her eyes met Harriett's. Dad attempted to fill the empty cavities of her memories during their ride home on that fateful day of the rescue. However, there was little Dad could tell her of the relationship between Harriet and her.

Harriet's countenance appeared sad whenever she glanced toward Ruth. How would she feel if Josh Jr. did not recognize her? Terrible. "I am relieved I was able to help save Dat—"

"Dat?" Harriet looked over at her husband, confusion written across her smooth face.

Jessup shrugged. "Our daughter has attached herself to the Amish lifestyle and language. It's easy to understand. She lived with her grandmother for the most part. It's normal for people suffering from dissociative amnesia."

"Of course." Harriet's expression strained as she searched Ruth's. "Your grandmother lived near the Mennonites and mimicked their lifestyle. You spent most of your adolescent years with her."

"I did? Why did I not live with you and Dat?" Harriet was leaving something out, but what? Ruth held her tongue. She mustn't appear nosy. "Now I understand why this life does not feel strange to me, why I feel at home with Martha and the boppli."

The noise of a horse and carriage coming up the drive alerted the people inside the farmhouse that the last visitors had arrived. Ruth rushed toward the doorway. Joshua, coming from the barn, helped Martha and her sister down. Their long black capes floated in the sharp winter wind. Their bonnets, which they had worn to protect their faces from the harshness of the cold, covered their eyes. *Like hollow*—Ruth stopped. A flashback of a dream came to her. Nonsense. She rushed to the stove and removed the turkey. In the quiet room, she heard Harriet talking to her dad.

"Jessup, I know enough about dissociative amnesia to be scared. You told me about one woman you treated who did not regain her full memory until five years later."

Harriet left her chair and approached Ruth as she busied herself with getting the serving bowls down. "I want to apologize to you. You see, we were never close—"

"I need to get the dinner on the table." Harriet seemed always to be in her way.

"Hello, everyone. I'm Martha and this is my schwester, Rachael."

Introductions were made, and Martha and her sister hurried to change from their wet clothes into dry ones. Harriet needed something to do besides watching Ruth's every move. Ruth reached up on the top shelf for the plates. "Could you set the table, please?"

Her dad smiled. "Good idea. Give Harriet something to do to occupy her time."

Harriet took the plates, muttering something beneath her breath.

Her dad sent Ruth a wink. "I can't be certain, but it looks like you are suffering from generalized dissociative amnesia."

"That's a long name to describe what I have," Ruth grumbled. She didn't feel the need to know. Especially not while she was trying to get dinner on the table.

He leaned over the counter. "You're an accomplished writer and editor of the *Cassell Herald* newspaper. It's only a matter of time before you remember everything."

Her dad reached for the silverware and napkins, walked to the table, and set them alongside the plates. "Now, all we need are the glasses."

"Ruth needs to see a physician." Evidently, Harriet needed instant answers. "Or maybe you could examine her. After all, you may be retired, but you're a practiced psychologist. You can treat our daughter."

"Treating family members is against the ethics of my profession." His face suddenly looked old and tired. "However, all a psychologist can do is prescribe time. There is no reason to hurry Ruth to a physician or psychologist. It will take her months to see them, Harriet, because they are all busy. The trauma and crime victims this Antichrist and New World Order have caused…"

"Doctoring these hoodlums and all those poor victims of these needless killings." Harriet paused. "I see your point, and I could not agree with you more, Jessup. What was I thinking? Our hospitals are not the same anymore. We can mend our Ruthie back together on our own." Harriet smiled. "Her memory will return when she needs it."

My stepmother is as fluid as water.

Harriet's smile hadn't reached her eyes, scrutinizing Ruth. She bit down on her lower lip. What type of relationship had she had with Stepmother? Oh, Joshua, I need your quiet strength right now. The thought of him was enough to send her heart into singing mode.

"My darling, there is a glow to your countenance. Oh my, I wish I could say I put it there, but I seriously doubt that," Harriet said.

"Her blush has something to do with one Amish widower, I believe," Jessup said. "The rescue not only freed the captives, but it freed a certain someone's feelings."

Ruth put her hands against her cheeks. They felt hot. "Because he's shown kindness to me, so I help any way I can."

Her stepmother and dad exchanged glances, grinning like two hyenas.

They think there is more than friendship to my and Joshua's relationship. Is there? She didn't know. After the rescue, she'd hoped he felt more for her than that of a companion for his son. Even though, maybe he'd propose. At times, he'd gaze at her like Josh Jr., brimming with contented bliss. Then suddenly, he'd become remote and guarded toward her.

Nothing relating to human emotions escaped Harriet's notice. "I think Josh needs a little push."

"Harriet, stay out of this," her dad warned.

A cold draft swept through the room. Joshua walked in, stomping the snow off his leather boots. Sitting down, he untied them and placed them neatly on the rubber mat, then shrugged off his coat. "Wonderful gut smells coming from your stove." His long strides made soft noises in socked feet. He extended his hands over the hot stove, inhaling deeply. "Hmm, gut I hurried back, ja, you miss me?"

Ruth dared not look up. Aware of the effects the heart-stopping grin on his handsome face had on her, coupled with his bantering words, she'd not be able to keep herself from reciprocating. That would be all her parents needed.

"Oh, Ruthie, I forgot to tell you," Harriet said, pretending to rearrange the napkins. "I met that nice man you dated."

Just then Martha and her sister walked into the room. They glanced at each other and then at Ruth.

"The one Mr. Ricker interviewed a while back. Mr. Rollins? Remember him? He's a lawyer in Cassell," Harriet continued. "He mentioned you. He belonged to the same hunt club and said you rode and dined together a couple of times. He's concerned about you. Said he was at the Johanssons' farm when you turned up missing."

"I can't recall." Ruth avoided Joshua's look.

"He's quite handsome. We had lunch together. He wanted to know everything he could about you and especially what the private investigator learned. My, that Mr. Rollins is one charming man. He has the cutest mustache, which adds just the right charisma to his square chin.

"Oh, and I heard from a few in the hunt club. A Maggie, and there was another one, oh, what was her name? Anyway, they said they're worried, too, and mentioned how popular Mr. Rollins was with the ladies, despite his quick temper. I tell you, what stood out about him was his thick raven black hair." She threw her head back and swept her coiffure.

"Black?" Ruth turned, walked toward the window seat, and plopped down. The man in her dreams had black hair.

"It upsets me to hear about any man Ruthie dated who had a quick temper," Dad said. "What else did Maggie and the other girls say, Harriet?"

"That bothered me, too. There was something else. His mouth looked funny. He had a deep scar. Said he hurt it during a hunt. But when I told Maggie about it, she said he didn't have any hunting accident."

Ruth blinked. A vision of a man with black hair walking past where she was hiding.

"That's enough, Harriet. The mind is a muscle and needs its rest, especially when hurt." Her dad patted Ruth on the shoulder.

Joshua hesitated before taking his seat at the table. "Did you tell Mr. Rollins anything about Ruth's whereabouts?"

"How could I? I didn't know where Ruthie was, only that she was probably with some Amish family—"

"Thankfully!" Her dad sent his wife a stern look. "Let's eat—"

"But Jessup—"

"Now, before it all gets cold." Her dad steered Harriet to her chair.

---

Joshua took his accustomed place at the head of the table. "Usually, Amish families say silent prayers. However, knowing how the English say theirs out loud, I shall do the same today." He bowed his head. "Lord, we may have planted the seed and seedlings, watered, and hoed, picked, and canned, but we know You give us the bountiful harvest. Lord, grant we reap a bountiful harvest in our lives and not bow before this Antichrist, but wait patiently for thee to return. Amen."

Ruth's pallor concerned him. He tried not to stare, but she barely ate a thing. He chewed his food thoughtfully, wondering how many Amish homes Rex Rollins had visited looking for Ruth.

"Daughter, you look tired."

"Yes, I am a little."

"Mammy." Josh Jr. cried out from the adjoining room.

"Oh, excuse me." Ruth hurried toward the child.

"Doesn't that mean Mommy?" Harriet said.

Joshua smiled. "Mammy is a word that has many meanings."

"Oh, okay, something like our name for nanny?" Jane said.

"Ja." Joshua studied Ruth's stepsister, Jane. Fashion-conscious like her mother, her nails manicured and tipped. Her hair cut in fashionable layers.

"Jessup, I want some time with Ruthie, alone."

"Harriet, what more could you possibly have to say?" Jessup hissed from the corner of his mouth, watching Ruth carrying Josh Jr. into the room. "Can't you see she's tired. After all, look at the feast she prepared for us."

"I won't keep her too long."

Joshua wished he could stop her. By the look that swept her beautiful face, Ruth didn't want to talk to Harriet.

Martha and her sister gathered the dinner plates. "Stay seated, please. We have dessert kumming."

He could see Harriet wasn't about to comply. She pulled at Ruth's arm. "Wait, I need to talk to you. I forgot to tell you something."

If ever there was a woman who could not manage her emotions, it was Harriet.

Ruth attempted to pull her arm away. "I need to get Josh Jr. something to eat."

"Those times I locked you in your room. Dear, it was only for your good. I want you to know that."

Martha gasped, dropping the dirty dishes into the sink with a clatter.

"What?" Jessup was on his feet. "When did this happen?"

Harriet ignored her husband's comment. She wrung her hands like something pricked her skin. Joshua grunted. More like a prickly conscience.

"Oh, Ruthie, I am so happy your father and I found you. I have so much I need to say. So much I want to make up for. Want your forgiveness for." Harriet bowed her head. "I wish I had accepted Jesus earlier. I am born again, and all my sins wiped away. I have lost my need for—you know."

"Nee, I don't." Ruth hugged Josh Jr. close. "What need is that?"

"My alcohol addiction." Harriet sighed. "There. I said it. When you were younger, you said you wanted me to accept Jesus so I could be happy, remember? I, I had other, more pressing issues going on in my life that inhibited it."

Joshua's and Ruth's eyes locked.

Jessup pried his wife's hands off Ruth. He had his wife by the shoulders now. "We'd better get you home."

Harriet shrugged his arms aside and turned toward Ruth, "After your mother died, I made myself available, so to speak, to your dad."

"Ja?" Ruth walked over and handed Josh Jr. to Joshua. Fear of rejection etched her face. The haunting past treading on their future. Hunching her shoulders, she walked to her dad. The chime of the grandfather clock in the corner of the parlor room the only sound breaking the silence.

"Let go of me, Jessup. I need to confess this. Maybe it might help Ruthie to remember." Harriet wiped a tear from her mascaraed eyes. She searched Ruth's face. "Only, I don't want you to remember me the way I was. I want you to see me in the new light of Christ's love."

Joshua bit his bottom lip. No wonder Ruth did not want to remember her former life. What had it been like for a young impressive teenage girl? Her mother dead and this alcoholic woman caring for nothing but her next drink?

Martha patted Ruth's hand. Ruth smiled gratefully at her.

"I, I want you to know that I absolutely love you like Jane and Paul." Harriet stretched out her hand toward her. "I wish I'd allowed you to hug me. That was very, very cruel on my part."

"Danke, Harriet." Ruth clasped Harriet's hand into hers. "It explains why Dat's love comes easier. Why I feel peace with my Amish family."

Pain seared Joshua's chest, seeing the hurt in her face. Oh, if there was only some way to ease her fears.

Ruth turned and gazed at Harriet, then at her siblings. "You, my schwester, Jane, and bruder, Paul, must have been gut to me."

Both hung their heads.

# Twenty-one

*"Go your way, Daniel, for the words are closed up and sealed till the time of the end. Many shall be purified, made white, and refined, but the wicked shall do wickedly; and none of the wicked shall understand, but the wise shall understand. Daniel 12:9–10*

Joshua wiped the sweat from his forehead. The hot July sun beat down relentlessly. Sheriff Baker had finally gotten around to wanting his independence from bartering, choosing to get his own chickens, milk, and transportation.

"How come the days spin faster away?" Baker said.

A half year had sped by like a whirlwind. What with helping his neighbors like Sheriff Baker, who liked to take time to chew on the latest news, Joshua struggled to complete his chores before sunset. Not that he did not want to help, it was just that—

"Gut morning, Sheriff Baker." The back door banged shut. Out walked Ruth carrying a basket of clean clothes and sheets ready to hang on their clothesline. The sun shining across her shoulders gave her face an angelic glow. Her white apron fluttered in the summer breezes. She waved.

"Good morning, Ruth," Baker replied, then whispered to Joshua, "She's the only woman I know that can look like a million bucks wearing a faded dress and a tattered apron."

"Ja," Joshua said, thinking about how the chain of events had locked him into a workload that gave him very little time to woo the woman of his dreams. Jessup had been helping Ruth to remember and him to be patient. He didn't tell Jessup all his distorted past. Somehow Jessup knew and told him Ruth's mind should not be overloaded with too many worries or major decisions. That was over six months ago. This was stretching his patience, for sure. Now, with only 251 days left of Daniel's 1290 days before the Lord returned, there was little time left for Joshua. He needed to get ahold of Jessup quick.

"Joshua? You okay?"

"Ja. What did you decide? The cow or you want the goat instead?"

"Look, my grandmother fed my mother on unpasteurized milk. We can survive drinking it straight from the cow, too."

"Amish do and are still around to talk about it," Joshua said. "Of course, when we sell our milk, we pasteurize it. If you like, I could trade you a goat."

"Goat milk? Does it taste like regular cow milk?"

Joshua pulled on his beard. "It depends on how it's cooled. What we do is to use a sterile stainless-steel bucket for the goat's milk. Get that bucket good and cold first. It kills all the taste and smell of the goat. Then keep the milk chilled. I know this as a fact, too; billy goats are easier to handle than bulls."

"Why would I want a billy goat? I want the nannies. They're the ones that give milk."

"Ja, but every April or May, you will have to breed a nanny or a cow to get enough milk—"

"This is confusing. Trade me a cow that's gentle that my wife or daughter can milk, and I'll be off."

"Sure. You will need to bring her back in the spring so I can breed her to my bull. I'll take the calf after he's weaned, and you'll have the milk your family needs all year long."

"Okay, it's a deal." He pulled out a wad of money. "How much?"

"I'd like to take out the price of the cow in labor. We are short laborers. We've three frolics coming up."

"Frolic?" The sheriff snorted. "Joshua, I don't have time for a dance. I need to build myself an icehouse."

"It's not a dance. We've got two houses and a barn to build. They're for the underground railroad Christians that the Patriots rescued from the cities. It is gut for us Amish these Antichrist followers only want the nice homes with electricity. And because of our carpentry skills, they leave us alone. Killing off the Jews and Christians has dented their pocketbooks too. Skilled laborers are few, as are doctors and nurses."

"Still, the way I figure the time is getting short before the Lord returns," Baker said. "I understand better why the Lord said in Matthew that people continued to build and marry right up to the day He returned." Baker looked down. "I don't rant and rave so much to my wife now about losing all our money in the bank. Seeing how that was the first thing this antichrist gang did, turn us into a socialistic world and took our money, houses, and anything else they wanted." He looked down as his wad of money and said, "I buried a couple thousand dollars in a jar in our yard, for just such a time. Little good it does me. Now, it's swap for this and barter for that. What I don't seem to have enough of is time."

Joshua knew that to be true enough. "Do you need a lesson on how to milk the cow? Do you have a place to put her where she'll be safe and have plenty of green grass to eat, Sheriff? There are a lot of poachers creeping about."

"Not sheriff anymore. I got me a place up in the hills where I've built a cabin for my family. If the WOP come by my place, they may find me, but they'll not find them. That brings me to something else we need to barter for. Do you have a horse you can sell me? I can't use my car, it has that GPS on it, and the tires on our bikes have worn through."

Joshua rubbed his chin. "No, but I'll check around. What you got to barter for?"

"I haven't got much of anything left; that's why I decided I'd better become a farmer." Baker rubbed his stubbled cheek. "If someone has some diesel fuel. I've got the equipment. Maybe I can work out something. I've got a family in need of a well bad."

"Let me see what I can come up with."

"Oh, and the word's out about the Brunswick family, heard they took the mark. Then turned coat on their neighbors. Real bad. The WOP picked those neighbors up last night."

"I'll pass the word. Have you heard anything about the Patriots?" Joshua asked.

"They took a beating a week ago. They managed to rescue the Mactonish and the Walsh families before anyone got hauled away. The Patriots lost five good men doing it. They're out of ammo and food."

Joshua shoved a peddle around with the toe of his boot, recalling his years as a soldier and officer. He always felt satisfaction when he'd rescued the oppressed. He knew that was the feeling that kept the Patriots going—doing good and combating evil. He was as helpless as his son. His hands were tied from doing anything more than pushing a plow. "I've got some food we stored up for these three-and-a-half years; I can help."

"How many more days before the Lord returns do you figure?"

Joshua stroked his beard. "I was just thinking about that. In the book of Daniel, the Lord gave himself a few more days than we may like. Daniel wrote 1290, then added, 'Blessed is he who waits and comes to the one thousand three hundred and thirty-five days.'"

"I guess that's why the book of Luke says no one knows the day or hour."

"Ja. I figure we've got 251 days left, give or take another forty-five."

Baker looked at him skeptically. "Sounds like you've be counting."

Was Baker trying to read his mind?

"Well, you don't want to mess up your wedding plans by getting killed. I know you want to fight as bad as I do. But leave the fighting to those who know how. The WOP is watching us like a hawk flying over a chicken coop."

"I'm tired of playing it safe. I want to marry Ruth, yet I want to fight for what I believe in. Blowing smoke does not help the chimney if it's plugged. Now is the time to fight."

"We have our work cut out for us here. Some of our shoes are getting worn through. We might need a little training in how to make new soles out of old shoes. Some English are plum out of bartering material."

Joshua smiled. "Don't worry, what are neighbors for but to help one another in trying times. How are your chickens holding out?"

"Good. The hens you sold me are giving us enough eggs to keep food on the table." Baker turned to leave. "But that rooster is getting downright mean. He bit my little girl and drew blood."

"Then you've got chicken and dumplings for supper, I'd say."

"But if I kill him, I won't have any eggs."

"You'll have eggs without that rooster, but they won't be fertile." With the blank look Baker gave him, Joshua explained. "You need a rooster to have chicks, that's all."

"But how do I go about—"

"The best way to do the killing neatly is to get yourself a hatchet, a board, and nail in two nails on either side. Then slide his neck in and wham him with the hatchet. That way, you can hold him down. If you let him run around, he'll bruise up his body. That's not good eating.

"Then, to get the feathers off, heat a kettle of hot water, about 130 degrees, and no hotter. Dip the dead bird in the pot, and the feathers will come off quickly."

"Why does the kettle have to be 130 degrees and no hotter?"

"Too hot, and the skin will peel off."

"I've lived among you Amish for forty years." Baker and Joshua strolled toward the barn. "And I still got lots to learn."

Joshua let out his milk cow, putting her calf in the stall. An awful lot of mooing erupted. The calf was eating her grain and hay, yet taking too much of her mother's milk. The Amish and English needed it to survive.

"Say, what about Ruth?" Baker said.

"What about her?" He glanced toward her. She was reaching up, pinning one of his shirts on the line. He could really imagine his arms wrapping around that slender waist of hers.

"When are you going to settle down and marry that little gal?" Baker nodded toward Ruth. "Next to the Antichrist and that New Order, you and Ruth are the hottest topics of conversation."

Joshua's passion warmed his face like a branding iron. How much longer could he hold his feelings for Ruth in check?

Recalling last Christmas and meeting Ruth's parents gave him a window into her past. So sweet and vulnerable, he had to hold himself back from sweeping her into his arms and whispering in her ear not to worry. He wanted to wipe away all her trepidations wrinkling her beautiful forehead. He dipped his hands into his coverall pockets and stomped into the barn.

Jessup said more than he cared to know about Ruth's previous years. Mother worried that if Joshua confided to Ruth regarding his tainted past, it might be more than her wounded mind could handle.

He'd assured Ruth that he'd love her no matter what she'd been or done. That he didn't care about her past—would she say the same to him when he disclosed the truth? He shoved the barn door open wider. What was the past to him but a shadow? A shadow could not harm him. Right? Then why did his troubled thoughts cause him sleepless nights? *Confess and ask forgiveness.*

He needed to tell Ruth the truth. Would Ruth feel the same toward him when she learned about his past?

"My wife said Ruth's planning to go to a singing?"

"Ja."

"What's that?" Baker asked.

"It's a party for single people."

"Will you be there? After all, you're single. I wouldn't let that pretty gal out of my sight if I were you."

Joshua bent down so Baker couldn't see that his words had walloped him where it hurt most. Ruth could meet a guy at the singing. The thought struck him square in the face.

"What if someone should spark an interest in Ruth?" Baker was on the same thought pattern.

His son had a strong liking for Ruth—as did his son's dad.

He nearly told Ruth his feelings after the daring rescue of her dad. Then her dad took it upon himself to tell Joshua about Ruth running away, being in and out of jail for drinking, drugs, and sorts. Her dad said not to take it personally if she should up and leave. That it was her nature.

"So, when's the marriage?" Baker replied impatiently.

How long had he gazed out the window of the barn like some star-struck lover? "I can't marry anyone that can't remember that she's engaged or not."

"Come on now. Her daddy says she wasn't married, being engaged is nothing, so what's holding you back?"

"Her dat doesn't know anything about the last four years of his daughter's life. He didn't even know anything about that Rex guy. His wife found that out hiring Mr. Ricker. That's not gut."

"Give Ruth a chance. Your son adores her, as does your mother."

"Look, did you come here to barter for that cow or bully me into getting married? These are serious times. I can't afford a wife. After all, I could get killed before sundown?"

"All the better reason not to dally."

Joshua walked to the north side of his barn. Burying his fists into his deep pockets, he gazed out the open barn doors at his green pastures and the little brook bubbling over the rocks some twenty feet away.

Baker followed. "We didn't know what we had until it was lost. Who would have dreamt allowing other countries like China to steal our technology and intellectual property would leave us second fiddle to them? To think, all those years ago the president allowed them to make our drugs and stock the components we need for our electrical grid. What were our political leaders thinking? Surely, they knew that someday those countries could use it against us."

Tugging at his beard, Joshua said, "I lived in your world for a while. What I learned made the hairs stand up on my head."

"When that first pandemic came along, it was the pivoting point. Coronavirus brought life, as we knew it, to a standstill. Our country was never the same after that. But what about that Antichrist guy? How did he get our power grid back on track like that?"

"Could be God allowing the devil to have his way on the earth, seeing how his time is short. The Bible talks about something like that happening. Who needs electricity anyway?"

"What I can't believe is how every time I think we've come to the last barrel of flour, somehow there's enough. Another wild turkey in the brush, another rabbit in our snare," Baker said. "Like the Almighty Himself is watching over us, making sure we get what we need to hang on to the end."

"The young lions lack and suffer hunger; but those who seek and trust the Lord shall not lack any good thing," Joshua said. "That's in Psalms. But you and I know that sooner or later, the WOP could make it to us before Jesus returns. The Antichrist can make war with the saints and overcome them. It says so in Revelation 13:7. 'And authority was given him over every tribe, tongue, and nation. All who dwell on the earth will worship him, whose names have not been written in the Book of Life of the Lamb.'"

Joshua chuckled. "Glad to see you're reading your survival manual, the Holy Bible."

"You best believe it. My whole family is! We plan to hightail it to the forests. And if they find us, then, we give them a speech about our Savior they won't forget. Anyways, thanks for the cow. Who did you say that might have a horse?"

"There's plenty of unbroken two-year-olds if you have a knack training a green horse to saddle and harness. However, I do have something you might be interested in."

They walked toward the out barn. "I don't have a horse to sell you. Would a donkey do? He's a little ornery, but you know Jesus' mother used a donkey. Maybe if you treat him nice and gentle, he'll soften up to you."

"I'll be trading in my comfortable Cadillac for a donkey and glad to do it. Who would have figured?" Baker walked around the animal, kind of summing him up as much as the donkey did him.

"Nice donkey," Baker said. "He could tote my supplies when I go to the cabin."

"How's the secret room coming?" Joshua asked.

"Mine's done. I'm just finishing up with the supplies. You know, I've heard looters are everywhere in the big cities. People are preying on the weak. But here, we've got law and order."

"Ja, a lot has been because of you, Sheriff."

"Now cut that out." Baker turned and slammed his fist on the fence. "I don't believe I didn't see it coming with Officer Smith. How could he do that to us?"

Joshua rested his hand on his friend's shoulder. "Don't take it to heart so."

Baker shook his head. He pushed himself away from the fence. "I hated to kill him, but he had it coming, trying to ambush us." He followed Joshua into the barn. Joshua reached for a halter for the donkey.

He poked a finger toward the cow Baker now held by the lead rope. "Make sure you milk her the same time each day. I milk mine at six a.m. and again at six p.m. Clean her udder before you start to milk her. You want a lesson on how to?"

Baker looked at him dubiously. "How hard can it be to milk a cow?"

"C'mon, let's see what you've got." Joshua pulled up a three-legged stool and motioned for Baker to sit down.

"Okay, grab hold of her teat and get in the rhythm like this." Joshua motioned with his right hand first, then the left, then the right, squeezing and tugging down on the cow's udder.

Baker tried it and nothing. "Hmm, not as easy as it looks."

"There's a method to it. You have to squeeze and pull at the same time."

Baker tried it again. There came a siz-siz noise of the steaming milk hitting the metal pan. "Never heard a more beautiful sound. This is different from what I thought. My, it's going to take a lot of milk to get that pail full."

"Once you get gut at it, you can teach your son, daughter, or wife to do the chore. Your wife will get gut butter from her too."

"Really? Cows give different kinds of milk. Say, you got any out there that gives chocolate latte?"

"I don't believe so." Joshua laughed. "But some cows' milk is richer than others, and it's easier to make cream and butter. Your wife won't have to churn it so long."

Baker kept milking. "Right, something else we need to learn. As soon as we get our icehouse finished in the basement, I'll bring my missus over, and maybe Martha can teach her."

"Uh, underground stays at 60 degrees. Guess it could be done with more insulation. Still, I think it will be hard to keep the ice from melting. Or you could build a small building, line the sides, top, and bottom with insulation and sawdust on the floor, and when the lake freezes, we'll all go out and cut the ice, then line the walls with blocks of ice. That will keep easy through the winter months and right through the hottest summer months. For now, you can use mine for your perishables."

"Thanks." Baker removed his hat and wiped his forehead. He bent over and began milking again.

"Yeah, this milking is hard on your back and arms; you'll find that out if you have more than five cows to milk at one sitting."

"I'll milk her some more when I get her home. About that donkey, you think I can ride it home leading the cow?"

"The donkey hasn't been ridden much. But she drives real gut. I could lend you my small wagon and pick the wagon up sometime next week."

"You'd do that for me?"

Ruth dipped inside the door of their cement building, what English would use as a garage, but where the Amish kept the wringer washing machine. She came out carrying another armload of fresh laundry. With clothespins in her pink-tipped lips, she stretched up to clip one of Joshua's pants on the clothesline. Her slender silhouette bathed in the sunlight as robins and bluebirds waved their wings above her.

"Yeah! I'm telling you, Joshua, don't let this one get away."

Joshua brought the straw brim of his hat low over his forehead and hunched his chin beneath the collar of his cotton shirt. "It's a gut thing you didn't bring the missus, or, you'd have a rough ride home."

Joshua showed Baker how to hook up the donkey then ducked into the barn to get the cow and tied the cow to the back of the wagon.

## LOVE'S FINAL SUNRISE

"Which way you headin' back?"

"Down the road, why? You got a better way?"

"I've made a trail through my property. Not too comfortable, but it keeps the Englishers who took the mark from spotting us and the WOP from seeing our goings-on."

"Have you received any mail?"

"No, neither Heydenreich nor the pony express has been here for a month now."

"Same. Everyone who could afford the expense or received the mark should have their electricity up by now. I wonder what's going on in the rest of the world." Baker took up the reins lying on the donkey's back.

Joshua pulled back on the reins. "As soon as you get mail, let me know. Mr. Jessup is planning on a trip to Cassell. He says his wife went to visit a friend and nurse her back to health. Mrs. Jessup is to write him exactly when she's ready to come home. I've told him I would need a couple of days to plan a trip like that."

"Now wait. You're not planning on going."

Joshua wasn't planning to sit back with the womenfolk and let the English do his fighting for him. "I'm going."

"Not without me, you're not! There's nothing and no one to keep you from getting knifed or shot down in those cities but God's grace. The antichrist's WOP and Marxists Movement is tearing America apart. They've annihilated what historical artifacts they haven't got to before. Looted and burned down buildings, it's terrible in the cities, I tell you.

"Listen to reason, Joshua. Let your womenfolk have their lady's day, and your frolics and go to your singings, but you leave the fighting to us English, you hear?" Baker turned his stormy eyes toward the mule. "Giddy up!"

Baker wasn't the boss of him. Ruth's voice, humming a familiar tune, floated his way. Baker had brought up a good point regarding that singing. It was time to come clean. It was now or never. He'd waited long enough.

# Twenty-two

*"Those who sow in tears shall reap in joy. He who continually goes forth weeping, Bearing seed for sowing, Shall doubtless come again with rejoicing, Bringing his sheaves with him." Psalm 126:5–6*

The last thing on Ruth's to-do list was going to that singing. After the church service, she spent the afternoon grooming the Standardbred mare. She missed horses. Her heart longed for one. She had spotty visions of her galloping across the hills on a milk-white mare. What a dreamer she was.

"It's okay that you're not white." She patted the Standardbred's glossy coat. She was a bay of a blood-red color. She had a sweet disposition and an even sweeter canter, considering she was more of a pacer and her expertise was trotting. Ruth hoped getting smelly might change Martha's mind and say she didn't have to attend after all.

She heard Martha's light steps before she spoke. With her arms akimbo, she said, "You need to clean up. You need a man and your own boppli to cuddle."

How Martha could read her thoughts amazed her. Ruth dropped her grooming tools into the box, feeling the emptiness. Josh Jr. found new independence with every birthday and plenty to get him in busy trouble. He was presently helping his daddy in the milk house.

"Martha, I do want a man and a boppli of my own." And her own house to clean and a place she felt belonged to her. Her dad's words stuck like a peach pit in her throat. *You know you'll get itchy feet again, so don't get these nice people to liking you too much. It's not Christian.*

"But my dat thinks I'll never change." She didn't need to ask if he'd given Joshua the same speech. She could see it in Joshua's eyes. A pain crossed her chest. "Did my dat, tell you, too, about my past life of running away when something didn't suit me?"

Martha sighed. "Ja, but you are not the same person. Komm now, you need to wash up and dress before Joshua returns."

"Dat believes his Frau is saved and capable of changing, but not his daughter."

Martha nodded. "People often accept some person's sins over others." She shrugged. "I do not understand this."

"I know in my heart Christ has done a miracle in me. He is my friend who sticks closer than a brother and my Father who loves me unconditionally."

"Ja, for sure and certain. Now komm."

"Most of the Amish women at the singing will be between eighteen and twenty years old," Ruth grumbled. "I don't feel like a mädel. I'm an old maid who has lost her flavor sitting on the shelf too long."

Martha laughed. "Nonsense. You are ripe for the picking, as my Mutter would say. You'll not sit by lonesome. This will be a wonderful gut time. You'll see." Martha looped her arm around Ruth's and giggled.

"Why don't you go to the singing with me? You have more spirit than I for this, and besides, you're single too."

Martha's eyes sparkled with youthfulness. "I'm young because of you. When you came to live with us, you gave me renewed hope and a reason to get up in the morning. You mustn't blame Joshua for not proposing—he's been afraid to hurt your progress. He didn't want to burden your poor mind with his troubles." She patted Ruth's hand, looking past the horizon. "He needs to unload his misery on the right mädel's ears." Martha's eyes bore into hers. "You are ready to accept that burden now, ja?"

"Ja. My past is just that—past worrying about."

# LOVE'S FINAL SUNRISE

The singing was in Johansson's large barn. The menfolk felt it the safest place. The married men had staked themselves outside. That was the norm now; womenfolk were chaperoned, what with the European Union and WOP poking about everywhere.

Ruth busied herself at the refreshment table. She didn't want the single men to notice her. A tall, good-looking widower from the next county had introduced himself earlier. He glanced her way again and started across the floor toward her.

The door to her right creaked open. The full moon glowed beams of soft light across the shoulders of a man who'd opened the barn door.

He stepped inside, fastening the handle against the wind with a thump.

"Joshua."

Hearing his name, in a split second, his stormy countenance flipped like a pancake on a hot grill.

Her heart skipped a beat.

The man from the opposite side of the room walked faster. Time stood still, and she waited with breathless anticipation to see who would get to her first.

With purposeful strides, Joshua overtook the would-be suiter and blocked the man's view of her. In deep low musical tones, he said, "I arrived in the nick of time, I see."

"But—I thought you didn't like singings?"

"Changed my mind." His lips parted in a conspiratorial grin.

She loved it when he smiled. It lit up his eyes to a sparkling glow like now, showering her with his warmth. She felt tingly all over.

"After all, I'm a single man. Ain't so?"

Time melted away, back to her first meeting with Joshua. That had been just under three years. He acted reserved, distant, like he was married. As if he thought Sara would burst through the door at any time. Ruth couldn't remember when Joshua stopped staring at the doorway.

Now, he sat beside her and sent her one of his half-moon smirks. Does he know how handsome that makes him? How his dimples accent his cheeks?

"I haven't been to a singing in over ten years. It was at one where I wooed Sara."

"Oh." She looked down. Sara. Of course, he was only reminiscing. Sara had been fair, soft-spoken, beautiful, and obedient. The opposite of Ruth. Whatever her past held, Dad told her it was not obedience. He'd often had to pick her up at the police station. She usually had narcotics in her possession, and more than once, he had to bail her out of jail. Joshua knew this because Dad felt he needed to confess it to him, oftentimes making it a point to ride over to confide in him.

Joshua took her hand. Suddenly, the harsh words, all the painful memories, melted within the warmth of his fingers. That was the third time he'd ever touched her this way. Oh, they had swiped shoulders now and then. He'd help her in and out of the buggy. But never an intentional touch like this—like that time they rescued her dad and the others. Then there was the time of birthing the Standardbred's foal. In the wee hours before dawn fully awakened, he took her into his warm arms that frosty day in April and gently kissed her forehead.

His hands now worked their way across her palms. "You know your dad told me about your youth."

Her breath caught in her throat. "I know."

"We all have pasts we wish we could forget. Is that what's bothering you?"

Ruth sighed. "The night is not long enough for me to say. Dat said he only wished to help me regain my memory." She looked up then, blinking back her tears. "Surely what Dat has told you of my earlier years is enough for you to wonder about the life I refuse to remember?" She looked away, unable to meet his eyes. "With what I have learned, I am afraid to know more. Perhaps that is why my brain chooses to forget."

"I'll not hold that against you. Most of us have a past we wish we could forget. Consider yourself lucky." He hunched his shoulders and refused to meet her eyes.

Suddenly Martha's words took on new meaning. "But, Joshua, you don't have anything in your past to regret? Or do you?"

He coaxed her forward. "Come on, I could use a little fresh air." She felt powerless within his grasp.

He pivoted her to the side of the large barn and through a narrow door that led outside. The stars twinkled down to them against a sea of black velvet. The Milky Way and the galaxy swept a glowing light and the man on the moon seemed to be smiling tonight.

"That is why Jesus tells us to ask for His forgiveness and then throw our sins away into the deepest sea. We must forget about them, as He does. See, you are luckier than others who are reminded of their past."

"My memory comes back to me in visions. I think because it is so terrible that my mind does not want to admit how bad—"

"I see a good heart. My son feels it, as do the animals. Brutus is not won over easily, yet he follows you around like a puppy on a leash." He took both her hands into his large ones. His eyes searched hers.

"I keep seeing another woman in my visions, someone like Martha. Kind, forgiving, and understanding. Only, I can't remember what happened to her. I asked my dat. He said I lived with Gran after Mother was killed by a drunk driver, that Gran attempted to raise me properly, but I rebelled against her—a vehicle ran over her and her buggy horse."

"You can't blame yourself."

She didn't deserve to be loved. Perhaps that's why Joshua held onto his Sara because she was lovely both inside and out. Not like Ruth with all her filthy baggage who only hurt those who loved her. "Even my own dat thinks me incapable of being different." She tried to lose her hands from his. "Don't you see, I'm no good. I hurt, even kill, the people who love me."

The night hid his facial expressions, but his voice gave him away. Low, hesitant, he stumbled over his words. "You don't know that for sure."

She struggled.

"Why do you persecute yourself like this?"

She flung his hands off and ran through the waist-high grass. Weeping, blinded by her tears, she stumbled over a rock. Joshua wrapped her like a blanket into his embrace. "If I could squeeze the fears from your body—I would!" He shook her gently. "Give God a chance to do His work. Give me a chance to prove to you Christ's miracle of forgiveness!"

Laying her head on his shoulder, she relinquished, absorbing his strength like a half-starved pup. "Gut. Now the truth is out."

He knew the worst, yet passion filled his eyes, and nothing seemed to squelch his desire to protect her. Why?

"All those men your dat told me about used you to advance their positions, their selfish desires."

"And Dat was sure Mr. Rollins was one of the same," Ruth said.

Joshua nodded. "Gut. Those who sow in tears shall reap in joy. Ja, you must sow to reap."

"Reap?" She knew she must look as confused as she felt with his remarks. "All I'm getting here is waterlogged."

"Waterlogged because before you knew Jesus, you were sowing to the devil. Ja, your conscience is awakened to the truth."

"I wasn't all that bad." How dare he.

"I know a sinner when I see one, Ruth, because I was one. A very, very bad one. 'Whoever has been born of God does not sin.'"

"Oh, now I get it. You can do whatever you want and call the rest of us devil followers?" Anger pulsed through her veins.

"Do you admit you need more than yourself to be happy?"

Her heart leaped inside of her bosom. "Yes," she whispered. "Remember, I went forward when your bishop asked."

"You realized something was missing in your life. Now you follow Jesus?"

Joshua somehow knew. He saw past flesh and blood, right into her soul. "Jesus may have forgiven me," Ruth whispered, "but I haven't forgiven myself."

"I know what you are going through because I was you. I was filled with guilt and regret for what I did. I wanted to jump into that grave with Sara. That's how riddled with guilt and sin I was."

"You?" She could not comprehend this. Joshua? The solid and strong, confident Joshua?

"I…I hesitated to tell you the truth about me because of your problems. But there is little time for us before the Lord returns to set up His kingdom." He sighed, looking longingly at her. "I've waited, my love, for you. Waited to confess the truth about me. That you might know the husband, father, and sinner that stands before you."

Was she wallowing in her own self-interest and oblivious of the hurt in others? Pain punctuated Joshua's eyes. "Go on."

"I carried my .22 in my right hand and my Bible in my left. I was armed and ready to shoot myself in the head. My Bible fell open to Leviticus 24:17 because I looked at it so often. 'Whoever kills any man shall surely be put to death.' I have killed men. I was a soldier in Afghanistan, and then I became a policeman in Detroit. I thought God was getting even with me for killing. That's why he took my Sara."

Ruth gasped.

"As sure as I stand here, this happened. I wanted children. A son I could teach and watch grow up. A daughter I could walk down the aisle someday. But Sara could not—past the fourth month. She told me she couldn't take another miscarriage, that she'd die—"

"Ah!" Ruth tried to pull away. He held her fast. She could not look at him. Her eyes searched the grass swaying in the breezes of the night wind.

"A soft voice whispered to me that night." He looked out. A sigh escaped his lips. "I remember the wind gently brushed the tops of my wheat field, and the wheat shucks rustled like a baby's rattle. At first, that's all that I heard.

"Then I heard the voice of God whispering in my thoughts, encouraging me. You see, Ruth, Christ died on that cross for my sins and yours. Jesus became our sin-bearer. He gives us the power to do good works in His name. If the devil comes against us, Christ gives us the grace to walk away from the guilt. 'For by grace alone you are saved.'

And that's why we are born again. 'That which is born of the Spirit is spirit.'" The wind picked up just then; the grasses bent beneath its invisible strokes.

"That day I rescued you and your horse I was seeking answers to my questions. You were the one God sent in answer to my requests."

"Me?"

"Remember? I told you my calling was here. Only, when Sara died, I felt I'd made a terrible mistake. Then you came along. You told me the temple had fallen, and the Judeans had fled to the mountains. When I returned home that day, the Holy Spirit led me to read John 3:17 and 18. 'For God did not send His Son into the world to condemn the world, but that the world through Him might be saved. He who believes in Him is not condemned.'" Joshua turned and gazed into the heavens. 'We are but a mist. I asked His forgiveness right then and asked Him to renew my heart in good works.

"I promised to obey him, to read His Bible, and He gave me the peace of mind I sought. Do you remember when Johannsson had me speak to the townspeople on how to survive without electricity? You asked to come?"

"Yes, I remember that night well."

"You said I made a difference in your decision to follow Jesus—right then I knew I was following my calling and on the right path."

Ruth thought she knew all she needed to know about what it took to be a Christian. Evidently, she did not. "You want me to give Jesus all my regrets, my past mistakes, my inhibitions?"

"Put your confidence and faith in Christ alone. If God wanted us to look back, He'd have given us eyes in the back of our head." He knelt, clasped his hands together, and bowed his head. The moon cast an iridescent glow on him, his golden hair the color of the wheat weaving a silent message as it fluttered in the wind.

"Like the wind, that is what the Spirit of God is like, unseen, yet everything eventually bows in His wake." Ruth knelt beside him, clasped her hands together, and said, "Lord, I know I'm born again, but the devil keeps needling me. Set me free from the fears of this demon of the past. When I do regain my memory, forgive me of those wrongdoings too. I accept by faith, believing you have forgiven me, and I promise to follow and obey you for the remainder of my life. Amen."

Joshua jumped to his feet and extended his arm toward her. She could sense his excitement. She did not need to see the grin creasing his square chin.

She felt her chains of depression her dad had unthoughtfully woven around her heart fall off. "I'm free from the chains of the past. So, devil beware!" She felt she could tackle anything that got in her way.

Joshua drew her into the shelter of his arms—warm, firm, trusting. "I love you!"

"This is all so surreal," she muttered. Joshua said what she had felt for months.

He kissed her lightly on her forehead. "We have to act faster than we'd like to, my darling. The days of the week speed quickly by, with One World Order Police picking our Christian numbers off like apples on a tree. He pulled her away, drinking in her face as a man might coming off the Sahara Desert. "Will you marry me?"

"But—"

"I am willing to accept what I know about you and have you be my bride and become a part of me."

He gazed into her eyes, as if to bind his words in her heart, and his words mingled with the whispers of the wind, prophetic in its meaning. "Let us not waste the moments we share today. Soon another year will speed by and we shall scarcely comprehend where the time has gone. "

## Twenty-three

*"And from the time that the daily sacrifice is taken away, and the abomination of desolation is set up, there shall be one thousand two hundred and ninety days. Blessed is he who waits, and comes to the one thousand three hundred and thirty-five days. But you, go your way till the end; for you shall rest, and will arise to your inheritance at the end of the days." Daniel 12:11–13*

What is wrong with me? Why do I allow these dreams of mine to hold my joy in my own prison of guilt? She wrapped her shawl around her shoulders. The sun was warm; the chill of mid-March only lingered in the shadows of the porch. Or was it the feeling of foreboding hanging in rafters about them? And like Joshua had predicted, what with the endless chores, worries of the terrorists, and harvesting of their food to feed the hungry mouths of themselves and their animals, seven and a half months had swept by—more anxieties, yet more miracles of God's love. Wild turkeys flocking into yards on Thanksgiving. Geese landing in yards on Christmas. God had not abandoned His people.

She could tell by the set of Joshua's shoulders, the angle his head, he was firmly set on his decision. She could not go with them to rescue her stepmother. What he didn't understand was—she'd rather die with him than live without him. Knowing of his great love for her, she persisted, hoping he'd change his mind. "Why can't I go?" Ruth searched Joshua's face. "After all, she's my stepmamm."

Joshua's expression softened, his eyes probing, questioning. She understood and couldn't hold him at fault. The fault lay totally on her shoulders. She'd given her word—and then had backed down on their wedding date. She reached up and encircled his neck, kissing him gently on his cheek. "Soon, my love." They would have been husband and wife—if she had not reneged.

She'd accepted his proposal at the singing. Joshua had waited until August, as was the custom, and had given her a beautiful hope chest as a gift and sent the bishop and deacon the proper credentials. They published this at the October Sunday service. Her name was read along with the other women who would be wed that fall. Joshua mailed some of the invitations, then hand delivered the rest of the wedding invitations to the closest houses. He apologized to her that it would not be the usual number of a hundred participants, but Ruth was happy just to be marrying him.

They decided on Thursday, November 16. Martha made her a beautiful blue dress she couldn't wait to wear proudly on her wedding day. Then it happened. Nightmares woke her up after midnight. Dark mysterious dreams of people shrouded in black hoods. But the worst of it—Martha and Josh Jr. were in her nightmare. Their frightened eyes followed her as she strode, donned in a black dress and veil, down a long aisle. She'd wake up crying, her nightgown completely drenched by sweat.

Now Joshua held her close.

She glanced at Sheriff Baker sitting in the wagon. He fidgeted with his hat impatiently. "Joshua, I'm sorry. Please try and understand." The time for Christ's arrival was drawing near. Ruth counted a short fourteen days left. She laid her head on his chest. What was God trying to tell her? She did not want Martha and Josh Jr. to die because of her. "I need to—"

"More promises, my love?" Joshua whispered.

She sighed. "Be patient with me a little longer." Between them, there was a silent agreement—but no date.

The back door of the kitchen slammed shut. Her dad hastened toward them. Joshua's jaw was set as ridged as the shafts connected to their horses and wagon. "You need to explain to your daughter why you are prohibiting her from coming with us, Mr. Jessup."

"Ruthie, Cassell City is not like it was." Dad threw his canvas bag into the wagon, beads of sweat wetting his forehead. It was only the second Wednesday in March, and not that warm. "The Antichrist's hangmen are running things. Rioters are burning and looting. There are no police, no order, and I don't know where your stepmother is. Three days ago, she contacted me that she was helping our church dispense the food they collected to pass out to their congregation.

"Then our sister church's pastor pledged allegiance to this prophet and the Antichrist. People who are not born again look at this man and become mesmerized into following him!

"The true Jesus followers fled to the hills. Others sought the underground railroad. Members of our congregation are in hiding, too. Joshua, Baker, and I are entering into this thing blindfolded. I feel bad enough asking anyone to follow me into this hell hole."

He took her shoulders in each of his strong hands. "I can't risk losing you. Not now. Not ever. Harriet would want me to keep you safe."

Stepmother. Most of Ruth's memory had returned. Only the night she'd lost her memory alluded her now. She knew Rex Rollins was instrumental. Exactly how, she did not have a clue.

A scene flashed through her mind. Harriet hugged and cuddled first Jane and then Paul; they laughed at her in sadistic pleasure.

When Harriet had drunk, it was worse. She'd lock Ruth in her room for an indefinite length of time... Ruth's legs buckled beneath her. Joshua came instantly to her side.

"What's wrong?"

Closing her eyes, she whispered, "I didn't know remembering could be painful." What did Jesus say? "If you have anything against anyone, forgive him, that your Father in heaven may also forgive you your trespasses." The sky and grass whirled like a cyclone before her eyes. Joshua scooped her up and carried her to the front porch, setting her down in the rocking chair, then kneeling beside her.

Her dad followed. Martha, seeing them, opened the front door. "What happened?"

"Ruth had another dizzy spell. Can you bring some water?" Joshua said.

When she laid her head back on the pillow rest, her dad wrapped an arm around her shoulders. "You shouldn't go. You're not well. Besides, Harriett wrote that she saw Rex Rollins in a produce store and—"

"I pray he didn't see her," Joshua blurted out.

Martha handed Ruth the glass of water. "You can help me here. We must prepare for our Saturday market day. I have over five dozen eggs and a half-dozen jars filled with vegetables and fruits that will bring a hefty bartering price. Maybe Joshua will komm, too." She looked up at her son. "You will be back by then?"

"Ja, I plan to."

"Would you like that?" Martha asked Ruth.

Ruth nodded. She liked the pampering, especially with those bad memories flooding her mind as if the devil decided to fling his poisonous darts into her flesh, hoping she would go back to him.

She quoted Scripture to put herself to sleep. Bible verses when she went about her chores. Bound the devil and his demons continuously in the name of her Savior Christ Jesus and laid claim to the power of the Holy Spirit. The devil would flee, only to return when she became weak.

Memories were not her friends. She knew now she left home because she felt unloved by Harriet. It was a battle of flesh versus the Holy Spirit.

Her flesh wanted her to revel, knowing that Harriet could possibly be locked up and had no one to help her. Ruth mouthed the correct words, yet her flesh was glad Harriet could be suffering, feeling the loss and helplessness Ruth once felt. Without food, water—not even a bathroom.

But now Harriet was saved and serving the Lord wherever she was needed, which had gotten her into this predicament. Ruth rested her head on Martha's soft hand. *Jesus, forgive me.*

Joshua rushed inside the house and back with a wet cloth and felt her forehead. "No fever." He laid the cloth on her sweating brow. "This might help you feel better."

Martha patted her shoulder. "That new plague has got us all jittery."

Ruth closed her eyes, praying the dizziness would leave. "When will you return?"

"By Friday evening at the latest." Joshua patted her hand.

"You'd better be," Ruth said good-naturedly. "You know your mamm. Saturday morning is her day to market, pick up supplies, and the latest news." She kissed his cheek. "I love you so; I can't think of waking and not seeing you at the kitchen table. Let's plan an April wedding, ja?"

Joshua wagged his forefinger in front of her startled eyes. "Nee. It's not happening. I know the workings of your mind. We will have it when I return. At least before Jesus returns, we will be husband and wife."

She flew into his waiting arms, holding him tightly. "Yes!"

"God willing." His lips mingled with hers, leaving her breathless, and then he sped down the steps of the porch.

She watched the wagon head out and waved.

"We shall pray for their safe return," Martha whispered. "Now you need to rest. I will prepare us a light dinner for this evening."

Rest was the last thing on Ruth's to-do list. She would rest when she got to heaven. She ran inside, snatched up her Bible, and hurried outside. The bluebirds and robins sang from branches that sprouted new life.

She sat down next to an apple tree and opened her Bible to Matthew 24, where Joshua had read last evening, and read for herself.

"And unless those days were shortened, no flesh would be saved; but for the elect's sake, those days will be shortened. Then if anyone says to you, 'Look, here *is* the Christ!' or 'There!' do not believe *it*. For false christs and false prophets will rise and show great signs and wonders to deceive, if possible, even the elect.... Therefore if they say to you, 'Look, He is in the desert!' do not go out; *or* 'Look, *He is* in the inner rooms!' do not believe *it*. For as the lightning comes from the east and flashes to the west, so also will the coming of the Son of Man be."

She looked up through the lattice of branches and whispered, "Everything's coming together, like the pieces of a puzzle. Like a large funnel that grows smaller toward its end to Christ's return."

Ruth fixed her eyes on the blue sky dotted with the cotton-ball clouds. "Lord, You're speaking to us through your Word on what to expect the next day and the day after that and—until You return."

A soft breeze flipped the pages of her Bible. "Who then is a faithful and wise servant, whom his master made ruler over his household, to give them food in due season? Blessed *is* that servant whom his master, when he comes, will find so doing."

She hugged her Bible to her bosom. Where was Harriet? What trap could Joshua, Baker, and Dad be getting themselves into? "Jesus, please keep everyone safe."

# Twenty-four

*"Beloved, do not believe every spirit, but test the spirits, whether they are of God; because many false prophets have gone out into the world. By this you know the Spirit of God: Every spirit that confesses that Jesus Christ has come in the flesh is of God, and every spirit that does not confess that Jesus Christ has come in the flesh is not of God. And this is the spirit of the Antichrist, which you have heard was coming."* 1 John 4:1–3

Joshua impatiently flipped the reins of his horses, listening to the conversation between Jessup and Baker.

They decided on the buggy. Betsy and Snowball pulled well together and if things got bad, Joshua could ride back for help.

"I know of a lane we can take the horses down and a couple of side roads," Jessup said, "when we get to the city."

"Ja, before we go, we best pray." They bowed their heads. "Lord, we have made You our refuge, the Most High, our dwelling place. Let no evil befall us. Give Your angels charge over us. Keep us in all our ways, and guide us to Mrs. Jessup. Amen!"

They traveled all day and into the night. The horses' shod feet clipped along the deserted dirt road at a fast pace. Joshua peered out from his Amish buggy; his quick eyes scanned the forests and darkened houses for anyone stirring.

Beams of light peeked out across the bleak sky from between jagged roofs as the rays of the rising sun swept away the night wind. He heard the stirrings of Ruth's father and Baker in the back seat, waking up. "Almost there."

After reaching town, they tried a half-dozen places, members of the underground and church Harriet and Jessup belonged to, and learned Mrs. Jessup had been captured by the WOP and where she had been taken.

Mr. Jessup peeked out from the back of the carriage. "Make a left here. The house is about two miles down this road. But be careful. It's a real steep decline. How are the horses doing?"

"Gut." Joshua noticed some men standing on the corner. Baker saw them, too. He unclipped his gun from his holster.

They passed by without a problem and pulled up to a red brick two-story home with a cement sculptured lion on either side of the porch. A pile of wood lay on the once well-groomed lawn, and a camping stove rested on the covered front porch, along with a bucket full of water.

"I see her!" Jessup said.

"Wait. Here, take this." Baker shoved his flashlight into his hands.

"Is this—"

"Yes. We need to know if these people have taken the mark. If they have, then we can't trust them."

"I know my wife; she'd die before she did."

Joshua didn't like it. He felt like a sitting duck waiting for a hunter's bullet. "Let's drive to the back and knock on the kitchen door, instead. I'll park my rig in that cluster of trees. From the front, you won't see it and we'll be able to leave easily."

"Good idea," Baker replied.

Once the horses were tied, Mr. Jessup jumped down and walked toward the back door and the window where he'd seen his wife.

Joshua followed a few feet behind. More wood, a garbage pail of apples, and a pile of discarded garbage in the back corner made it a good haven for varmints. Then he noticed the army-issued tent. That's strange.

Joshua kept his eyes on the tent. He was waiting for a face to appear in the open flap. "Something doesn't feel right," he whispered his misgivings to Baker.

A woman slipped through the half-opened back door, an infant in her arms and a two-year-old by her side. She swooped into Jessup's arms in a quick embrace. He pulled her and the children toward Joshua.

"Your timing is impeccable. The house owners and the WOP army are away due to some fire up on Main Street," Mrs. Jessup said.

They hurried to the buggy, and Jessup helped his wife and the two-year-old into buggy. She clutched the baby to her chest. She cooed softly while she patted the little girl's head. She kissed the girl on her forehead, her eyes wet. "We're going to a nice place." She looked at Joshua with terror-brimmed eyes. "They'll be back any minute. You can't imagine how terrible it is here."

"Is there anyone else in the house?"

"No. Part of the reason they spared me is that I can cook and sew. No one in that house knows how to do either. All they ever did was shop, eat out, and use the microwave. Please hurry. If they find us, it will mean certain death."

Joshua trotted his horses out. "Know of any quiet side roads?"

"Yes, make a left here," Harriet said. "This is a half-forgotten farm lane the Christians have been using." She held the baby to her.

Big wet tears rolled down Mrs. Jessup's shallow cheeks, her sobs racking her shoulders and chest. "Pray for our congregation. Pray they got away from the WOP. Not even Hitler and Stalin can compete with this Antichrist. He might appear handsome and debonair, but—"

"You saw him? This Antichrist?" Baker asked.

"Yes! He appeared at one of our home church services. Big as life! I looked up. He was standing at our makeshift altar along with the prophet—but I didn't see what Mary saw. I swear, I saw Satan incarnate." She turned toward her husband and buried her head into his coat. "Jessup, remember Mary? The lady who follows the church laws religiously and told us this born-again mania is hype?"

"Yeah."

"It was at her house we had our service. She sat next to me. She *believed* this imposter. I pointed to the Bible passage about how Jesus said not to be deceived—she wouldn't look down to read it! Said this man is the king and would rule the universe forever and ever and that we should pay homage to him! Then she reiterated what the prophet said, that this global warming was because of the Christians.

"This prophet said, 'To stop these dust storms, droughts, tornadoes, floods, locusts, and pandemics, we must annihilate all who will not pledge allegiance to the king. Find your closest WOP and help rid yourselves of these confused Christians and Jews who are sadly deceived into believing this false Jewish Christ is coming down from heaven to save them.'

"Before I could say more to Mary, the WOP stormed in. Me, and these poor children saw their mother and daddy—"

"Mrs. Jessup?" Joshua said. The children's eyes were as big as saucers, listening and watching to see what would happen to them next.

"Dear things, the two-year-old has terrible nightmares."

Baker patted the little girl on the head. "Understand, I have to do this." He shone his flashlight on the little girl. She was clean, then the infant. And, lastly, Mrs. Jessup. "Sorry, ma'am. I've learned the hard way what this antichrist group is capable of."

"I understand." She sobbed. Her husband held her close. "Our Ruthie's safe. She saved you. Now her friends have saved me."

"Ruth wanted to come," Mr. Jessup said, "but I wouldn't let her."

"Oh, dear, I forgot to tell you. Rex Rollins has a personal vendetta against our daughter. He has the mark. He's the head of the Cassell unit and determined to send every Christian in Michigan to the re-education camp, sometimes conducting experiments with the captives before beheading them. And if some people do accept the mark, then they implant them with computer chips and mechanical parts to be stronger. Remember Private Investigator Ricker?"

"Ja."

"He must be one of the captains in the Patriot group as well as the head of the underground railroad because Rollins is looking for him.

# LOVE'S FINAL SUNRISE

Rollins came here to the house four times, hoping to catch Ricker."

Harriet covered her face with her hands. "I… I feel they're keeping me alive, using me as a decoy, hoping to catch you. You see, they know you're part of the underground, Sheriff Baker, and they won't stop until they have killed you and everyone else."

"Humpf. Sooner or later, it was inevitable." Baker shrugged. "I told my wife to head to the cabin. Hope she listened."

The baby whimpered, then burst into a full-blown cry. "There, there, little one. Shush."

The cresting sunbeams escaped from a tall, siloed barn and shone their golden rays on the horses' sparkling harness.

Two shadows separated from the building and stepped into the path of the buggy. Were they men or women? One person had a nose ring. Both sported a mohawk hair style. One was wearing some sort of a skirt, and the other had leather pants on.

"Hey, we could use a ride, mister; what about it?"

"Don't stop," Baker hissed. He stretched out his hand, revealing what he hoped looked like his badge. "Sorry, on official business."

Evidently, they didn't buy the phony badge. The tall one dressed in leather pants pulled out a bowie knife from his belt. "This is official business too."

Baker flashed his light. Six hundred sixty-six gleamed on their foreheads.

"Sorry, gents, you're bad business. Don't come any closer, or I'll shoot to kill." His gun gleamed in the sunlight.

"Whoa, big daddy. There are plenty more of me; you'll not get out of here that easy."

"We didn't plan to get out of here that easy, but we do plan on getting out. Move, or I'll make a few more holes on that face of yours you weren't planning on."

Joshua drew out the whip from the holder next to him, in case these men had any thoughts of not obeying.

The guys backed away and Joshua slapped his reins. The horses broke into a canter, climbing the hill. Ahead, the countryside stretched out like a welcoming friend. Or so they thought. The dirt road grew rutted and mud-soaked, but it had been an unusually dry spring. A strange odor assaulted their nostrils.

"What *is* that smell?" Jessup asked.

"Death." Joshua looked out toward where the smell was strongest. A field of corpses met his eyes.

"What the—" Baker covered his nose and mouth with his hand.

"Harriet, was this because of the plague, or was it the WOP killings?" Jessup asked.

"Probably both," she said. "The hospitals are overloaded with cases, and I heard they didn't know where to put the corpses."

They drove on for hours, well past noonday. Then they spotted two rows of marching men and women dressed in prison garments, not more than a half-mile ahead of them. Two men on bay horses, one ahead and the other behind, led the group. They hadn't noticed them. Joshua pulled up. Checking his options, he decided not to pass them. The fewer people to know their whereabouts, the better.

He headed his team down the hill toward a clump of trees and got out. "We're going to wait until those men leave. Let's try and get a little sleep. We'll leave first sight of daylight." Running his hand across his horses' necks and down to their shoulders, he gave a little pinch to their skin. Dehydrated. "My horses are exhausted. They need water. A little pasture grass won't hurt either." He unhitched them.

"Look, there's a creek beyond those trees." Baker jumped down. "I'll take them down for you."

"Oh, dear me." Harriet cried. "We need to get back to Ruthie quickly."

Jessup turned. "Why?"

"I don't think I said anything that would lead Rollins to Ruthie. But now, thinking back, I wonder." The baby stirred in her arms. She rocked it gently back to sleep. "He's crafty. When I went to the market, he'd be there. He was pleasant and polite and seemed lonely, wanting someone to talk with.

"He'd asked me about the Amish lifestyle. When they did their baking and when they went to market. Little things like that. He never asked any direct questions about Ruthie. But he did get me to talk about Christmas and what we did."

"I'm hungry," the little girl said.

Joshua helped the little girl down, then drew out his knapsack packed to the brim with sandwiches and handed her one.

Harriet followed her husband to a large oak. Sitting down, she cooed and rocked the baby, attempting to coax him back to sleep.

There was something Harriet wasn't saying. "What else did Rex ask you?"

"Oh, random things, Joshua, like do Amish work on saddles and such." She squirmed. "Then I…I did something foolish."

Joshua walked closer. "We all do; go on."

She fumbled with the blankets layering the infant. "It was hard bartering for my vegetables while pretending I didn't know what he did to Ruthie. He's so cocky at times. He had the nerve to ask me when I'd see Ruthie again, could he come along? I, well, my temper got the best of me and I blurted out, 'Doesn't it matter to you that our Ruthie has no memory of her past? For almost three and a half years? Just what did you do to her?'"

Jessup sucked in a breath. "Harriet, you didn't."

She turned on him in a woman's scorn. "Jessup, I thought maybe I could get him to confess or at least blurt out that he thought he killed her—or something!"

"What did he say?" Joshua kept his voice low, consoling.

"He sneered at me and said, 'Where is my little Ruthie?' I told him he was the last person I'd tell." She sobbed. "Then at the church service, Rollins pulled me aside from the other Christians that were being— you know." She put a hand to her eyes, wiping away her tears. "When I went to join them in line, he said, 'Where do you think you're going?' 'To join my fellow patriots,' I told him.

"He laughed at me! He called over a super-soldier and he handcuffed me. Rollins said, 'I'm placing you under house arrest until I get the information I need from you.' Jessup, I'm sorry, I should have fled with some of the other Christians to the underground railroad."

"It wouldn't be hard for Rollins to know that the best time to meet Ruth was on market day," Joshua said.

"Okay, let's all try and sleep. I'll take the first watch. Let's plan to leave before dawn." Joshua watched everyone lie down. It would be a restless night for all.

# Twenty-five

*"Finally, my brethren, be strong in the Lord and in the power of His might. Put on the whole armor of God, that you may be able to stand against the wiles of the devil. For we do not wrestle against flesh and blood, but against principalities, against powers, against the rulers of the darkness of this age...." Ephesians 6:10–12*

Ruth wiped at the cereal on Josh Jr.'s lips. It's Saturday. What's happened to Joshua and Dad? Why aren't they back?

Robins and bluebirds outside their kitchen window sang a shrill tune this morning that mimicked Martha's chattering. Market day was a monumental time. Bartering their produce determined what they would eat and wear in the coming months. Ruth sipped her coffee thoughtfully. Her imagination worked overtime, fearing the worst.

"Ruth? Are you ready?"

She met Martha's kind, however, apprehensive eyes.

"What's wrong? You grow more thoughtful with every passing day."

"I...I fear something might have happened to Joshua and Father."

"We leave the worrying to God. Ja? We prayed when we sent them off. Now we give it to God."

Ruth folded and refolded her fingers. Last night a dream had awakened her in the middle of the night. She hurriedly struck a match and by a single candle's glow, read Scripture that confirmed to her Jesus wanted her to confess all to Joshua of what she remembered before she took her wedding vows. She couldn't. She'd lose him. It is one thing killing to save the oppressed, quite another when you kill an innocent babe."

Martha looked at her knowingly. "I think there is something you are hiding. Confess all. It does the soul gut."

Ruth jumped up. "We'd best get to town." She hurried toward her bedroom. "Let me get my cape, then I'm ready."

Martha stepped outside into the bright sunlight. "This day is warm enough to fry an egg on the roof. Whoever heard of a Michigan March being this warm?"

Ruth gathered up her cape as well as Martha's and Josh's coats. "We'll need a covering when the sun goes down." A chill covered her heart before she had taken five steps. She looked around the room before closing the door as if memorizing the cheery red-checkered tablecloth and bright curtains hanging like a flag of greeting on the windows. This place had brought her a peace she had never experienced. "Lord, forgive my deceit," she prayed before closing the door.

"Such a woebegone face! Why do you act as if you're leaving for good?"

Ruth handed Josh Jr. to Martha and ducked her head as she stepped into the buggy. "Something is wrong. I can feel it. Dat and Joshua should have been back from Cassell by now."

Martha kissed her grandson on the forehead, and handed him back to Ruth. He stretched out his arms, yawned, and settled back into the crook of Ruth's embrace.

"Maybe Joshua's getting something for his intended bride and is waiting for us in town. After all, he'll go right by Owenson on his way back from Cassell." Martha picked up the reins. "Giddy up." Obediently the Standardbred trotted down the drive and onto the road.

"Martha, I can't marry Joshua until he knows everything about my past and who I am."

"Hmm." Martha turned her sharp eyes toward her. "Why, Kind, you've known who you are for some time." Then she was back slapping the whip in the air and singing out, "This is the day the Lord has made. I think I need to trade my eggs for some flour and baking soda, or else we'll be eating eggs and milk all month."

"Didn't Joshua tell us not to go into town without him? That it had become too dangerous?"

"For sure and certain. But I was reading about the coming of God's kingdom in Luke this morning. That was where my fingers took me, and what struck me was that God wants us to go right on enjoying life until His return. Especially marrying the one you love!"

"Strange, I read it this morning too, but what stuck with me was, 'Whoever seeks to save his life will lose it, and whoever loses his life will preserve it.'"

Martha shrugged. "That too. Still, our God loves us, and He loves a good romance best." She gave her a wink. "Your mamm has requested you wear her wedding dress. She had it cleaned and pressed. Your dat brought it with him."

"Oh, but you've made me a beautiful blue one," Ruth said. "I don't want to upset my stepmom, but shouldn't I, as an Amish bride, be married in Amish blue?" She felt the pains of guilt wash over her. She had wished Harriot ill, but now look at the kindness her stepmom had done her. "Oh, I don't want to disappoint anyone."

Martha patted her hands. "Not to worry. We will work this out for the gut. Joshua told me he wants the marriage soon. We will try for this Thursday. That is gut. I need to make this a proper wedding. I will pick up some baking things to make you a gut wedding cake."

There was no easy way to tell the truth. Ruth kissed the sleeping Josh on his forehead and blurted out, "You can't imagine how bad I was."

"True." Martha patted her knee. "God, through what His Son did on the cross, has completely forgiven you of everything. But you see, Ruth, as Joshua has already told you, you must forgive yourself. The devil uses guilt to keep us from what the cross of Christ did in shedding His blood as the sacrifice for our sins."

*They don't know what sin is like—I do.* If Martha knew, she would turn away from me and never talk to me again. "Jesus has asked me to trust Him and tell Joshua all I—"

"God and Jesus are not going to let you down. No sirree. Now, do you love my son, and do you love Jesus?"

Ruth bit down on her bottom lip and nodded. "With all my body and soul."

"That is all Joshua and you need to have for a happy-ever-after." Martha took the buggy whip and cracked it over the horse's rump. "We'll all do fine. God and His Son have us surrounded with His angels; you wait and see. We're ready to face whatever lies ahead for us—even at Owenson."

"Aren't you a little worried about those—"

"We've started early in the morning, and most of the ruffians are still in their beds sleeping off last night's liquor. What I can't understand is with all the food shortages, why is there always a bountiful supply of spirits?"

Ruth adjusted her kapp as the wagon slowed down, reaching Mr. Brinkman's lumber mill and general store. She breathed deeply, remembering Joshua's words that Mr. Brinkman and now Mr. Brunswick had taken the mark. She said a silent prayer that they would all get home safely this Saturday, especially Joshua.

---

Because of the men and women dressed in prison garments and the guards on horses, they had to wait longer than Joshua wished to and were forced to take an alternate route that would make them a day late in returning home. "Stay here. I'll scout the area."

"What's up?" Baker said. Jessup joined him.

"I'm going to go on ahead. Here's the knapsack. There are enough sandwiches and water for at least another day. If I don't come back, then you better find another route to take back home." He left, leaving the two staring after him.

He wished he knew where Rollins was. Planning to capture them—or Ruth? With the sun peeking over the horizon, he prayed Mother had not left for the market. "Lord, please let me get to Ruth before

Rollins gets his dirty hands on her."

He took to the woods and meadows, keeping an eye on the road. Then he heard something. Crawling up the hill, he looked out.

Hmm, looked like the same group from yesterday. What type of prisoners were they? Or maybe they weren't prisoners at all. Just Christians taken away to who knows where?

He counted three guards. He was downwind from them. He didn't know for sure that would benefit him; it did when tracking a deer for their venison meat during the winter months.

What was that? He crawled closer. The early rays of sunshine glinted eerily off a large iron hatchet embedded in a log.

The group of thirty or so men, women, and children bound in leather straps huddled together. Thin, raggedly clothed children no older than his son clutched an older person's hand. Joshua clawed the dirt in front of him. *Lord, help me save them.*

He clenched his knife between his teeth and crawled closer, keeping in the tall grass. He'd take the first WOP guard down with his knife so as not to alert the others. The man with tattoos across his neck and arms didn't know what hit him. Joshua dragged his body toward the trees and then crawled to the next guard. One of the prisoners spotted him.

He put his finger to his lips.

One of the guards yelled out for someone. Most likely the guard he'd just knocked out. The guard started toward him. He motioned for the other guard to follow.

Joshua sneaked lower into the weeds. Sticks, dried grass, and dead leaves tickled his nostrils. He held his breath and counted to ten. Then peering through the tall grass, he watched the two guards as they talked. They walked back to the group standing among the trees.

The two guards turned around. Hmm, are they waiting for someone? It seemed strange that they were standing around like they had nothing to do but chop off thirty or forty heads.

A truck with three rubber wheels and one steel rim roared down the one-lane trail.

Two civilian men and two soldiers got out. One of the soldiers set up a folding table and two chairs. The two important-looking men were dressed in black suits and carried notebooks. The men opened their pads; the tallest of them removed a pen from his chest pocket. The other man, who had a mop of hair on his head and a beard to match, opened his black folder and yelled, "Mr. Tyrone. Mr. Samuel Tyrone, step forward."

A large man, his hands bound with a rope that traveled upwards and wrapped his neck, walked forward.

"You've had a chance to think about your decision of following this Jewish Jesus or worship the true king and pledge allegiance to him alone forever and ever. Do you want to be free?"

The man named Tyrone nodded.

The taller man spoke. "Sign here. Your lands, homes, and personal belongings will be restored to you. We'll give you new clothes and implant you with a chip that will make you a super-soldier and super-human. Wouldn't you like that?"

Tyrone leveled his shoulders, looked the man straight in this face, and said, "Of course, I want to be free. Only, I follow the one true God and His Son, Christ Jesus. You had better consider your options or face the eternal damnation of hell."

He held up a string of knots between his bound wrists that resembled the rosery Joshua had once seen, only this was longer. Mr. Tyrone smiled. "See this? The large knots represent years, the middle-sized knots represent months, and the small knots represent days. Jesus is coming. There are nine or ten days left.

"We who have been faithful will meet Christ in the air!" He pointed his finger toward the men in black. "You and your Antichrist will remain on Earth to face Christ's wrath when the blood will flow as high as a horse's bridle!"

The tallest man jumped forward and grabbed the counting rope. He flung it aside. "You know this date? How—"

"The book of Daniel, '*There shall be* one thousand two hundred and ninety days. Blessed is he who waits, and comes to the one thousand three hundred and thirty-five days—"

"No, no, no!" The short man in the black suit made a lunge for him. Tyrone stepped away, and the man fell like a black blob to the ground.

"Enough of this," the tall man yelled. "Bring Tyrone's family forward. The WOP will be here soon, and I want these beheadings finished before they get here."

A small woman who hardly came to her husband's shoulder walked forward. Four towheaded children ranging in height like steps on a church porch followed behind her. The smallest of the children ran ahead. "Daddy!"

The littlest boy jumped forward, and Jones knelt, he kissed him on each cheek.

By this time, the short man had regained some composure and walked back to his table. He plopped himself down in his chair and banged his fist on the table like a child having a temper tantrum.

The tall man's demeanor resembled a demonic sneer. "Executioner, I want you to slice off his hands, then slice the boy's throat slowly—"

"No!" Tyrone leaped onto the man holding the hatchet and wrestled him to the ground. The little boy ran to his mother. The guards rushed forward, jumped on Jones, and wrestled him to his feet. The noose around his neck tightened, and Jones gasped for air.

"Undo the noose." The tall man rubbed his hands. "Prepare the fires for the branding of the entire family."

"God said, 'I will give you a mouth and wisdom…and they will put some of you to death.' But not a hair of our heads shall be lost. Lord God, be it according to Your will!"

"Your God doesn't care about you. Weren't you supposed to be raptured before this tribulation stuff began?"

"The Bible says we will see 'the Son of Man coming in a cloud with power and great glory.' That's when the rapture will take place. Not before."

The tall man leaned forward and whispered, "Really? This Jewish imposter is going to show up in nine or ten days? Can't you see your

God tricked you into believing about this Jewish Messiah coming back in the clouds for you?"

"He is the sacrificial Lamb that made it possible for us to be forgiven and to go to heaven. Jesus Christ—"

"Don't say that name," the tall man demanded. "Be reasonable. You don't want to see your son hurt, yet this fake Jew you worship left you here to be tortured and experience an agonizing death? Where's that love you Christians always talk about?"

"Our Lord and Savior, Jesus Christ, died on the cross for us!" the woman boldly declared.

"I said don't say that name!" The men threw up their hands, blocking their ears.

"Yes. The cross of Christ offends you because you know of its power over sin and the grave." The woman stepped forward. "For God so loved the world that He gave His only begotten Son, that whoever believes in Him should not perish but have everlasting life."

"Daddy." The little boy pulled on his father's sleeve. "Don't worry. I won't yell much." He walked over to the executioner and took his hand. "Come on, let's get this over with."

Adrenaline pumped through Joshua's veins like a raging bull. *God, what do You want me to do?*

The executioner sneered. Jones fell to his knees as did his wife and children, their hands clasped in prayer. "'All who desire to live godly in Christ Jesus will suffer persecution.' Lord, help us to remain strong."

The executioner laid the child's small hands on the log. "Your head will be next."

The boy's golden hair gleamed in the breaking daylight, reminding Joshua of his son. He sprang up, grabbed the knife from between his teeth, and rushed the man. He slit the executioner's throat as neatly as he would an animal. *God forgive me!*

"Get him, get him, you fool," the tall man yelled.

A truck drove up with a company of soldiers in it. One soldier drew out his gun. Joshua ducked, then lowered his head and rammed him like a bull. The tumble knocked them both to the ground. Around the grassy turf they wrestled. The guard was strong, super-human strong with a wild animal strength. *Jesus, give me strength.* He aimed his thumbs for the guard's eyes.

"Grrr!"

Joshua flipped him onto his belly like a pancake on the griddle. It was easier to kill, be it animal or human, without the victim staring at him.

Yells and screams pierced the crisp air around him. Soldiers jumped to the ground and surrounded him. Then Baker and Jessup were there, slitting the ropes on the captives.

Joshua finished the guard and jumped up to see Jones and the other captives fighting for their lives. He, Jessup, and Baker rushed the guards. Fists against flesh resounded in Joshua's ears. Bullets rang out and the smell of gunpowder floated past his nostrils. One guard took careful aim at the boy. Joshua lunged toward him, hoping to be a human shield before he could pull the trigger.

A huge man shoved him away. He tumbled down the hill, and all he could see was the man's stream of fire-yellow hair—Gabriel? Where the blazes had he come from?

Behind trees, valleys, and swamps, an army of men swarmed them. They toted guns, knives, and pitchforks, and attacked the well-armed men of the Antichrist.

Side by side, they fought. In the end, they won.

Joshua couldn't believe the transpired events. The men who had come from the shadows of the forest walked forward. "Who are—"

"The Patriots."

Joshua looked around for Gabriel. He spotted him and walked toward the clump of trees.

"Ja, thought that was you," Joshua said. "Danke for saving my life."

Gabriel bowed gallantly. The man looked more and more to be out of his element in this twenty-first century. Gabriel resembled a picture Joshua had seen in a painting once of a centurion during Jesus's time.

"Where's Ruth?" Gabriel's stabbing hazel eyes met Joshua's.

"She stayed back at the house and is safe with my Mutter."

"Not anymore. As it was in Job, the devil wagered and bargained with God before he was cast out of God's presence—for her soul. Only, her life is not all you will lose."

Could Joshua trust him? Of all the people outside his Ordnung, Gabriel appeared to be the most trustworthy. He'd come to his aid twice now. Could it be a coincidence? Was he, as his name denoted, an avenging angel from God? He wasn't going to take chances, especially not with Ruth. "She's a good Amish mädel."

Gabriel's mouth twisted into a knowing smile. "She will remember all her past—"

"What?" Joshua shook with anger, holding his temper in check with difficulty. "Well, so? She's given her life to Jesus Christ."

Gabriel looked at him down the bridge of his large nose. "Her faith will be tested. Pray she will triumph and remain true to her calling."

"Joshua? Who are you talking to?" Harriet stepped forward. "Look who I found."

Joshua turned. "Detective Ricker, why am I not surprised? So, you must know Gabriel."

"Who?"

"Gabriel—He's gone." Joshua shrugged.

"I can see that." Detective Ricker looked around. "I don't know of any Gabriel in our group."

"Honestly, I don't know how you gents found us—but I'm mighty glad you showed up when you did."

# Twenty-six

*"You are all sons of light and sons of the day. We are not of the night nor of darkness. Therefore let us not sleep, as others do, but let us watch and be sober...putting on the breastplate of faith and love, and as a helmet the hope of salvation."* 1 Thessalonians 5:5-6,8

Rollins patted a little girl's head and used the opportunity to peek at the woman's face. He searched the throngs of buggies pulling into the general store and cussed. These Amish all looked alike with their black buggies and blue dresses. To see a woman's features, you had to step right in front of her.

At first, he searched the faces of the single women without kids pulling at their skirts. Then he thought, what if Ruth married? What if she had a baby? This might be harder than he thought. Children and babies were everywhere, like a population explosion. No abortion clinics here.

A familiar figure left the crowd of curious onlookers.

"What are you doing here?" Johansson's dislike for him was evident. "You can't be here for anything but trouble."

Mr. Johansson had not changed. His booming voice and even sharper tongue stopped every pedestrian within ten feet. Rollins flicked his wrist and placed his well-manicured index finger to Johansson's broad chest. "You had best mind your p's and q's with me. I'm the head man of WOP in Cassell, and I'm planning to be head of the state of Michigan. I do not take to troublemakers. I can make your life a positive hell, if you get my drift."

"You might as well get your feet wet 'cause that's where you're headin' to for eternity."

"I'll enjoy seeing your head dismembered from that thick stubborn neck of yours."

Johansson laughed. "You know, I should be thanking you. My religion used to be a sideline with me. That is, until you antichrist people took over. Yeah, I realized Jesus meant more to me than a cushy lifestyle. Much more than living on this earth without Him." Johansson spat in the dirt, right in front of Rollins's shiny black boots. "The thought of sharing the same bunk in the hereafter with the likes of you made me feel dirty and filthy from the inside out."

"You're interfering with the wrong man," Rollins growled.

Johansson crossed his arms, looked down his nose, and sniffed. "Something here smells rotten through and through."

"Well, someone will be dead soon enough." Rollins snickered.

"There is a God of this universe, and it ain't you or that hokey-pokey man who likes to imagine he can raise the dead." Johansson poked Rollins in the chest so hard he stumbled backward. "My God cared enough to send His only Son, Jesus Christ, to save me, a down-right sorry-faced sinner."

Rollins blocked his ears. "Don't say that name."

Johansson leaned over and hissed. "Jesus Christ is Lord of lords and King of kings!"

"Why, you—"

"You got a problem with this guy?" Heydenreich joined Johansson.

"Nothing that I can't handle." Johansson and Heydenreich strolled into the General Store.

Rollins looked around for the WOP. No. Keep cool. If he alerted the guards, then Ruthie would run, and he'd lose his chance to nab her. This time he wasn't going to allow his temper to get the better of him. Besides, Johansson wasn't his job. It was Brinkman's.

Rollins stormed into the lumber store adjacent to the General Store. "Where's Brinkman?"

The cashier had all he could handle to tally up the bartering of the ever-increasing line of customers. "He's in his office at the top of the stairs."

Rollins took the wooden steps two at a time, into the office that overlooked the store. A large picture window ran along the southern section of the office and framed an antique cherry-wood desk.

With the fury of a hurricane, Rollins stood over him. Brinkman slinked deeper into his swivel chair. "Mr. Rollins, what brings you to Owenson?"

Rollins grabbed Brinkman's shirt collar and jerked him forward. "All I want to know is why haven't you had Johansson arrested by the WOP?"

"For what?"

"He's a threat to the government. That's what."

Rollins threw Brinkman down so hard his swivel chair spun around several times.

That seemed to knock some grit into Brinkman's backbone. "You want to know why? Because I wouldn't see daylight again. You don't get these people in Owenson. They got themselves a vigilante group that calls themselves the Patriots. These people live by their own set of rules here. They wouldn't find any piece of my body left. You want to arrest him, be my guest."

"That's not my job."

"Really? I give it to you. Go ahead, or are you too chicken to prey on a real man? Is your expertise in defenseless women and children?"

"Why, I should—"

"What do you have in mind?" Brinkman drew out his revolver and leaned back in his chair. "Let me give it to you straight. You'll need a full-fledged army to win here. Now get your threats and your carcass out of my office."

Rollins threw up his arms, innocence lapping his face like a dog's tongue. "Sure, partner, I see your point. Now that I have the total picture, I understand. Here, let's shake on it." Rollins extended his arm. Brinkman laid his gun on the desk.

"No, don't get up. I'll come to you." Walking closer, Rollins pushed Brinkman's chair hard. The ball-bearing wheels rolled straight toward the broad window. Brinkman, unbalanced, tried to rise. Rollins slammed it into the picture window. The glass cracked with the weight of man and chair. Brinkman's cry blended with the cracking glass panels as he fell to his death below.

Rollins took the steps two at a time in his hurry to escape. Two WOP policemen waited for him at the bottom. Rollins rushed through the doorway and bumped into a woman.

"Ah!" She fell onto the wooden walkway into a heap of cloth.

Rollins hoisted her to her feet. "What do you mean pushing Brinkman out that window." He slapped her face.

---

"Ah!" Ruth held her cheek, feeling a welt forming. Her eyes met her assailant's. "Rex Rollins, I should have known. What are you doing here? Unhand me, or I'll tell the police how you tried to kill me." She gasped at what she had said. The glee in his eyes confirmed her fears. For the past three-and a-half years she had tried to see the face of the man who attempted to kill her. Of all times for her to regain that last piece of her memory, this was not it.

Johansson rushed to her defense. "Let go of her!"

"She's under arrest for the murder of Mr. Brinkman."

"What?" Heydenreich said. "She was here, and we can vouch for her. You were the one running down the stairs like the guilty polecat you are. I can find at least a half-dozen bystanders who can testify they saw you through the store window pushing—"

"That's the way it looked like to me," the WOP policeman said.

Rollins removed his badge from his pocket with Head Superintendent written in red across it and displayed it to the WOP. Then said to Johansson and Heydenreich, "You calling me a liar?"

"Yeah, we are."

Rollins looked out at the gathering crowd, his arms crossed. "Looks like I need to send in the super-soldier unit. These WOP policemen have been compromised."

A murmur went around the crowd.

"I don't want any trouble from any one of you, or else your families will suffer, you hear me? You want to see your wives and children hauled off to the re-education facility? You ready for that?"

God, help me. Ruth squeezed her eyes shut. I can't allow my friends to get hurt because of me. She looked back into the gentle eyes of Johansson and smiled. "Don't fear. My God will deliver me." She allowed Rex to lead her down the steps of the porch.

The warm sun that felt comforting on Ruth's face earlier now resembled a firing squad's spotlight. She straightened her shoulders and prayed. This was not the time for her to cringe before her captor. God can turn all things to good.

Rex shoved her toward the car. "I can't believe you killed Mr. Brinkman like that. It's straight to the re-education facility for you."

The two officers who knew of her innocence did not utter a word.

"Send for the super-soldiers," Rex barked. "I want those people beheaded NOW!"

A flood of memories rushed into Ruth's head. She remembered the paper she had worked for and the abuse she'd endured from Rex.

The men, the alcohol, the drugs, the baby she aborted... She didn't like the woman she saw in her past. Was there a way to disown that part of her life and keep only the good parts?

She prayed fervently. What had Martha said? Hadn't Joshua prayed with her in the wheat field, and hadn't she accepted Christ and been born again, born anew? Yes, that's right, her sins had all been washed away by the blood Jesus shed on Calvary, washed clean and pure as the driven snow on a winter's eve.

Her past was behind her; her future was in God's hands, and so was her present. Hot tears rolled down her cheeks and dropped onto her bound hands. Lord, help me do what You want with the time I have left on Earth.

The car labored up the steep hills toward Pigeon. This was not the way to the re-education facility. Was he heading to the old mansion? Would it become a prison for her final days on Earth? Martha, Josh Jr.—Joshua! Her heart wrenched within her bosom. Lord, help me. Thy will be done to me. Please comfort, Joshua. Oh, Lord, don't delay in Your return. We can't hold out much longer.

# Twenty-seven

*"A king shall arise, Having fierce features, Who understands sinister schemes. His power shall be mighty, but not by his own power; He shall destroy fearfully, And shall prosper and thrive; He shall destroy the mighty, and also the holy people. Through his cunning He shall cause deceit to prosper under his rule." Daniel 8:23b–25a*

Dragged from the car, Ruth was thrown into a room dark as pitch. She could not see her hands before her. The musty smell of the room attacked her nostrils. She coughed. Her hands still bound, she crawled forward, sweeping her hands across the floor and feeling her way in the darkness. When she reached a stone wall, she rose to her knees. The rough irregular crevices must be rocks. A cellar, a basement? "Hello? Anyone else here?"

The drip, drip, drip of water was her answer. Was this to be her new dwelling place? For how long? Would Joshua find her? Something bit her foot. She screamed. Lifting her hands to her mouth, she bit down hard, hindering another scream, and clasped her hands in prayer.

Hours crept by.

A thread of light appeared somewhere behind her, then back to darkness. From out of the blackness came a voice. "Do you need any more time to decide, Ruthie?"

She slid along the wall, away from his voice. "Decide what?"

"If you prefer this to be your new home—my dungeon—or to sup with me in the elegant dining room where we can discuss better accommodations?" Rex's fiendish laughter bounced against the stone walls as did his flashlight seeking her. His nails clawed at her bound wrists, dragging her forward. "Fighting me will get you nowhere."

He dragged her up the steps. At the top she heard the creaking of a door. She blinked against the sudden bright light of the hallway adorned with sparkling crystal chandeliers. Doorways stood ajar to beckoning rooms ornately furnished. This wasn't the mansion. She was passing through wide hallways and glittering dome-shaped cathedral-like ceilings. Where was she, and how would Joshua find her?

They went up another stairway. She stepped into a large room where a king-size bed with a satin bedspread and pillows in delicately scrolled satin cases sprawled along a cherry-paneled wall. Lying on the shiny bedspread was a ball gown, slippers, gloves, and a tiara. In the corner near a picture window sat a Queen Anne desk. In the opposite corner, she could see the powder room. He unbound her wrists.

"Take a bath. You stink."

"What do you expect me to smell like after you stuck me in that ill-smelling dungeon?"

"I don't want your lip! Get dressed. I'll be back in an hour."

He slammed the door. She heard a key turn in the lock. She waited for his footsteps to recede and then ran toward the window. Bolted shut. It wouldn't have done her any good if she could have opened it. She was three stories up. She rushed to the door, praying that it hadn't locked. She pulled at it until her arms hurt.

She must not allow fear to overcome her faith. Believe. The moments before dawn are always the darkest. God had a plan, and she needed to have faith. Jesus spent forty days and forty nights alone, praying in the wilderness without anything to eat. Every time Satan used Scripture, Jesus replied with Scripture, it is written. "And I know my devil's name is Rex Rollins."

☼

A vast table lavishly adorned with sparkling crystal and delicate china greeted her eyes.

Rex, impeccably groomed, kissed her hand. "I'm so sorry for the way I treated you. Can you forgive me, my darling?"

He held her chair out, nodding his head for her to sit. "You look lovely, my dear. You have no idea how much I have missed you. Have you missed me—maybe a little?"

"I had amnesia."

A man dressed in a tuxedo appeared with their plates of food. His stiff movements and blank face made her think of a mummy. He set their plates before them then retreated from the room. As the night continued, the courses advanced one after another until finally dessert arrived. The servant, devoid of all emotion throughout the evening, alarmed her. The knot in her stomach tightened. What had happened to this man? Was Rex hoping to do the same to her? *Lord, make every word I utter be Yours.* The night of her narrow escape came vividly to her mind. He could become a maniac in the blink of an eye.

After dessert, Rex wiped his mouth, stood, then sat in a chair closer to hers. "Ruthie, I've missed you." He patted his chest. "There's a hollow spot where my heart once was. I wish I could erase that night from my memory. I can't believe I said and did those terrible things to you."

He raised her to stand near him. Drawing her close, he muttered in her ear. "You have no idea how hurting you hurt me." He kissed her cheek and whispered in her ear. "You are my only love; I could never love another like I love you. Show me, my sweet, that you love me. Take the mark; I will take it with you."

The thought of taking that beast's mark sent stabs like an icy knife blade through her heart. She shuddered. Meeting Rex's mesmerizing eyes, she felt she was looking into a snake's trance. "You have not taken it?"

His lips parted over perfect white teeth into a captivating smile. "I've been waiting—for you, love."

"Really? That's hard to believe—that you could become captain of the Antichrist's WOP without taking the six-six-six mark."

Rex's arm shook ever so slightly. "I will do it all over again, with you."

"You are as much as a liar as the one you serve. Jesus Christ is my Lord and Savior."

"Then you must forgive me. If you don't forgive those who trespass against you, He won't forgive you your trespasses."

"I do forgive you."

"Then prove it by marrying me and taking the mark."

She struggled in his grasp. "No! Never! Let go of me!" His arms held her firmly.

"You haven't forgiven me. You can always ask God's forgiveness. This way, you'll prove you have forgiven me, and your God promises to forgive you seven times seventy."

"It is written, 'to him who knows to do good and does not do it, to him it is sin.'"

A slinky smile covered his distress. "My god killed your Jewish prophet on the cross!"

"My God designed a plan to help His creation after your god, the devil, attempted to have us banished from our Creator, the one true God! 'He shall bruise your head, and you shall bruise His heel.... For as in Adam all died, even so in Christ all shall be made alive.'"

"Don't say that name!" He blocked his ears for a moment, then lowered his hands. "My god sent fire down from heaven, and he made a statue speak."

"Apostle John warned of this very thing over a thousand years before in Revelation. He wrote to the Christians all about the false prophet and Antichrist who would show great signs to deceive, if possible, the elect."

An animal growl erupted deep in Rex's throat. His mouth moved, but he couldn't speak. When he did, it was with a different voice, not his own. "You were mine before you were His. I can give you fine foods, silks, and jewels. Worship me."

"I am a child of the Most High God, and His Son, Jesus, redeemed me through the blood He shed on the cross of Calvary."

His face turned fiery red; his eyes burned into hers. "Don't say that name around me. Ever! Do you hear me? My government forbids this. It is written, 'Render unto Caesar what is Caesar's…therefore to all their due…customs to whom customs, fear to whom fear, honor to whom honor."

"It is also written, 'We ought to obey God rather than men. The God of our fathers raised up Jesus—'"

He thrust her away "You're no better than me." His steps echoed in her ears, beating a war drum. "I will marry you, and you will receive the same—"

"Aaaah!" Her eyes spotted the mark on his hand, the number of the devil 666. It glowed in the light of candelabras on the tables and the sconces blinking on the walls.

"Do you have any idea what awaits you, rejecting me?"

"I have found peace, and I gladly lay down my life for Jesus as He did for me so many years before."

"So, my little coward, you no longer want to run away?"

"I have found a cause to believe in, a reason for why I was born, and someone who loves me for who I am—"

"A pretty speech, my dear. Bravo!" His fingers wrapped her wrist in a crushing grasp. "I would applaud your decision, but as you can see, my hands are busy. Let's see if I can change your mind."

In her billowing ball gown, she stumbled to keep up with him as he dragged her across the room, down a flight of wooden stairs, and then stone stairways. She smelled the odor that had assaulted her nostrils earlier.

Down, down, down they went. The darkness engulfed her. The smell was suffocating and wreaked of filth, debris, and mold.

Rex fished in his pocket for a key. The door creaked open. He lit a match to the kerosene lamp sitting on a shelf, and she stepped in.

"Ruth!" Martha ran forward.

Josh Jr. clutched her gown. "I'm scared. I want to go home."

"Count me in, too," Johansson said.

"Me too," Heydenreich added.

# Twenty-eight

*"All who dwell on the earth will worship him, whose names have not been written in the Book of Life of the Lamb slain from the foundation of the world. If anyone has an ear, let him hear. He who leads into captivity shall go into captivity; he who kills with the sword must be killed with the sword. Here is the patience and the faith of the saints." Revelations 13:8–10*

"Tell me again." Joshua snatched a breath, attempting to calm his pent-up emotions.

"It happened so fast. I…don't know if I can remember." The proprietor glanced at Joshua's fists. "Ruth Jessup pushed Mr. Brinkman out the window. Mr. Rollins said so."

"I want to know what you saw. Who came running down the stairs from Brinkman's room? Ruth or Rex Rollins?" Joshua tightened his hands into stronger chokehold on him, then realized his temper was overcoming his judgment and released him. "I'm sorry."

The proprietor rubbed his neck. "That's better. It was Mr. Rollins that went upstairs. Then I heard the window break, and here he comes skipping steps in his hurry to run out the door. But he hauled your lady friend away all the same, and the WOP didn't argue with him."

"Which way did Rollins take her?"

"Toward Pigeon." A man of medium build with a full-grown beard stepped forward.

"Tobie James is my name." He pointed a shaking finger down the road in the direction Rollins had gone. Then he looked around, his eyes jackrabbiting about the room. "Follow me."

This guy was nervous as a man who poached a dozen eggs. Joshua followed James as he zigzagged through the city's back alleys to a house and down the stairs into a basement-like room.

"We can talk here." James sat down in a straight-back chair and mopped his brow. "The super-soldiers killed two women before you got here. They have the people scared out of their wits." Puffing out in broken English, he continued. "Your mother and son, they were taken, too. That woman, Ruth, I don't think she knows that."

*God, lead me to them.* Could they be at the old cathedral—that's what the locals called it—renovated to house retired bishops? No, it couldn't be there. Not the Gilead House. Didn't he hear about a lightning fire burning it to the ground? Then where? "Thanks. Oh, I need a horse. My friends dropped me off here. Do you have one I can buy or rent?"

"Come to think of it, I have a beaut." James led the way to his barn.

"Hosanna!" Joshua couldn't believe it.

Hearing her name, Hosanna looked up from munching on her hay, pricking her ears forward.

He felt her soft muzzle nudge his arm. That first day he and Ruth met. He knew then. This horse was different. Had grit, she did. The thought encouraged him. "How did you happen to come across Hosanna? I know the lady who owns her. So, who did you purchase her from?"

"At an auction. You wouldn't have recognized her. She was thin and ill-kept. I think they hired her out."

"You'll soon be home, girl." Joshua felt encouraged. God was looking after them. "How much do you want for her?"

"I'll take some flour and potatoes—any meat you can spare. That should cover the feed I put in her to get her back to health. Oh, if you can throw in a couple of laying hens, I'd be grateful. My family is down to their last potato."

"Sure. You'll have that, and I'll throw in some venison." Joshua was about to leave—

"Wait!" James walked forward. "Johansson and Heydenreich took off like madmen after the men who abducted your family. That's all I can tell you." His hand was shaking as he shook Joshua's.

He patted him on the shoulder. "Jesus is coming soon."

James wiped his brow. Something was bothering him. "Most of us ran when the headhunters started swinging their ax. We didn't even try to fight them off. That's the hardest part. Knowing you let your neighbors down and you ran like scared mice. Huddling underground, anywhere, to get away from the truth about yourself."

James inhaled a shuddering breath, hand swabbing his dirty cheeks. "If you had looked closer, you'd see that the proprietor of the general store took the mark. I know I'm a doomed man, but I can't live with what I've done."

"Keep your faith anchored on God, James." Joshua shoved his hands deep into his pockets. His fingers landed on something. The New Testament he had found in the burned-out remains of a fire pit. "Here, the cover's a little burned at the edges, but the pages are okay." He handed it to him.

"It's a Gideon pocket Bible."

"Look up Ephesians 6 and take up the armor of God." Joshua squeezed his shoulder. "You'll find what you need to be in God's army. You can do this."

"Remember, this is not our home. Jesus will come and set our home up soon! Keep on fighting the good fight of faith." Joshua turned to leave, then paused. "Oh, and that smoke smell on that Bible is to remind you of the fire the devil and his demons will be thrown into when Jesus returns."

---

"I've missed you, my little coward," Rex said.

"You missed me? The feeling is not mutual." Ruth eyed the front door that opened to the beautiful outdoors—to her freedom from this nightmare. "If you love me like you said you do, you'd release my friends. Then maybe—" She snuggled up to him, gritting her teeth in distaste as she kissed him on the cheek.

"Really?" His cold eyes stared into hers. "Prove you love me first. Become like me."

Her heart skipped a beat. Not happening.

"Take the mark."

A knock on the door broke Rex's concentration. Had he hoped to mesmerize her into agreeing to taking the devil's brand?

Grabbing her arm, he walked toward the massive wooden front door that crested in a half-moon shape at its crown. It depicted the fourteen-foot medieval castle of yore, as did the rest of the house. Now all Rex needed to finish his diabolical reign was a drawbridge and some charging knights. He already had his dungeon.

The heavy clasp screamed open, and Rex peered out, then smiled. He swung the door wide. "About time. What took you so long?"

"Those are some stubborn people living in that obscure little Owenson. We killed two. One woman fought me. Look what she did." The newcomer pointed to his arm, which bore two huge teeth marks. "I could get rabies from a bite like that."

"What happened then?"

The man shrugged. "The rest scattered like a bunch of chickens on roasting day."

"What? How many took the mark?"

A man with massive arms shrugged.

"No! No!" Rex stamped his booted foot so hard the lamp on the adjacent table jumped. "Tell me you took care of that—little matter?"

"Sure, boss." He looked down at his cellphone. After reading the text, he glanced up and nodded. "They've located him, and as we speak, that, uh, that little matter—consider it completed."

Rex confidently washed his eyes over Ruth's frame. "I've got the one that can sway those obstinate Christians into believing in our king and One World Order, don't I, Ruthie?"

"I will not receive the mark, nor marry you, Rex."

## LOVE'S FINAL SUNRISE

His laughter grew fiendish. The men joined him. His face closed in on her, his snake-eyes growing more liquid as his tongue whipped out from beneath his thin lips, licking her cheek. "We'll see, my bride. We'll see." He pulled her along. His nails dug in the soft flesh of her wrist as he dragged her up the two flights of a circular stairway, past the room she'd changed her clothes in, and toward another flight of stairs. He kicked open a door. The attic beams poked upwards, and the small window overlooking the front drive had wrought-iron scrollwork that weaved a patchwork of birds of prey.

A woman with black hair, black lipstick and long, pointed fingernails looked at Ruth curiously.

"Of course, black fingernail polish." Ruth turned. She would not allow Rex the thrill of seeing her cringe. "What is this, a horror flick?"

"Enough with your smart tongue, or I'll cut it off. Might be to my advantage, then I won't have to listen to you telling me about that Jesus freak." He shoved her, and she landed on the four-poster bed. The rough skin of her fingers snagged in the black webbing of a headdress.

"Get that wedding gown on her and be quick about it. I've lost my patience with her." His boots resounded across the wooden floor like a medicine man's death rattle. Grabbing her from the bed, he yanked her to him and growled deep in his throat. "I want what's rightfully mine." His fingers wrapped around her throat like a snake's body. She felt his wet tongue in her mouth, nearly choking her. He drew back, and she spat at him.

The woman cackled like the old banty hen on Joshua's farm.

"Joshua."

Rex turned. "He's dead. There is no one to save you now. Get over him."

"Never! And I'll never give alliance to your false god over my true God and Jesus Christ, His Son!"

"I told you not to say that word." His cold, clammy fingers held her chin. "Understand this—in a little while, you won't have a tongue in your head to worship Him with."

"Then I'll worship Jesus with my thoughts."

Joshua checked out the places he knew in Pigeon. Nothing. He got off his horse and knelt, clasping his hands. "Lord, please help me find Ruth, my mother, and son. Lead me to them, Lord."

"There he is, grab him!"

Joshua swung himself onto Hosanna and urged her into a run. "So much for kneeling in prayer, Hosanna." Weaving through the birch and pines might lose them; it was his only chance to outrun the Antichrist's WOP. The miles clicked by. His horse lathered from running. He and Hosanna needed rest, food, and drink, but where? As it was, he'd hide among the shadows of the pines and maples like a hunted coyote for hours.

There, that farmhouse, was it Amish or English? His horse nickered, stumbling through the underbrush. "Poor girl, you're exhausted." He'd have to chance it. Hosanna needed tending.

He quietly entered the barn and rubbed her down. Careful not to give her too much water. The hay smelled good. Hosanna thought so too. "Wish I could join you." His stomach rumbled. The barn door creaked open.

"Who are you?" demanded a man sporting coveralls, a beard, and an Amish hat.

Was he Amish? No way of knowing. Many Englishers liked to dress like them, as did many deceived Christians, and went over to worshiping this false god.

"Sir, a wanderer seeking rest."

"I don't need any trouble with the WOP. Heard they got those zombies with them now, those European biological super-soldiers."

The noise from outside filtered through the wooden walls. "Spread out, men! He must be in here."

# Twenty-nine

*"Here is the patience of the saints; here are those who keep the commandments of God and the faith of Jesus. Then I heard a voice from heaven saying to me, 'Write: "Blessed are the dead who die in the Lord from now on."' 'Yes,' says the Spirit, 'that they may rest from their labors, and their works follow them." Revelations 14:12–13*

The black webbing of Ruth's veil pricked her work-worn fingers. "I'm wedding the devil's advocate on Sunday. How sick is that?"

Her long blackbird-colored gown glistened like a vulture's beak in the candelabras lining the stairway. The organ played the low keys of some dismal sonnet she had never heard of before, but it reminded her of the funeral for a devil worshiper she once attended.

"Lord," she whispered, "is there no way to escape this nightmare?"

*Be strong in the Lord and the power of His might.*

God wants me dressed in the armor of God. Yes! My waist with truth, the breastplate of righteous... the shield of faith so I can quench all the fiery darts of my soon-to-be husband. She covered her face with her hands.

She clutched to her bosom the dried-out flowers that comprised her bouquet. The shriveled petals left their remnants on her dress.

"I am reaping what I have sown." The lies she had told, the men, the booze, the drugs, all of it had caught up with her. God, forgive me of it all. Even the things I would not admit to Joshua and You.

The tall, wooden front doors swung open to reveal a torch-lined walkway leading to an altar. Below her stood Martha, Johansson, Heydenreich, and her precious Josh Jr. The men were dressed in black robes; their hoods cloaked most of their faces. Martha had on a black dress with a matching bonnet that hid her eyes. *My dream. I'm living my dream!*

Josh Jr. clutched the folds of Martha's dress and buried his head. *Lord, give me strength.*

The altar was draped in black satin. On a backdrop of red roses and baby's breath draped an upside-down crucifix. She wanted to run—Martha's look stopped her. She glanced at Josh Jr. Martha was trying to tell her something. She tilted her head slightly, not wanting to alert Rex.

Off to the side was a sawed-off stump. A large man, his head covered in a black mask, watched her, one hand fastened around an ax. Was Rex planning to begin their reception with head-cutting entertainment? She cringed.

---

That was a narrow escape. "Gabriel, my man, where to now?" Joshua looked over at the seven-foot hunk of a man and waited. "You've got a knack for showing up at the right time. Say, you have any idea where I should look to find Ruth?"

"You must do this on your own. Remember, God looks on the inside of man, not the outward appearance. What at first glance seems to be true—is often not."

Joshua pondered this. Gabriel was not allowing his emotions to giveaway what he knew.

"The devil and his advocates like to mimic God. But they always do the opposite. For instance, God is all about forgiveness. Satan is all about revenge and hate. Jesus will come from the east, so I'd look west. For the darkest-looking building you can find etching a black gothic mark upon God's heavens."

"The Gilead House. Then it didn't burn down?"

# LOVE'S FINAL SUNRISE

"No. It's there."

"Hosea 6:8, of course! 'Gilead *is* a city of evildoers *And* defiled with blood.' That sounds like the right place for Rex to take up residence."

Joshua headed Hosanna down the broad path leading to the century-old house that was once used as a cathedral, then became a retired bishop's home and later used by the devil worshipper, Gilead. His horse's hooves pounded the turf as his heart pounded the space between his ribs and flesh.

The place had a reputation for animal sacrifices and plain weirdness. It drew the teens like a magnet. Now, where was that deer path he traversed as an Amish youth to get a closer look at the castle-like structure? There it was!

The path was covered with thorny vines and saplings sprouting from the rich dirt dotting the trail. He bent low in the saddle and plowed through the maze of underbrush. After dismounting, he tied Hosanna.

Torches belched black smoke toward the setting sunlight, distorting the tranquil sapphire of the night skies. Looks like some sort of ceremony is going on. He crept closer.

---

Ruth paced her steps to the music. When she reached the altar, Rex offered her his arm and stepped beside her. "I've waited impatiently for this moment."

His glance flickered to the right of the altar where a fire burned. A man dressed in a black suit held a branding iron in his left hand. The numbers six, six, six glowed red in the dim light. It was apparent what Rex intended to do.

"Rex, I cannot continue this charade. I'm sorry you feel such strong affection for me."

The corner of his lip snarled upwards. "Don't tell me you love that Amish man. He's dead. Would you like me to produce his head to prove it to you?"

Her knees shook with fear and foreboding. Joshua's dead. She willed herself not to cry. "Let my friends go, Rex."

Rex's hands went to her neck and brought her face closer. His lips swept hers. His hands slowly worked their way down her bare shoulders. "Give me a moment of what we once enjoyed. No matter your decision, I will allow your friends to go free."

Is he telling me the truth? One way to find out. She stepped into his embrace. He smelled like dead fish. His lips were as slimy as a snake. She shuddered. Still, she willed herself to kiss him deeply.

"Hmmm." Their lips separated, and he smiled. "I doubt your Amish farmer made you feel anything like this. So, your decision is for me?"

She paused and stepped away. Now the truth. Would he release her friends? "Rex, I have given you a chance. My old life and my old desires are replaced with God's will and God's desires. Will you honor your promise and let my friends go?"

His sweet-honey voice plunged three octaves to low, dark, and threatening. "What a beautiful speech, my dear. From you of all people who have your own child's blood and your grandmother's—"

"Aaaah! I remember. You killed my grandmother." Rex's confession nearly three-and-a-half years before came in waves upon waves, flooding her thoughts.

"Ha, ha."

*Forgive!*

"Sure you want to be a Christian, my little coward?"

"God forgave me for not obeying His Ten Commandments. Jesus washed me clean from my sins. Yes, I forgive you, Rex."

"Stop it! Stop it!" Rex spun her around. "Your God is weak, whereas mine is strong. I'll show you what happens to those who refuse to receive my king's commands."

He dragged her to stand in front of Johansson, Heydenreich, Martha, and Josh Jr.

"Johansson and Heydenreich, have you made up your minds? Are you going to be wise like Ruthie and accept my king of the universe? Pledge allegiance and take his mark. The king of the universe and our New World Order will open its doors to you."

"Ruth, tell me you didn't?" Johansson said.

She shook her head. "Of course, I—"

"Shut up!" Rex hissed.

"Never," Johansson spat out. "Jesus will return to set up His kingdom on Earth and put your god into the great lake of fire!"

"Your days are numbered," Heydenreich said.

Rex's face turned dark and threatening. "Take them to the chopping block."

Ruth fell at Rex's feet. "No, no, please."

Rex laid his hand on her head. "There, there, my love. Johansson and Heydenreich had their chance to repent."

She sobbed, glancing up at Martha and Josh Jr. The boy hid his face in Martha's skirts.

Rex placed one knee down beside her and pulled her head up so she had to watch Johansson's beheading. The swipe of the ax sliced through her heart. She thought she would faint from the sight. Then she felt it—a knife cleverly concealed in Rex's boot top.

Rex turned to watch Heydenreich kneel.

She held onto his leg. Lowering her head, she reached for the knife while clutching his leg as if for support. Rex bent over. "This a lovely wedding gift for me, dear. I love blood."

"I can't believe I'm hearing this," Martha said.

"With your own ears." Rex poked his angry face into Martha's. "Remember it." Rex turned to watch the beheading and tripped over Ruth's arm.

She hurried for the knife, briefly fumbling it, then concealing it within the pocket of her dress. The ax swept down.

Rex laughed.

"Ruthie, I have something special planned for our reception. But first, you get to watch your friends Martha and that sweet little boy over there beheaded."

The motion of a man running across the yard appeared in her peripheral vision. Joshua? She turned Rex's way. "Why do you want to do this?"

Joshua attacked the axman and lunged toward another guard. Then someone shouted.

Rex sprang into action. "Get him! I want him alive!"

"Dat!" Josh Jr. ran toward his father as fast as his little legs could go. Straight toward the armed guards.

"No!" Joshua, who had bolted into the woods, ran back, stretching his arms toward his son.

"God, help me." Ruth ran forward, but Rex pulled her into his embrace.

"There, there, my beautiful wife-to-be."

Ruth sobbed and looked up, right into Joshua's glance.

"How could you?" Joshua's face, red with anger, spat out the words as he fought against the three guards who held him.

She cringed. *Oh, God, even if they did manage to get out of this alive, he would never trust her, let alone love her again.* She glanced at Martha and hung her head. She, too, thought the worst of Ruth, that she was ready to denounce the true God for this false impersonator.

"I thought you changed. You let God, Jesus Christ, and His Holy Spirit down. You even let—" Joshua gazed down at a trail of bloody scenes, the dried leaves. "Johansson and Heydenreich get killed!"

"You don't know me." Ruth hung her head. *They believed her ruse.*

"You're twice the sinner you were," Joshua yelled. "You had a choice, and you choose the easy way. This man as your groom, and you've accepted his false god."

Rex laughed wickedly. "You have met the true Ruthie. We are a pair of bookends and belong together."

"As we belong together." Martha joined her son and grandson. Her eyes sent piecing shockwaves through Ruth. "My sin was to lie for you."

Ruth had one hope for Joshua and his family. One thin thread of hope. She stood on her tippy toes and kissed Rex on his cheek. Just the way he liked it. "Rex, dear, let these crybabies go so we can enjoy our wedding feast. We've spent enough time on them." She circled her arms around his waist. She prayed Rex would not notice the bulge of the knife she'd hidden in the pocket of her wedding dress. She placed her lips in her most becoming pout. "Please, my husband-to-be, tell your WOP guards to unhand Joshua and his crybaby family."

"Ah! My Ruthie has come back to me. If that would make you happy." Checking to see that Joshua was already bound, he said, "Leave us, men. Go and enjoy the good eats—drink yourselves into drunkenness, you deserve it for a job well done!"

Rex gave her a lingering kiss. Ruth felt his exotic ecstasy, his lust and desire for her as he kissed her. She could also feel the tension of his lips. What was he up to now?

"Go into the house, to our bedroom chambers, and I will join you momentarily."

"No. Come now."

Rex had not removed his eyes from Joshua. She stealthily pulled the knife from her pocket.

"I have some business needing attention." His evil eyes laughed into hers. "I shall have the best wedding present I could ever imagine." He touched her cheek. "Someday, you shall thank me for this."

She circled her left arm around his waist, the knife in her right hand. "I desire you—now."

"I desire more than you, my dear. I want—the heads of this family that have caused me untold distress. Remember, my love. I never forget a wrong done against me. Revenge is my sweet nectar. What my body gets nourishment from."

"Oh, my love, kiss me before my passion wears thin."

Bending forward, as their lips united, she sunk the knife deep into his heart.

"Mmm!" He tried to disengage their lips. His hand pushed her away. She put her foot behind his and pushed him backward. They fell together in a heap.

The guards turned and smiled. They must have thought she and Rex frolicked in lovemaking among the browned leaves and feathers of grass poking through.

Joshua struggled against his bindings.

"Come on, men, you heard our general, let's eat."

The WOP soldiers walked toward the table laden with liquor and food.

She removed the knife from Rex's chest and tossed it toward Joshua. Josh Jr. smiled at her, running over and retrieving it.

"Give it to Daddy—Run!" she whispered. "Don't stop running until you get home."

---

Joshua hesitated. Had it all been a play-act? He took a step toward Ruth. Martha stopped him. "Son, komm!"

He hung his head, uncertain, feeling the handle of the bloodied knife. Still, he had to get his family out of here. Joshua glanced back, from the safety of the woods. She was lying over Rollins—kissing him? But the bloodied knife? He glanced at the guards; seconds were ticking away. Little time left him to rescue his family.

He hoisted up Josh Jr. and ran with Martha fast upon his heels toward his horse. Hosanna nickered low. He handed Josh Jr. to Martha long enough to jump into the saddle. Martha handed Josh Jr. back, then he gave her his arm.

"Can your horse ride us all?"

"She will have to. Here, put your foot on my boot, and I'll hoist you up behind me."

All that filled his ears was the galloping gait of Hosanna as they sped through the forests and meadows with only the moon's rays and stars to guide them. Had Ruth meant what she said? Or had it been a ploy to get him and his family to safety? Whose blood was on that knife? That kiss she gave Rex was real enough. Still, Gabriel had warned him to look to the inside, to the heart, and not outward appearances.

A band of men overtook them. "Hold up!"

God, don't let it be the WOP. Josh Jr. had fallen asleep over an hour ago. His soft angelic face lifted in a half-moon smile. Suddenly, he was wide-awake. "Mommy said for us to run."

"What?"

The man saluted. Detective Ricker rode up. "Were you successful in finding the headquarters of the WOP ring in this area?"

Joshua nodded, hugging his son to him. Then Ruth had devised a ploy to get him and his family to safety. "I can show you the way. But my family needs to get safely home."

"Pete?" Detective Ricker said to one of his Patriots. "Can you see them home?"

"Yes, sir!"

"Does anyone here have a spare horse?" Ricker said.

Joshua placed Josh Jr. into Martha's arms. He kissed his son's forehead gently, recalling how closely they came to being beheaded. Then waving his mother and son goodbye, he headed Hosanna west.

"Follow him, men, and be quiet. We don't want to alert any WOP as to our whereabouts," Ricker ordered.

They followed the trail Joshua vacated and came into the clearing. It had to be about two a.m. Poor Johansson's and Heydenreich's bodies remained where they fell. Torch flames lit the black sky with an indescribable eeriness and smell. Something was burning on their altar.

Joshua and the Patriots crept closer. Black-hooded men with torches and swords marched around the altar in a sort of ritual. A figure lay prostrate—Rex Rollins.

"He's dead?" Joshua could not wrap his head around this. "Ruth killed him—Where's Ruth?"

He looked toward the old gothic mansion, trying to remember the years before when, as a teen, he and his Amish friends roamed these woods and the outbuilding of the mansion's fortress. The basement—it was more like a dungeon, with its dirt floors and chains bolted into the stone walls. "Follow me, men."

Glancing back at the stump doused with the blood of martyrs, he wondered if he led these brave patriots to sure death.

The musty smell of mold, mice, and mud met his nostrils. He could hear some of the WOP upstairs, arguing. Probably about who would be their next leader.

The drip, drip of water met his ears. He waited, hoping his eyes would accustom themselves to the blackness of the room. "Listen."

Someone wept—another voice. A muffled voice answered. Joshua rushed toward the sound.

A single candle illuminated the dungeon-like room that housed two children, a woman, and a man. Evidently a family. He put a hand to his lips and whispered, "Don't worry, we came to free you."

"Praise our good Lord." The woman clutched his sleeve. "Take care of that poor girl in the next cell. They did some awful things to her, trying to get her to tell her friend's whereabouts."

"Beat her until she fainted," the man said.

"Ruth!" Joshua was beside himself. Draped in her black gown, she stood spread eagle. Her hands and legs locked in iron cuffs to a chain on either side embedded in the stone wall. The back of her dress had been ripped open, disclosing whip marks.

"Ruth? Ruth? It's Joshua."

She looked up. "Joshua? Forgive me." Her head fell forward.

# Thirty

*"He who overcomes shall inherit all things, and I will be his God and he shall be My son. But the cowardly, unbelieving, abominable, murderers, sexually immoral, sorcerers, idolaters, and all liars shall have their part in the lake which burns with fire and brimstone, which is the second death." Revelation 21:7–8*

Joshua held Ruth close. His family safe as they could be at home during the last days of the Antichrist's reign. His eyes swallowed her hole with his desire.

"Joshua, I was afraid I'd never see you again. That you would never know—"

"There's been enough talk." He took her into his arms. Strong, unyielding to anything but the truth of God's Word. The bindings of his coat pressed against the folds of her dress. His beard tickled her mouth. Lingering for a breathless moment, his lips leisurely sent their message of fidelity, unity, and finality to her thirsty soul. Yes, kindred souls, united in the bondage of battle and the endless ecstasy of truth. No one in her past life had ever kissed her thus. She swirled in the pleasure as his lips traveled to her chin, then her neck as if eternity had arrived miraculously, and she was spinning around in the ecstasy of his love.

Joshua smiled.

She rested her hands on his heart.

"What are we waiting for now? Marry me."

"Yes, Joshua. But first I need to tell you all the truth about me."

Grabbing a shuddering breath, she whispered, "I was raped when a teen, and I aborted my baby. I killed an innocent child." She sobbed, her tears wetting his shirt. He stroked her hair.

"Gut. Everything is confessed. I understand why you hesitated to tell me. God forgives you as He forgave me and the people I killed." His lips swept hers, then he looked deeply into her eyes. "I understand why it took so long for you to confess. I, too, deserve condemnation, but because of God's grace, I have absolution. I don't deserve to be happy—but I embrace this, as I do God's infinite love! He paid the price for us and offered Himself up for such a sin as ours. And now, the moment I have longed for—has arrived!"

---

Ruth looked down at her lace and satin wedding gown, admiring how it gleamed in the sunlight. The bishop had waved the requirements for wearing blue, but he was happy the wedding fell on a Tuesday, when all good Amish people got married. And to the bishop's calculations, Jesus could return in six days—but he was happy to wait if God decided to delay his arrival.

"Could there be a more perfect day for a wedding?" Martha said.

Harriet squirmed with pride. "I don't believe I looked half as pretty as Ruth when I wore that dress. Oh, this is so wonderful!"

Jane giggled and whispered to Ruth. "You really made Mom happy wearing her dress."

"It is gut to see her so happy." Ruth hugged Jane and noticed Paul was in deep conversation with Joshua. It was unimaginable to her that through all those trying years of adolescence, the Scripture verses Gran taught her found ground to grow in.

As the wedding march echoed through the doorstep, Jane, her maid of honor, stepped through the doorway, then through the trellis of roses and down the aisle to their friends awaiting them.

"Well, daughter, ready?"

"Yes!" She took her father's arm and walked through the doorway to her new life, smelling the sweet perfume of the roses arching above her head. She felt she had wings on her feet walking down the white ribbon of fabric toward her betrothed.

Joshua stood tall and looked so handsome in his Amish clothes.

Solemn-faced Josh Jr. cupped his little hands about the tiny pillow as he carried their rings importantly toward the altar.

"A threefold cord is not quickly broken. Pledge ye this day to let God be your guide through this ordained union you, as free wills, enter into this union of matrimony. Joshua, will you take Ruth Jessup as your lawfully wedded wife?"

Joshua's eyes spoke the words before he uttered them. "Yes, I do, with all my heart. And may our Savior Christ Jesus be with us throughout our lives."

"Ruth Jessup, do you take Joshua Stutzman as your lawfully wedded husband?"

Tears welled into her eyes and, looking into his, she said, "Yes from this day forward and throughout eternity."

"I pronounce you husband and wife."

He swept her into his warm embrace. His lips blended with hers, tipping her like a string to his bow.

"Oh, this is so beautiful," Martha said, clutching her tissue in one hand as her fingers wrapped around Josh Jr.'s with the other. Josh's free hand reached toward Ruth. His eyes gleamed with love. "You are my true mamm now."

"Did you hear that?" Mrs. Jessup said. Bending down, she kissed him on his forehead. "And I'm your new Granny."

A modest supper with close friends followed. Wonderful, except for the guard posted outside their farmhouse door and the one up the road to alert the group if the WOP was coming.

Ruth chewed her food thoughtfully. This moment was theirs to share with her family and friends. Sunlight washed their forms as happy children played together in the green grass. So different from the dungeon pits.

In a brief interlude, Ruth whispered to Joshua. "Jesus heard my prayers. I wondered how God could rescue me from myself."

The day wove into evening, with a glorious sunset illuminating the western sky. Joshua's eyes melted into hers. He stood, offering her his hand. Shyly, she joined hers with his.

Lifting her into his strong arms, he carried her down the stone steps toward the *dawdi haus* prepared for them. The wind brushed Ruth's cheek. Joshua's booted feet crushed the gravel beneath his steps. He smiled down at her, his eyes like the stars gleaming in the velvety night.

The train of her stepmother's wedding gown whisked tiny dust clouds behind Joshua's eager steps. Shyness overtook her. The door to the *dawdi haus*, no contest to Joshua's intent, swung open to reveal a soft fire in the hearth, a sitting room with a love seat, a rocking chair, and Joshua's man chair.

The focal point of the room, the four-poster bed with the lace canopy. That had to be my stepmother's idea. Ruth smiled. She had always wanted one when she was growing up. Stepmother told her someday she would get her one. Someday had arrived.

Gently, Joshua laid her on the bed done up in a pink and blue wedding quilt that Martha made. The large window adjacent to the bed was open, and the night wind blew a tentacle of hair across her forehead. Joshua's fingers, feather-light, stroked her. He kissed the spot where one of her tendrils lay.

Her gran told her that God wanted every woman to keep the marriage bed sacred. To wait until the union between a man and woman was blessed by God.

God heard her prayers. He made this experience new. He made the moment memorable, beyond belief.

Joshua stood. His eyes fixed on her as his thumbs flipped open the buttons on his shirt. Reaching down, he unlaced his shoes and then slipped out of his socks. His body glowing in the moonlight.

A patchwork of dreams melted together. She had taken many wrong turns throughout her life. How had she ended up here, safe and loved? *Yes, we are God's workmanship, created in Christ Jesus for good works, which God prepared beforehand that we should walk in.*

## LOVE'S FINAL SUNRISE

She rose from the bed, her eyes beseeching. "Joshua."

Their minds were on the same path. "It will not be long now, my love. 'And the Spirit and the bride say, "come!" And let him who thirsts come. Whoever desires, let him take the water of life freely.'"

Her heart sang a new tune. Kindred spirits they were—united in the bonds of matrimony and Christ's redeeming love.

A tug of Joshua's fingers loosened her hair from its combs. Cascades of curls bounced on her shoulders. His fingers weaved through her silky strands. He gently pulled her wedding dress off her shoulders. The silky clouds of fabric floated to the glistening floor.

His belt undone, he stepped out of the last piece of his clothing. She was caught in his arms and the ecstasy of their unity.

Shyness overcame her. She hesitated. Then his arms caught her, sweeping the remainder of her fears away. Night wove on in a tapestry of touch and sonnets of love, made more memorable knowing that it could be their last.

---

"What happened? It's been over 1,290 days! Where is Jesus?"

The booming voices in Joshua's big room echoed against the walls and deafened his retort. Everyone was yelling at once, and no one wanted to hear answers unless it was spiked by the trumpet sound of Jesus' return. He was as disheartened as they. With days turning into weeks and still no sign of the Lord's return, he understood their feelings, but not enough to give up hope.

"Silence!" He banged his hammer on the piece of wood he had placed on his table for such a purpose. Baker waved his arms in the air and tried to get everyone's attention. The people lulled enough for Joshua to speak.

"Remember, no one knows the day or hour, not even the angels in heaven, no not even our Savior, Jesus, just God our Father. I know He gave Daniel a timetable, and I know you all have been counting off the years, months, and days of the 1,290. Well, remember that in Daniel,

God gave himself an additional forty-five-day leeway!"

"But, Joshua," said a man who stood up, wringing his hat. "This is the twenty-seventh day over the 1,290! How much longer? My wife is thinking we have no choice but to take the mark, maybe—"

"No! That's just what the devil, that great deceiver, is hoping for! Now, look; remember the parable of the ten virgins, the five wise and the five foolish? Remember, the bridegroom tarried. Well, so what that our bridegroom is delayed. He's worth waiting for!"

Everyone applauded.

"Joshua's right! Jesus is coming, so let's trim our lamps and wait for him," Baker said.

"Let us all pray and fast, after all, tomorrow's Easter! Don't allow the devil get a toehold into your minds. There could be twenty or so more days we might have to wait for Jesus—then again, He could come tonight! He says to watch, and don't go to bed naked. I really don't care to see your, umm, you know!"

---

"Joshua, I thought you did wonderfully gut today." Ruth hugged his arm as they watched their friends and neighbors leave. "What do you want me to prepare for supper?"

He turned and smiled. "Your gut bread will be fine for me."

"Sounds gut to me." She sighed. "The days have come and gone so fast I hardly had time to cook and clean anyway. I didn't get the clothes on the line today to dry them, what with cleaning the house and cooking something for everyone to eat for your impromptu meeting. I'll probably have to go to sleep in my wedding gown."

"Well, it's white." Joshua laughed. His gleaming eyes met hers. "About all it's good for on a farm is to be used as a nightdress."

"Ja, that's for sure. Only, whatever you do, don't tell Harriet. She's planning for Jane to wear it on her wedding day."

"Hmm, hope Jane plans to get married quick like, 'cause when the Good Lord makes up His mind—He waits for no one!"

# Thirty-one

*"Now I saw heaven opened, and behold, a white horse. And He who sat on him was called Faithful and True, and in righteousness He judges and makes war. His eyes were like a flame of fire, and on His head were many crowns. He had a name written that no one knew except Himself. He was clothed with a robe dipped in blood, and His name is called The Word of God. And the armies of heaven, clothed in fine linen, white and clean, followed Him on white horses." Revelations 19:11–14*

The rumbling awoke Ruth. Their marital bed shook beneath their bodies, vibrating out of control. "Is it an earthquake?"

The night's blackness met their curious gazes. An eclipse covered the moon, a shroud of foreboding. She couldn't see her hand before her face. How terrible hell must be.

"We need to get dressed." Joshua fumbled for their clothing.

Ruth had only her wedding dress from the day before to wear.

"Look, a shooting star," Joshua yelled.

"Oh my. Not just one. Look. The stars are falling!"

Joshua wrapped his arms around her. "It will not be long now, my love. Jesus is coming. Let us go outside to greet Him."

The wind picked up and blew her long hair and wedding gown as they faced the eastern sky with anticipation.

"I knew the time was short for Christ's return," Joshua said.

Ruth nodded. "As in the days before the flood, they were eating and drinking, marrying and giving in marriage, until the day that Noah entered the ark, and did not know until the flood came and took them all away."

"Do you see that?" Joshua pointed toward the eastern sky.

"Why it looks like—"

A trumpet rumbled the sky.

"Look! On that white cloud—it must be Jesus! I can see a golden crown on his head and a sharp sickle in his hand!"

Ruth was airborne. Joshua was next to her. She reached out, and Joshua clasped her hand into his. Josh Jr. and Martha joined them.

An angel came and thrust his sickle into the earth, and blood came out of the winepress, up to the horses' bridles.

Gabriel said, "Watch, here come the seven last plagues, only then will the wrath of God be complete." Everyone stood on a sea of glass. There was her mother and grandmother, and they were singing as it was written in Revelation 15:3. Joshua and Ruth joined them. "Great and marvelous are Your works, Lord God Almighty!"

They watched as loathsome sores came on the people who had the mark of the beast and worshiped his image. Then the waters were turned to blood. The men were scorched with the sun's fire. They gnawed their tongues because the pain was so intense! Then great hail from heaven fell. They blasphemed God with every hailstone that fell upon them!

A voice that came from nowhere but consumed them quoted Revelation 19:7-8, "Let us be glad and rejoice and give Him glory, for the marriage of the Lamb has come, and His wife has made herself ready. And to her it was granted to be arrayed in fine linen, clean and bright for the fine linen is the righteous acts of the saints."

Instantly, their clothes transformed into glowing linen.

Gabriel smiled at them. "Here's Hosanna! Mount up, Ruth. You, too, Joshua. Here are your horses, Martha and Josh Jr. We're in the Lord's army now and will be part of this last battle against evil!"

Hosanna neighed shrilly. Ruth hugged her neck. "Oh, praise Jesus. Hosanna, you're white and radiant!"

"It's time to show that Antichrist, Satan, and his demons, and all who took the mark, that Jesus Christ is no mealy-mouthed King. Yes, the wrath of God is great. Here come the seven angels with the seven bowls of judgments, the seven last plagues, for in them the wrath of God is complete. For they have shed the blood of saints and prophets, and Jesus will give them blood to drink for it is their just due."

"Really?" Ruth fingered the folds of her sparkling white linen gown. "That doesn't sound much like the forgiving Savior I grew up learning about."

Gabriel patted her arm. "People had their choice, Ruth, which road they chose to tread and whom they wanted to follow. They don't have a choice in the consequences of their decisions."

"Oh my, will God judge us? I read about that in Revelation."

Joshua nodded, then bent low and whispered. "I remember. We are judged according to our works, by the things which are written in the books."

"Oh no." Ruth hung her head.

Gabriel smiled. "Do not fear, Ruth, you and all who accepted through faith His forgiving grace have been redeemed by the shed blood of Jesus Christ. Your sins have been wiped clean and forgiven before the eyes of God. But, yes, your good works will not go unrecognized.

"The great white throne judgment will not happen until after a thousand years of reign while Satan and his followers are chained and bound into the bottomless pit."

Ruth eased into her saddle. A gasp of relief escaped her lips as truth opened her mind. "God knew my tears and pain beforehand."

"The Scriptures say He knows the numbers of the hairs on our head—you can imagine His all-encompassing love—as if you're His *only* daughter." Joshua reached for her hand and squeezed it. "But our Father doesn't want robots. We make our own choices.

"That's what makes you and me different from those who received the mark, our faith in Christ and the forgiveness and righteousness we freely received from Him by turning our backs on sin, following His commandments, and receiving His Holy Spirit to help us resist temptation." He turned. "Gabriel, how come God never forgave the angels who followed Lucifer?"

Gabriel groaned. "Because we angels never had a tempter as you. Those angels freely chose to follow the so-named angel of light, Lucifer, the Antichrist, who wanted to claim God's creation, made in His image—humans.

"Satan devised a plan to claim dominion over mankind, hurting God by conquering His shining achievement, the apple of His eye, you. Satan hated everything God stood for: purity, sinlessness, and unconditional love."

"God loved me when I was a sinner and gave His Son to die for me!" Ruth said.

The wind whipped her hair as lightning slashed through the menacing clouds. Out of the darkness galloped a milk-white stallion, spouting fire from his nostrils, and the Man astride him—was Jesus!

Only it wasn't the compliant Savior she'd seen in pictures. Or the crucified Savior hanging on a wooden cross.

This Jesus had a fire in his eyes, and his mouth was woven in a determined line. She remembered a passage she'd read in Revelation 19: "Now out of His mouth goes a sharp sword, that with it He should strike the nations. And He Himself will rule them with a rod of iron. He Himself treads the winepress of the fierceness and wrath of Almighty God. And He has on *His* robe and on His thigh a name written: KING OF KINGS AND LORD OF LORDS."

The Antichrist and the armies of the earth gathered to make war against Jesus and His army. Ruth felt no fear. She was ready to die for her Lord and Savior. Hosanna trembled with anticipation, and Joshua readied his lance.

They captured the Antichrist and his prophet, and they were cast alive into the lake of fire burning with brimstone. The rest were killed with the sword and the birds were filled with their flesh.

Ruth watched puzzled. "I remember reading about this."

Then a voice spoke. "Then *I saw* the souls of those who had been beheaded for their witness to Jesus and for the word of God, who had not worshiped the beast or its image, and had not received *his* mark on their foreheads or on their hands. And they lived and reigned with Christ for a thousand years."

"That's us!" Joshua said.

Gabriel gave Joshua a high five.

"Who are you anyway? You always seem to be intercepting my passes and—"

"I'm your guardian angel."

"I should have known," Joshua muttered.

"What are you complaining about? I saved you from a few head-hunters, if you recall, so you could attain your bride. Here I thought I'd have it easy, protecting an Amish guy." Gabriel huffed. "Hardly. It wasn't an easy task keeping your body intact the way you enjoyed joining every squabble known to man. You acted like you were the avenging angel and not me!"

"As you know firsthand, I'm no great guy—so why me?"

"God devised a way for you to help Ruth find her way back to Him. Satan and his demons tried to obstruct God's plan by eliminating you before your calling was completed. I was sent to make sure that didn't happen. And just think, we'll be together here for an eternity. Forever and ever."

"I'll amen that." Joshua raised his arm, and Gabriel and Ruth clasped it.

"Amen, Jesus!" Ruth seconded. Then she saw Satan's opposing army, mammoth in size and Rex Rollins was right in front.

Joshua rubbed his hands together. "I've been waiting for this moment! Just think, I'm riding in Christ's army!"

"The beast and the kings of the earth and their armies have gathered together to make war against us!" Gabriel huffed. "As if they had a chance against the Lord of lords and King of kings."

She and Joshua rode side by side. "Look, there's Johansson and Heydenreich. Wow, look at those glows encircling their heads. My, they look so wonderful gut content."

Joshua reached over and squeezed her hand. "Forever and ever! It's love's final sunrise, for there is no need of the sun or moon to shine, the glory of God illuminates, and Jesus is our light!"

"And the nations of those who are saved shall walk in its light," Gabriel repeated where Joshua left off in Revelation.

Ruth looked at Rex, his eyes burning with hate for Jesus, then turned away. "Thank you, Lord, that the wings of an eagle persevered over evil, and only because of Your mercy to us, the USA, the world!"

"Say," Joshua looked over to Ruth and winked. "What's our next mission, Gabriel? You got any idea?"

"Nope, but I'm sure God has a doozy of one waiting for us."

# Author's Note

My objective in writing ***Love's Final Sunrise*** was not to change the views of my readers regarding the end times. What I do hope my readers will glean from ***Love's Final Sunrise*** is an exuberance to spread the good word about Jesus. Tell your loved ones and friends that in order to enjoy the fullness of life, a personal relationship with Christ Jesus is a must as Jesus told Nicodemus in John 3:3 "Most assuredly, I say to you, unless one is born again, he cannot see the kingdom of God." Becoming born again and knowing their name is written in God's Lamb's Book of Life is eternal, which God reaffirms in Revelation 3:5, "He who overcomes shall be clothed in white garments, and I will not blot out his name from the Book of Life; but I will confess his name before My Father and before His angels."

Revelation 13:8 "All who dwell on the earth will worship him, **whose names have not been written** in the Book of Life" (emphasis added).

My main objective in writing *Love's Final Sunrise* is to warn Christ's elect. Many a night, I have awakened with a start to jot down Scripture verses running through my head. Always with the same theme—*warn the elect*. As the prophet Ezekiel became the watchmen for the house of Israel, Christians are the watchmen for America. We have freedoms that other countries do not share. Let your voices be heard. Victory is ours through our Lord and Savior, Jesus Christ.

Through His Holy Spirit, God teaches Christians and Jews how to be victorious. Revelation 14:12 says, "…here *are* those who keep the commandments of God and the faith of Jesus."

God and His Son, Jesus, give protection through His Word. Matthew 24:24 says that "false christs and false prophets will rise and show great signs and wonders *to deceive,* if possible, *even the elect."* (emphasis added).

Over and over, God is protecting us.

"And unless those days were shortened, no flesh would be saved; but for *the elect's sake those days will be shortened"* (Matthew 24:22, emphasis added). Also, His Word states, "Take heed that *you be not deceived"* (Luke 21:8, emphasis added).

"Those who do wickedly against the covenant he shall corrupt with flattery; **but the people who know their God shall be strong, and carry out** *great exploits"* (Daniel 11:32, bold added).

It's as if God and Jesus are standing on the sidelines and cheering for us. Only, with our free will the choice is ours! "And shall God not avenge *His own elect…?* I tell you that He will avenge them speedily. Nevertheless, *when the Son of Man comes will He really find faith on the earth?"* (Luke 18:7-8, emphasis added).

God is God. At the appointed time, we shall learn just what every end-time Scripture in the Bible meant. Until then, sit back and enjoy *Love's Final Sunrise* while learning selected God-inspired verses and enjoy the lifestyle of the Old Order Amish who provide first-hand knowledge on how Christians can live in a volatile society without conforming! God Bless.

I can remember, like some of you might, that our great grandparents as well as our grandparents lived without modern conveniences like cars, electricity, computers, Facebook, and (heaven forbid) our cell phones, as the Amish continue to do.

The Amish build homes, barns, and harvest crops by harnessing their neighbors' aid. They easily barter for life's necessities, while surviving in an off-the-grid environment.

I first met this Amish community while working as a staff writer for the *Michigan Traveler Magazine.* I have since written articles for numerous publications, especially the editorial section of *The Tri-City Times, and LA* (Lapeer Area) *View Newspapers,* regarding the Amish of Michigan.

The Amish, a Protestant religious group developed from the Mennonites, came to America around 1720 to escape severe persecution in the Netherlands, Germany, and Switzerland. Many made their home in Pennsylvania. Presently, the Amish live in communities in twenty-two states throughout America. Nowhere else in the world today do large populations of Amish live but here in the United States, inheriting, as many have, freedom to live and worship as they choose.

In 1987, the first "Old Order" of Amish families moved to Michigan. Their manner of speech, dress, and lives are different from ours, worlds apart, yet remarkably similar to their late 1700s patrons who followed a literal interpretation of the Bible. Progress has stood still here, with no electricity, indoor bathrooms, refrigerators, cars, tractors, and no rubber on their implements' wheels.

I have not lost my relationship with the Amish. We employ an Amish blacksmith for my four Arabian horses. The Amish erected our horse arena, put in our wood floors, and taught my husband and me how they survive and thrive in the twenty-first century without electricity, computers, cell phones, and modern conveniences.

I wrote this beautiful love story as a hands-on approach for enterprising Christians to endure through Satan's lies and life's trials.

I apologize for anyone taking offense with my words. However, I am encouraged as well as enheartened reading Jesus' words in Matthew 11:25 "I thank You, Father, Lord of heaven and earth, that You have hidden these things from *the* wise and prudent and have revealed them to babes." Here are a few handy Amish recipes, compliments of Naomie:

### Mommy's Noodles

One quart of egg yokes. Beat well.
Add two cups of boiling water, mix.

Add 16 cups of flour all at once. Mix and let stand 10 minutes covered. Then continue to make noodles using a noodle grinder.

### Zucchini Patties

1 cup shredded Zucchini
¼ cup chopped onions
½ cup whole wheat flour
½ cup crushed crackers
½ cup milk
1 tsp baking power
1 tsp salt
¼ tsp garlic powder
1 egg

Mix as you would pancakes and fry in pan with oil or butter. Delicious with maple syrup or chicken gravy.

### Breakfast Casserole, a favorite

18 eggs, beaten
1 onion
Bacon, ham, or sausage
1 can cream of mushroom soup
18 slices bread, cubed
Salt and pepper to taste
6 cups of milk
Butter
crushed cornflakes
Cheese

Heat oven to 350 degrees; beat eggs, add bacon, ham, or sausage. Add salt and pepper, onion, milk, and cream of mushroom soup. Mix well. Add bread. Leave in refrigerator overnight. Next morning, when almost ready put cheese slices on top, then a layer of cornflakes. Pour melted butter on top of everything. (Put in oven again. Bake uncovered.) Very Good!

### Chilly Day Stew

Into a kettle of boiling water, chop one nice fat carrot. Add 4 medium chopped onions, one qt. diced potatoes. Sprinkle over this 2 tablespoons rice, 2 tablespoons macaroni, and 1 tsp salt. Add water to cover. Let cook slowly, till tender. Add 1 pint or more good rich cream or substitute butter and milk. Heat. But do not boil again. Serve with crackers or hot toast.

### Butterscotch Pudding

1 cup brown sugar
1 cup cornstarch
2 tablespoons flour
2 tablespoons instant butterscotch pudding
2 eggs beaten
½ cup of milk

Heat three cups of milk to boiling. Mix rest of ingredients and add milk. Very Good!

## HOME REMEDIES

For Cold or Sore Throat
2 cups of tomato juice
2 tablespoons vinegar
2 tablespoons honey
2 tsp red pepper
Mix and boil
Note: you can use only 1 tsp. red pepper if you want.

### For Pesky Deer

1 cup milk
1 egg
½ cup oil

Beat well and stir in 2 tbsp. dish soap. Put in 1 gallon water and spray at perimeter of garden—or wherever to keep deer away!

### Trail Bologna

Mix 2 lbs. tender quick, 1 ½ c. salt and 2 tsp salt petre with 100 lbs. meat. Grind and let stand 2 to 4 days. Then add the following:
2 oz. pepper
3 lbs. powdered milk
4 oz. gr. Coriander
4 tsp. garlic
Approx. 4 ½ qt. water
1 cup liquid smoke
4 tsp. mace-may take more or less water, just depends on dryness of meat. Grind again, two times. (pressure cook one hour at 10 lbs.)

# Acknowledgments

Charles Hadden Spurgeon spoke from his pulpit on May 25, 1879, that heaven is "A prepared place for a prepared people." Truly, John 14:2 attests to this. Spurgeon's words spoken some 143 years ago are truer today than at any other time in history.

"In my Father's house are many mansions; if it were not so, I would have told you. I go to prepare a place for you. And if I go and prepare a place for you, I will come again and receive you to Myself; that where I am, there you may be also."

I did not write *Love's Final Sunrise* as a feel-good novel. Though, I guarantee, you will feel the inspirational exaltation of Christ's satisfying peace when you finish the final chapter. There are more Biblical references in this novel than in any of my previous six novels. Delving into the history of this novel, I was taken aback when I realized I had finished the manuscript and sent out the proposal back in 2019. The only publishing company brave enough to tackle the opposing current disproving waves of society was CrossRiver Media Group.

Through the onslaught of her husband's illness and her four teenagers' proms, graduations, college, and prospective partners, **Tamara Clymer** still managed to keep CrossRiver galloping forward. She even took my call regarding *Love's Final Sunrise*.

This is the first Amish futuristic novel that CrossRiver has done. But Tamara chose the right editor for CrossRiver. The new and unknown is nothing different for **Debra L. Butterfield**, who thrives on challenges.

Perhaps it's a throwback from her Marine years.

What an indivisible twosome these ladies make! *Love's Final Sunrise* was decidedly a challenge for me to write and for Tamara to give her blessing to publish and for Debra to edit. Our viewpoints, as are those of many of my family and coworkers, are as different as are the interpretations of the Bible. After all, not even all the Jews who studied the Scriptures accepted Jesus Christ as the Son of God! *Love's Final Sunrise* is a work of fiction, so sit back and enjoy a good what-if mystery!

I asked my Amish friend what the Old Order Amish say regarding the end of the age and the current social unrest in relation to the Bible. He said it's like a funnel—swirling closer and closer to Christ's coming.

My heartfelt thanks to Norman and his lovely wife Naomi, who supplied numerous data regarding their Old Order Amish community. Continuous thanks to my Amish friends, **Ada, Ephraim, Ella, Ernest, Ada, Ellen, Anna, Barbara, Millie, Melvin, Bennie, Eli, Jonas, Mary, Danny, Mary, Isaac, Joe,** and **Rosemary,** who supplied numerous amounts of data on how they live without electricity, heat their homes, cook their meals, make their clothing, raise their children, farm their fields, and how they attend church without entering a church building. Naomi supplied me with delicious recipes passed down through the years from mother to daughter. Norman was always ready to help me with their Old Order language. The Amish invited us to their butchering, caning, haying, house and barn raising, and horse auctions. Yes, and even a funeral for our dear friend helped me to put the Amish feel"into this work of fiction.

Heartfelt thanks go to my CrossRiver family and **DeeDee Lake** whose bubbly personality connects, inspires, and encourages us somewhat befuddled authors to try unknown spheres of social networking.

Most especially my heartfelt thanks go to my dear, wonderful, and faithful **readers**. Because without your encouragement I could not continue. **Charlene,** or Charlie as we all know her, came right at a God moment remarking that placing Bible verses into my novels inspired readers to get out their Bibles out and read the Scriptures! That is all I want and desire. To inspire and encourage my readers to a close and intimate contact with our Lord and Savior Jesus Christ. My words can't save anyone—but His can!

Thanks also go to my ever-encouraging husband, **Edward**. You can't imagine how much I appreciate you reading and rereading this novel. I also treasure the encouraging words I received from my son, **Derek**, and daughter, **Kimberly**. I have a renewed hope that my grandchildren **Zander, Logan, Annabelle,** and **Willow** will glean wisdom and encouragement from *Love's Final Sunrise* and stand against the inevitable life trials to come.

Most of all, I praise our Lord God and Savior Jesus Christ who, because of His great love for us, is preparing a place for his prepared people! God Bless!

# ABOUT THE AUTHOR

Catherine Ulrich Brakefield is an ardent receiver of Christ's rejuvenating love, as well as a hopeless romantic and patriot. She skillfully intertwines these elements into her writing as the author of *Wilted Dandelions, Love's Final Sunrise, Swept into Destiny, Destiny's Whirwind, Destiny of Heart,* and *Waltz with Destiny* inspirational historical romances; and *Images of America, The Lapeer Area.* Her most recent history book is *Images of America, Eastern Lapeer County.* Catherine, former staff writer for *Michigan Traveler Magazine,* has freelanced for numerous publications. She has had dozens of short stories published as well. Catherine spent three weeks driving across the western part of the United States, meeting her extended family of Americans. This trip inspired her inspirational historical romance *Wilted Dandelions.*

Catherine enjoys horseback riding, swimming, camping, and traveling the byroads across America. She lives in Michigan with her husband, Edward, of forty years, and her Arabian horses. Her children grown and married, she and Edward are the blessed recipients of two handsome grandsons and two beautiful granddaughters.

CatherineUlrichBrakefield.com<br>
Facebook.com/CatherineUlrichBrakefield<br>
Twitter.com/CUBrakefield

# Surviving Carmelita

When Josie's world implodes there is only one place to go.

Available in bookstores and from online retailers.

**CR** CrossRiver Media
www.crossrivermedia.com

# More Great Fiction from CrossRiver Media

## Swept into Destiny

Maggie Gatlan may be a Southern belle on the outside, but inside she's a rebel. Then she meets a man who captures her heart. As the battle between North and South rages, Maggie is forced to make a difficult decision. She must choose between her love for the South and her growing feelings for the hardworking and handsome Union solder, Ben McConnell. Will their love survive or die on the battlefield? Award-winning inspirational historical fiction author Catherine Ulrich Brakefield weaves fiction with real life create this antebellum romance, the first book in the Destiny series.

## Love Calls the Shots

Dr. Saige Westbrook seeks a prestigious cardiology position but worries her farm-girl upbringing won't fit in with the upscale office blue bloods Dr. Aiden Littlefield—goofball extraordinaire—asks Saige to marry him and join him on the mission field. And Dr. Gray Addington is tired of upper crust society and his controlling girlfriend. The three doctors get acquainted while volunteering at a free clinic, but jealousy leads to disaster. As one man lies on the edge of death, Saige bargains with God for his life. And she can't break her oath to God—even if means relinquishing true love.

## Claiming Her Inheritance

A shooting, a stampede, a snakebite... Sally Clark has received an inheritance of a lifetime, but first she has to survive living on the ranch in Montana. Chase Reynolds is astounded that his father has willed one-third of their ranch to a total stranger. Who is this woman and what hold did she have over his dad? What Sally and Chase discover is beyond their imagination and wields far greater consequences than the inheritance.

# Books that build battle-ready faith.

*Cross River*

| | |
|---|---|
| HANDS FULL | FRICK |
| THE GRACE IMPACT | NANCY KAY GRACE |
| THE BENEFIT PACKAGE | CLYMER |
| ABBA'S ANSWERS | BUTTEFRFIELD |
| ABBA'S PROMISE | BUTTEFRFIELD |
| SURVIVING CARMELITA | MIURA |
| Marriage Conversations | KRAFVE |
| BETHANY'S CALENDAR | ELAINE MARIE COOPER |
| GROWING IN CHRIST | HYLTON |
| SWEPT INTO DESTINY | BRAKEFIELD |

Available in bookstores and from online retailers.

CROSSRIVERMEDIA.COM

## If you enjoyed this book, will you consider sharing it with others?

- Please mention the book on Facebook, Instagram, Pinterest, or another social media site.

- Recommend this book to your small group, book club, and workplace.

- Head over to Facebook.com/CrossRiverMedia, 'Like' the page and post a comment as to what you enjoyed the most.

- Pick up a copy for someone you know who would be challenged or encouraged by this message.

- Write a review on your favorite ebook platform.

- To learn about our latest releases subscribe to our newsletter at CrossRiverMedia.com.

Made in the USA
Columbia, SC
16 July 2023